W9-AFV-645

Protector of the Small

Lady Knight

Tortall Books
By Tamora Pierce

The Song of the Lioness Quartet

Alanna: The First Adventure

In the Hand of the Goddess

The Woman Who Rides Like a Man

Lioness Rampant

THE IMMORTALS QUARTET

Wild Magic

Wolf-Speaker

Emperor Mage

The Realms of the Gods

Protector of the Small

First Test

Page

Squire

Lady Knight

Protector of the Small

Lady Knight

TAMORA PIERCE

Random House New York

Published in the United States by Random House Children's Books,
a division of Random House, Inc., New York, and simultaneously in Canada by
Random House of Canada Limited, Toronto.

www.randomhouse.com/teens

Library of Congress Cataloging-in-Publication Data
Pierce, Tamora.
Lady knight / by Tamora Pierce.
p. cm. — (Protector of the small ; #4)
Sequel to: Squire.
SUMMARY: When she became a knight, eighteen-year-old Kel hoped to be given a combat post, but instead she finds herself named commander of an outpost of refugees, where she must face the unnatural forces of the evil Blayce.
ISBN 0-375-81465-5 (trade) — ISBN 0-375-914645-X (lib. bdg.)
[1. Knights and knighthood—Fiction. 2. Fantasy.] I. Title.
PZ7.P61464 Lad 2002 [Fic]—dc21 2002069862

Printed in the United States of America
10 9 8 7 6 5 4 3 2

To the people of New York City,

I always knew the great sacrifice and kindness

my neighbors are capable of,

but now the rest of the country knows, too.

CONTENTS

Protector of the Small

Lady Knight

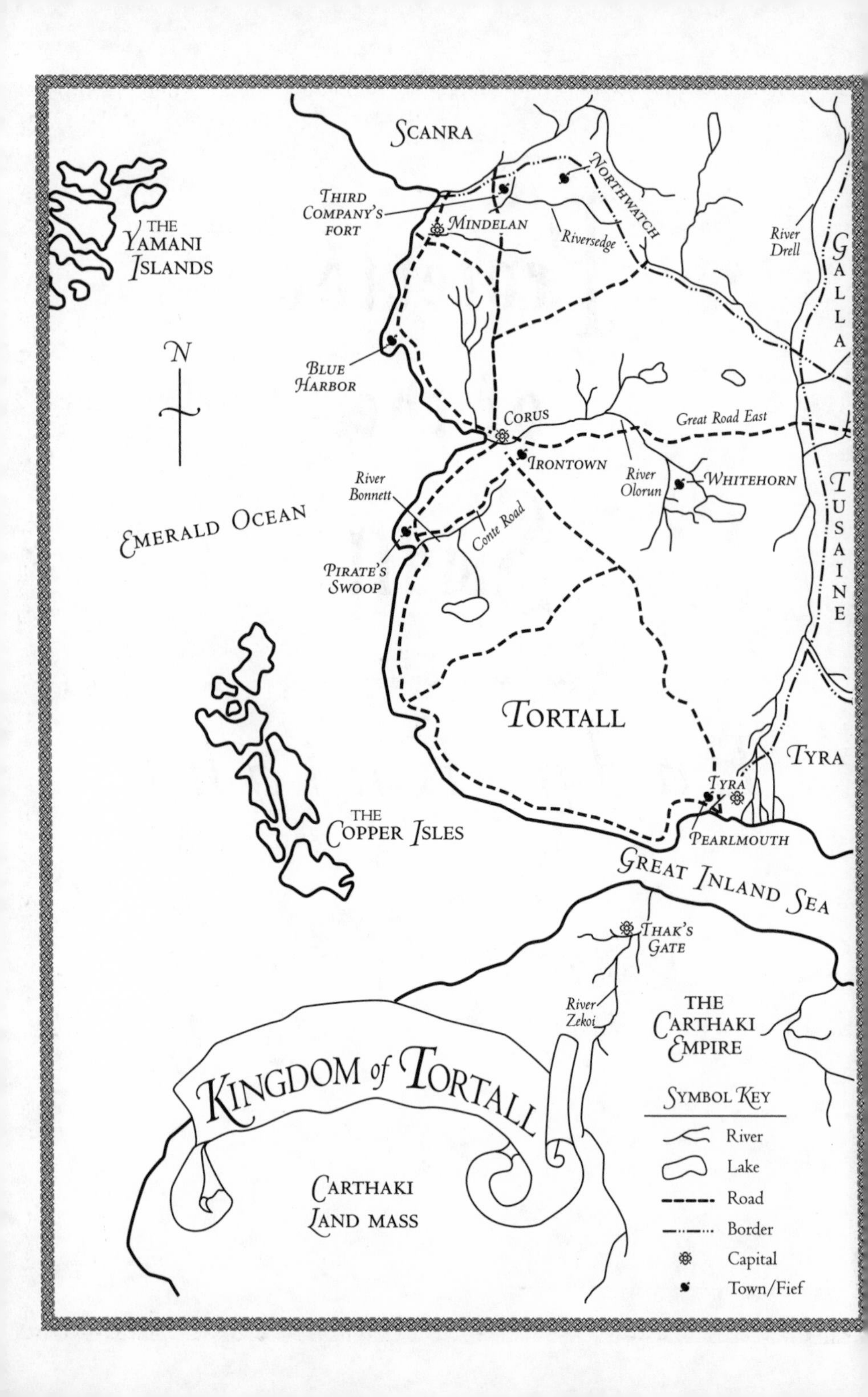
Scanra
Third Company's fort
Mindelan
Northwatch
Riversedge
River Drell
Galla
The Yamani Islands
N
Blue Harbor
Corus
Great Road East
Irontown
River Olorun
Whitehorn
River Bonnett
Conte Road
Tusaine
Emerald Ocean
Pirate's Swoop
Tortall
Tyra
Tyra
Pearlmouth
The Copper Isles
Great Inland Sea
Thak's Gate
River Zekoi
The Carthaki Empire
Kingdom of Tortall
Symbol Key
River
Lake
Road
Border
Capital
Town/Fief
Carthaki Land mass

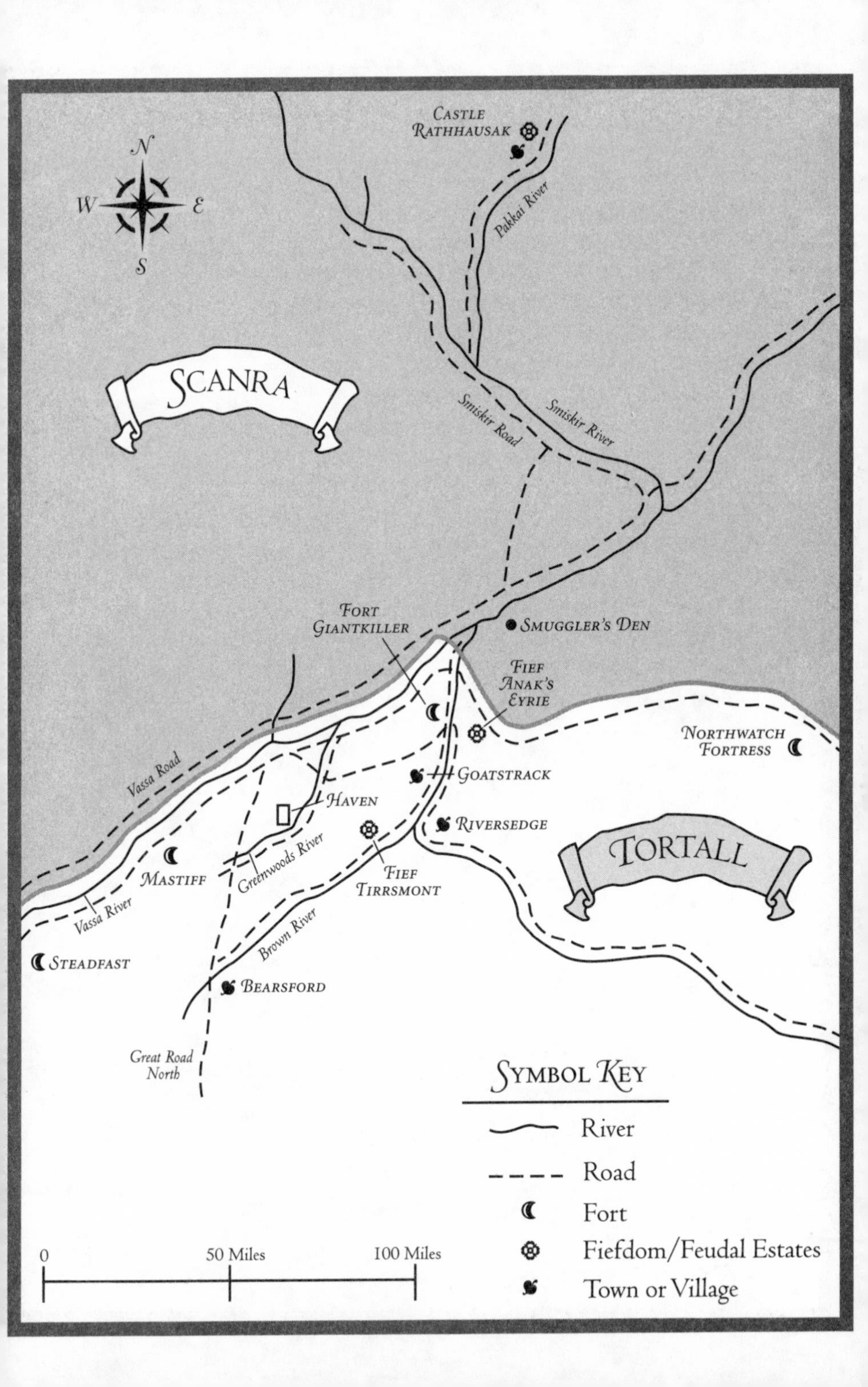
Castle Rathhausak
N
W
E
S
Pakkai River
Scanra
Smiskir Road
Smiskir River
Fort Giantkiller
Smuggler's Den
Fief Anak's Eyrie
Northwatch Fortress
Goatstrack
Vassa Road
Haven
Riversedge
Tortall
Mastiff
Greenwoods River
Fief Tirrsmont
Vassa River
Brown River
Steadfast
Bearsford
Great Road North
Symbol Key
River
Road
Fort
Fiefdom/Feudal Estates
Town or Village
0
50 Miles
100 Miles

Mid-March,
Corus,
the capital of Tortall;
in the 21st year of the reign of
Jonathan IV and Thayet, his Queen,
460 H.E. (Human Era)

I
STORM WARNINGS

Keladry of Mindelan lay with the comfortable black blanket of sleep wrapped around her. Then, against the blackness, light moved and strengthened to show twelve large, vaguely rat- or insectlike metal creatures, devices built for murder. The killing devices were magical machines made of iron-coated giants' bones, chains, pulleys, dagger-fingers and -toes, and a long, whiplike tail. The seven-foot-tall devices stood motionless in a half circle as the light revealed what lay at their feet: a pile of dead children.

With the devices and the bodies visible, the light spread to find the man who seemed to be the master of the creations. To Keladry of Mindelan, known as Kel, he was the Nothing Man. He was almost two feet shorter than the killing devices, long-nosed and narrow-mouthed, with small, rapidly blinking eyes and dull brown hair. His dark robe was marked with stains and burns; his hair was unkempt. He always gnawed a fingernail, or scratched a pimple, or shifted from foot to foot.

Once that image—devices, bodies, man—was complete, Kel woke. She stared at the shadowed ceiling and cursed the Chamber of the Ordeal. The Chamber had shown Kel this vision, or variations of it, after her formal Ordeal of knighthood. As far as Kel knew, no one else had been given any visions of people to be found once a squire was knighted. As everyone she knew understood it, the Ordeal was straightforward enough. The Chamber forced would-be knights to live through their fears. If they did this without making a sound, they were released, to be proclaimed knights, and that was the end of the matter.

Kel was different. Three or four times a week, the Chamber sent her this dream. It was a reminder of the task it had set her. After her Ordeal, before the Chamber set her free, it had shown her the killing devices, the Nothing Man, and the dead children. It had demanded that Kel stop it all.

Kel guessed that the Nothing Man would be in Scanra, to the north, since the killing devices had appeared during Scanran raids on Tortall last summer. Trapped in the capital by a hard winter, with travel to the border nearly impossible, Kel had lived with growing tension. She had to ride north as soon as the mountain passes opened if she was to sneak into Scanra and begin her search for the Nothing Man. Every moment she remained in Tortall invited the growing risk that the king would issue orders to most knights, including Kel, to defend the northern border. The moment Kel got those orders, she would be trapped. She had vowed to defend the realm and obey its monarchs, which would mean fighting soldiers, not hunting for a mage whose location was unknown.

"Maybe I'll get lucky. Maybe I'll ride out one day and find there's a line of killing devices from the palace right up to the Nothing Man's door," she grumbled, easing herself out from under her covers. Kel never threw off her blankets. With a number of sparrows and her dog sharing her bed, she might smother a friend if she hurried. Even taking care, she heard muffled cheeps of protest. "Sorry," she told her companions, and set her feet on the cold flagstones of her floor.

She made her way across her dark room and opened the shutters on one of her windows. Before her lay a courtyard and a stable where the men of the King's Own kept their horses. The torches that lit the courtyard were nearly out. The pearly radiance that came to the eastern sky in the hour before dawn fell over snow, stable, and the edges of the palace wall beyond.

The scant light showed a big girl of eighteen, broad-shouldered and solid-waisted, with straight mouse-brown hair cut short below her earlobes and across her forehead. She had a dreamer's hazel eyes, set beneath long, curling lashes, odd in contrast to the many fine scars on her hands and the muscles that flexed and bunched under her nightshirt. Her nose was still unbroken and delicate after eight years of palace combat training, her lips full and quicker to smile than frown. Determination filled every inch of her strong body.

Motion in the shadows at the base of the courtyard wall caught her eye. Kel gasped as a winged creature waddled out into the open courtyard, as ungainly on its feet as a vulture. The flickering torchlight caught and sparked along the edges of metal feathers on wings and legs. Steel legs, flexible and limber, ended in steel-clawed feet. Between the metal wings and above the metal legs and feet was human flesh, naked, hairless, grimy, and in this case, male.

The Stormwing looked at Kel and grinned, baring sharp steel teeth. His face was lumpy and unattractive, marked by a large nose, small eyes, and a thin upper lip with a full lower one. He had the taunting smile of someone born impudent. "Startle you, did I?" he inquired.

Kel thanked the gods that the cold protected her sensitive nose, banishing most of the Stormwing's foul stench. Stormwings loved battlefields, where they tore corpses to pieces, urinated on them, smeared them with dung, then rolled in the mess. The result was a nauseating odor that made even the strongest stomach rebel. Her teachers had explained that the purpose of Stormwings was to make people think twice before they chose to fight, knowing what might happen to the dead when Stormwings arrived. So far they hadn't done much good as far as Kel could see: people still fought battles and killed each other, Stormwings or no. Tortall's Stormwing population was thriving. But this was the first time she'd seen one on palace grounds.

Kel glared at him. "Get out of here, you nasty thing! Shoo!"

"Is that any way to greet a future companion?" demanded the Stormwing, raising thin brown brows. "You people are getting ready to stage an entertainment for our benefit up north. You'll be seeing a lot of us this year."

"Not if I can help it," Kel retorted. Grimly she walked across her dark room, stubbing her toe on the trunk at the foot of her bed. She cursed and limped over to the racks where she kept her weapons. When she found her bow and a quiver of arrows, she strung the bow and hopped back to her window. She placed the quiver on her window seat and put an arrow on the string. Outside, the courtyard was empty. The Stormwing's footprints in the snow ended right under Kel's window.

Scowling, Kel looked up and around. There he was, perched on the peak of the stable roof, a steel-dressed portent of war. Kel raised her bow. She wouldn't actually kill the creature, just make him go away.

He looked down at her, cackled, and took to the air, spiraling out of Kel's range. He flipped his tail at her three times in a mockery of a wave, then sailed away over the palace wall.

"I *hate* those things," grumbled Kel as she removed the bowstring. The thought of anyone's dead body providing Stormwings with entertainment gave her the shudders. And she knew chances were good that *she* might become a Stormwing toy very soon.

There was no point in going back to sleep now. Instead, Kel cleaned up, dressed, and took down her glaive. It was her favorite weapon, a wooden staff five feet long, filled in iron, cored with lead, and capped by eighteen inches of curved, razor-sharp steel. Banishing all thoughts, opening herself to movement, she began the first steps, thrusts, lunges, and spins of the most complicated combat pattern dance she knew.

Her dog, Jump, grumbled and crawled out of bed. He leaped out of one of the open windows to empty his bladder. The sparrows, fluffed up and piping their own complaints, fluttered outside to visit their kinfolk around the palace.

Raoul of Goldenlake and Malorie's Peak, Kel's former knight-master and present taskmaster, was not in his study when Kel arrived there after breakfast. Another morning conference, she thought, and sat down with chalk and slate to calculate the number of wagons they'd need to move the King's Own's supplies up to the Scanran border. She was nearly done when Lord Raoul came in, a sheaf of papers in one ham-sized fist.

"We're in it for certain," he told Kel. He was a big man, heavily muscled from years of service with the Own. His ruddy face was lit with snapping black eyes and topped with black curls. Like Kel, he was dressed for comfort in tunic, shirt, breeches, and boots in shades of maroon, brown, and cream. He slammed his bulk into one of the chairs facing the desk where she worked. "You know, I thank the gods every day that Daine is on our side," he informed Kel. "If ever we've needed a mage who can get animals to spy and carry messages, it's now."

Kel nodded. Unlike other generations, hers did not have to wait for Scanran information until the mountain passes cleared each year. Daine, known as the Wildmage, shared a magical bond with animals, one that endured even when she was not with them. For three years her eagles, hawks, owls, pigeons, and geese had carried tidings south while the land slept through winter snows, allowing

Tortall to prepare for the latest moves in Scanra.

"Important news, I take it?" Kel asked.

"I'm glad you're sitting down," Raoul said. "The Scanrans have a new king."

Kel shrugged. Rulership in Scanra was always changing. The clan lords were unruly and proud; few dynasties ruled for more than a generation or two. This one hadn't even lasted a full generation. She was surprised that Raoul would be concerned about yet another king on what was called the Bloody Throne. Far more worrisome was the threat that had emerged a couple of years before, a warlord named Maggur Rathhausak. He had studied combat in realms with real armies, not raiding bands. Serving as one clan's warlord, he had conducted enough successful raids in Tortall that other clans had asked him to lead their fighters as well. With more warriors he had won more victories and brought home more loot and slaves, enough to bribe other clans to swear allegiance to him. It was Rathhausak that the Tortallans prepared to fight this year, not the ruling council in Hamrkeng or its king.

"So they'll be fighting each other all summer instead of . . ." Kel let her voice trail off as Raoul shook his head. "Sir?" she asked, unsure of his meaning.

"Maggur Rathhausak," Raoul told her. "He's brought *all* Scanra's clans into his grip. This year he'll have a real army to send against us. A real army, trained for army-style battle, instead of a basketful of raiding parties. Plus however many of those killing devices he can send along to cut our people to shreds. The messages from the north report at least fifty of the things, wrapped up in canvas and waiting for the spell that will make them move again."

Kel set her chalk and slate down. Then she swallowed and asked, "The council let Maggur take over?"

"They weren't given a choice. Maggur had nine clans under his banner last year. The word is he smuggled them into the capital at Hamrkeng after the summer fighting and, well, persuaded all the clans to make him king." Raoul tossed his papers on the desk with a sigh. "We knew it was to be war this summer, but we thought we'd be facing half the warriors in the country, not all. Jonathan's sending messengers out to all the lords of his council. He wants our army to start north as soon as we can manage it." The big man grinned, exposing all his teeth, wolflike. "We'll prepare the warmest reception for our northern brothers that we can. Once they cross our border, they'll think they've marched into a bake oven, by Mithros."

Kel stared blindly at the papers Raoul had just thrown onto the desk. It was decision time: await the Crown's orders, or slip away to wait for the northern passes to clear so she could track down the Nothing Man? She didn't know enough; that was the problem. She needed information, and there was only one place she could think of to get it. "Sir, has anybody ever entered the Chamber of the Ordeal a second time?"

For a moment the only sound was the crackle of the fire in the hearth. Raoul froze. At length he said, "I must tell the bathhouse barber to clean my ears tomorrow. I could have sworn you just asked me if anyone has ever returned to the Chamber of the Ordeal. That's not funny, Kel."

"I didn't mean to be funny, sir," she replied. Shortly

after her Ordeal and knighthood, Raoul had commanded her to address him by his first name, but "sir" was as close as she could bring herself. She clenched her hands so he couldn't see them shake. "I'm serious. I need to know if you've ever heard of anyone going back there."

"No," Raoul said firmly. "No one's been mad enough to consider it. Most folk can tell if once is more than enough. Why in the name of the Great Mother Goddess do you ask?"

Kel swallowed. If he didn't like her question, he really wouldn't like what she was about to say. "I need to talk to it."

Raoul rubbed his face with one hand. "*You* need to talk to it," he repeated.

Kel nodded. "Sir, you know me," she reminded him. "I wouldn't ask anything silly, not when you bring such important news. But I have to know if I can enter the Chamber again. I need to find something out."

"You're right, I do know you," Raoul said glumly. "No, no, you wouldn't jest at a time like this. I'm afraid you're stuck, though. No one has been allowed back inside that thing in all history. No one would ever *want* to go back. You'll just have to settle for what you got in there the first time." He held her questioning eyes with his own anxious ones.

Kel wished that she could explain, but she couldn't. Knights were forbidden to tell what had taken place during their Ordeal. "I didn't mean to worry you, sir," she told him at last.

Raoul scowled at her. "Don't frighten me like that

again. I've put far too much work into you to see you go mad now." He looked around. "What were we doing last?"

"Wagon requisitions, sir," she replied as she held up her slate.

He took it and reviewed her numbers. "Let's finish this now. I won't be able to work on them this afternoon—the council will be meeting."

Kel fetched the papers he needed. "There was a Stormwing in the courtyard this morning," she remarked as she laid them out. "I think he already knows how bad things will be this summer."

Raoul grunted. "I wouldn't be surprised. They probably smell it. Now what's this scrawl? I can't read Aiden's writing." They spent the rest of the morning at work, sorting through the endless details that had to be settled before the men of the King's Own rode north to war.

After lunch Kel saw to her horses, stabled in the building the Stormwing had turned into his momentary perch. There were hostlers, whose job it was to mind the hundreds of horses kept at the palace, but Kel preferred to see to her riding mount, Hoshi, and her warhorse, Peachblossom, herself. The work was soothing and gave her time to think.

Jump watched as she tended the horses. The scruffy dog had put in an appearance at Kel's side about midmorning, clearly recovered from having his morning's sleep interrupted by Kel and a Stormwing.

Jump was not a typical palace dog, being neither a silky, combed, small type favored by ladies nor a wolf- or boar-hound breed prized by lords. Jump was a stocky, short-haired dog of medium size, a combat veteran. His left ear was a tatter. His dense fur was mostly white, raised or dented in places where it grew over old scars. Black splotches covered most of the pink skin of his nose, his only whole ear, and his rump. His tail was a jaunty war banner, broken in two places and healed crooked. Jump's axe-shaped head was made for clamping on to an enemy with jaws that would not let go. He had small, black, triangular eyes that, like those of any creature who'd spent a lot of time with Daine the Wildmage, were far more intelligent than those of animals who hadn't.

"I need more information," Kel murmured to Jump as she mucked out Hoshi's stall. "And soon, before the king orders us out with the army. I certainly can't tell the king I won't go. He'll want to know why, and I can't talk about what happened during my Ordeal."

Jump whuffed softly in understanding.

Her horses tended, Kel reported to a palace library. There, she and the other knights who were her year-mates (young men who had begun their page studies when she had) practiced the Scanran tongue. Many Scanrans spoke Common, the language used in all the Eastern Lands between the Inland Sea and the Roof of the World, but the study of Scanran would help those who fought them to read their messages and interpret private conversations.

After lessons Kel spent her time as best she could. She cared for her weapons and armor, worked on her sword and staff skills in one of the practice courtyards, ate supper with her friends, and finally read in her room. When the watch cried the time at the hour after midnight, she closed her book and left her room, with Jump at her heels.

The palace halls were deserted. Wall torches in iron cressets burned low. Kel did not see another soul. In normal times the nobility would be at parties; not this year. The coming war dictated their hours now. They retired before midnight after evenings spent figuring what goods and labor they could spare for the coming bloody summer. Even the servants, always the last to sleep, were abed. It was like walking in a dream through an empty palace. Kel shivered and grabbed a torch from the wall as she passed the Hall of Crowns.

It was a good idea. No lights burned in the corridor that led to her destination. The Chapel of the Ordeal was used only at Midwinter, when squires took their final step to a shield. Now it was shut and ignored. Still, the chapel's door was never locked. Kel shut it once she and Jump were inside. There was no need to post a guard: over the centuries, thieves and anyone else whose motives were questionable had been found outside the chapel door, reduced to dried flesh and bone by the Chamber's immeasurable power.

Once a year during her term as a squire, Kel had visited the Chamber to try her will against it. On those visits she had confined her encounter with it to touching the door. To converse with the thing, she suspected that she had to go all the way inside once again.

Kel set her torch in a cresset near the altar. Its flickering light danced over the room: benches, the plain stone floor, the altar with its gold candlesticks and cloth, and the large gold sun disk, the symbol of the god Mithros. To the right of the disk was the iron door to the Chamber of the Ordeal.

At first Kel could not make her legs go forward. She had never had a painless experience from the Chamber. In the grip of its power she had lived through the death of loved ones, been crippled and useless, and been forced to stand by as horrors unfolded.

"This is crazy," she told Jump. The dog wagged his tail, making a soft thwapping noise that seemed loud in the quiet chapel.

"You wait here," Kel told him. She ordered her body to move. It obeyed: she had spent years shaping it to her will. She stepped up to the iron door. It swung back noiselessly into a small, dark room with no windows or furnishings of any kind.

Kel trembled, cold to the bone with fear. At last she walked into the Chamber. The door closed, leaving her in complete darkness.

She stood on a flat, bare plain without a tree, stream, or animal to be seen. It was all bare earth, with no grass or stones to interrupt the boring view.

"What is this place?" she asked aloud. Squires were forbidden to speak during the Ordeal, but surely this was different. In an odd way, this was more like a social visit than an Ordeal. "Do you live here?"

It is as close as your human mind can perceive it. *The Chamber's ghostlike voice always spoke in Kel's head without sounding in her ears.*

Kel thrust her hands into her pockets. "I don't see why you haven't done something with it," she informed the Chamber. "No furnishings, no trees or birds . . . If you're going to bring people here, you ought to make things look a bit nicer."

A feeling like a sigh whiffled through Kel's skull. Mortal, what do you want? *demanded the Chamber. Its face—the face cut into the keystone over the inside of the iron door—formed in the dirt in front of her. It was lined and sexless, with lips so thin as to be nearly invisible. The deep-set eyes glinted yellow at Kel.* The task you have been set is perfectly clear. You will know it when you find it.

Kel shook her head. "That's no good. I must know when and where. And I'd like another look at the little Nothing Man, if you please."

Instantly the dirt beneath her was gone, the air of the plain turned to shadow, as if she dreamed again. She fell like a feather, lightly, slipping to and fro in the wind. When she landed, she was set on her feet as gently and tidily as she could have hoped.

During her Ordeal she had seen the Chamber's idea of her task as an image on the wall in a corner of the gray stone room. Now she was living the image, standing in a room like a cross between a smithy and a mage's studio. Unlike her vision and the dreams that had followed it, this place was absolutely and completely real. Behind her, a forge held a bed of fiery coal. An anvil and several other metalworking tools lay nearby. Along one wall stood open cupboards filled with dried herbs, crystals, books, tools, glass bottles, and porcelain jars. Between her and the cupboards was a large stone worktable with gutters on the sides. It was covered with black stains. To her left was another, smaller, kitchen-style hearth set into the wall. Its fire had burned out.

Kel inhaled. Scents flooded her nose: lavender, jasmine, and vervain; damp stone; mold; and under it all, the coppery hint of old blood.

There he was, scrawny and fidgeting as he stood beside the worktable chewing a fingernail. Kel shrank back.

It is safe, *the Chamber said.* He cannot see you.

The Nothing Man was just as she remembered, just as he'd been in all those dreams she'd had since Midwinter. There was nothing new to be learned from this appearance.

In the shadows to Kel's right, metal glinted. She gulped and backed up as a killing device walked out of the shadows, dragging a child's body. The devices also looked just as she remembered, both from her Ordeal and from a bloody day the previous summer when she and a squad of men from the King's Own had managed to kill one. The device was made to give anyone who saw it nightmares. Its curved black metal head swiveled back and forth, with only a thin groove to show where a human neck would be. Long, deep pits served as its eyes. Its metal visor-lips could pop open to reveal clashing, sharp steel teeth. Both sets of limbs, upper and lower, had three hinged joints and ended in nimble dagger-fingers or -toes. Its whiplike steel tail switched; the spiked ball that capped it flashed in the torchlight.

The little man flapped an impatient hand. The machine left the room through a door on Kel's right, towing its pitiful burden.

Moments after it was gone, a big man came in. He was tall enough to have to stoop to get through the door. His graying blond hair hung below his shoulders. A close-cropped graying blond beard framed narrow lips. Brown eyes looked out over a long, straight nose. He wore a huntsman's buff-colored shirt, a brown leather jerkin, and brown leather breeches stuffed into calf-high boots. At his belt hung axe and dagger. He stopped in front of the Nothing Man and hooked his thumbs over his belt.

"We just shipped twenty more to King Maggur. That leaves you with ten, Master Blayce," he said, his voice a deep baritone. He spoke Scanran. "Barely enough to make it to spring."

Blayce, *Kel thought intently.*

"It'll do, Stenmun," Blayce replied. His voice was a stumbling whine, his Scanran atrocious. "Maggur knows—"

Suddenly Kel was back in the Chamber's dreary home. She spared a glance around—did she see a tree in the distance?—before she turned to glare at the face in the pale stone. "Where is he?" she demanded. "Look, Maggur Rathhausak is king now. He'll march once Scanra thaws out. The king will be sending the army—that includes me—north as soon as he can. You have to tell me where to look so I can leave before that happens! If I go now, I won't be disobeying the king. We mortals call that treason."

I cannot, *the Chamber said.*

Kel disagreed with a phrase she had learned from soldiers.

I am not part of your idea of time, *the Chamber told her. Apparently her language had not offended it.* You mortals are like fish swimming in a globe of glass. That globe is your world. You do not see beyond it. I am all around that globe, everywhere at once. I am in your yesterdays and tomorrows just as I am in your today, and it all looks the same to me. I only know you will find yourself in that one's path. When you do, you must stop him. He perverts life and the living. That must not continue. *Its tone changed;*

later, Kel would think the thing had been disgruntled. I thought you would like the warning.

Kel crossed her arms over her chest, disgusted. "So you don't know when I'll see that piece of human waste. The Nothing Man. Blayce. Or that warrior of his, what's his name? Stenmun."

No.

"And you don't know where they are."

Your ideas of countries and borders are meaningless to me.

"But you thought I'd be happy to know that the one who's making the killing devices, who's murdering children, will come my way. Sometime. Someplace."

You must right the balance between mortals and the divine, the balance that is my reason to exist. That creature defies life and death. I require you to put a stop to it. Your satisfaction is not my concern.

Kel wanted to scream her frustration, but years of hiding her emotions at the Yamani court stopped her. Besides, screaming was a spoiled child's response, never hers. And as a knight at eighteen, she was supposed to act like an adult, whatever that meant. She tried one last time. "The sooner, the better."

You will meet him, and you will fix this. Now go away. *The iron door swung open.*

"Can I at least talk to people about it? Tell them that you showed me this?" she demanded.

If you think they will believe you. You are not considered to be a seer or a mage, and your own mages know the name of Blayce already. They just cannot find him.

Kel responded with another word learned from soldiers and walked out of the Chamber.

* * *

The news of Maggur's coronation in Scanra sped the process of gathering Tortallan fighters and supplies. Preparation for war filled the hours at the palace. Every knight not already assigned was summoned to the throne room. The king and queen told the knights that they were now in military service to the Crown for the length of the war and gave them their instructions. Kel remained under Lord Raoul's orders for the moment. She readied her own gear as she helped him assemble all that his men would require.

Weather mages turned their attention to the northern mountains. A week later they told the monarchs that while it would be hard going, Tortall's army could move out. The next day the warriors readied for departure in the guest-houses and fields around the Great Road North, assembling knights, men of the King's Own, six Groups of the Queen's Riders, ten companies of soldiers from the regular army, and wagon after wagon of supplies. It would take three times longer to reach their border posts than if they waited another two weeks for the sleet, snow, and mud of the northern roads to clear. But it would be worth the trouble if they could be in place when the Scanrans came to call.

At dawn on the first morning of the last week of March, the army's vanguard of knights and lords of the realm set off for the border. Kel rode Hoshi, with Jump in one of her saddlebags and sparrows clinging to every part of her and her equipment. On the bluffs north of the city she murmured a soft prayer to Mithros for victory and one to the Goddess for the wounded to come. She was starting a prayer to Sakuyo, the Yamani god of jokes and tricks, when Lord Raoul snarled a curse. She looked at him, startled: he was riding just in front of her with the King's Champion, Alanna, the realm's only other lady knight, and Duke Baird of Queenscove, chief of the realm's healers and father of Kel's best friend, Neal. Everyone else turned in their saddles to see what could make the easygoing Raoul so angry. He was pointing a finger that shook with rage.

Below them lay the city of Corus, sprawled on both sides of the Olorun River. Across from them on the high ground south of the river lay the royal palace, its domes and towers clear in the growing light of sunrise.

Above the palace flew Stormwings by the hundreds, males and females, like a swarm of hornets. The sun bounced off their steel feathers and claws, shooting beams at anyone who looked on. Higher the Stormwings rose. Slowly, lazily, they wheeled over the capital city, then streamed north over the army as if they pointed the way to battle.

2
TOBE

Riding with Third Company of the King's Own, Kel had spent plenty of time slogging through mud and slush. She was used to that. It was her frequent riding companions, Prince Roald and Sir Nealan of Queenscove, who sometimes made her wish her family had stayed in the Yamani Islands. The bitter conditions were echoed by the moods of both young men. They were betrothed and in love with the women they were to marry. They moped. Kel tried to make them think of other things, but the moment conversation lagged, they returned to the contemplation of their Yamani loved ones.

Kel felt sorrier for Prince Roald. Two years older than Kel, the prince was to have married Princess Shinkokami in mid-May, before the arrival of word that Maggur had taken the Scanran throne. Instead of an expensive ceremony, he and Shinko had decided to put their wedding off.

Both showed cheerful faces to the public, saying they had traded rose petals for arrows to arm their soldiers, but to their close friends their disappointment was plain.

Neal, usually dramatic in love, would not talk about his lady, Yukimi, at all. It was such a change from his normal behavior that Kel was convinced he truly loved her Yamani friend. Before, he'd made high tragedy of his beautiful crushes and his own heartbreak, but not this time. Not over a plump and peppery Yamani.

With Roald on one side and Neal on the other, Kel had to wonder about her own sweetheart, Cleon of Kennan. They hadn't seen each other in over a year. A knight two years older than Kel, he was stuck in a northern border outpost, where he had been assigned to teach the locals how to defend themselves. He'd been unable to get or send letters during both winters. Had he forgotten her? She wasn't even sure if he knew she'd survived her Ordeal.

I'll write him when I know where I'm to be posted, she promised herself. Maybe we'll even be assigned to the same place. I'd like that.

She smiled at the idea. They'd never gotten much time alone: something had always interrupted. Perhaps by now he'd be over his impractical idea that he wanted them to marry before they made love, as proper young noblemen did with proper young noblewomen.

Nothing would come of waiting to marry. Years ago, Cleon's mother had arranged his marriage to a young noblewoman with a fine dowry. Cleon thought that, given time, he might convince his mother that Kel would make a better wife. Kel was not so sure. As the youngest daughter of a family that was not wealthy, her dowry was small. She was also not ready to marry. She'd only just gotten her shield; there was so much to do before she could think of settling down. Cleon loved her, wanted to have children by her. She wanted love and children, too—someday. Not now. Not with Scanra ready for all-out war against Tortall. Not with a future that included Blayce the Nothing Man.

Romance wasn't the only thing to think about, but it was more pleasant than reality. Knights used their powerful mounts and the wagons of armor, tack, and weapons to break trail through snow and ice, clearing the way for the foot soldiers of the regular army. It was slow going.

At least Peachblossom, Kel's infamous, temperamental warhorse, behaved. He was a strawberry roan: reddish hide flecked with white, and red-brown stockings, face, mane, and tail. Eight years with Kel had cured him of his tendency to attack others. It was only when they got held up and he was bored that Kel caught him eyeing Neal, his favorite target. When that happened, Kel excused herself and rode ahead to join Lord Raoul or Lady Alanna.

To everyone's relief, the countryside offered dry quarters for the military. War parties rode north so regularly that local farmers made extra money by letting soldiers bed down in their barns. Officers and knights slept at Crown wayhouses. These large inns provided snug quarters and plentiful food, doubly welcome after a day in the cold and wet. Often villages encircled the wayhouses, offering shops and more places to find shelter for the night.

Each day as she walked into the comfort of a wayhouse, Kel hoped the Stormwings that flew above the army found only cold, damp perches for the night. She wished them ice-covered wings and frostbite in their human flesh. Each morning she saw the flash of their steel feathers and heard their jeering calls as the army marched on. And each morning their numbers were as great as they'd been the day before.

Kel had been on the road ten days when they stopped in Queensgrace for the night. The Jug and Fire was the largest of three wayhouses there, so large that even first-year knights had rooms to themselves. By the time Kel got to her room after tending her mounts, a hot bath awaited her. She soaked until the mud and ice were out of her pores, then dried herself, dressed in clean clothes, and went down to eat with her friends. Except for the conversation of the villagers, who had come to see the nobles, the only sounds were the clatter of cutlery and occasional quiet requests for butter, salt, or the refill of a tankard.

Kel finished and thrust her plate back with a grateful sigh. A bowl of winter fruit sat on the table she shared with Neal and her year-mates, reminding her of her horses. They deserved a treat after that day's work. She scooped up two apples and excused herself.

A shortcut through the kitchens meant she was outside for only a couple of yards rather than the width of the large courtyard. It also meant she entered the stable unnoticed, through a side door rather than the main entrance.

The long building lay in shadow, the lanterns being lit only around the front entrance. The horses dozed, glad to be under shelter. Kel was letting her eyes adjust to what light there was when she heard the hard *whump!* of leather on flesh, and a child's yell.

"I tol' ye about foolin' around the horses when there's work to be done," a man snarled. He stood two rows of stalls over from Kel, his back to her. He raised his right hand; a leather strap dangled from his fist. "You're supposed to be in that kitchen washin' up, you thankless rat turd!" Down plunged the hand; again, the sound of a blow as it struck, and a yelp.

Kel strode quickly but silently across the distance between her and the man. The next time he drew his arm back, she seized it in one iron-fingered hand, digging her nails deep into the tender flesh between the bones of his wrist.

"You *dare—*" the innkeeper growled, turning to look at her. He was bigger than Kel, unshaven and slope-shouldered. His muscle came from hoisting kegs and beating servants, not from eight years of combat training. His eyes roved from Kel's set face to her personal badge, a gray owl on a blue field for House Mindelan, and below it, Kel's own ornament of crossed glaives in cream lined with gold. There were two stripes of color for the border—the inner ring cream, the outer blue. They meant she was a distaff, or female, knight.

The innkeeper knew who she was. That information spread quickly everywhere Kel went. "This's no business of yours, lady," he said, trying to yank free of her. "Look, he's allus ditchin' chores, never minds his work. Likely he's out here to steal. Leave me deal with him."

The boy, who sat huddled in a corner of the empty stall, leaped up and spat at the innkeeper's feet. He then bolted across the aisle and into the next stall.

"No!" shouted Kel, but it was too late. The boy slipped

in manure and skidded to a halt under Peachblossom's indignant nose. "Peachblossom, leave him be! Boy, he's mean, get out *now*!" While the gelding had learned to live near others like a civilized creature, he could not be approached by just anyone.

Peachblossom lowered his muzzle to sniff the ragged scrap of humanity before him. The boy waited, perfectly still, as the big gelding whuffled through his guest's hair and under his arms, then gently lipped the boy's nose. Kel waited, horrified, for the shriek of agony that would come when Peachblossom bit.

The shriek never came. Peachblossom continued to inspect the newcomer inch by inch.

"Milady, you oughtn't go between a man an' his servants," the innkeeper said, trying to be agreeable. "I'll never get him to do proper work now." He tried to wrest his hand from Kel's grip. She tightened her muscles, digging even deeper into his wrist. He couldn't shake her loose, and he was afraid to anger a noble by striking her.

As he struggled, Kel inspected the skinny urchin who had so bewitched Peachblossom. The shadows around the lad's deep-set blue eyes were not all from lack of sleep. There was an old black eye, a newer bruise on one cheekbone, and a scabbed cut across his sloping nose. The boy glared at the innkeeper, his chin square and determined. There were new welts on his arms and back visible through holes in his shirt. A slit in half-rotten breeches revealed a long, recent bruise. He was barefoot, his feet red and chapped. His matted hair might be blond if it were clean.

As she watched, he reached up and gently stroked Peachblossom's muzzle.

Horse magic, Kel thought. It has to be. And this idiot treats a lad that useful like a whipping boy. She looked at the innkeeper. Fury boiled in her veins, but she kept her face calm, allowing no emotion to escape. It was a skill she had perfected. "Tell me he is not your son," she said mildly.

The innkeeper made a face. "That stray pup? We took him in of charity, fed and clothed him, and gave him a home. He works here. I've the right to discipline him as I please."

"You would lose that right if he weren't forced to depend on you. He'd be long gone." Her voice was still pleasant. Her inner self, the sensible part, shrieked that she had no business doing what she was about to do. She was on her way to a war; boys took much more looking after than sparrows, dogs, or horses.

"Let him starve? That would be cruel," the man insisted. Looking at him, Kel realized that he believed it. "He's got no family. Where can he go?" demanded the innkeeper. "But he can't just leave work. Boys need discipline. Elsewise he'll go as bad as the feckless Scanran slut that whelped him an' left him on the midwife's step."

"If he was left with the midwife, how did he come to you?" Kel asked.

"She died. We bid for the boy's indenture. Paid for seven years, we did. Been more trouble than he's worth, but we're gods-fearin' folk, an' charity be a virtue." The man looked piously toward the ceiling, then at Kel. "Forgive my sayin' so, milady, but this be no affair of yours."

Kel released him. "I think the district magistrate would find your treatment of this boy to be very much *his* affair," she informed the man. "Under the law indentured servants have some rights. What did you pay when you bid for his services?"

"You can't buy his contract," protested the innkeeper. "It ain't for sale."

Kel wrapped both hands in his tunic and dragged his face down to hers. "Either tell me, or I visit the magistrate tomorrow, and you'll have no say in the matter," she informed him. "This boy is an indentured servant, not a slave. Accept my coin now, or have him taken with no payment tomorrow, it's all the same to me."

When the innkeeper looked away, she released him, knowing she had won.

"Two copper nobles," growled the man.

"One," said the boy grimly. "Only one, an' I been workin' for 'im for three year."

"Lyin' little rat!" snapped the innkeeper, darting to Peachblossom's stall. The gelding lunged without touching the boy at his feet and snapped, teeth clicking together just in front of the innkeeper's face. The man tried to run backward and fell, ashen under his whiskers.

Kel looked in her belt purse. She wouldn't have paid a copper bit for ten boys in that condition, but she wanted to be rid of the innkeeper. She held up two copper nobles. "I'll take his indenture papers before you have this. Get them, right now."

The man fled the stable.

Kel sighed and walked into Peachblossom's stall. "You're getting slow," she informed the gelding. "Time was you'd have had his whole arm in your teeth."

Peachblossom snorted in derision and backed up.

"Not that I'd mind," Kel admitted, looking at the lad. "A good bite would keep him from hitting people with that arm for a while. But I suppose it would make a fuss." She propped her hands on her hips, disgusted with herself. Why had she done this?

Even as she asked herself if she'd run mad, she knew that she couldn't have done anything else.

Kel inspected the boy. Clothes, particularly shoes, were required. His present rags would have to be burned. He needed a bath and a haircut. He probably had lice. Shaving his head and scrubbing him with lice-killing soap would eliminate that problem. He didn't look old enough to need shaving anywhere else. And he needed a healer.

Kel looked over at Hoshi's stall, where Jump gnawed a bone. Chances were that it had not been intended for his supper, since there was quite a bit of meat on it. She only hoped the inn's staff didn't know who the thief was.

"Jump, will you get Neal, please?" Kel asked the dog. Jump thrust his bone under the straw, then trotted out of the stable. The boy followed the dog's movements with wide eyes but made no comment that might draw Kel's attention.

"What's your name?" she asked. "And how old are you?"

The boy retreated under Peachblossom's belly. He watched her warily from between the gelding's forelegs. After a moment he said, "Tobe, miss. Tobeis Boon. I think I'm nine."

Kel repeated, "Boon?"

The boy nodded. "Auld Eulama said I musta been a boon to someun, though she din't know who."

"Eulama?" asked Kel.

"Midwife as reared me, best's she knowed."

Kel scratched her head. "Whose opinion is that?" she inquired, intrigued by his frank way of talking. "That she did the best she knew?"

"All Queensgrace, lady. They all say't. Way they talk, it din't do me much good." It seemed Tobeis—Tobe—was as intrigued by Kel as she was by him. He inched forward.

Kel indicated the boy's guardian. "It's not so long ago that I convinced him not to savage everyone in reach. I've known him eight years. I was sure he'd kill you."

"Aww, he's a good un." Tobe wrapped a casual hand around as much of Peachblossom's right foreleg as he could manage. "Ain't nobody likes Alvik—me master there."

Here came Alvik himself with a writing board, a quill, an ink pot, a sheet of grimy paper, sealing wax, and a candle. Kel briskly signed Tobe's indenture papers, handed over the coins, and watched the innkeeper also sign, then seal the document. As soon as Kel had the completed bill of sale in hand, Alvik fled. He passed Neal and Jump on their way in.

"You know, Mindelan, our lives would be easier if the dog just broke down and talked," Kel's friend announced. "I was winning that card game." He glared down at Jump. "There was no need to grab me."

Kel smiled. "If you're not bleeding, he was being nice, and it's not fair for you to play cards with ordinary folk." To Tobe she explained, "He remembers all the cards dealt."

Neal looked to see who she spoke to, and stared. "Kel, that monster has a boy under his belly."

"That monster hasn't touched him," replied Kel. Neal

had every reason to expect the worst of the big gelding. "Will you take a look at the boy? Tobe—Tobeis Boon, this is my friend Neal." She didn't give Neal's titles, not wanting to make the boy uncomfortable. "Tobe, my friend is a healer. I want him to look at you."

"Not while he's in there," protested Neal.

At the same time the boy said, "He's no healer, just some noble."

Neal glared at Tobe. "I'm a healer *and* a noble." He looked at Kel. "What have you done now, Mindelan?"

Kel shrugged. "I need a servant. Tobe seemed to want a change, so I hired him away from the innkeeper."

"You mean he's another of your strays," Neal pointed out. "Didn't that griffin teach you anything?"

"Griffin?" Tobe asked, scooting a little forward of Peachblossom's legs. "You saw a griffin?"

Kel smiled. "I'll tell you about it if you'll let Neal have a look at you."

Tobe eyed Neal with considerable suspicion. "Folk like him don't touch the likes of me."

"If you knew how I spent my squiredom, you'd know the likes of you are *most* of what I ended up touching," Neal informed him. "I can get rid of your lice and fleas," he added as Tobe scratched himself.

"Cannot," retorted the boy.

"Can too," Neal replied. "The handiest spell I ever learned."

Convinced that Neal would talk the boy around, Kel went to see about having a hot bath drawn and carried up to her room.

"Miss, you shouldna bother with that un," the maid she

paid for the service commented. "He's a gutter rat, as like to bite a helpin' hand as not."

Thinking of Peachblossom and the baby griffin she'd once cared for, Kel replied, "If he does, it won't be the first time."

When Neal brought Tobe to her room, Kel was just donning the oiled canvas cloak and broad-brimmed hat she used to keep off the rain. Under the cloak she wore a quilted coat made by her former maid, Lalasa, now a dressmaker. Lalasa had spared no effort on the coat for the mistress who had given her a start in business. By the time Kel had tied the cloak around her neck, she was sweating.

"Here he is." Neal pushed open Kel's door to admit Jump and Tobe. "Did you order supper for him?"

"I remember that much from my own healings, thank you," Kel replied. "I appreciate your seeing to him, Neal."

Her friend waved a hand in dismissal and left, closing the door. Kel regarded her new servant. "You see that?" She pointed to the tub that sat squarely in front of the hearth. "It's a bath. You climb in and you don't climb out and eat before you're clean. Scrub all over, understand?" Hanging on to Tobe, she saw that Neal had done well: the boy's weals and scabbed-over cuts showed now as pink, healthy, new skin. "There's soap in that bowl. Use it," she continued. "The little pick is to clean under your nails. Remember your hair, your ears, and your private parts." She released him.

The boy went to the tub, stuck a finger in the water, and glared at Kel. "It's hot!" he exclaimed.

"Don't expect hot baths *every* night," she told him,

straight-faced. She could see that he was dismayed at the thought of washing in hot water. "But you'll do this on your own, or I'll do it for you, with a scrub brush. My servants are clean."

Tobe hung his head. "Yes, lady."

Kel pointed to the bed, where she had set out drying cloths and one of her spare shirts. "Dry with those and put that on for now," she said. "Don't wear your old things."

"Not even me loincloth?" he asked, horrified.

"You're getting fresh ones. *Clean* ones," she said, immovable. "I'm off to take care of that now. When you're dry, wrap up in a blanket and look outside—the maid will leave a tray with your supper by the door. I got a pallet for you"—she pointed to it, on the side of the hearth opposite the table—"so you can go to bed. You'll be sleepy after a decent supper and Neal's magicking."

"Yes, lady," replied the boy. He was glum but resigned to fresh clothes and a bath. He glanced around the room, his eyes widening at the sight of her glaive propped in a corner. "What pigsticker is *that*?"

Kel smiled. "It's a Yamani *naginata*—we call it a glaive. I learned to use one in the islands, and it's the weapon I'm best with. Clothes, off. Bath, now, Tobe."

He gaped, then exclaimed, "With a girl lookin' on? Lady, some places a fellow's got to draw the line!"

"Very true," Kel replied solemnly, trying not to grin. "Don't give Jump any food. He's had one good meal already tonight."

Jump, sprawled between the tub and the fire, belched and scratched an ear. His belly was plump with stolen meat.

Kel rested a hand on Tobe's shoulder. "You'll do as I ask?"

He nodded without meeting her eyes.

Kel guessed what was on his mind. "I'll never beat you, Tobe," she said quietly. "Ever. I may dunk you in the tub and scrub you myself if I come back to find you only washed here and there, but you won't bleed, you won't bruise, and you won't hobble out of this room. Understand?"

He looked up into her face. "Why do this, lady?" he asked, curious. "I'm on'y a nameless whelp, with the mark of Scanra on me. What am I to the likes of you?"

Kel thought her reply over before she gave it. This could be the most important talk she would have with Tobe. She wanted to be sure that she said the right things. "Well, Peachblossom likes you," she answered slowly. "He's a fine judge of folk, Peachblossom. Except Neal. He's prejudiced about Neal."

"He just likes the way Neal squeaks when he's bit," Tobe explained.

Kel tucked away a smile. It sounded like something Peachblossom would think. "And for the rest? I do it because I can. I've been treated badly, and I didn't like it. And I hate bullies. Now pile those rags by the door and wash up. The water's getting cold." Not waiting for him to point out that cooler water didn't seem so bad, she walked out and closed the door. She listened for a moment, waiting until she heard splashes and a small yelp.

He's funny, she thought, striding down the hall. I like how he speaks his mind. Alvik didn't beat that from him, praise Mithros.

At the top of the stairs, Kel halted. Below her, out of sight, she could hear Neal: ". . . broken finger, half-healed broken arm, cracked ribs, and assorted healed breaks. I'm giving your name to the magistrate. I'll recommend he look in on you often, to see the treatment you give your other servants."

"Yes, milord, of course, milord." That was Innkeeper Alvik's unmistakable voice, oily and mocking at the same time. "I'm sure my friend the magistrate will be oh so quick to 'look in on' me, as you say, once you're down the road. Just you worry about Scanra. They'll be making it so hot for you there, you'll be hard put to remember us Queensgrace folk."

"Yes, well, I thought of that," Neal said, his voice quiet but hard. "So here's something on account, something your magistrate can't undo."

She heard a rustle of cloth. Alvik gasped. "Forcing a magic on me is a Crown offense!"

"Who will impress the Crown more, swine? The oldest son of Baird of Queenscove, or you?" asked Neal cruelly. "And did my spell hurt?"

"Noooo," Alvik replied, dragging the sound out. Kel imagined he was checking his body for harm.

"It won't," Neal said. "At least, as long as you don't hit anyone. When you do, well, you'll feel the blow as if you struck yourself. Clever spell, don't you think? I got the idea from something the Chamber of the Ordeal did once." Neal's voice went colder. "Mind what I say, innkeeper. When you strike a servant, a child, your wife, your own body will take the punishment. Mithros cut me down if I lie."

"All this over a whore's brat!" snarled the innkeeper. "You nobles are mad!"

"The whore's brat is worth far more than you." Neal's voice was a low rumble at the bottom of the stairs. "*He's* got courage. You have none. Get out of my sight."

Kel waited for the innkeeper to flee to his kitchen and Neal to return to the common room before she descended. It was useless to say anything to Neal. He would just be embarrassed that he'd been caught doing a good deed. He liked to play the cynical, heartless noble, but it was all for show. Kel wouldn't ruin it for him.

It was a long ride to the wagonloads of goods for those made homeless by the Scanrans. Her lantern, hung from a pole to light Hoshi's way, provided scant light as icy rain sizzled on its tin hood. Other riders were out, members of the army camped on either side of the road for miles. Thanks to their directions, Kel found the wagons in a village two miles off the Great Road North. They were drawn up beside one of the large, barnlike buildings raised by the Crown to shelter troops and equipment on the road. In peaceful years local folk used the buildings to hold extra wood, grain, animals, and even people made homeless by natural disasters.

The miserable-looking guards who watched the wagons scowled at Kel but fetched the quartermaster. Once Kel placed money in his palm, the quartermaster allowed her to open the crates and barrels in a wagonload of boys' clothes.

The wagon's canvas hood kept off the weather as Kel went through the containers. Tobe looked to be about ten, but he was a runty ten, just an inch or two over four feet, bony and undersized from a life of cheap, scant rations. She chose carefully until she had three each of loincloths, sashes, shirts, breeches, and pairs of stockings, three pairs of shoes that might fit, a worn but serviceable coat, and a floppy-brimmed hat. If she was going to lead Tobe into battlelands, the least she could do was see him properly clothed. The army tailors could take in shirts and breeches to fit him properly; the cobblers could adjust his shoes. Once she had bundled everything into a burlap sack, Kel mounted Hoshi, giving a copper noble to the soldier who had kept the mare inside a shelter, out of the wet. As the rain turned to sleet, they plodded back to Queensgrace.

In Kel's room, Tobe sat dozing against the wall, afloat in her shirt. When Kel shut the door, his eyes flew open, sky-blue in a pale face. "I don't care if you was drunk or mad or takin' poppy or rainbow dream or laugh powder, you bought my bond and signed your name and paid money for me and you can't return me to ol' Alvik," he told her without taking a breath. He inhaled, then continued, "If you try I'll run off 'n' steal 'n' when I'm caught I'll say I belong to you so they'll want satisfaction from you. I *mean* it! You can't blame drink or drug or anything and then get rid of me because *I won't go.*"

Kel waited for him to run out of words as water trickled off her hat and cloak onto the mat by the door. She gave Tobe a moment after he stopped talking, to make sure he was done, before she asked, "What is *that* about?"

"See?" he cried. "You forgot me already—me, Tobeis

Boon, whose bond you bought tonight. I *knew* you was drunk or takin' a drug or mad. But here I am an' here I stay. You need me, to, to carry your wine jug, an' cut the poppy brick for you to smoke, an', an' make sure you eat—"

Kel raised her eyebrows. "Quiet," she said in the calm, firm tone she had learned from Lord Raoul.

Tobe blinked and closed his mouth.

Kel walked over and blew into his face so he could smell her liquor- and drug-free breath. "I'm not drunk," she told him. "I take no drugs. If I'm mad, it's in ways that don't concern you. I went out to get you clothes, Tobe. You can't go north wearing only a shirt."

She tossed the sack onto her bed and walked back to the puddle she'd left by the door, then struggled to undo the tie on her hat. Her fingers were stiff with cold even after grooming Hoshi and treating her to a hot mash.

When she removed the hat, a pair of small, scarred hands took it and leaned it against the wall to dry. Once Kel had shed the cloak, Tobe hung it from a peg, then knelt to remove her boots. "I *have* clothes," he said, wrestling off one boot while Kel braced herself.

"I saw," she replied, eyeing the heap they made on the floor. "I wouldn't let a cat have kittens on them. I ought to take Alvik before a magistrate anyway. Your bond says you get two full suits of clothes, a coat, and a sturdy pair of shoes every year."

"It does?" he asked, falling on his rump with her boot in his hands.

Kel reached inside her tunic and pulled out his indenture papers. "Right there," she told him, pointing to the paragraph. When Tobe frowned, she knew Alvik had neglected something else. "You can't read, can you?" she asked.

"Alvik said I din't need no schoolin', 'acos I was too stupid to learn," Tobe informed Kel, searching for a cloth to wipe her boots with. He was practiced at this: the innkeeper had taught him to look after guests' belongings as well as their horses, Kel supposed.

"Lessons," she said, folding the papers once more. "After we're settled in the north." She yawned. "Wake me at dawn. We'll try those clothes on you then. And I'm not sure about the, the"—she yawned again—"shoes. I'm not sure these will fit. If we stop on the way, perhaps . . ."

She looked around, exhaustion addling her brain. Her normal bedtime on the road was much earlier than this. She eyed the door, her dripping hat and cloak, her boots, Tobe.

"Lady?" he asked quietly. "Sounds like you mean to do all manner of things for *me*. What was you wishful of me doin' for *you*?"

"Oh, that," Kel said, realizing that she hadn't told him what duties he would have. "You'll look after my horses and belongings, and in four years you'll be free." A will, she realized. I need to make a will so he can be freed if I'm slain. She picked up her water pitcher and drank from the rim. "For that, I am duty bound to see that you are fed, clothed, and educated. We'll settle things like days off. You'll learn how to clean armor and weapons. That ought to keep you busy enough."

He nodded. "Yes, lady."

"Very well. Go to bed. I'm exhausted." Unbuttoning her shirt, she realized he hadn't moved. "Bed," she said firmly. "Cover your head till I say you can come out. I won't undress while you watch."

She took her nightshirt out of a saddlebag and finished changing once Tobe was on his pallet with his eyes hidden. In the end, she had to uncover him. He'd gone to sleep with the blanket over his head. Kel banked the fire and blew out the last candle that burned in the room.

The killing device moved in her dreams. Blayce the Nothing Man watched it. He pointed to a child who cowered under his worktable: it was Tobe. The metal thing reached under the table and dragged the boy out.

Kel sat up, gasping, sweat-soaked. It was still dark, still night. The rain had stopped. She was at an inn on the Great Road North, riding to war.

"Lady," Tobe asked, his voice clear, "what's Blayce? What's Stenmun?"

"A nightmare and his dog," Kel replied, wiping her face on her sleeve. "Go back to sleep."

The rain returned in the morning. The army's commanders decided it would be foolish to move on. Kel used the day to finish supplying Tobe, making sure that what he had fit properly. Tobe protested the need for more than one set of clothes and for any shoes, saying that she shouldn't spend money on him.

"Do you want to make me look bad?" she demanded at last. "People judge a mistress by how well her servants are dressed. Do you want folk to say I'm miserly, or that I don't know my duty?"

"Alvik never cared," Tobe pointed out as he fed the sparrows cracked corn.

"He isn't noble-born," Kel retorted. "I am. You'll be dressed properly, and that's that."

At least she could afford the sewing and shoe fitting. She had an income, more than she had thought she'd get as the poorly dowered youngest daughter of a large family. For her service in the war she received a purse from the Crown every two weeks. Raoul had advised her on investments, which had multiplied both a legal fine once paid to her and her portion of Lalasa's earnings. Lalasa had insisted on that payment, saying that she would not have been able to grow rich off royal custom if not for her old mistress. It was an argument Kel had yet to win. And it did mean that she could outfit Tobe without emptying her purse, a venture Lalasa would approve.

The rain ended that night. The army set out at dawn, Tobe riding pillion with Kel. Once they were under way, Kel rode back along the line of march until she found the wagon that held the gear of the first-year knights, including Hoshi's tack, spare saddle blankets, weapons, and all Kel needed to tend her arms and armor. She opened the canvas cover on the wagon and slung the boy inside with one arm.

"There's blankets under that saddle, and meat and cheese in that pack," she informed him. "Bundle up. It's a cold ride. I'll get you when we stop for the night." She didn't wait for his answer but tied the cover and returned to her friends.

They ate lunch on horseback as cold rain fell again. Knights and squires huddled in the saddle, miserable despite broad-brimmed hats and oiled cloaks to keep the wet out. Kel had extra warmth from Jump and the sparrows, who had ducked under her cloak the moment the rain had returned.

They were crossing a pocket of a valley when Neal poked Kel and pointed. In the trees to their left, a small figure moved through the undergrowth, following them. Kel twitched Peachblossom off the road and into the woods, cutting Tobe off. He stared up at her, his chin set.

"I left you in the wagon so you wouldn't get soaked," Kel informed him. He was muddy from toes to knees. "Are you mad?"

Tobe shook his head.

"Then why do this?" she asked, patiently. "You're no good to either of us if you get sick or fall behind."

"Folk took interest in me 'afore, lady," replied the boy. "A merchant and a priestess. Soon as I was gone from their sight, they forgot I was alive. Sometimes I think I jus' dreamed you. If I don't see you, mayhap you'll vanish."

"I'm too solid to be a dream. Besides, I paid two copper nobles for your bond," Kel reminded him. "Not to mention what we laid out for the sewing and the cobbler."

"Folk've given me nobles jus' for holdin' the stirrup when they mounted up," Tobe informed her. "Some is so rich, a noble means as much to them as a copper bit to ol' Alvik."

Kel sighed. "I'm not rich," she said, but it was for the sake of argument. Compared with this mule-headed scrap of boyhood, she *was* rich. It was all she could do not to smile. She recognized the determination in those bright blue eyes. It matched her own.

She evicted the sparrows from the shelter of her cloak and reached a hand down. When he gripped it, Kel swung the boy up behind her. "Not a word of complaint," she told him. "Get under my cloak. It'll keep the rain off."

This order he obeyed. Kel waited for the sparrows to tuck themselves under the front of her cloak, then urged Peachblossom back to their place in line.

Neal, seeing her approach, opened his mouth.

"Not one word," Kel warned. "Tobe and I have reached an understanding."

Neal's lips twitched. "Why do I have the feeling you did most of the understanding?"

"Why do I have the feeling that if you give me a hard time, I'll tell all of our year-mates your family nickname is Meathead?" Kel replied in kind.

"You resort to common insult because you have no stronger arguments to offer," retorted Neal. When Kel opened her mouth, Neal raised a hand to silence her. "Nevertheless, I concede."

"Good," Kel said. "That's that."

"You got anything to eat?" inquired a voice from inside her cloak.

April 1–14, 460
near the Scanran border

3
LONG, COLD ROAD

It was well past dark when they reached their next stop, the village of Wolfwood. "We're here for a few days," Raoul told the younger knights. "Lady Alanna and the troops for the coast leave us here. So will the troops and knights meant for the eastern border. Maybe we'll even be here long enough to dry out."

"What's dry?" asked Faleron of King's Reach wearily.

"Good question," Lady Alanna said, stretching to get the kinks out of her spine. She and Neal chorused, "Next question." The lady grinned at her former squire. "You rode with me too long, Queenscove," she pointed out.

"And I learned things every step of the way, lady knight," said Neal with a bow.

Tobe offered to groom Peachblossom and Hoshi. Kel watched as the boy worked.

"You think he's a horse mage?" Neal murmured. He'd

tended his mounts and was ready to go inside. "He's got wild magic with horses?"

"It seems so," Kel admitted, gathering her saddlebags. "Look how easy Peachblossom is with him." Satisfied that Tobe needed no help, she followed Neal into the wayhouse, Jump and the sparrows trailing behind.

Messengers had warned their hosts of their arrival. There was a tub of hot water in Kel's room. She scrubbed, changed, then went to find her charge. She found Tobe in Peachblossom's stall, though both the gelding and Hoshi had been groomed and fed.

"You'll sleep in my chamber like last night. There's a tub there now. Go wash," she ordered. "The servants take meals in the east wing of the house. Eat properly, vegetables as well as meat. And drink some milk."

Tobe grinned at her. "He said last night you're a bear for vegetables—Sir Nealan, that is. Auld Eulama were the same." He went to do as he was told. Kel returned to the wayhouse, thinking. They needed to come to an understanding. She couldn't let him walk, but she didn't like to share a saddle. Perhaps he could ride Hoshi? Normally Kel would have ridden the mare on a journey like this, but she needed Peachblossom's strength to help open the road in spots. Hoshi would barely notice Tobe's weight, and she would keep him out of the mud.

In the common room, Kel picked at her supper, too weary to eat. She was about to go to her room when someone came in. A servant rushed forward to take his wet things; the innkeeper followed to see what the new guest required.

The newcomer was a big fellow, a knight from his

tunic badge, with red curly hair and gray eyes. Kel froze. It was Cleon of Kennan, her sweetheart. But something was wrong. She looked at him and saw a brawny knight she knew. Where was the joy of looking at him that she had felt the last time they met? Cleon was as attractive as ever, but he didn't make her skin tingle as he once had.

Kel bit her lip. As a page she'd thought she was hopelessly in love with Neal. Then, a newly made squire, she'd spent a summer with Lord Raoul and Third Company. Seeing Neal after months of separation, she'd found he looked like just another man, not the bright center of her heart. Now it had happened again. She and Cleon had kissed, had yearned for time and privacy in which to become lovers. He'd wanted to marry her, though she was not sure that she wanted marriage. Here he was, but she didn't feel warm and eager at the sight of him. Friendship was there, but passion was gone.

Worse, a part of her wasn't surprised by the change. They'd been apart for such a long time, with only letters to keep their feelings alive. So much had happened, too much, all of it more vivid and recent than her memories of him. She didn't want Cleon as a lover now, of that she was sure. There was work to be done. She wanted no lovers until she had settled the Nothing Man's account.

Kel looked down at her plate. Maybe Cleon wouldn't see her.

Merric of Hollyrose, at the end of her table, jumped to his feet. "Cleon!" he yelled. Everyone looked at the newcomer and called out greetings. Prince Roald waved him over. Kel fixed a smile on her face.

Cleon too smiled when he saw Kel, but he didn't seem

to notice that Neal offered him a seat beside her. Instead, Cleon took a chair near the prince.

"Why are you here?" asked Faleron of King's Reach. He was one of the knights destined to defend the seacoast. "You're headed the wrong way."

Cleon glanced at Kel, then looked at Faleron. "I got a mage message asking me to come home soonest. You've heard there's flooding in the southwest hills?"

Faleron, whose home was near Cleon's, sighed. "It's bad," he said. "Father said a lot of fiefdoms lost their entire stores of grain—oh, no. Yours?"

Cleon nodded, his mouth a grim line. "The Lictas River went over its banks and wiped out our storehouses. I've got to help Mother raise funds so our people can plant this year."

Kel met Cleon's eyes. They had often talked about his home. She knew his estates were short of money.

Abruptly, Cleon stood. "May I have a word, Kel? Alone?"

She couldn't refuse. Her thoughts tumbled as she followed him outside. They stood under the eaves that sheltered the inn's door, the wind blowing rain onto them. She wondered if he'd noticed she hadn't moved to kiss him, then realized that he had not tried to kiss her, either. Suddenly she knew what was coming.

"I've just one way to get coin for grain and the livestock we lost, Kel," he said. "The moneylenders only give Mother polite regrets. I have to marry Ermelian of Aminar or my people will starve this winter." He turned away. "I'm so sorry. I'd thought, if we had time . . ."

Relief poured through Kel. She wouldn't have to hurt him. "We knew our chances weren't good," she said over the rattle of sheaves of rain. "We did talk about it."

"I *know*," he said hoarsely, standing with his back to her. "Even knowing I couldn't break the betrothal honorably, I went ahead and dreamed. That's the problem with being able to think. It means you wish for things you can't have."

Kel wished she could comfort him. Even beyond kisses, he was her friend. She laid a hand on his back. "Cleon—"

"Don't." He twitched away from her touch. "I can't— I'm as good as married now. It wouldn't be right."

Relief flooded her again. Cleon was too honorable to kiss her or let her touch him now that he'd agreed to his marriage. She felt shallow, coldhearted, and sorry for him.

"You said you liked her, when we were on progress," she reminded him. "You said she's nice. It could be much worse. People do find happiness, when they're married to someone good."

The awful grinding sound that came from his throat was supposed to be a laugh. "That's you, Kel, making the best of it," he said. He rubbed his eyes with his arm before he turned to face her. "You're right. I saw her while we were on progress. It was after you left to help that village after the earthquake. She *is* nice. She's also pretty and kind. Some of our friends can't say as much about the wives arranged for them. She just isn't you. She isn't my friend, or my comrade." He tried to smile.

Kel's heart hurt. Cleon *was* still her friend, if not her

lover. "Come inside," she told him. "Dry out, and eat. We'll do our duty, like we're supposed to. And we can be friends, surely. Nothing changes that."

"No," he whispered. "Nothing will ever change that." He raised a hand as if to touch her cheek, then lowered it and went inside.

Kel didn't cry for her friend and the sudden, hard changes in their lives until she was safe in bed and Tobe was lightly snoring on his pallet. She thought she'd muffled herself until he said, "It's awright, lady. I'd be ascairt, too, goin' off for savages to shoot at."

Kel choked, dried her eyes on her nightshirt sleeve, and turned onto her back. "It's not the war, Tobe," she replied. She groped for the handkerchief on her bedside table, sat up, and blew her nose. "I've been shot at. I can bear it. I'm crying because my friend is unhappy and everything is changing."

"Is that what you're 'posed to do?" he asked. "Cry for your friends, though they ain't dead? Cry when things change?"

"If the changes are hard ones," Kel replied. "If they take away the things you knew were good." She wiped her nose, trying to decide what else to say. How could he not know about sorrow for a friend? "Don't you cry when your friends are hurt?"

"Dunno," he said. "Never had no friends, 'cept maybe Auld Eulama, an' she only cried when the drink was in her."

Kel sat breathless for a moment. Tobe sounded as if this was all he'd ever expected his world to be.

"You have friends now," she told him. "And with luck,

Peachblossom and Jump and I won't do any crying for you."

"I hope not, lady," he said. From the rustle of cloth, she guessed he was preparing to go back to sleep. "It don't sound like any kind of fun."

Cleon left in the morning. Two days later the army split. One part was bound for the western coast. Another turned east. The rest, including Kel, Neal, and Tobe, turned north with fully half of the army that had left Corus. Tobe, now with his own cloak and hat to shed the rain, rode Hoshi as Kel's personal groom. Watching him made Kel feel good. Tobe looked like a proper boy at last, not a little old man in a child's body.

Ten days later General Vanget haMinch, supreme commander of Tortall's northern defenses, met them in Bearsford, the last fortress town on the Great Road North before the border. His presence told Kel how important it was to get the new forces into position quickly. Normally they would have gone to headquarters at Northwatch Fortress to receive their orders.

Vanget wasted no time in giving out assignments. Two days after they reached Bearsford, Kel, the other first-year knights, and fifty senior knights accompanied Duke Baird and his healers to Fort Giantkiller. Lord Wyldon of Cavall, Kel's former training master, commanded there; he would give out their final postings. Lord Raoul would ride a day or two with them before he turned west to take command at Fort Steadfast.

"Do you know where these forts are?" Kel asked him as the last of the army prepared to break up.

"I've been informed," Raoul said drily. "You actually know where Giantkiller is. Third Company named the fort we built with them last summer that, supposedly in honor of me." He made a face. Third Company of the King's Own had waited until Raoul wasn't there to protest before they named the fort. Raoul continued, "Vanget moved Third Company to Steadfast. He's sending regular army troops to Fort Giantkiller."

He hugged Kel briefly. "Gods all bless, Kel. Trust your instincts—they're good. Try to survive the summer. I don't want your mother or Alanna coming after me if you get killed."

Kel grinned as he swung into the saddle. She wished she were going with him, but she knew that everyone who mattered wanted to see how she did without his protection.

"Lady knight, come on," Neal called. "Let's go see if the Stump's forgotten us."

Kel mounted up. "Don't call Lord Wyldon that," she told him as they rode out of Bearsford. "I doubt he's forgotten you. He never threatened anyone else that he'd tie his tongue in a knot."

"Threats are the last resort of a man with no vocabulary," Neal said, nose in the air.

"Well, *I* have a vocabulary," said his father, riding behind them. "I have often wished I could tie your tongue in a knot. Several of them. I can describe them, if you like."

"It's my fate to be misunderstood," Neal announced. He fell back to ride with the more sympathetic Merric.

As the knights shifted riding order, Kel found herself beside Duke Baird. She had often seen Neal's father for healing after her fights in the palace and felt comfortable enough to talk to him. "Your grace, if you don't mind my asking, what are you doing here?" she inquired. "As the royal healer, shouldn't you be in Corus?"

"My assistant has to show whether or not he can step into my office," Neal's father replied. He was a tall, lanky man. His eyes, a darker green than Neal's, were set in deep sockets. His hair was redder than his son's, but his nose was the same. "It's time to see if he can handle the nobility alone. And I have experience in the layout of refugee camps."

"Refugee camps?" Kel repeated.

"When villages are destroyed and there are too many people for single lords to take in, someone must care for them. That's particularly true here, where people scrabble to feed their own." He gestured toward their surroundings: thick woods and stony ridges, the unforgiving north. "We need camps for the refugees. We also need field hospitals for the wounded now that we're faced with all-out war."

For a moment Kel said nothing, thinking of the grim picture he'd just painted. Could she bear the sight of hundreds who'd been cast from their homes? "How do you stand it, your grace?" she asked quietly.

"By doing the best I can," Baird replied, as quiet as Kel. "By remembering my wife, my daughters, and the sons I have left. I can't afford to brood. Too many people need me." He sighed. "I worry about Neal," he confessed. "He tries to hide it, but he's sensitive."

Kel nodded. Baird was right.

"If you are placed together, will you watch him?" asked Baird suddenly. "He respects you, despite the difference in your ages. You're sensible and levelheaded. He listens to you."

Kel stared at the duke, then nodded again. "I will look out for him if I can," she replied honestly.

They reached Fief Tirrsmont at twilight and spent the night behind the castle's gray stone walls. The lord of Tirrsmont pleaded scant room inside the buildings of his inner bailey. He also pleaded scant food, though he feasted Duke Baird and two of the senior knights, along with his own family, on suckling pig, saffron rice, and other delicacies.

Camped in the outer bailey, the army was jammed in among thin, ragged survivors of last year's fighting who were housed there. Kel looked into the commoners' haunted eyes and felt rage burn her heart. Most of the newcomers' rations of porridge and bacon went to the refugees. They accepted the food in silence and fled.

"How can they treat their own people so shabbily?" Kel asked Neal. "The lord and his family look well fed."

"You worry too much about commoners," remarked Quinden of Marti's Hill, who shared the first-years' fire. "They always look as pathetic as they can so we'll feed them. I've never met a commoner who doesn't beg while they hide what they've stolen from you."

"You're an obnoxious canker-blossom," Neal snapped. "Go ooze somewhere else."

"On your way, Quinden," added Merric. "Before we help you along."

Quinden spat into their fire to further express his opinion, then wandered off.

"I pity the folk of Marti's Hill when he inherits," murmured Kel.

In the morning they rode on to Fort Giantkiller. This was country that Kel knew, though the trees were bare and the ground clothed in snow and ice. They were entering the patrol area she had covered the year before with Third Company. This was hard land, with little farming soil. Any wealth came from the fur trade, silver mines, logging, and fishing. They might have trouble feeding themselves if supply trains didn't arrive. On the bright side, the enemy would have even more trouble staying fed, with the mighty Vassa River at their backs to cut off supplies from Scanra.

Some daylight remained when they reached Fort Giantkiller. Kel saw many changes. The fort had been turned from a quickly built home for a company of over one hundred into a fortress with two encircling walls. An abatis had been installed on the outer wall: a number of logs sharpened on the forward end, planted in the side of the ditch. They made a thorny barrier that horses would balk at trying to jump. Watchtowers now stood at each corner of the inner wall. The Tortallan flag snapped in the wind. Below it flapped the commanding officer's banner, a rearing black dog with a black sword in its paws on a white field bordered in gold: the arms of Fief Cavall. Below it were the flags of the army brigade charged with the defense of the district.

Inside, Kel saw even more changes. Third Company's tents were gone, replaced by two-story log buildings. Giantkiller now housed at least five hundred men, their horses, and supplies. Lord Wyldon had taken command of the district when Kel and Lord Raoul had ridden south for her Ordeal. He must have rushed to get all his troops decently housed before winter put a stop to most outdoor work.

"Kel, Kel!" someone cried. A stocky young man barreled into her, flinging strong arms around her to give her a crushing squeeze.

"Mithros save us, I'd forgotten the Brat," Quinden muttered behind Kel.

Kel looked down an inch into a familiar round face and laughed. Owen of Jesslaw's gray eyes blazed with delight; a grin revealed wide-spaced front teeth. His cap of brown curls tumbled over his forehead. As Wyldon's squire, he wore his master's badge. "We knew you couldn't hold the border alone, so we came to lend a hand," she said as he released her. Owen's wild courage was a byword among the pages and squires; he would throw himself into a fight even when he was outnumbered.

"Neal, you came!" Owen cried as he crouched to scratch the gleeful Jump's lone ear. Sparrows swirled around his head as he did so, cheeping their own welcome. "Merric, Seaver, Esmond, you're here!" He looked up, saw Duke Baird, and straightened abruptly. "My lord duke, welcome to Fort Giantkiller," he said with a graceful bow. "Forgive my inattention. If I may take your mount, your grace?"

"Mithros save us, the Stump broke him to bridle," Neal said, his voice dry as he dismounted. "I thought it was impossible."

"Do not let me catch that nickname on your lips as long as you are under the man's command," Duke Baird told Neal sternly as he gave his reins to Owen. "You owe him the appearance of respect, not to mention proper obedience."

Neal met his father's gaze, scowled, then bowed silently. Owen whistled softly; Kel, too, was astounded. She had thought nothing could make Neal back down so quickly.

" 'Scuse me, lady." Kel turned. There stood Tobe with Hoshi's reins. "I'll take 'im now."

Kel gave Peachblossom's reins to Tobe. "Check his hooves, please?" she asked.

"Yes, lady," the boy said. He headed toward the stables, gelding and mare in tow.

"Who was *that*?" The shocked whisper came from Owen. Kel glanced at him: her friend stared gape-jawed at Tobe. "Did you see that? He just—Peachblossom! He just took Peachblossom, and Peachblossom *went*!"

Kel smiled. "That's Tobe," she explained. "He is good with horses."

Duke Baird cleared his throat. "Did my lord Wyldon say what was to be done with us?" he inquired tactfully. A proper squire would have bustled the duke away at the first opportunity. Kel was relieved that Lord Wyldon hadn't changed Owen completely.

"Your grace, forgive me," Owen said with a deep bow. "My lord is out riding patrol yet, but I am to show you where you will sleep and ask if you will dine with him later. To the knights who accompany you"—he bowed to the group that stood behind the duke and Kel—"he sends greetings. Lukin will show you to your quarters"—he beckoned a soldier forward—"and lead you to supper when you choose. My lord asks you to remain in the officers' mess hall after supper. He will send for you to talk of your assignments."

Lukin bowed and beckoned; other soldiers swarmed forward to take charge of the newcomers. Kel, Jump, and the sparrows followed them as Owen guided Duke Baird to headquarters.

Over supper with the officers in their mess hall, the newly arrived knights got some idea of what they would face when the fighting began. So interesting was the talk that Kel didn't realize immediately that Owen came from time to time to lead knights from the mess hall. When he gathered up three at once, she realized he was taking them to Wyldon for orders.

Kel watched as Owen led the knights away. The men's backs were straight under their tunics, their air businesslike as they left. Were any afraid? she wondered. Did they have unsettled dreams of war, as she did? Were any hoping for a post in a fortified place with orders that kept them from battle? Some would get part of the district to guard, with squads of soldiers to command and a small fort to build. Others would go to Wyldon's new fortress between Giantkiller and Steadfast, to the town of Riversedge, or to the castles, to be placed under a senior commander. Some would remain here.

Owen came for Quinden, Seaver, and Esmond, then for Neal and Merric. Suddenly Kel realized that she was the last newly arrived knight to be called. A fist clenched in her belly. She didn't like this. She didn't like it at all.

Wyldon of Cavall had not wanted a girl page. He thought females had no place in battle, Alanna the Lioness and lady knights of the past notwithstanding. He had wanted to send Kel home, then shocked everyone, including himself, when he'd allowed her to stay after a year's probation. Once he'd decided she would remain, he'd taught her as thoroughly as he taught the boys. But he had also said, often, that girls didn't belong in combat, even if they did have good combat skills. Doubt entered Kel's heart. What if he planned to keep her safe with him?

She hadn't become a knight to be safe.

Owen came for her at last. She followed him across the torchlit yard between mess hall and headquarters, her feet crunching the ice that rimmed the ruts in the ground. Surely if Wyldon planned to give Kel a safe assignment, Owen would know and warn her. Owen was a terrible liar, even when he lied by omission. Instead, he bubbled over with plans. Before he entered Wyldon's office and announced her, he'd predicted that they'd send the Scanrans back to their longhouses in a trice. He left, closing the door behind him.

Inside Wyldon's office, Kel studied her old training master. The crow's-feet around Wyldon's hard, dark eyes had deepened, as had the lines at the corners of his firm, well-carved mouth. The scar that ran from the corner of his right eye into his short cropped hair was puffy, which meant it probably ached in the night's raw damp. If it hurt, then certainly the arm that had also been savaged by a killer winged horse called a hurrok would be in pain, too.

Silver gleamed in the hair at Wyldon's temples. His bald pate shone in the light of a globe spelled by mages to cast steady light. Wyldon's skin was chapped, like everyone else's, by northern weather. His cream wool shirt was neat and plain, as was the brown quilted tunic he wore. Kel knew his breeches and boots would also be made for warmth and comfort, not elegance.

"Have a seat, lady knight," he said. "Wine? Or cider?"

Kel sat in the chair before his desk. Despite her fear of what was coming, she was deeply pleased that this man she respected used her new title. "Cider, please, my lord." Recently she had found that wine or liquor gave her ferocious, nauseous headaches. She was happy to give up spirits; she hadn't liked the loose, careless feelings they gave her.

Wyldon poured cups for both of them, then raised his in a toast. "To your shield."

Kel smiled. "To my fine instructors," she replied. They both sipped. The cider, touched with spices, was very good.

Wyldon leaned back in his chair. "I won't dance about," he said. "I'm giving you the hardest assignment of any knight in this district. I think you will hate it, and perhaps me."

Kel's skin tingled. So the news *was* bad. She set her cup on his desk and straightened. "My lord?"

"General Vanget has asked me to build and staff a refugee camp in addition to the new fort. As soon as it's ready, we'll take about three hundred refugees, all ages, from Tirrsmont, Anak's Eyrie, Riversedge, Goatstrack village, and outlying districts. About two hundred more will arrive once fighting begins. Maybe seven hundred in all by summer's end." He reached for a map of the countryside before him and tapped it with a blunt fore-finger. "The only ground I can get for it is an open piece of elk-dung valley between Fiefs Tirrsmont and Anak's

Eyrie, on the Greenwoods River. There's the river for water, and flat ground for planting if no one expects to grow more than enough to survive. There's fortified high ground now, and troops to defend it. My new fort, Mastiff, will be here, on the other side of these hills. We'll patrol as much as we can, to keep Scanrans from getting very far, but there's just too much empty ground and too much forest to plug all our gaps."

Kel nodded. From her experience the year before, she knew how easy it was for the enemy to slip by Tortall's defenders."

"I tried to get land farther south," Wyldon continued. "The nobles there say they pity the refugees and send old clothes, tools, perhaps some grain, but they don't want all those extra mouths on their lands, hunting their game."

So her worst fears were true. He didn't want her in combat. Instead, she was relegated to the protection of refugees. It wasn't *right.* She had more real fighting experience than any first-year knight, even Neal. If she had to wait to pursue the mysterious Blayce and his guard dog, Stenmun, she wanted to spend that time fighting.

She swallowed hard to fight off the urge to cry, then cleared her throat. A knight didn't complain. A knight did her duty even when the duty was unpleasant. Even when everyone would say Wyldon had so little confidence in her that he was tucking her away behind the front lines.

"Who's to command this place, sir?" she asked, forcing her voice to remain even, her features smooth and calm.

Wyldon raised his brows. "You are."

For a moment her ears felt very strange. That feeling

promptly spread to the rest of her. "Forgive me, my lord, but—I could have sworn that you said *I* will be in command."

"I did." Wyldon's eyes were direct. "It's work, Mindelan. Half of the men I can spare to build and guard the camp are convicts. They agreed to fight if we took them from the quarries and mines. They must be watched and further trained. All have mage marks to expose them as convicts if they run, so you shouldn't worry about desertions, unless they're fool enough to go to Scanra. The other half of the men I could find"—he shrugged—"I did my best."

Kel looked at her hands as thoughts tumbled wildly in her head. She voiced the first thought that came to mind. "I expected to serve under an experienced warrior. In combat."

"You are more useful with the refugees. You will have advisors. Duke Baird will reside with you temporarily, to help in matters both medical and social," Wyldon said drily.

Panic rose in her chest. "Sir, I'm only eighteen; I don't know anything about refugee camps! Everyone says it, first-year knights are so green, we're better off plowed and planted with something useful!"

"You are not a typical first-year," Wyldon replied firmly. "The Knight Commander of the King's Own trained you in matters like supply, the building and defense of a fort, and how to command. You helped him recruit new personnel for the Own, and he says your work in supply and logistics is superior."

The words fell out before Kel could stop them: "He also trained me for *battle.*" About to apologize, she closed her lips tightly. She had meant it.

Wyldon rubbed his bad arm, staring into the distance for a long moment before he said, "If this were last summer's war, I wouldn't expect much danger. Raids don't get far without help. But this isn't last summer's war. The border will vanish. King Maggur wants to keep the ground he takes. There is no safe zone within a hundred miles of the border. You'll see combat. I guarantee that."

Kel met Wyldon's eyes with hers. "Sir, you'll have forts and patrols close to the Vassa—between me and the enemy. I still feel like you're trying to keep me safe. That's not why I became a knight."

Wyldon sighed, levered himself out of his chair, and went to the door. "Come with me."

Outside, Wyldon led the way to a large building near the rear wall. Its windows, covered with hides to keep out the weather, leaked bits of light. Wyldon found the door and entered, Kel on his heels.

The large building was filled with sound: conversation, babies' and children's crying, the clatter of wood. Rows of three-tiered bunk beds lined the walls. There were lofts overhead on either side, with railings to keep anyone from falling to the ground floor. Rope strung across the open space between them held drying laundry. Bags of winter fruits, garlic, bundles of dried herbs, and vegetables also hung from the rails. The air was filled with the scent of rarely washed human, burned food, cooking fat, and animal urine. Cats and dogs hid in the shadows, lay on the beds, or played with anyone who would bother. At the far end of the barracks a giant hearth provided warmth and cooking fire.

Silence fell as the door closed behind Kel and Wyldon. Those people closest to them went quiet, staring at the district commander and his tall companion. Face after face turned, half hidden by shadow, fitfully lit by lamps or hearth fire. Children and adults appeared between gaps in the loft railings to see why the room below had gone still.

"If you've come to share supper, my lord, we've none to spare," announced a woman by the fire. "We ate it all and could have eaten more."

She walked forward. There had been more of her once, from the way her stained red wool dress hung on her stocky body. Her eyes were brown and heavy-lidded, the eyes of someone who had seen hard times. Age had scored deep lines around her nose and mouth. Her nose was broad and fleshy at the tip, her lower lip fuller than the upper, giving her a look of dissatisfaction. A kerchief of black wool kept reddish brown hair from her face; a black wool shawl hung from her elbows.

She stopped before Wyldon and Kel. "Giving this pup a look at the unfortunate?" she asked, her husky voice scornful. "Something for the lad to write home about?"

It seemed the woman thought she was a boy. Kel looked down at her bosom. She wore a quilted tunic, which hid her small breasts, and it had been so long since a knight had worn the double ring on her badge that most wouldn't know it signified a lady knight.

"Good evening, Mistress Fanche," Wyldon said courteously. "This is one of the knights who has come to defend the border, Lady Knight Keladry of Mindelan. Lady Keladry, Fanche Weir."

His voice was loud enough that everyone nearby heard. For a moment there was no sound. Then a whispered rattle of talk broke out, spreading to fill the room. Kel heard "lady knight" repeated over and over.

Kel bowed to Fanche, glancing at the woman's left ring finger. Fanche wore a ring of black braid: she was a widow.

"Fanche's husband Gothar was the Goatstrack miller," Wyldon explained.

"'Was' bakes no bread," Fanche said. "I'm single enough now, and I've work to do." She returned to the hearth to stir whatever simmered in the biggest pot.

"The Scanrans hit Goatstrack last October—burned the mill, killed the miller and their daughters," explained Wyldon softly. "Thirty-seven dead in the entire village. Fanche mustered those who remained and got them here, fighting Scanrans the whole distance. She saved fifty-eight lives."

"She's a handful, that one," commented the man who now stood by Wyldon's elbow. He was shorter than Kel, unshaven, with ears that stuck out and an impish glint in his blue eyes. He was going bald in an unfortunate way, losing strands of brown hair in clumps, giving his crown the look of a field gone to weeds. He was weathered, the sun having put deep crow's-feet by his eyes and two long creases down either cheek. Like Fanche—like all the refugees—he wore clothes that would have fit someone with more meat on his bones. He stood casually, hands dug into his pockets. "Gods, I love a tough woman," he admitted.

"You have your work cut out with her," Wyldon said with a chuckle.

"Oh, well, I like work," the man replied.

Kel, startled, looked from him to Wyldon. Her training master always stood on dignity; Neal's epithet, the Stump, was justified. Never had she heard Wyldon laugh or joke. Never had she seen him smile for amusement's sake, as he did now.

He's happy, she realized, stunned. Training us—that was his duty. But he didn't like it. He's comfortable here, in the dirt and the cold, with people to defend.

"Keladry of Mindelan, Saefas Plowman," Wyldon said. "He's a trapper."

The man bowed. "Not from Goatstrack, so I've had little time to wear her down," he said with a grin. "The way Squire Owen tells it, milady, you're ten feet tall and eat ogres."

Kel smiled. She could see that Owen would like this man. "I shrank in my last hot bath," she replied. "I'm very disheartened by it."

People came over to be introduced. So did others as word spread that the realm's second female knight was present. They spoke to Wyldon, asking for news as they eyed Kel. All bore the signs of hard times: clothes that were too loose, ragged, and stained; skin that had once covered more flesh. Their eyes were haunted by family and friends who were dead, crippled, enslaved, or missing.

At last Wyldon bade the refugees good-night and led Kel back to headquarters. Inside, he knelt to poke up the fire. "I hear you have a new servant."

"Yessir," Kel replied. She watched the play of firelight

over Wyldon's features. "You took me there because you wanted me to feel badly for them, enough that I would take the command. But all you have to do is order me."

"Sometimes it's better to have understanding than obedience," Wyldon informed her. He got to his feet with a grimace. "I know this is not what you wanted. No matter what I say, you and others will think this is a dungheap assignment."

He sat in a chair and motioned for Kel to sit opposite him. She did so gratefully. The long day's ride and the time standing with the refugees had made her ache.

"The truth is, you are the only one I can trust to do this job properly," Wyldon explained. "You care enough about commoners to do the task well. I did consider Queenscove, but he is much too fair. He shares his sarcasm and his inability to abide fools with all, regardless of rank. If they didn't kill him within two weeks, I'd have to see if he was drugging their water." He winced as he flexed the hand on his bad arm. "Anyone else will order them about, create more resentment, and turn the place into a shambles—or pursue his own amusements and leave them to get into trouble."

Kel rubbed her face. He was right. She'd heard her peers' opinions of commoners, had been accused of caring too much about them. Not so long ago, she had learned that the maximum punishment given to a noble who'd arranged the kidnapping of another noble's servant was a fine, to compensate for the loss of the servant's work. That law was being changed, but there were others like it. A noble owed a duty to those who served him, but such duty was not glorious. Fairness and consideration were unnecessary; the affairs and pride of commoners were unimportant. The noble who worried too much about them was somehow weak. Kel knew her world. Her respect for common blood was a rarity. Her father's grandparents were merchants. Every branch of their family save his was still merchants to the bone. Perhaps it was also because her parents, as diplomats, were so used to seeing other points of view, foreign or Tortallan, that they had passed their attitudes on to their children.

She also knew Wyldon was right about Neal.

"Well?" her former training master inquired. "Will you do this, Keladry of Mindelan?"

Blayce! she thought, suddenly panicked. The Nothing Man! If I'm pinned to a camp, how will I find him? How will I stop him?

She remembered those thin faces in the barracks, child and adult alike. She remembered Tirrsmont, crammed with people. Looking at Wyldon, she saw trust in his face, the face of a man she respected as much as she did her father and Lord Raoul.

Kel sighed. "I'll do it, my lord."

Her first task was to choose supplies. Wyldon cautioned her not to get greedy. The next morning he sent Owen with her to write down her choices. When they reached the storehouse, Kel stopped to look at her unusually quiet friend. Owen wouldn't meet her eyes.

She put her hand under his chin, startled to feel the scrape of newly shaved whiskers, and made him look at her. "You didn't know," she said.

Owen grimaced. Words tumbled from his mouth:

"Kel, I swear I didn't! He told me this morning. He—he *apologized,* for keeping something important from me, he said, 'specially when I have to learn about making camps like this, but he said you'd see it on my face, and he wanted to talk to you first. Kel, if I knew, I'd've argued him out of it. Well, I'd've tried to," he amended as Kel took her hand away from his chin. "He's hard to argue with. But I *would've* tried! I'm so sorry!"

Kel grinned. "Of course he wouldn't tell you," she informed him. "You're the worst liar I know, even if you're just not saying anything. You ought to feel virtuous, that he knows you can't lie."

"I feel like a failure," Owen confessed. "A true friend would have found out and warned you."

"How?" Kel asked reasonably, leading the way into the storehouse. "Search his papers? That's hardly proper. And what could I have done if you'd told me? Run off? Stop fussing." She opened the shutters, admitting the morning light so they could see the rows of goods. Her sparrows flew in. Some perched on Owen; others zipped around the stacked supplies, as if taking their own inventory.

"But Kel, making you a, a nursemaid!" protested Owen, stroking a male sparrow's black collar with a gentle finger. "When you're a better warrior than anybody but my lord! And Lord Raoul, and the Lioness," he added, belatedly remembering that there might be others Kel would think were better. "It's just not right!"

"My lord says I'll see plenty of fighting," Kel told him.

Owen studied her for a long moment. Whatever he sought in her face, he seemed to find it. "Anything you want me to do, Kel, you let me know," he told her seriously.

He gripped her arm for a moment, then let go. "Anything I can do to help."

For a moment they looked at one another, Owen's gaze firm, Kel's thoughtful. He's growing up, she thought, surprised. And he's growing up well.

She patted his shoulder, then surveyed the storehouse. "For now I need a quartermaster," she said. They might never talk about what had just passed, but neither would they forget it. "Someone who can say what's reasonable to draw for my people."

"Be right back," Owen promised, and trotted out the door.

Tobe and Jump came in as he left, Tobe directing a scowl at Owen's back. "I can do anything he might do," Tobe informed Kel.

She clasped his shoulder, amused and yet flattered. "I need you for other things, Tobe," she informed him. "We've a lot of work ahead."

4
KEL TAKES COMMAND

With the men who had built the camp—soldiers, convict soldiers, and refugees—already in residence, Kel saw no reason to linger at Fort Giantkiller. She needed a thorough view of her new home and its surroundings before the bulk of her charges arrived. Once they did, she would be short on time.

Two days after her arrival at Giantkiller, she left at the head of a train that included Duke Baird, Lord Wyldon, Neal, Merric, and Owen, as well as the supplies she had taken with the quartermaster's approval. She had been disconcerted to find that Neal, the camp's healer, and Merric, their patrol captain, would technically be under her command. Neal didn't seem to mind, but Neal never reacted like most people. On the other hand, she would have to be extra careful with Merric. She wasn't sure that *she* would like being under the command of one of her year-mates.

Once the train was assembled, Giantkiller's defenders opened the gates of the inner and outer walls. Lord Wyldon gave the signal, and they rode out in a rumble of hooves, the jingle of harnesses, and the creak of wagon wheels.

A pure, beautiful voice rose in the crisp air, singing an old northern song about the waking of the sun. Startled, Kel looked for the singer. It was Tobe, his face alight as he sang. A deeper voice joined his, then others: the song was a common one, though the words might vary from region to region. Above the baritone, bass, and tenor voices of the men and older boys soared Tobe's perfect soprano. Even Kel, Wyldon, and Baird sang, their voices soft. Only Neal scowled at his saddle horn, still not awake.

Giantkiller's refugees clustered around the gates to watch them go. Fanche had been quite vocal when she had learned who was to command their new home. The kindest phrase she'd used was "wet-behind-the-ears southerner." If the gods were good, perhaps Fanche would change her mind. If they weren't, Kel would have a long time to get the formidable woman on her side.

"When people tell me a knight's job is all glory, I laugh, and laugh, and laugh," Lord Raoul had once told Kel. "Sometimes I can stop laughing before they edge away and talk about soothing drinks."

She knew what he meant.

Still, when Tobe started the next song, about the stag who met the Goddess as Maiden, Kel sang along.

* * *

April was a chancy month in the north. Normally few Tortallans would try to build or march here until May, but the news of King Maggur's arrival on the throne had forced their hand. Kel had plenty of time to observe the once-familiar countryside while the men wrestled the wagons out of one muddy dip after another. It took her a little while to place the landmarks: she had been here last in the summer, when the woods and hills were alive with birds, animals, and insects. Now it was cold and grim. Patches of snow lay under the groves of pine trees, but here and there she could see a courageous green bud or sprout. Some of the hardier songbirds were returning from the south. Those birds who had stayed through the winter perched on tree limbs and in hollows, waiting for things to warm up.

Between Fort Giantkiller and Kel's future home was a series of rocky hills, one or two of which might actually be called a mountain. The road was tucked deep between them, enough so that once they reached it, they were on solid frozen ground once again. They lost no more time pulling their wagons from the mud.

On the far side of the hills, they found the next valley also dotted with patches of melting snow and heavy stretches of pines and newly budding trees. They kept to the road until Wyldon pointed something out to Kel. She raised her spyglass, a gift from Lady Alanna, to her eye and looked. There, on a rise of perhaps twenty feet, stood a log palisade. That was it: her first command. Men and sledges moved along the road that climbed diagonally across the face of the rise, bringing in logs. Every ten feet along the top of the wall stood guards in regular army maroon, each wearing a conical helm, each carrying a bow. The travelers heard a distant horn call: they'd been spotted.

Wyldon's trumpeter replied with the call that signaled they were friends.

Kel continued to eye her new home. Above the fort she saw the Tortallan flag, a silver blade and crown on a royal-blue field. Suddenly another flag climbed the mast from inside the fort until it flew just below the national banner. It was a square of dusty blue with a double border of cream and blue. The device at its center was familiar: gray owl and cream glaives bordered in gold. It was Kel's own insignia, the flag of the commander of the fort.

She lowered her spyglass and took her time as she collapsed it and set it just so into its pouch until her leaping emotions were under control. Who at the camp would have known she was coming and gone to the trouble to create a flag for her?

As the supply train drew closer, they saw the Greenwoods River at the base of the high ground. The ice was breaking up, the water cold and swift as it tore chunks away. The river was a little over twenty feet wide; Kel judged it to be normally fifteen feet deep at most. The spring meltwater would keep it high and swift for now.

They crossed the Greenwoods on a sturdy wooden bridge. It was the only one Kel saw in either direction. She looked at it before they crossed. Flat black disks called mage blasts were fixed on the piles and underside of the bracing planks. Even a non-mage could make the things explode by snapping the thin, flat piece of wood that was the key to the spell. The blasts would then drop the bridge, and anyone on it, into the river.

As a moat, this was fairly good. No enemy would be able to cross the Greenwoods within miles of the camp as long as the spring floods continued. Kel had spent the previous night studying the maps of her new command. In summer the river could be forded, but only ten miles upstream and thirty miles downstream. She devoutly hoped the army could stop the enemy by then.

Their company rode up the sloping road around to the north face of the camp: the river-moat protected the gateless eastern and southern sides of the enclosure. Rocky, inhospitable hills gave some protection to the west. North toward the forest was a squad of ten soldiers guarding a sledge piled with logs. The sounds of hammers and saws grew louder as the riders reached the top and the large gates swung open. Remembering her last encounter with a hammer, Kel winced and entered the camp.

The great expanse of open ground inside the walls was a mess of churned mud, crates, plank walkways, and equipment in between raw wooden platforms that looked to be floors for future barracks. Kel noted a well on her left and another on her right, both covered with wooden lids. Near the right-hand well stood a barracks with the army's flag hung over the door and a large stable behind it. Beyond those stood two complete long, wooden two-story buildings and a third that was nearly done. These would house the refugees.

On her left, beside the gate, was the guard shack. Beyond it, in front of the other well, stood a two-story headquarters that would serve as office and residence for her, Neal, Merric, Tobe, and, for now, Duke Baird. She checked the half-finished building behind it on her camp map. It would be the infirmary, big enough to serve their sick or wounded. Behind that was a second low building, a woodshed for the infirmary and the mess hall and cookhouse near the center of the camp. Against the rear wall, Kel noted storage sheds and what was unmistakably a latrine. According to her map, this one could seat ten at a time.

Ground space for future buildings was marked by pegs and ribbon or, in some places, complete wooden floors. The flagpole rose at the very center of the camp, with four sets of double stocks at its base. Kel looked up at the flags and shook her head. Her flag looked very brave. She wished she felt the same way. She sensed the men's eyes on her as they worked and couldn't help but wonder what they made of her.

A man in army maroon who wore his gray hair cropped short trotted down one of the wooden staircases that led to the walkway that lined the upper wall. He strode briskly along planks laid on the mud to halt before Lord Wyldon. Kel noted the newcomer wore a yellow band on each arm, embroidered with crossed black swords, a regular army captain's insignia.

He came to attention before Wyldon and saluted. "My lord."

Wyldon returned the salute and began the introductions. "Captain Hobard Elbridge, I present his grace Duke Baird of Queenscove, chief of the royal healers." Elbridge bowed. Wyldon continued, "Here is Lady Knight Keladry of Mindelan, who will relieve you here as commander, Sir Nealan of Queenscove, who will be camp healer, and Sir Merric of Hollyrose, in charge of camp security."

The captain bowed to each of them. Looking around, he found a man who wore a sergeant's black circle and dot on his armbands and beckoned him over. "Your grace, my lord Wyldon, sir knights, Sergeant Landwin here will take charge of your things and show you where you're to sleep."

Kel watched the men follow the sergeant, wishing she didn't feel so bereft as they disappeared into headquarters.

"Lady knight, what would you have us do here?" Elbridge inquired. "Will you address the men? Tour what we have? Review the country? I have keys to give you, of course, and I must familiarize you with the state of affairs here. The camp is unnamed. We thought to leave that to you."

Kel dismounted from Hoshi to hide her confusion. Wyldon had given her no advice about how to actually *take* command, and this man seemed determined to dump everything into her lap at once. "How long are you with us, Captain Elbridge?"

"It's my hope to ride on to the new fort in the morning, milady," he said, his face unreadable, "but of course I'll stay as long as you have need of me."

Kel looked around. The soldiers had come to take charge of the horses and supply wagons, leading the free mounts toward the stable and directing the drivers of the wagons to the storehouses. Only Tobe remained with Peachblossom and the packhorse assigned to Kel by the Crown. The sparrows and Jump rode on the pack-horse, watching Kel and the captain with almost human intensity.

"Is there any time during the day when the men are all assembled?" Kel asked. "Suppertime, perhaps?"

"Aye, milady. Lunch most of them take where they work."

Kel passed Hoshi's reins to Tobe. "You may as well tend the horses, Tobe, and bring my things to my quarters."

"Very good, my lady," he said, bowing in the saddle before he accepted Hoshi's rein.

Somebody gave him lessons in manners, Kel thought, amused, before she looked at Elbridge again. "Why don't we tour the camp and you tell me how things are," she suggested. "Let the men work unhindered—there's time enough to talk at supper."

Elbridge fumbled at his belt until what looked like a small bundle of sticks came free in his hand. Bowing, he offered them to Kel. "Lady knight, I surrender this camp to you. Here are the keys to the mage blasts."

She blinked for a moment, then accepted the keys. Each was strung on a leather thong, secured to a ring, and labeled with the location of its mage blast. Now she alone could set off the blasts that would explode and drop the bridge into the river.

"And here are the keys to this place." Elbridge gave Kel an iron ring. More conventional keys dangled from it. "Allow me to show you where they are used."

She had not expected the place to be so big, or that so much work would already be done. She said as much to her escort.

"They did it inside, most of it," the captain explained as they walked through the soldiers' barracks. "Cobbled the floors together in sections in a barn at a homestead nearby—the house was burned, but we could use the barn. They worked all winter, planing boards, whittling pegs, cutting shingles, making nails. These northmen are the fastest woodworkers I've laid eyes on. They say they're used to it, just not so much at one time."

Outside, he led her toward the flagpole. "That long key's for the stocks," he said, pointing them out. They framed the pole, with room for two men on each. Two yards beyond them was a flogging post. "Here's another symbol of your office," he explained, handing over a cowhide whip. Kel nearly dropped it in her distaste but hid her feelings behind her very best Yamani mask. She didn't want to feel the leather in her hand, so she hung it from her dagger hilt.

"These convict guards, they need a touch of the lash," the captain informed her. "It's the only thing they understand."

"Will they fight?" Kel asked as they walked on.

"If they don't want to end up collared and on the march back to Scanra they will," he replied. "They know it. I trained them and the builders on weapons this winter, same as my own men. The convicts' weapons are locked up in headquarters unless there's need. I don't know about Sir Nealan as a healer, but tell him he can't let them come whining to him whenever they've a scratch. These prisoners take any excuse to get off work, and they love it when the healer's a soft touch."

With every word Kel disliked the man more and more. Obviously he was good at his job. The proof was everywhere she looked. His manner itched her, though.

He didn't talk about others as if they were human, only animals to be driven.

"There's so much room," she commented as he pointed out the pens where livestock was kept and the ground that would serve the cookhouse as a small garden. "I didn't understand from the map just how much space we have."

"It'll fill up soon, with civilians bringing their clutter and animals," the captain replied. "But it's true we've more to work with than we thought last fall. That's Master Salmalín's doing. My lord was showing him this place, saying how it was the best location for a camp. Master Salmalín opens his mouth and says—something, I don't know what." The captain shuddered. "It—it made my bones ache. The ground close to the hills, it dropped about fifty feet. And the ground here starts rising up like an inchworm crawls. Suddenly we've twice the high ground to build on as we had before. Mages." Elbridge shook his head. "Very well, you can see we've storage sheds enough, and the latrines beyond." He led her through the rest of the camp. Stopping at its rear, he asked, "Have you questions?"

"Not really," Kel told him. "I would like to go over the walls, if you don't mind."

Elbridge looked at her, his face impossible to read. "These northern woodsmen know what they're doing, lady knight."

"I'm sure they do," she replied politely. "I just want a full view."

She circled the camp once inside the wall on the ground, testing the trees that formed it, finding them hard and sound. The gate was also very well built and would take plenty of battering, if it came to that. She went to the first set of stairs and climbed to the top, not looking at the open air outside the rail. At the end of her page term, she had conquered her fear of heights, at least as far as being able to climb without either freezing or vomiting. Still, she would never like them.

On the walkway, she inspected its boards. They were as sound as the wall itself and placed low enough that the top of the wall would give her soldiers protection from enemy archers.

Since the guards were there, the captain introduced them. Kel shook hands with each man, looking him in the eye. Whispers ran the circuit of the wall but Kel refused to try to hear what was being said. She had been through this before, too. These men would respect her, or not, over time. There was nothing she could do now to win them over. She didn't even try, beyond a smile and a firm handshake. She was responsible for their lives, not their affections. Did it scare them to know a green girl was in charge here? Or did they feel safe this far from the border?

She did not feel safe, for all that this was a well-built refuge. She knew the heavy forests that ranged on either side of the Greenwoods River north of the camp. Last summer had taught her just how many of the enemy could sneak by in such forests. This strong camp might not be enough.

It all depended on the Scanrans, their numbers, their allies, and their strange magic that turned chain, iron-coated bone, and iron sheets into killing devices. Kel wouldn't be able to guard hundreds of civilians with the forty soldiers Wyldon had promised her. The refugees had to be trained to fight, not just the men, but the women, even the older children. Her next shipment of supplies had to include weapons if the refugees had none of their own.

In a day or two she'd start riding the country until she knew it like her palm. She'd make sure the refugees and soldiers knew it, too. Standing over the gate, she stared blankly into the distance as she made plans. They'd have to know the roads and trails to Forts Mastiff, Steadfast, and Giantkiller, and their escape routes to the south. She was lucky to have local people inside her walls. They'd know the hidden and not-so-hidden trails, bogs, pitfalls, and canyons around here, as well as the best hunting and fishing areas.

She realized the captain was speaking. "What? I'm sorry, Captain Elbridge. I was thinking."

A corner of his mouth twitched—in amusement or scorn? wondered Kel. "I was asking if the lady knight had chosen a name," Elbridge repeated.

"A name for what?" Kel asked, looking at him blankly.

"This place. We call it 'this miserable mudpit,' but my lady will be living here. It's your privilege to name it as you like," explained the captain.

Kel turned, her hands jammed into her breeches pockets, and surveyed her command. Men crawled over beams, hammered, sawed, unloaded wagons, called out to each other, visited the latrines. Wyldon, Baird, Neal, and Merric were emerging from headquarters. She glanced at the road below: here came the sledge with its military guard and its load of cut trees.

"I suppose 'Mudpit' is a little depressing," she admitted. "I'll have to think about it."

The captain bowed. "Very good, milady."

They descended the stairs near the guard shack as the gates swung open. The sledge made its slow way inside the walls.

"I see you've conducted your first inspection," Wyldon said to Kel. "What do you think?"

"Captain Elbridge has done far more than I could imagine," Kel said honestly. For a hard, cold fish, she thought. "I'll be hard put to keep up his good work." As soon as I've thrown his whip into the compost heap, where it'll be of use, she added silently.

"We've plenty of work to do in the infirmary," Duke Baird said. "But I've seen the plans. It looks good."

Elbridge shrugged. "It's these northern woodsmen. If they could find a way to eat trees as well as work them, they'd be rich men. Still, I confess, I'll be pleased to be working only with soldiers again. These civilians are too contrary for my taste."

He, Baird, and Wyldon turned away to discuss matters relating to the new Fort Mastiff while Neal and Merric automatically looked at Kel. "I feel as ready for all this as a babe who picks up a sword," Merric said with a twisted smile. "Of course, Neal is ready—"

"Mithros save us, they'll allow just any freak of nature up here, won't they?" a familiar male voice proclaimed. Kel, Merric, and Neal turned to see the speaker. One of the sledge guards, a tall, broad-shouldered young man, dismounted from his horse. Bright blue eyes blazed and a broad grin flashed in a face splattered with mud. Under other mud Kel could see the familiar tunic, chain mail, and armband of a sergeant in the King's Own. "Meathead!" he called, handing his reins to a guard. "They sent you out with no keeper?"

Neal laughed and strode forward to hug the slightly taller man despite the mud. Kel almost ran to the newcomer as well, remembering just in time that a commander couldn't throw herself at an old friend. She knew Domitan of Masbolle, Neal's cousin and a sergeant of the King's Own, very well indeed. They'd become friends during her four years with the King's Own. She'd had a terrible, unreturned, crush on him—he was handsome, mud or no.

Neal pushed Dom away. "Insubordinate!" he scoffed. "That's *Sir* Meathead, to you. What have you been doing, chasing mudhoppers?"

"It's a skin treatment. I've gotten so chapped here in the north," retorted Dom. He turned to Kel and bowed. "Lady knight," he said, and straightened with a wide grin. "You did it. We knew you would."

Kel reached out her hand; they clasped forearms, Dom squeezing hers tightly before he let go.

Another voice sounded out. "Squire Kel—I mean, lady knight!" The other men who'd been guarding the sledge came over. Kel cheerfully shook hands with each of them, Dom's squad in the King's Own. One hot day the previous summer, at a place called Forgotten Well, she had commanded these men after an arrow shot had put Dom out of action. Both Wolset and Fulcher now wore mud-splashed armbands with the circle mark for a corporal. Dom had lost one corporal before he'd been wounded; the second was killed after Kel took command. She'd given Wolset a field promotion to corporal for keeping his head, and Dom had confirmed it. Two of the other six men before her she did not know. They simply bowed to her and stayed back, watching with interest.

"What are you doing here, anyway?" she asked Dom when the greetings were over.

"Lord Wyldon asked for one of our squads to work here till the place is finished, since we've been in the area almost a year. It's just coincidence that my boys got tapped," Dom told her. "Have you seen Giantkiller? Just when we got the place all fixed up, the regular army kicked us out. I bet they ruined all of our chair cushions."

"I noticed a sad lack of taste," Neal said in his usual drawl, "but I figured it was left over from when the King's Own lived there."

Dom grinned, then looked at Kel. "Do you like your flag?" he asked.

She smiled at him with all the gratitude in her heart. "I love it," she told him.

"He don't get *all* the credit," Corporal Wolset said. "It was me that thought of it."

"And you what nearly ruined the embroidering," retorted Corporal Fulcher.

Dom cleared his throat. "Here comes command. We'll talk later, Lady Kel, Sir Meathead." He waved his squad back to the sledge. They helped the civilians unload the logs.

"That was friendly," Merric remarked, folding his arms.

"They're from Third Company," Kel said. "We rode together for four years."

"Dom's squad fought one of the metal killing devices under Kel's command." Neal's voice sounded clearly over the racket of nearby hammers and saws. His wry tone told Kel what he thought of her not mentioning such important specifics. "Dom got shot; they lost two men."

"And it took all of us to beat the cursed thing," Kel retorted, wishing Neal hadn't spoken. It seemed like bragging, even if it was Neal's comment, not hers.

"*You* fought one of those things?" Elbridge demanded, hard eyes fixed on Kel.

She was starting to feel cross. She didn't want to boast. Wolset had trapped the thing's head as the other men roped its limbs. Still, she didn't appreciate the captain's disbelief, either. "Together with Sergeant Domitan's squad, captain," she replied, locking her hands behind her back as a reminder to keep her face and voice bland and polite. "None of us wants to repeat it."

"Mithros witness that," murmured Duke Baird.

Wyldon and the captain murmured the ritual reply "So mote it be," Neal and Merric just a syllable behind them. Kel said nothing. She didn't think anything she said to Mithros on the subject of the killing devices would stop the war god from allowing more of them to swarm over the border that summer.

After lunch, Wyldon, Kel, Merric, the captain, Owen, and a squad rode out to view the land immediately around the fort, returning with Elbridge's regular patrol as the sun vanished behind the western mountains.

That night the soldiers who rode with Lord Wyldon took supper in the barracks where they slept. Those who would remain to guard the camp—recovering wounded men, convicts, and such whole soldiers as Wyldon could spare—Dom's squad, and the civilian loggers, carpenters, smiths, and men-of-all-work took their supper in the mess hall. The nobles, Captain Elbridge, and Dom shared a table at one end of the building.

Listening to the men talk, Kel wished that Dom and his squad were to stay all summer, and not just because he was easy on the eyes. Cleaned up and wearing a fresh blue tunic, Dom was fair-skinned, with Neal's curved brows and that same long nose, wide at the tip. Dom had a relaxed, comfortable charm that made anyone feel confident. That charm could help to ease Kel's dealings with the men she had to command. Dom would influence those who believed Kel to be no warrior. Like Raoul, Dom had always taken Kel's fighting skills as a matter of course. He would make it clear to any doubters that she pulled her weight in a fight or a march. She knew that she couldn't depend on Dom, though. Once the real fighting began, he would return to Fort Steadfast and Raoul.

Over supper, news from the palace and the border was traded. Kel let the others do the talking as she sneaked bits of meat to Jump. At last Lord Wyldon pushed his plate away. Duke Baird had finished some time ago, and Captain Elbridge was nearly done.

"Keladry," Wyldon said quietly. "Time."

"Yessir," Kel said automatically. She extracted herself from her seat between Neal and Merric, then wiped her hands on a handkerchief. For a moment she nearly forgot and raised her hands to check her hair but stopped herself in time. It would not do for men whom she was to command to see her do something so feminine when her mind should be on business.

I can't do this, she thought desperately as she took a

last swig of cider and set down her cup. I'm eighteen! Someone should be commanding *me,* not the other way around! Wyldon's trusting me with their lives, and me with the paint still wet on my shield. . . .

Somehow her feet and legs carried her down the long rows of men and tables, past Tobe and Saefas to the open part of the hall. Before her now sat four squads of soldiers, forty men in uniform, and about sixty-five civilians who were all refugees. These were the first people she had to deal with in her new position, and they would carry their impression of her to those who would arrive soon.

Kel looked for something to stand on and found a wooden box. She wiggled it when she put it in position, just to make sure it could bear her weight. The men, who had watched her come their way, chuckled quietly.

Kel looked up and smiled. "There's so much of me," she explained. "It would be undignified if I stepped on it and it broke."

Another, louder chuckle rose from them. One of the knots in her chest came undone. Just like the men of Third Company, they liked a joke at an officer's expense. Carefully she stepped onto the box: it held her. She waited as men set down their forks and knives.

As she waited, she looked them over, face by face. None of them, not even the healthiest soldier, was untouched by the hard times of recent years. She recognized the convict soldiers: they bore a silver circle on their foreheads. It would shine under hair, mud, or face paint; it could not be cut out with a knife. The only way to remove it was to use spells that were carefully guarded by palace magistrates. Even without the mark, Kel would have known the convicts. They were the thinnest of all, hollow-eyed and gaunt-cheeked. Right now they looked to be near exhaustion from a day of guard duty and unloading wagons.

She would have to feed them up if they were to manage any serious fighting. They were criminals, of course. They'd no doubt deserved their sentences to the mines and quarries. She'd known two men who had been sentenced to prison, and she'd hated them for their crime. Presumably the men here were guilty of the same or worse, but surely the officers knew starved men had no strength to fight.

One convict stood and walked between the tables, peering at Kel.

"You, there," Captain Elbridge called. He fell silent; Kel guessed that Wyldon had told him to let her manage this. She kept her eyes on the approaching man. There was gray in his coarse-cut black hair, gray in the stubble on his chin, too. His nose was a long prow of bone, his eyes shadows in their sockets. From the darkness of his skin and from his features, he was kin to the tribes of the southern desert. He was too pale to be full-blooded Bazhir, and as he drew closer she saw his eyes were gray, not brown. His uniform was patched and worn; of course they wouldn't give convicts the best, she realized. That irritated her. Are they supposed to come here to fight and die quickly, so we can make more room in the quarries and mines? she wondered, keeping her face mild and blank.

"Can I help you, soldier?" she asked when he stopped a yard from her.

He rubbed his chin with bony fingers. "I begs pardon

for my forwardness, lady knight," he said, awkwardly gallant, "but was you anywheres near the River Hasteren in summer, seven years gone? Hill country?"

"Yes," Kel replied, puzzled. "Lord Wyldon took the pages there for summer exercises in camping and field craft."

"You seen any fighting, them days?" the man asked. "Nothin' big, just a scramble, like. With hillmen?"

Now Kel was curious as well as puzzled. "We rode with the army when they cleaned out some hill bandit nests," she replied. "And some friends of mine and I got into a little trouble, which is how we learned bandits were in the area."

"I knew it!" he cried, jubilant. "I *thought* 'twas you, but there's more of you now. You should've seen the likes of her, boys," he said, turning toward the other convicts as he pointed at Kel. "We was all outlaws, livin' on the edges, and this bunch of pages stumbled into our camp. We chased 'em back in a canyon, and *her*"—he jabbed his finger at Kel—"she gutted ol' Breakbone Dell, and him the meanest dog skinner you'd ever hope to meet. Stood there afoot, her and her spear, cool as meltwater with Breakbone ridin' down on her with that neck-cutter sword of his. First time she got 'im in the leg, second in the tripes, and he was done. Her and six lads held us all back, just them. There she was, eyes like stone and that bloody spear in her hand. Lady." He bowed deep.

Kel looked at him, not sure what to say. Finally she asked, "What's your name, soldier?"

"Me? Gilab Lofts—Gil. Lady. It's—it's good to see you well." He bowed again and returned to his seat, whispering with the men on either side of him.

Kel waited for them to quiet once again before she said ruefully, "I'm not sure that being known for gutting a man is exactly a recommendation for a commander."

"It is in the north!" cried someone. Several men laughed outright; others grinned. Kel felt the very air in the room lighten.

"Well, perhaps it is," she admitted. "I've been away all winter, so I may have forgotten." This time they were quick to fall quiet, curious to hear what she would say. "So you *won't* be calling me the girl that gutted Breakbone, my name is Keladry of Mindelan. Lady Knight Keladry of Mindelan. And it's no good thinking I'm a southerner who'll squeak at the sight of a mountain, either. My home fief is almost due west of here, by the sea. I'm a northerner by birth."

She surveyed them, making sure they were with her now. She'd thought long and hard about what she could say. Back at Giantkiller she'd imagined herself delivering a blood-stirring speech full of fire and dreams that would have them all on their feet, cheering her, ready to take on the entire Scanran army. That had lasted all of two breaths; then she had giggled at her own folly. She didn't have fiery speeches in her; they would make her extremely uncomfortable if she had. In the end, she'd decided to keep it short and simple.

"You all know why we're here," she told them. "You know the enemy. He will be on us soon. When he comes, we will fight not for some glorious cause, but to survive. The gods have given us time to prepare, and we must take advantage of every moment of it. Once the enemy comes, how safe we'll be is determined by these walls and the people in them.

"You've built our home well. It's true what they say, that northern woodsmen build the very best." That made the civilians happy; they grinned and clapped one another on the back. Kel smiled. When it was quiet again, she continued. "We'll finish building together. The more we do before our guests come, the more time we'll have for weapons training with everyone, including civilians, who can hold a bow—or a spear." The convicts chuckled. She went on, "If you have problems, or questions—officers, note this—you will see me every day. You must tell me. I won't know anything if you don't speak up, and if it's something that can be fixed, I'd as soon fix it right away. You look at me and see I'm young. *I* look at me and see I'm young." All of them laughed as their eyes remained fixed on her. "I *have* seen combat in my years as squire to the Knight Commander of the King's Own. And I'm willing to learn more, if you will be my teachers."

Kel took a deep breath. "That's all I have to say. We'll hammer the rest out as we build this haven for those who have lost their homes. Now I'll let you go to your beds. Tomorrow comes soon." She looked down, then had an idea. "Who's the best woodworker here? Signs, and suchlike?"

There was a murmur among the civilians. They pointed at one man, a burly fellow with straggly red hair.

"First thing in the morning, will you make us a sign? It's got to be large enough to be read across the river. It should carry the word 'Haven.' Not Fort, just Haven. Because that's what we are." The man nodded as a pleased murmur swept through the room. "I thank you for your attention," Kel said, and stepped off the box.

The men began to rise from their benches. Brief words of welcome and greeting followed Kel as, limp with the release of tension, she walked back to the seated nobles. Tobe patted her arm awkwardly when she passed; she rested a hand on his bony shoulder. When Kel met Wyldon's eyes, he nodded, once, in approval. Neal clapped her on the back; Merric punched her shoulder lightly; Dom bowed his head.

"Now all I have to do is live up to it," she pointed out to her friends, and collapsed onto the bench.

April 15–23, 460
the refugee camp
on the Greenwoods River

5
CLERKS

The next day Kel rose before dawn and used the quiet time before sunrise to take her glaive outside onto ground still hard from the night's cold. There she practiced, working her way through the complex pattern dances that were combinations of strikes, blocks, and feints strung together so the warrior could build strength and stamina with each step. When she finished, she cleaned the glaive and stowed it in her tiny bedchamber. After that she went to the mess hall, where the morning cooks had started breakfast. As they stirred porridge, fried ham, and set out bowls of honey, bread, and pitchers of milk, Kel thought about her day.

Baird, Wyldon, Merric, and Elbridge took their breakfast in headquarters with Owen to serve them. Neal staggered to the cookhouse after the dawn trumpet sounded. "Figured you'd be here," he said, yawning, as he slumped onto the bench across from her. Tobe, then Dom arrived shortly after he did.

Wyldon, Elbridge, and Owen rode north after breakfast, taking the extra soldiers and several wagons of supplies on to the new fort, Mastiff. Before they left, Wyldon and Kel settled on a schedule of meetings and messages so they would keep up to date with one another.

Once the district commander, his squire, and the captain had gone, Haven's residents learned that their officers ate not in headquarters, as the captain had, but in the mess hall: Baird and Merric joined Kel and Neal on that second day. Once everyone was at least half awake, they discussed the day's schedule, making plans so they didn't interfere with each other's duties.

Kel's first act was to put herself on all the work lists to cook, wash up, clean out latrines, do laundry at the river, and serve on guard detail and patrols. This was something she'd learned from Raoul: if the commander did something, few would object to performing the same job. The only lists she did not put herself on were hunting and fishing: they were popular with everyone in camp. Whatever she did, Tobe was somewhere close by, passing tools, helping as she lifted heavy objects, scrubbing, feeding animals. As they stood watch, pounded sheets, or dumped noxious tubs into the honey wagon and went out to bury its contents, men would drift by for a word or two. Some of it was complaints. Most was just a quick greeting or question, a way to size up the new commander. Kel made sure to answer each of the men courteously.

She tried to put herself on carpentry detail only to be politely refused. The third day the carpenters said no, she demanded to know why. She had experience, after all. She didn't want the men to think she would do some chores and not others, though she knew she was a terrible woodworker. The master carpenter explained politely that Sergeant Dom had said Kel was a disaster with hammer, axe, or saw, and they did not have wood or nails to spare. Kel spotted Dom up on the walkway, grinning down at her. He'd seen her approach the carpenters. She gestured rudely at him. She also stopped asking the carpenters for work with considerable private relief.

Each night, everyone—nobles, men of the Own, camp soldiers, and civilians—took supper in the cookhouse. Each night, Kel ate at a different table. At first the men were wary, not sure if she had come to lecture or to eavesdrop. They soon relaxed. Kel was very good at eating as if she thought about nothing else. As the men got more comfortable, they talked to her. They told her of their families, their experiences in the north, and their guesses as to the enemy's next move. Kel fixed faces with names and what she knew of each man in her mind.

She also bet on the contests held in the early evening: archery matches, footraces, and wrestling. When Merric suggested the time would be put to better use if the men continued to work, Duke Baird replied before Kel did.

"They need play, Merric," the healer explained. "People need a release for tension. They need a reminder that not all the world is a fearful, war-shadowed place."

The next evening, Merric joined the archery competition and came in third.

After games, the men formed small groups, building little fires around the bunkhouses and barracks. Kel, Neal, and Merric used that time to meet in the headquarters dining room to plan and to read any correspondence or reports. These came in almost every day. Couriers spelled to be invisible and noiseless brought messages from Forts Steadfast, Mastiff, Giantkiller, and Northwatch. The three young knights read each one and wrote their own reports in reply. Sometimes they just listened as the men sang, particularly when Tobe's unmistakable voice soared into the night sky.

Kel looked forward to those nighttime songs. They made her relax. She could appreciate the stars, the growing softness in the air, and the scents of wet earth and coming spring without thinking of everything she had yet to do, or of Blayce out there making his devices. The mage was never far from her thoughts, but each time she caught herself grinding her teeth because she wasn't hunting him, she forced her mind back to Haven. The safety of its residents came first, at least for now.

Between work details she took out groups of refugees and convict soldiers to train with bow, staff, and sword. The regular soldiers were used to training with their officers and comrades; she was only underfoot with them. The refugees and convicts had been made nervous by the barking sergeants. Kel gentled them along, suggesting without insults, showing them the exercises she'd done to strengthen her own body. Tobe helped her there. Her students were reassured by her patience with her young servant, watching her show him the way to master the small curved bow she'd found for him.

One by one, bunkhouses and storage sheds went up and the infirmary was completed. The first furniture to be built were the cots and stools for the infirmary, then the beds for the bunkhouses. Baird and Neal readied the infirmary. Baird also rode out on one of Merric's patrols to mark the best places to bury the waste collected in tubs under the latrines. As he did, Neal spelled the latrines to keep any sickness inside the tubs. He thoroughly explained to Kel and the men that human waste bred powerful disease and must be carefully disposed of.

Neal also began a thorough examination of Haven's residents, spotting future health problems, strengthening weak lungs and hearts, working cures on sniffles, sores, and splinters. One day after he'd checked one of their two squads of convicts, Kel took him for a ride outside the walls. She had watched the signs of Neal's blooming temper and knew he needed a break. If he was going to explode, she wanted him outside, far from the hearing of anyone else.

"There's no excuse for it, none," he yelled, green eyes blazing, once they were on the far side of the river. "Yes, they're criminals, but they're supposed to be soldiers now. You don't send a man with a hole in his heart to fight! You might as well execute him and have done with it!"

Kel listened and kept Neal talking until he calmed down. Sergeants Vidur and Oluf, regular army soliders who commanded the convicts, were hard. They had already told Kel that her ban on flogging was a sign of female weakness. She knew they would take their anger out on their men if Neal turned his scalding tongue on them. There was only so much Kel might do about the way the sergeants handled their troops. She preferred to avoid battles with them now so she would have authority with them later if she needed to use it.

They never say it's one thing to be given command by your superiors and another to be given it by the men under you, she thought as she and Neal rode back to Haven. You have to decide what's important and what you have to let go. They can pretend to take your orders, then dawdle, or lose equipment, or claim they misunderstood, and laugh behind your back when you get frustrated. We're told the commoners will respect our nobility and our shields, but they don't, mostly. They only pretend to.

Kel could understand that. She had seen the way many nobles dealt with commoners. No wonder the common folk responded as slowly and awkwardly as they could. Her sympathy made her careful with those she commanded, soldiers and refugees alike. She found ways to firmly suggest things to the men so that they came to believe that what she'd asked had been their own idea all along. It meant she didn't need to use physical punishment as a goad.

Tobe waited by the gate to take the reins of their horses as they rode back into camp. "You'll be all right?" Kel asked Neal, a hand on his shoulder.

"Don't worry, Kel," he said. "I won't make your job harder. You probably won't see me or Father at supper, though. We're going to try to fix that man's heart. It's—"

"Milady!" called Sergeant Connac, who had the command of the watch on the walls. "We got company!"

Kel and Neal raced up the closest steps to the walkway. Kel didn't even notice the open air to her left, though normally she was always aware of it, the last echo of her old fear of heights. Her skin prickled as she reached the top of the wall. Had the enemy come already?

She turned to order the men to close the gate, but Sergeant Connac had already done so. Let him do his job, she scolded herself. You have enough of your own to do.

On her first complete day at Haven, she had lent her precious spyglass to the sergeant commanding the watch. Now Connac passed it to her and pointed east. A line of horsemen and wagons approached on the Giantkiller road, led by a rider on a black-and-white horse, the kind known as piebald. Behind him on a lead rein plodded a bay cob laden with packs. An assortment of wagons followed.

Kel frowned. They'd gotten no word of exactly when the refugees would begin to come. With the enemy and their mages due to arrive any day, she might be looking at an elaborate illusion, one that would trick them into opening the gates.

She passed the spyglass to Neal. "Is that an illusion?" she demanded.

Neal put the glass to his eye and adjusted it. Suddenly he yelped and turned away, pushing the spyglass at Kel with one hand as he rubbed his eyes with the other.

"Neal?" she asked, horrified. What if he'd been magically attacked? "Neal, are you all right?"

"Oh, I'm fine," he grumbled. He groped in his breeches pockets, gave up, and wiped his eyes on his sleeve. He was squinting; tears streamed down his cheeks. Kel produced one of her many pocket handkerchiefs and thrust it into his hand. "Thank you," Neal said, blotting his eyes. "He's got warning and alarm magics around that train for—

Mithros, it's got to be at least fifty yards. I couldn't manage ten feet. Those are our refugees, all right, and Master Numair at the front."

Kel's jaw dropped. "Numair Salmalín?"

"That's who I said," her friend replied, grumpy. "I'd know the look of his Gift anywhere, even if it didn't half blind me. You thought he was an illusion?"

"We've had no word the refugees were on the move," Kel reminded him. "And disguising Scanrans as a refugee train would be a good way to get them close enough for an attack."

"Well, that's no disguise. And since when do *you* need a mage to see through illusions?" Neal inquired. "Where's that griffin-feather band?"

Kel blinked at him. "Band?" she asked. Then she remembered: last year she'd learned that if she held griffin feathers over her eyes, she could see through magical illusions. She had promptly stitched a number of the feathers she had gotten for looking after a baby griffin onto a cloth band. When tied over her forehead and ears, it gave her protection from magical falsehoods. Neal had helped her test it, which was how they knew the band also protected Kel from spoken magic. "The griffin band," she said, understanding. "Well, yes, I have it . . ." She realized what she was about to say and closed her mouth, feeling sheepish.

"Where?" Neal prodded.

Kel cleared her throat. "In my room."

"Where it will do you much good, I'll wager," Neal replied. "It looks like our guests should be here soon. Time to warn everyone we'll have company for supper."

Kel looked around for Jump or Tobe and found the boy. "Tobe, in the kit I use to clean my weapons you'll find a red silk bag. Would you get it for me, please?" Tobe nodded and clattered down the steps.

"I'm going back to the surgery," Neal said, returning Kel's handkerchief. "Father and I are ready to work on that man's heart."

"Good luck," Kel said, then looked at Sergeant Connac. "We'd best tell everyone," she said. "Send a rider out to Sir Merric, so he doesn't think we're having trouble."

"Don't you worry, milady," the man assured her. "We'll have the new folk settled before you can say 'Gods all bless.'"

Kel, the griffin-feather band now on her belt in its pouch, was helping unload a cart when she spotted one of the cooks nearby. His eyes were fixed on her. She handed off a crate and turned to him. "What is it, Einur?" she asked.

The man cleared his throat and scuffed the ground with his shoe. "Milady, if, if I might be havin' a word," he said after a moment's hesitation.

"So are the men all after you, then, milady?" demanded Fanche. She stood in the door of the barracks where her people were to stay, hands on hips, brown eyes mocking. "Couldn't find a husband in the south, so you came here to pick and choose."

Einur turned on her with a glare. "You ain't been here these last weeks, so you keep silent till you know who you're talkin' of. She's been workin' curst hard—"

"Enough," Kel ordered, secretly pleased by his defense

of her. She took him by the arm and led him a few yards away from the cart and Fanche. "None of that," she told him. "Let's not start any brawls."

"But milady, she's wrong," protested Einur. "She's not seen you laboring like one of us."

"She'll get her chance," Kel said firmly. "What did you need to say?"

"Oh." Einur grimaced. "Lady, it might, it might be easier, if, if you great folk took supper at headquarters, like the captain done. At least until—well, just for a time."

Now it was Kel's turn to prop her hands on her hips. "Spit it out, Einur, there's work to do. Why change our meals?"

The man scratched his head. Finally he muttered, so quietly Kel had to lean in to hear, "Till that mage is gone." The word "mage" sounded like curdled milk in his mouth.

"Which mage? We've got sev—" Then she saw it. "You mean Master Numair."

Miserable, Einur nodded.

"But he's a fine man," protested Kel. "He taught Sir Nealan and Sir Merric and me. He's a little scatterbrained, to be sure, but he is a black robe—"

Einur raised pleading eyes to Kel's. "Milady, you wasn't here that time he croaked and the land just moved around, like giant snakes was under it. He makes us nervous, and nervous cooks burn soup."

Kel had not missed that "us." "All the cooks feel this way?" she asked.

Einur nodded.

"We'll need someone to serve, if we're to be formal," she pointed out.

"Your boy says he'll help," replied the cook instantly.

Kel sighed. "Very well. Notify everyone who's to dine at headquarters. I have to talk to the new people in the morning, you know. I wanted to do it like I talked to you men, only over breakfast."

"We can send for you, when folk are finishing in the morning."

Kel smiled crookedly. "An answer for everything, it seems. Go on, then. Back to work."

"Bless you, lady," the cook said with a deep bow. "Thank you."

Kel went back to the business of unpacking the wagon. Once that was finished, she went in search of Fanche. The woman was outside her building, helping a man and a girl to build a firepit and line it with stones. While the cooks would manage for the entire camp that night, normally the inhabitants of each building would fix their own meals outside their sleeping quarters. Kel had thought it would be good for the refugees to build their own firepits. It might help them to feel part of their new home.

"Mistress Fanche, I would like a word in private, if you please," she said as the older woman set the stone she carried in place.

Fanche looked up at Kel, hair in her face. "I'm busy."

Kel held Fanche's eyes with her own. "If you please, Mistress Fanche."

The woman straightened and dusted off her hands, then followed Kel down the long strip of earth between the refugee barracks. When Kel reached the open ground between the buildings and the wall, she turned and faced the older woman.

Kel had put a great deal of thought into this moment, knowing that she and Fanche would have such a conversation at some point. Kel preferred to do it right away, at the first chance offered, before Fanche got settled and confident here. Only once before had Kel dealt with someone who didn't accept that she had been appointed to lead, but she didn't think physical force would do the task here. Fanche was no anxious soldier who doubted a squire's ability to command. Fanche was worthy of respect, the headwoman of the Goatstrack refugees and the one who had kept them together on the flight to Giantkiller. So far, her experience of lords and ladies was that they collected taxes and refused to share their wealth and lands with homeless people. Force would be just what Fanche expected of a noble.

As Fanche opened her mouth, ready to attack first, Kel said, "It doesn't matter what you think of me. If you have a criticism or an insult you'd like to deliver, then take me aside and tell me, I don't care. Though I must say, I do get bored with folk claiming I became a knight either because I'm a slut or I'm desperate for a husband. You'd think people would *try* to be a little more original. I'm surprised to hear such talk from you."

Fanche grimaced. "Why? Because I'm another woman, and everyone knows women are sweet and helpful with each other? Because we're all sisters under the Goddess?"

Kel met her eyes steadily. "No. Because I expected you to know what it's like, to be a woman and command. Lord Wyldon said you rallied your people when Goatstrack fell. You took charge and fought till you got them to Giantkiller. I *know* you must have had men who argued and balked and nearly got you all killed. I'd hoped you'd see you and I are in the same boat, and keep your disagreements between the two of us."

"You break my heart, little girl," Fanche replied. "So they told you to command here. You know what you command? A killing ground. Those northern leeches will batten on us whenever they like. Gods forbid our mighty nobles would pay to feed and guard us inside those stone walls that *our* families built. They can always replace commoners. So they give us walls of twigs, protector knights so green I can smell the sap, and a handful of guards recovering from wounds or half dead from the mines."

Kel shrugged. "Don't you think I know that?" she asked. "I see it just as plain as you. What I'd like *you* to see is that if we aren't all united inside these walls, noble and common, soldiers and cooks, male and female, then the enemy will take us all. So think about that, will you? And insult me in private." Kel waited for the woman to reply. There was no way to guess the thoughts behind the woman's tired brown eyes. When she said nothing, Kel nodded. "Welcome to Haven, Mistress Fanche."

She walked back to headquarters, where she found Numair lounging on the bench outside her small office. There was a lot of him to lounge. With his legs stretched out before him, he nearly blocked the narrow hall through the building. "Master Numair, I'm sorry—you should have sent someone to find me," she apologized as he got to his feet. "It *was* me you wanted, wasn't it?" He might only be daydreaming, or thinking.

Numair smiled. "Yes, I am here to see you. I have

dispatches for you from Raoul, Wyldon, and Vanget. I also brought you clerks." He pointed through the open door opposite Kel's office.

Clerks? she wondered, peering at the newcomers in the room. Do I need clerks?

Three men, five teenaged boys, and two young women, all in the pale gray outer robes of the royal bureaucrat, were there. They had shifted tables and benches and set out slates, ink pots, sheaves of paper, and other tools of their trade. Then Kel understood. Clerks made lists, wrote letters, kept accounts, drew up work rosters—all the things she did now.

"Gods be thanked," she told Numair with relief. "The way the soldiers carry on when you ask them to write things down, you'd think it was worse than fighting. I've been doing a lot of it myself rather than argue with them. Excuse me."

She went over to the open doorway. "Well met!" she told the clerks. They turned, startled, obviously not knowing who she was. "I'm Keladry of Mindelan, in charge of things here. Welcome." The two women bowed first, then the men and boys. "Let me or Nealan of Queenscove know what you require, and we'll see about getting it for you. You can sleep upstairs. My boy Tobe will get you cots and whatever else you need." She glanced at the sparrow on her shoulder—she always seemed to have at least one with her. "Bring Tobe?" she asked the bird. The sparrow cheeped and flew off.

"Thank you, lady knight," the oldest man said to Kel. "We look forward to serving you. I am Zamiel. These are my colleagues . . ." As he named them, each one bowed.

When Tobe arrived, Kel turned the clerks over to him and led Numair into her office. "Tobe will see them right. Please"—she indicated one of the rough chairs—"sit down. You say you have dispatches?"

Reaching into the saddlebag he carried, the mage produced folded and sealed documents. "This is for you, and this, and this." He turned them over to Kel and took the offered chair.

Kel sat and, with a murmured apology to her guest, cracked the seals on the documents and began to read. Once she finished, she re-read them all. They held a mixed lot of news.

The topmost dispatch came from Raoul. He requested that Dom and his squad go to Fort Steadfast. The serious fighting was about to begin. Already King Maggur had sent an army to besiege the port city of Frasrlund, at the mouth of the Vassa River.

General Vanget wrote that the enemy was everywhere, from the seacoast to the Gallan border. In addition to besieged Frasrlund, Seabeth and Seajen had fought off ship raids. Raoul's Fort Steadfast had turned back a probing attack of about two hundred warriors. Along the northeastern border, small parties of Scanrans had all struck on the same day, resulting in major tangles as the army tried to defend every threatened village and fort. The City of the Gods on the same border reported killing devices seen in their hills. Kel imagined armies on the move and hated the walls that surrounded her, keeping her from the *real* fight.

Pouting about it won't help me in the least, she told herself.

Lord Wyldon wrote that Numair carried a verbal report to be heard by Kel, Neal, Merric, and Duke Baird. He also wrote that enemy patrols had been seen near Fort Mastiff, but none had been caught. Finally, he told Kel it was time for her to report in person about Haven's progress. He expected her and an escort at Fort Mastiff in seven days, when he would have more supplies for her. In the meantime, the refugees from Tirrsmont and Anak's Eyrie were on the road and should reach Haven soon.

"My lord says you have spoken messages to deliver?" Kel asked Numair. "Can they wait until after supper? That way you'll have all of us together."

Numair smiled. It was the first time he'd ever really met Kel's eyes. In all her years at the palace and with Raoul, she'd had little to do with this quiet mage, apart from lessons and one memorable encounter during a fight with bullies. Numair was both scattered and brilliant. He would begin a lesson on illusion runes only to be sidetracked by the habits of basilisks or the nature of tides in the air. Now Kel got a tiny glimpse of what lay under his vague exterior, and she could not make herself look away.

He blinked, and she was free. "Of course," he told Kel. "It will be far easier to talk with all of you at once."

Her mind scrambled to remember what he was talking about. "Oh . . . oh, yes." She frowned, relieved and intrigued. No mage had ever affected her like that. "Sir, can other mages do what you just did—hold someone with their eyes?"

"I did?" he asked, startled, then sighed. "I'm sorry, I

must have, for you to mention it. I was just thinking that you are a good choice for this post. I apologize for, ah, forgetting. If a typical mage wants to hold your attention, usually he needs something bright and shiny in his hands. He'll play with it, catching the light. You'll be unable to look away, or to refuse his orders, until he releases you. Or she. Didn't I teach you pages about that?"

"I don't recall it if you did, sir," Kel admitted sheepishly.

"We have to make sure they are taught that, first thing every year. It can be done with something as ordinary as a coin. You have to watch for it, and not be trapped. Listen, Keladry, I'm not just a courier. I want to spell your walls and gates while I'm here. I must see the areas I need to protect. Could you get someone to give me the tour?"

"If you don't mind interruptions, I'll take you around," offered Kel.

Numair smiled. "I would appreciate that. I'm sure by now you know every nook and cranny here."

They were a third of the way around the inside wall, having been interrupted by no fewer than five newcomers with questions for Kel, when she heard familiar loud peeping. Three sparrows zipped over the wall crying the alarm and homed in on Kel. From the gate the trumpeter also sounded an alarm. Those soldiers who had been doing chores or relaxing after lunch grabbed their weapons and raced up the stairs to the wall. Numair followed the soldiers, his long legs quickly covering the ground between him and the nearest stair.

Kel ran to headquarters, meeting Tobe near the gate.

He clutched Kel's mail shirt and helm. Her quiver of arrows was slung over his bony shoulder, dangling almost to the ground. Jump, beside him, gripped Kel's bow in his jaws.

Kel slid into the mail shirt, donned the plain open helm, and accepted bow and quiver from her helpers. "Tobe, find Saefas," she ordered the boy. "Tell him I said to get everyone who can use a bow on the ramparts."

Tobe nodded and ran. Kel, Jump, and her sparrows climbed to the walkway over the gate. There she took a moment to string her bow.

Connac, the sergeant in command of the watch, passed the spyglass to her. "There, milady," he said, pointing. Kel looked. The enemy galloped across the open meadows on the western side of the valley. With one ear she listened to the horn calls as special combinations told Merric and his patrol of the attack. More trumpet blasts summoned those who had been plowing the fields east of the river. They raced across the bridge and up the inclined road to the gate.

With the glass to her eye, Kel did a rough count of the foe. This was a raiding party of thirty or so warriors, mounted on nimble, shaggy-coated horses. Among the warriors, two wore the pointed fur hats of shamans, or mages. Fumbling one-handed at her belt, Kel drew out the griffin-feather band. Sergeant Connac took the glass and her helm. Kel tied the band in place and slid the helm on over it. "Two shamans," she told the sergeant.

"Shall I get my lord duke and Sir Neal?" he asked.

Kel shook her head. "I doubt we'll need them." She jerked her head to indicate Numair. He stood on the wall that directly faced the oncoming Scanrans, his full shirt-sleeves flapping in the brisk spring wind.

The sergeant chuckled. "They'll wish they'da stayed in bed today," he told Kel.

"You may be right," she replied, hearing new voices and the rattle of shod feet clambering up wooden stairs. She glanced around. Refugees carrying bows, men and women alike, had come to join the soldiers on the ramparts.

"Lady knight, orders?" asked Dom, coming over to her. He and his squad had been guarding the plowmen. They had been the last to enter the fort. Now the heavy gates were closed and barred.

"Keep your horses ready in case you need to make a sally from the gate, Sergeant Domitan," Kel said. "Up here, dispose of your men as you see fit. You know where they'll do the most good." She looked at Connac. "See that the refugee archers take instructions from the nearest soldier," she told him. "You may want to distribute the refugees better."

The civilian archers, knowing the enemy came from the north, had all gone to the northern ramparts. The sergeant would spread them out around the entire wall, in case the enemy had split up to attack from two or even three directions.

An arrow arched into the air, striking the ground dozens of yards before the closest horseman. "Don't shoot till the sergeants give the command!" Kel shouted, pitching her voice as Raoul had taught her to carry over distance and noise. "Don't waste arrows! Wait for the command!"

"Did they teach you that voice special?" murmured a

familiar voice in her ear. "Or did you pick it up yourself?"

Kel looked at Fanche. She was glad to see the woman carried a strung longbow and a quiver of very businesslike arrows. "They teach it special. Choose a spot and take your orders from the nearest soldier," she said as she watched the enemy. "Wait to shoot till the command, then pick your shots." When she glanced back a moment later, she saw Fanche had walked over to the center of the gate and was listening to a soldier.

Relieved that Fanche hadn't argued, Kel put the spyglass to her eye.

The raiders were fifty yards from the northern wall. Another twenty-five yards would bring them to the base of the rising ground. She suspected they would split up then, some to come up the gate road from the east, others to climb the rising ground and attack the gate directly. It was what she would do.

"On the north wall, loose at my command," she cried, lowering her spyglass.

Thoughts tumbled through her mind as they had when she and Dom's squad had battled a killing device and when she and her friends had fought off hill bandits. The gate should be on the eastern or southern wall, she realized. We could squeeze them between the height and the river then. Too late to fix that now.

She judged the enemy's distance, her hands trembling, her palms covered with sweat. They were nearly thirty yards back, about to split up. "Loose!" she cried.

Her people's arrows whistled through the air. Four Scanran horses went down. Kel winced for the horses. Two other Scanrans fell from their saddles and were trampled.

Four more reeled, arrows sticking in their bodies.

We have good archers here, Kel thought with relief. Three raiders still galloped toward the eastern wall. One of them went down, an arrow in his throat: it was Fanche's.

The two shamans, who had stayed safe at the back of the raiders, had gone to work, creating a mingled blue and yellow fog. Kel, about to shout a warning to Numair, bit her tongue. He would know far better than she what magic unfolded. She glanced at him as he raised his hands. Black lightning edged with white streaked from his fingers, lancing toward the shamans. Kel didn't see the result; she heard trumpet calls from the south. Merric had gotten the alarm. He was in the woods to the west of the camp, the enemy in his sight.

Dom and Sergeant Connac had stayed close by in case she had orders for them. She did. She didn't have to make them up, after all, not when she, Merric, Dom, and the sergeants had spent their evenings working out plans to counter different kinds of assault. "Signal Merric to move north and be ready for our attack," she told Connac. "Sergeant Oluf's squad and Sergeant Domitan's, mount up," she directed: Oluf commanded one of the convict squads. "Prepare to ride out at my signal. Archers on the north wall," she yelled, "pick your shots and loose at will!"

Dom gathered his soldiers with an ear-piercing whistle. Kel heard the clatter of boots as the men of the Own ran for their waiting mounts. Dom clapped her on the shoulder and murmured in her ear, "You sound just like Lord Raoul." Kel grinned, then returned her attention to the enemy as Dom raced down the stairs. Connac hand-signaled Sergeant Oluf and his squad to join the attack.

Horn calls soared from Haven's trumpeters, telling Merric his part of the plan.

Numair's spell had done its work: flames rose from the ground at the enemy's rear. There was no sign of either shaman in that large blaze. He'd burned them out of existence.

The Scanrans milled at the foot of the high ground as the north wall archers pelted them with arrows. When the enemy started to draw back, Kel thought they were about to run, but she was wrong. They regrouped, sent half their number to try the road in the east, and prepared to climb directly to the gate once more.

"Hold your arrows," Kel shouted. Out of the corner of her eye she saw a soldier grab Fanche's bow arm to stop her from shooting again. In the distance she heard Merric's horn call. He was ready.

She nodded to Sergeant Connac, who bellowed, "On the gate!" Timbers creaked as a handful of civilians hauled one leaf of the massive gate open just wide enough to allow two riders to pass at a time. Dom and Sergeant Oluf led the charge while trumpeters signaled their attack. From the woods to Kel's left she heard Merric's trumpeter reply. His patrol squad streamed out of the woods at the gallop, Merric in the lead, fully armored, his sword unsheathed. He smashed into the Scanran flank. The attackers from Haven rode down to hammer the enemy from the front. The tide of battle had turned.

Screams tore the air. Kel whirled, putting the spyglass to her eye. Soldiers and civilians alike hacked at black, insectlike arms as they reached over the top of the east wall. One soldier's hand flew into the air, cut from his arm.

The screams and shouts of warning came from those who didn't need all their air to fight.

"Crossbow," said Kel. She thrust the spyglass at Connac.

The sergeant didn't wait to ask questions. He took the spyglass, unslung his quiver, and gave it and the crossbow to Kel. She handed over her longbow and quiver, then raced down the walkway, heart pounding in her throat as the domed helms of two killing devices showed above the eastern wall.

6
DEFENSE PLANS

Other civilians and soldiers on the walkway had turned to see what was happening. Kel shoved one corporal back toward the wall. "Keep your post!" she yelled, doing the same to a pair of civilians who stood gawping. "Do you want the enemy to come up this way while you stare?"

She barreled down the wall, shoving those who didn't listen back into their places, ordering them to watch the enemy outside. The crossbow was already set, a bolt in the notch. She wasted a breath on regrets for her griffin-fletched arrows, which seemed to aim themselves, and made the turn onto the eastern walkway.

"Move!" she snapped, thrusting onlookers aside. Ahead, a knot of soldiers and civilians battled the killing devices. It was disastrous. The things were quick, and the fighters had almost no protection against them. A man went down, gutted by a dagger-hand. A soldier flew off the walkway to the ground twenty feet below.

Kel yanked civilians and soldiers away from the closest device, which was only half over the wall. She leveled her bow at its helm, just five feet away, and pulled the trigger. Crossbow bolts, heavy enough to punch through armor, were devastating at such short range. This bolt slammed into the head-dome of the device to punch through the thick iron. Kel lunged within reach of the three-jointed arms, prayed, and grabbed the bolt, yanking it out of the device. It left a small, round hole.

Something white and vaporous flowed out of the opening, crying like a child. The wind shredded the spirit as the device went dead in a clatter of metal and chains.

Kel fumbled for her quiver, dropping two bolts before she finally grasped one. "Get back!" she yelled at those who fought the remaining device. *"Now!"*

They obeyed. One refugee wasn't quick enough; the device cut him lengthwise from behind as he turned to flee. This monster had made it onto the walkway. Sparrows fluttered around the narrow pits that served as its eyes, confusing it. Kel shot from just six feet away, but the thing turned its head. The bolt hit at an angle and bounced off, leaving only a scratch in the metal. The device shook its head and faced Kel. White-lipped, she grabbed the quiver and sought another bolt with trembling fingers.

"Look out!" Saefas shouted from the far side of the thing. He'd gotten a big axe and was guarding civilians until they could make it down the nearest stair. "Lady, look out!"

Kel glanced up and threw herself back. A sledgeload of logs, raised from the ground by magic the color of glittering black fire—Numair's Gift—hung over the killing device. As Kel dodged, Numair's magic dropped the logs. They slammed the metal creature and the walkway on which it stood down onto the ground behind an unoccupied barracks.

Wasting no time, Kel raced down the flight of stairs behind her, where the walkway was undamaged. She set a bolt in the crossbow's notch and yanked the heavy string to the trigger as she reached the heap of logs. It shifted. A claw-hand shot out of a gap. Logs rolled and tumbled as the device fought its way out from under them. As soon as she saw the head-dome, Kel shot and hit squarely. She lurched over the treacherous logs until she could yank the bolt free. The trapped spirit that fueled the killing device escaped, crying for its mother. Once it had fled, the logs and the thing under them were still.

As she was about to remove her helmet, Kel remembered that this wasn't the only fight she had to worry about. She ran toward the gate, trying to ignore trembling knees and rolling stomach as the effect of fighting the devices hit her. They could have cut her to pieces, mail shirt or no. They *had* cut up some of her people.

Connac, still at his post over the gate, was looking for her. As soon as he saw her, he gave the hand sign for "battle won." Kel sagged for a moment, relief making her giddy. But it would not do for her people to see her lose her strength, even if they were safe for now. Somehow she found the strength to walk on to the gate. Tobe met her halfway, a water flask in his hands. Until she saw it, Kel hadn't realized how thirsty she was. She drained it and smiled at him. It was good to know that when she needed him, Tobe was always there without argument or complaint. Part of his eagerness to help was still his worry that she would vanish, she knew, but she also liked to think it was because the little old man in him approved of the way she did things.

"I don't know how I managed before you came along," she said, handing the empty flask back to him. "I did a good day's work when I hired you."

Tobe swiped at his face with one hand, embarrassed, and went for more water as Kel dragged herself up the stairs to the watch post. Below, her men were checking the enemy on the ground. They gave the mercy stroke to those too badly hurt for the healers to tend or to those Scanrans who begged for it. None of them wanted to be made a prisoner. Like Kel's Yamani friends, Scanrans thought surrender was a loss of honor that could never be recovered. Most preferred to die fighting.

To hide the trembling of her fingers, Kel polished the lens of the spyglass with a handkerchief. She accepted a ladle of water from Sergeant Connac and drank it, then returned her gaze to the field below. Merric, his patrol, and the squad of soldiers from Haven were on their way up the inclined road. Dom hand-signaled Kel, asking for permission to check the north woods. Kel signaled for him to go ahead but take care. Connac was right. This battle was done.

"Nets," she said abruptly, turning to survey the camp. People were laying out those who had been killed when the devices came over the wall. "Maybe nets would do it."

"Milady?" asked Connac.

"I want nets made," she said as Tobe reached her with

a newly filled water flask. She gulped half of it. "Hemp, yes, but metal, too. Chain, wire, rods . . . Let's salvage what we can from those devices for a start. The nets should measure twenty feet by twenty feet, and we'll keep two for each side of the wall. And I want five pickaxes for each wall, equally spaced, where folk can get at them."

"You think they'll help with the devices?" Connac wanted to know.

"Those things can cut hemp, but metal woven into it ought to slow them down," she said, putting the stopper into her flask. "Gods willing, it'll slow them a bit so that someone can get close enough to crack their heads with the pickaxe, and let the magic out."

"It's a good idea," Numair said. He looked disheveled and sweaty but lively enough. Kel handed over her flask. The mage drained it. "I'll help make the nets."

"You'll have to train the soldiers on them," Fanche pointed out as she unstrung her bow. "Drill them. They'll only get one chance to trap 'em, those devices move so fast."

Kel nodded. "We'll drill them till they drop," she promised absently, watching as Merric and his fighters rode through the gates. "And not just the soldiers. Anyone who can fight." The new refugees who weren't helping to carry the wounded to the infirmary or weeping for those killed on the road thanked the soldiers who'd saved their lives.

Perhaps now was the best time to speak to the newcomers and to the other civilians, Kel thought, before they learned that a fifth of their soldiers would be returning to

Fort Steadfast in the morning. Kel looked at Tobe. "Would you tell Master Zamiel—that's the new head clerk—I need four of his people, with note-taking materials, at the flagpole?" she asked. "I'll need them to write up training rosters."

The boy nodded and ran to do her bidding. Kel looked at Fanche, who observed her with a crooked smile.

"Amused?" Kel asked, feeling tired. "I could use a joke."

Fanche shook her head. "I was just thinking that maybe you're worth your feed." She poked Saefas in the ribs with an elbow. "Let's get our folk over to that pole."

Saefas waved to Kel and trotted down the stairs after Fanche.

"Kel?" Merric called from below. He'd removed his helmet to empty his water flask. His normally copper hair was dark and matted with sweat. His bright blue eyes glittered in his pale face. "I'm taking another patrol out for a look at the south woods."

"Go, and be careful," Kel told him. Merric nodded and began to reassemble his men.

After a moment spent watching them, Kel began to walk around the upper wall, talking to each person there, soldier and civilian, thanking them for their service as she took the opportunity to inspect the ground. She didn't want any more surprises. Fortunately, none seemed to be available. When she reached the gap in the walkway, she climbed down the stairs, walked around the tumbled heap of logs atop the device, and climbed up to finish her inspection of her people and their surroundings.

One of the Goatstrack refugee girls found Kel after she

had returned to the walkway over the gate. "Mistress Fanche says they're waiting," she said, panting from the trot up the stair.

Kel refilled her flask at the well and followed her to the flagpole, Jump at their heels. As she made her way through the cluster of refugees, she listened to the trumpet signals that came over the wall. Patrols had found no more of the enemy lurking in the north or south woods. A knot she hadn't noticed in her gut loosened. She'd been afraid there would be more Scanrans out there, waiting for them to relax after they'd beaten off one attack.

Kel stepped up onto a bench so everyone could see her, nodding to the four gray-robed clerks who stood nearby. "If each of you will take a place at one of the stocks?" she asked them. The clerks obeyed as Kel waited for the people around her to quiet down. When she had their attention, she called, "How many of you shoot bows?" she asked. "Raise your hands. I want anyone over the age of ten or so, no matter if your shooting is good or bad."

Hands went up in response. "All of you, sign up with . . ." Kel pointed to the female clerk at the southern stocks.

"Hildurra Ward," the woman said, getting to her feet to bow.

"When I'm done talking, give Mistress Hildurra your names," Kel ordered them. "How many can use a sling?" More hands went up, including those of girls and boys who looked to be under thirteen. Mountain children, who watched the family herds, learned to use slings to fight off predators. She assigned those people to a clerk, then did the same for those who could wield a staff or pitchfork.

Those who were skilled with more than one weapon Kel directed to sign up on all the appropriate lists. "No doubt you're wondering why I ask this," Kel went on, looking into the many faces turned up to her. "Or perhaps you've guessed already. Tomorrow, after breakfast, we start holding weapons training for you."

A moan went up from the refugees.

Kel waited for them to be quiet, taking a drink of water as she did so. When they were silent, she continued, very much aware of the soldiers watching from the ramparts. "Training can't be put off. We're not a fort, we're a refugee camp. That means we don't have as many soldiers as the forts, and one-quarter of our men will always be out on patrol. If we're to defend ourselves properly, we need everyone who can use a weapon. I'll put your training-group assignments up in the mess hall in the morning." She smiled ruefully. "I had meant to give you time to settle in, but as you see, the enemy had other plans."

A mutter of curses ran through the crowd.

"One more group I need," Kel went on. "Young people who are good with horses, who can saddle them. Hands."

Hands shot up all through the gathering.

"Sign up with our neglected clerk," she said, pointing out a boy not much older than Tobe who wore the blue ribbon trim on his sleeves that indicated he was an apprentice. "You saw how little warning we get. The moment any of you who work this detail hears the signal for an attack, drop whatever you're doing, head for the stables, and start saddling horses. You'll have a trainer when you report to the stable tomorrow, someone to check your work and teach you better ways to do it. Soldiers shouldn't waste time finding their weapons *and* saddling up. Understood?"

The young people nodded with considerably more enthusiasm than had the adults.

Silver flashed in the sky overhead. Kel looked up. Stormwings glided over Haven, bound for the dead who lay on the valley floor. She flexed her hands into fists. It didn't matter that only Scanran dead lay out there. They had fought as their own nobles had ordered. They deserved better than the treatment Stormwings would give them.

"Now," Kel said, bracing herself for a fight, "I need a burial detail to go out with me."

"Leave 'em t'rot!" cried a man. Others added their approval.

Kel put her hands on her hips and waited until they were quiet. "Then, sir, you shall plow the section where the bodies are, two days hence," she said mildly. "The feel of a plow as it hits rotting flesh and bone must be . . . interesting."

Some of her audience turned green.

"Bodies mean sickness in the water and the ground," Kel said more crisply. "We won't have it. Burial detail volunteers can report to me. If no one volunteers, I will choose some." She looked them over and decided the news that they would also need to fill out work lists could wait. "That's it. Burial volunteers, let's get moving."

Kel wiped her hands on her napkin yet again as the cooks took the last supper dishes from the headquarters common room. For the first time she wished she had perfume. The odor of Stormwings and death clung to her despite a pre-supper wash and change of clothes.

As the last cook left with the last dish, she made herself put the napkin down and observed her companions. Merric, Dom, and the sergeants all had a goblet of wine before them. The mages—Baird, Numair, Neal—had similar goblets, but theirs were filled with cider, as was Kel's. Baird and Neal looked fresher than she had expected after an afternoon spent keeping the soldier with the hole in his heart comfortable while they tended the wounded. Still, she had to remember that they couldn't be allowed to overwork.

Assistants, Kel thought, watching the healers. There are midwives in the Goatstrack company. Maybe the new people have a healer or two. Lord Wyldon's gift of clerks had made her realize that people didn't have to do each and every thing themselves. "Why weren't we taught about clerks?" she heard herself ask. The men grinned.

"Regular knights don't need 'em," Merric said, sipping his wine.

"It's true," Dom added. "You only really need clerks at company level. Till then, you do your own paperwork." He made a face as the others laughed. "Kel, you know I've got my orders, right?" he asked, meeting Kel's eyes with his very blue ones.

I'm going to miss looking at him, she thought. And I'm going to miss his support. Dom always backs me up. "Yes, Lord Raoul wrote me," she replied. To the others she explained, "Dom's squad's to report back to Fort Steadfast. War's officially declared."

"If you hadn't said so, however would we guess?"

drawled Neal. "Oh, wait, now I remember—I saw dead Scanrans lying about somewhere."

"They were more interesting when they were alive," Merric told him grimly.

"I'll take your word for it, thanks all the same." Neal raised his cup in a silent toast.

Kel looked at Numair. "Master Numair, you said you have other messages to give?"

The mage drew a circle at the center of the table with a quill, then etched signs along its sparkling edge. When he snapped his fingers, an image sprang to life within the circle, standing a foot tall. Kel grimaced. It was a killing device.

"In addition to the two killed here today, nineteen of these things have been reported in the country between the City of the Gods and Seabeth," Numair said quietly. "Nineteen that we are sure of. Villagers near Sigis Hold caught one in the kind of pit they use to trap bears, then shoveled it full of oil, hay, and coal and burned it until it half melted. None of the others have been taken, well, 'alive' is the best term. But we finally know more about who is creating them."

He sighed and rubbed his temples. "The City of the Gods expelled a mage student, Blayce Younger of Galla, six years ago. The charges were necromancy, particularly the enslavement of the spirits of the dead. It seems he has an aptitude for it."

"So he uses his *aptitude* to kill children," Kel whispered through numb lips. "He murders them and uses their spirits to fuel the killing devices." Around the table everyone but Numair and Kel drew the sign against evil—an *X* with a straight line through it: a six-pointed star—on his chest. *It isn't going to do you any good*, Kel thought, watching them. *And Master Numair knows it, too.*

"You sound sure," Numair said, his long, dark eyes sharp as he looked at Kel.

"I was there when three of the things were killed," she reminded him. "The white vapors that come out of their heads? They have the voices of children." *I don't have to mention the Chamber now*, she thought with some relief. *They know who's doing it, they have his name, and that's the only useful thing* I *know. So I'm not doing harm to their search for him by not speaking up.*

"He could use any spirit," Baird pointed out, his mouth twisted in disgust. "I wager he uses those of captive foreigners so Maggur will ignore, and make his own people ignore, what this Blayce does." He drained his cider. Neal refilled his cup. "It disgusts me," whispered Baird, "what people allow, if they think those who commit vile acts can help them to achieve some goal."

Numair snapped his fingers and the device at the center of the table vanished. He reached over and rubbed a hand over the glittering circle, retrieving its power. "All this means that refugee camps are just storehouses of fuel for Blayce. We've sent a request south for wagons to take every refugee out of reach of the border," he said. "I think I've explained things in frank enough terms that even the Council of Lords and the Council of Commons will see there's no choice. They'll vote us the funds and find the land to house them. His majesty says he won't let the councils adjourn for the summer until they do. Until then, we'll have to manage as best we can."

"But we know who's responsible," Merric pointed out. "And these devices could change the course of this war. Surely we ought to be sending teams of assassins to settle this Blayce."

"Do we know where he is?" asked Dom. "There's an awful lot of Scanra out there, and most of it's straight up and down."

Numair shook his head. "All we know is that he's not in the capital at Hamrkeng. Our spies searched the place from cellar to attic. He's not with King Maggur."

"And anyone who might know is too scared to talk," murmured Neal.

"That's the size of it," Numair admitted. "We'll continue to search, and to bolster the defenses of the camps. At least Haven can look to someone who's killed three devices." He nodded at Kel.

"With lots of help," she reminded him automatically.

All of them sat, eyes somber, arms crossed over their chests or cupped around their goblets.

I needed to know where Blayce was so I could find him before I got tied down here, Kel thought ferociously at the distant Chamber of the Ordeal. But you wouldn't tell me. You aren't of *my* time. Now I have to defend these people from his creations, and with what? Scant magic, forty soldiers, half of them convicts, and a bunch of civilians used to hunting and shooing wolves from their flocks. Curse your stone heart.

"Stones," she said aloud. Everyone looked at her. "Let's start moving stones to the base of the raised ground here, start piling them up. It's easy to climb dirt," she explained as Neal opened his mouth to argue. "Didn't we see that today? And then they just claw their way up wood. Stones at least make a smooth surface. The killing devices' claws will slip on stone." Neal closed his mouth. Seeing that the men continued to stare at her, Kel went on, "That's how the Yamanis build their castles. They cover everything from the wall straight down below the moat in stone. We can't cut it flat, maybe, but we can make the climb up these heights much harder."

"Wyldon made a good choice when he put you in command here," Duke Baird said with a tired smile. "He knows you have a fresh way of looking at things."

Kel glanced at Merric. She knew her being in command here was a sore point with him, though her job was the refugees and his was the patrols and command of the soldiers outside Haven's walls. Merric smiled crookedly, raised his goblet to her in a mocking toast, and finished its contents.

"I can help," Numair said abruptly. "I can move large rocks more quickly than muscle and oxen can do it, at least."

"Not the Sorcerer's Dance!" cried Neal. "That one is so old it creaks!"

"The spell may creak as much as it likes, if it works," Numair replied calmly. "What would you use?"

They began to argue magic. Dom and Merric stood with groans; Kel did likewise. If the mages even noticed they were leaving, they gave no sign of it.

Kel bade Merric good-night and promised Dom she would see him and his squad off in the morning. Then she looked at the extra clump of shadow by the rear door. "Tobe?"

He stepped into the light of the few cressets on the walls. "He said Blayce. Is that *your* Blayce, lady? The one as makes you talk in your sleep?"

Kel sighed. "Yes, it is."

Tobe shook his head. "No wonder you've got nightmares."

"If you'd sleep in a room of your own, you wouldn't hear them," Kel pointed out. This was an old discussion. Tobe refused to trade his pallet by her hearth for a real bed and room. "And what are you doing, eavesdropping?" she wanted to know. "That was a closed-door meeting. No listening allowed."

Tobe gave Kel his best "don't you know *anything*?" look. "I'm in service, lady," he said patiently. "When you're in service, you have to eavesdrop. Elsewise your masters get up to things and you get took by surprise."

Kel had begun to recognize the signs of another conversation she could not win. She switched tactics. "You should be in bed," she informed him.

"So should you," he retorted. "But them scribblers is still working, and they asked me to say, they're wishful of seeing you. Do I tell 'em to stuff their wishfulness?"

Kel rubbed her eyes. "No, I'll see them," she replied. "Off to bed, Tobe."

He vanished into her rooms. Kel walked into the clerks' office. They were all working, but when they saw her, they scrambled to their feet and bowed.

"My lady, there was no time for proper introductions today," said the oldest, a man. "I am Zamiel Fairview of Blue Harbor. This is my colleague Hildurra Ward, and my apprentice, Gragur Marten." Kel recognized them from the gathering at the flagpole, as she recognized Master Traver and Mistress Thurdie. She did her best to fix the other clerks' names and faces in her mind but knew she'd have to be reminded of them later. She was tired.

"What may I do for you?" Kel asked, with the feeling that this wasn't simply a matter of introductions.

"We hope to take just a little of your time, if you please, lady knight," replied Zamiel. "We have suggestions that may ease everyone's lot."

Kel bit her lip. Hadn't her day been long enough?

A sigh escaped her. Wyldon had trusted her to do this task—all of it—properly. She returned the clerks' bows. "I am at your service," she told them.

7
TIRRSMONT REFUGEES

When Kel left headquarters the next morning, she found the camp shrouded in fog. The sound of a recorder wound its way through the veils of mist, an aimless song that raised goose bumps on her skin. She traced it to the wall that looked to the western mountains. Numair stood on the ramparts, the soldiers at his sides moving away from him. The mage played the tune on a slender, hand-carved recorder.

She knew better than to interrupt a mage at work. Instead, she did her glaive practice, trying to ignore the piping, and walked around the camp before she entered the headquarters meeting room. A sleepy cook was setting bread, cheese, honey, and butter on the table. "We appreciate your letting him eat here, Lady Kel," he told her with a yawn. "Do you hear him? Mages." About to spit on the floor to express his opinion, he caught Kel's eye and thought the better of it.

"Even when he is trying to protect you?" she asked mildly.

"*Especially* then," the man said with feeling. "They save their scariest tricks for when they want to help folk." He bowed and went to fetch the rest of breakfast.

She saw Dom's squad and Merric's patrol on their way, then returned to the mess hall to discuss mundane things like work rosters with the newly arrived refugees. Once the fog burned off, she took weapons groups—one bow, one staff—outside the gate for practice. First she assigned one soldier and one experienced civilian as teachers to each group, then she worked in the ranks, keeping her own skills warm.

Back in Haven after training, she broke up three fights, two among children, one between two women over who was first in the latrine line. It was the magic thickening the air that made people edgy, Kel knew. She had just sorted out an argument between carpenters when she felt the physical effects of Numair's work. The ground began to quiver under her feet.

Stones, she thought, awed. I should have guessed there would be a lot of them. The sparrows came, shrieking, to whirl around Kel's head. They settled on every part of her they could find. Kel saw a white streak that was Jump scrambling into headquarters. Tobe, normally dauntless, wasn't far behind him.

Kel made herself walk calmly and confidently through camp, stopping often to assure everyone this was no earthquake but a protection spell. When she climbed to the rampart on the west wall, Baird and Neal were already there. In the distance, Numair walked, playing the recorder like a demented piper, leading a swarm of boulders, many taller than he was. "Is this one of those black-robe mage things?" she asked Neal and his father as they looked on.

"Even child mages can learn the Sorcerer's Dance," Neal replied scornfully. "An idiot couldn't get it wrong."

"It's the magnitude that has you acting like a bear with a burr under his tail," Baird replied gently. "If you or I worked the Dance, we could move logs, or a handful of wagons, for a mile or two. Numair called boulders from ten miles away."

"Show-off," grumbled Neal.

The duke leaned against the wall, his eyes on the sight below. "Numair told me once he has to blow on a candle flame to put it out," he said. "If he uses his Gift, the candle explodes. We have shaped our power to cut single veins if we must. Numair has to do big projects or nothing. You might show more tolerance."

Kel left father and son to it, shaking her head, and retreated to the mess hall. She was able to eat very little of her lunch as person after person, civilian and soldier, came to hear from her that this rumbling was neither an attack nor a natural disaster. She finally gave up on eating and took a group of slingers out to practice in the meadow across the bridge.

She could have saved herself the trouble. No one could practice once Numair came into view around the northern edge of the fort at the base of the high ground. He trailed boulders like chicks as he played that strange tune, with flourishes, on his recorder. At each flourish, the rearmost boulders dropped away, to roll up the slope below the walls. Ten feet up they would halt and settle into their new home. At the point where Haven's road crossed the high ground, Numair played only the basic tune until the rocks had rolled over and past the road. Once they were clear, he began to pipe them up onto the high ground again, one after another.

Kel sent her charges back to Haven and steeled herself to follow the mage. The sparrows, seeing where she meant to go, abandoned her for the safety of the walls. Kel tailed Numair around the south edge of the high ground, picking her way along the scant margin of earth between stones and the river. Wobbling, she braced herself against a chunk of granite, then yanked her hand away. The newly moved stone was warm.

She found Numair on the west side of Haven, his boulders used up. He, too, looked used up. His dark skin was gray-blue. He leaned, gasping, against one of the stones.

Kel took her water bottle to the mage. Numair grunted his surprise, then drank it dry. "Thank you," he croaked.

Kel went back to the river and touched the cork Neal had spelled for her to the water. When the cork didn't glow, she knew the water was safe to drink. She filled the bottle, then stripped off her tunic and soaked it in the river. Numair emptied the bottle a second time. He wiped his face, then wrung the waterlogged tunic out over his head and back. Kel went to the river for a second refill. When she returned, Numair offered her a dry, unwrinkled tunic.

"I thought you couldn't do small magics," she said,

trading the water for her tunic. She pulled it on and refastened her belt over it.

"Depends on the magic, and what I have left," Numair said. This time he only sipped from the bottle and returned it half full. Kel slung it on her belt. "Don't worry, I'm not drained," the mage assured her. "And I have stones I've filled with extra power to draw on if more company comes to call. Kel, I need to show you something. Come here, on my other side."

Kel frowned but did as he told her, walking from his left to his right.

"Now look behind you, between the rocks."

Kel looked. He'd left a large gap between two stones where she saw not earth but darkness.

"Daine made me promise to put a bolt hole large enough for the camp's animals to escape in every fort I come across," Numair explained. "The upper opening is inside the storage shed next to the latrine."

"Master Numair, the enemy could find this tunnel as quickly as our animals!" Kel objected, shocked. What if those brutes yesterday had found their way in here?

"I shielded each opening with signs only another black robe would even sense, let alone have the power to break. I just raised the protections now so you could know it's here." Numair made a sign. Before Kel's startled eyes the dark gap vanished, replaced by reddish brown dirt.

When she tried to put a hand between the rocks, she couldn't. The dirt felt solid. "You're sure no one can whistle a little charm and find this?" she demanded. "Scanran shamans have lots of nasty little whistle magics."

"I know," replied Numair calmly. "You have to trust me, Lady Kel. I'd suggest letting Neal and Merric know, at least. Daine worries about animals, but it's also a way to get a message out, if you are besieged. Jump is clever enough to get word to Lord Wyldon, if need be."

Kel smiled. "Yes, he is. And never mind the 'lady'—it's just Kel."

"As you like," Numair replied, stretching. He twisted from side to side, his spine cracking. "I'd suggest you get your people to put smaller stones above these all around the high ground, just in case."

"One of the clerks is already drawing up a schedule," Kel said, and grinned. "I *love* clerks. I'd marry them all if I could."

"You're easily pleased." They walked back around the river toward the gate road. "If anyone ever asks me what to give you for Midwinter, I'll just tell them, clerks."

"I won't *always* need them," Kel said.

"Very true. While I'm here, I'll finish spelling the walls and the gate. I bought some very nice fire-ban charms in Riversedge. I had to add to their potency, but it will be hard for anyone to burn you out of Haven."

They continued to discuss magical protection as they walked the rim of ground between the boulders and the river, then continued to the gate road. They were halfway up the steep incline when an eagle screamed high overhead. Kel would have ignored it, but the eagle's next scream sounded *much* closer.

Numair dragged off his tunic, clumsily wrapping it around his left arm. He was grinning. Kel looked up and gasped. A golden eagle spiraled down from the sky. Numair extended his wrapped arm, and the eagle landed on it with authority.

"So you found me, dear one," Numair said, and kissed the creature on the beak. "I've missed you."

Kel guessed who the eagle must be as the bird preened Numair's hair with its murderous beak. This had to be Numair's lover and Kel's friend, Daine the Wildmage. Kel had seen her as a golden eagle more than once.

"Welcome to Haven, Daine," Kel said politely. "Have you any news?"

The bird shook its head and returned to preening Numair.

"Will you excuse us?" he asked. "She likes to be private when she changes back to human." Without waiting for a reply, he strode on up the incline.

When Kel walked through the gate, she found a small group of young people waiting for her, with Tobe at the fore. All of them held spears in uncertain grips.

Kel frowned. "Tobe, what's this?" she asked.

"'Tis folly," Sergeant Vidur, that day's watch commander, remarked in a scornful voice. He was in charge of one of the convict squads, as hard a man as his friend Oluf. "Askin' you to waste time on this lot when you've other things to do."

Tobe ignored him. "Lady, we was hopin' you'd teach us to fight with spears like you do with your pigsticker." He nodded at his companions. "I showed 'um it—the glaive—and we know there's no more, but won't spears work 'most as good?"

"Just say the word, milady, and I'll run 'em back to their dams," Vidur told Kel.

She wasn't sure if the sergeant's attitude annoyed her or if she just admired young people who wanted to learn pole arms. "Get me a saw," she ordered Tobe, holding out a hand for his spear. He passed it to her and raced away.

"There's a big difference between using a spear as a casting weapon and as a combat weapon," she explained to the boy's companions. "It's like staff fighting, with a bit extra at the end of it. If we're to do this, we need to shorten your weapons." She inspected the five young people. Two looked to be about twelve, another thirteen, the two oldest fifteen or sixteen. She recognized one of them, the girl refugee who had summoned Kel to the flagpole meeting the day before. "What's your name?" Kel asked her.

The girl seemed to forget she wore tattered breeches; she curtsied, hanging on to her spear with one hand. "Loesia, if it please your ladyship."

"Well, Loesia, have your parents granted permission for you to take this time to practice weapons?" asked Kel. "Have any of you *asked* your parents?"

"We got none, milady." The girl who spoke up was one of the youngest, her face pale and sharp-chinned under brown hair awkwardly cut.

"They was killed or taken by raiders," added one of the boys. "The Goatstrack folk took us in, like, and let us eat from they pot."

" 'Acos my lord told 'em to," said another girl. "*An'* gave 'em extry food to not begrudge us."

It made Kel's heart hurt. None of the youngsters

wanted pity, though. All met her eyes as if they defied her to comment. "Well, if you have trouble now, eat with the soldiers," she said. "I'll fix that with the cooks."

"Old Fanche ain't so bad," said the boy who had not spoken yet. "She's fair."

"She smacked Yanmari with a spoon when she woulda fed just her own with the extra," added the girl who'd told Kel they were orphaned.

Tobe arrived with a saw, panting. Jump followed him. Kel exchanged Tobe's spear for the tool and led the youngsters down the gate road to the practice field on the far side of the bridge. Once there, Kel shortened each spear to match the bearer's height while the group borrowed extra bales of hay from the peasant archers who practiced nearby. Once the bales were set as targets, Kel began to teach her group the basics of holding, blocking, and thrusting with a spear.

They broke off when the archers did as the sun disappeared behind the distant western mountains. Kel followed the young people and the archers back to Haven, content with a day well spent. She liked teaching youngsters, she realized. She had noticed it before, when she had helped her maid and some younger pages improve their fighting skills. A pity she couldn't afford to take on and equip a squire—she would love to do for someone else what Lord Raoul had done for her.

"I'll say this for them, they're determined," a familiar voice commented at her elbow. It was Connac, who'd been training the archers.

"Who is determined, Sergeant Connac?" asked Kel.

"All of them, mine and yours. New recruits in the army, sometimes you need a switch to wake 'em up, impress on 'em this is all serious business. Not our refugees." The sergeant scratched his head. "Even your little 'uns—I was watching. They want to learn." He sighed. "They'll spoil me for plain recruits, once this is over."

"We can thank the Scanrans that they *are* serious," Kel replied as they passed through the gates. "You don't usually need to teach mountain people a lesson twice." She asked the gate sergeant, "Is Sir Merric in, and all the workers?"

The man saluted. "You're the last of 'em, milady."

Kel nodded. "Close up for the night, then."

As Kel bade the two sergeants good-night, the heavy gates slowly swung shut. She knew she shouldn't sigh with relief at the thud of the bar when it dropped into place, but she did anyway. At least it was some extra insurance against nighttime surprises.

The next morning dawned gray and cloudy, the skies threatening a drizzle. Kel and Tobe, followed by Jump and the sparrows, left headquarters early. Kel wanted to show Tobe the bolt hole Numair had left for them. Tobe was determined to practice his training when his lady did. They were in the middle of exercises, Kel with her glaive, Tobe with his spear, when their dog and sparrow audience left them.

Kel refused to break her concentration to see where they had gotten to—she was used to them watching her entire routine—but once she had washed up and pulled on her tunic, she went in search of them. She found them, and what looked to be all of the camp's dogs and cats and at least thirty sparrows, clustered around and on Daine. The Wildmage sat cross-legged in the corner formed by the north and east walls, surrounded by animals, serving many of them as a perch. Her eyes were closed, her hands palm-up on her knees.

Not a feather rustled, not a cat scratched, not a dog yawned. There was something taking place that made the hair stand on the back of Kel's neck. It made the air around the animals tingle. She beat a fast retreat. Scanrans and killing devices she could face, but this was something different, something she didn't understand. Daine would tell her what it was, and until then, Kel would find someplace else to be.

Kel was at the training field by the river with her morning archers when she heard the Haven trumpets call the alert, followed by the signal that friends had been sighted. Friends or no, she hustled the archers back to Haven, then raced up the steps to the ramparts, Jump and Tobe at her heels. She had fumbled the griffin-feather band out of its pouch as she ran up the incline. Now she tied it so part was on her forehead above her eyes and part lay across her ears, then accepted the spyglass from another of her sergeants, Yngvar. Calls to answer Haven's had come from the west.

Kel trotted over to the western ramparts, where Numair and Neal stood peering into the distance. "It's the Tirrsmont refugees, I believe," Numair said.

Kel saw the approaching riders and nodded. Two regular army squads guarded a train of people and wagons. Not nearly enough soldiers, not with the enemy in and out, she thought, swallowing anger. Nice of my lord of Tirrsmont to spare *any* guards, I suppose.

She handed the spyglass to Neal and slipped off the feather band, rolling it up. No matter what punishment they took, her griffin feathers never broke or cracked. "Neal, if you're done fixing that man's heart, let's start your physical examinations with these people," she suggested. "They didn't look so good when we passed through Tirrsmont."

"No, they did not," he said grimly. "I'll talk to Father and Master Zamiel right now."

"Zamiel?" Kel was not sure what the head clerk had to do with medical examinations.

Neal shook his head at her. "If we record who they are as they come in, then we can draw up a schedule for them to visit the nice healers," he said gently, as if she were simple. "Everything else here must be scheduled. Wouldn't it be lovely if we did the same?"

"You don't respect me," Kel told him with her sourest glare.

Neal grinned. "I respect you heaps, lady knight. I'd've thrown myself off a bridge, getting this assignment. You, you're there with lists and plans. You listen to every flap-mouthed bumpkin who thinks he can do your task better, and you answer with a smile and thanks. Why, you've inspired me to be a blessing to my fellow bumpkin, just like you." He fluttered his fingers in delicate farewell and trotted down the stairs.

"I can turn him into something for you, if you like," Numair murmured, startling a laugh out of Kel.

"He was actually complimenting me," she told the

mage. "It happens so rarely, I'd hate to see him turned into anything for it." She looked sidelong at the man. Neither he nor Daine had come to supper the previous night. "Daine seems very well after her journey," she remarked slyly. She wouldn't ask him what Daine was up to now; she knew Daine would tell her when she wished.

"I hate it when we're separated for weeks," Numair replied seriously, unaware that Kel might be teasing him for having vanished once his lover arrived. "I feel like half of me is missing. I know she takes risks out there, and nothing I can do will stop her. When I scold, she promises she won't do it again, but once she's back in action, she can't help herself. She'd do anything for the realm, however risky."

Kel looked up at Numair, surprised. "You wouldn't?"

"Of course I would," Numair replied, squinting at the Tirrsmont party. "But that's different. That's me." The day's threatened drizzle began. He raised a hand. His Gift streamed from his fingers, widening as it went. He closed his hand into a fist, breaking off his connection to the sheet of magical fire. It flowed through the air until it stopped and hovered over the oncoming refugees. Kel put up her spyglass. Numair's creation hung over the entire train, keeping it dry.

He's sweet, Kel thought, fascinated. I had no notion!

By the time she reached the gate, Master Zamiel and three other clerks had set up desks under canvas awnings, clear of the sweep of the gates as they opened. All Kel had to do was approve Sergeant Yngvar's request for permission to admit the newcomers. She watched the refugees stream in from a place on the ramparts. The fresh arrivals would soon get into the habit of seeking her out for every complaint and cramp. She'd delay that for now.

Curious, she glanced inside to the corner where north and east walls met. The heap of dogs, cats, and sparrows that covered and spread around Daine was still there.

Kel was in the mess hall, just sitting down with a bowl of venison stew, a slice of bread, and a wedge of cheese, when Zamiel found her. "Eighty-six in all, milady," Zamiel reported. "Two more than we expected."

Kel accepted a mug of cider from Tobe. "One of their sergeants told me two of the women had babies, one back at Tirrsmont, one on the road. The mother who had the baby on the road means to name her Haven. That baby's a girl," she added, thinking the clerk would want to know this detail.

Zamiel sniffed, which seemed to be an opinion of people who had girl babies in wagons, and went to get his own lunch. The new refugees, their belongings stowed in their assigned barracks, filtered into the cookhouse. They must smell the cauldrons, thought Kel. Huge pots of stew had been cooking for more than a day. "That'll fill 'em up fast, milady," Einur the cook told her. "Hard to beat a good stew with turnips, carrots, and onions for that, for all it takes forever to cook."

Watching the newcomers eat, Kel hoped they'd made enough. The Tirrsmont people looked as if they hadn't had a proper meal in months.

A group of them walked down the aisle between the long tables, led by a man in his fifties. His clothes had originally been better. They were trimmed with tags of fur, the fine cloth stained and splotched with mud and grease. He was starting to go bald, but he combed the springy iron-gray hair on top of his head forward to hide the retreat of his hairline. The man's mouth formed a thin, straight line. His nose was an arrow pointing down. His brown eyes narrowed as he scanned the mess hall.

He stopped at the table where Kel, Zamiel, Tobe, and some off-duty soldiers ate. "Where's this so-called commander, this knight we're told is in charge?" he demanded, folding his arms over his chest.

Kel, startled, looked up at him. She'd just taken a hearty bite of stew, more than was mannerly. There was no way she could answer until she chewed the stubborn chunk of venison in her mouth. She felt like a child caught at misbehavior.

"You, there, clerk!" snapped the man. "I want to see this knight and I want him now. Some green lad, fresh out of the Chamber, that's good enough for the likes of us, is it?"

"Sir," Zamiel began with a look at Kel.

The man cut him off. "I won't have this. Dragged off our lands, holed up like rabbits in a hutch all winter, and now this place! We are the larger group—why did the Goatstrack rabble get first choice of residence? Those buildings aren't fit for barns, all green wood and cracks between the boards. I'm an important man, with friends in Corus. I demand proper treatment!"

Kel gave up on her venison. She covered her mouth with her hands and pretended to cough so she could spit the meat into her palms. Quickly she dropped it on the floor, hoping no one had seen. She glanced at Zamiel. He sat, hands folded in his lap, eyes down, cowed by the newcomer. The soldiers at the table watched Kel to see what she'd do.

Kel got to her feet. Zamiel and the soldier who shared her bench pushed back so she could stand comfortably. Taking up her goblet, Kel drank the cider in it.

The Tirrsmont man continued, "These nobles shuffle us about, lining their pockets with money that's meant for us and taking their pleasure whilst we live with common farmers—"

A woman stood on tiptoe and whispered urgently in his ear, pointing to the Mindelan badge on Kel's tunic.

The man scowled at Kel *"You?"* he said in clear disbelief. "You are the commander of this camp? Impossible! I will not be governed by a, a shameless girl, a chit who's no better than she ought to be!"

The insult to Kel, the claim that she was nearly a prostitute, brought the soldiers growling to their feet. Kel gave them the hand signal to return to their seats, though she secretly appreciated their championship of her. Then she leaned forward and braced her fists on the table. Though her veins hummed with anger, she made herself smile mockingly as she looked at the Tirrsmont women. "Mistresses, have you ever noticed that when we disagree with a male—I hesitate to say 'man'—or find ourselves in a position *over* males, the first comment they make is always about our reputations or our monthlies?"

One of the new women snorted. Others snickered.

Kel looked at the man, who was momentarily speechless. "If I disagree with you, should I place blame on the misworkings of your manhood? Or do I refrain from so serious an insult"—she made a face—"far more serious, of course, than your hint that I am a whore. Because *my* mother taught me courtesy, I only suggest that my monthlies will come long after your hair has escaped your head entirely."

That brought a laugh from most of the Tirrsmont refugees and guffaws from Kel's soldiers.

Kel hardened her face. "I am Keladry of Mindelan, lady knight and the commander of Haven," she said icily. "My reputation is no concern of yours. What is your name?"

The man drew himself up. "Idrius Valestone, fur merchant."

"Here you are just another refugee, Idrius Valestone," Kel informed him. "Subject to the laws that govern this camp. While I command, you will address me with respect, understand? If you have complaints about me, address them to my lord Wyldon of Cavall, the district commander. Until you get his reply, keep your opinions of me to yourself. You are dismissed."

"My lady, please!" It was a woman who stood close to Idrius's elbow. "He wasn't thinking—"

"Then he had best learn," Kel remarked. "Who are you?"

"His wife," the woman said. She was a plain creature, face chapped by wind and cold, thin-lipped, with nearly straight black brows and greasy brown hair. Her orange dress was patched and stained, like those of the other refugees. The brown shawl around her shoulders was as worn as the rest of her.

"'His wife' is an odd name," Kel replied.

"Olka," the woman answered. "Olka Valestone."

"I demand to speak to my lord Wyldon immediately." Idrius glared at his wife, who looked down. "Today!" the man continued.

Kel sat on her bench again and speared a hunk of venison in her bowl. "Go, with my blessing. If you follow the road across the Greenwoods River and north, then ride west on the Vassa road, you should reach Fort Mastiff by midnight. That's his headquarters."

"I will need a horse and an escort," Idrius pointed out.

Kel raised her brows. "I can't spare them. You may not have noticed, but we are at war. I need every guard and every horse to protect this camp."

"I *demand* a horse and escort!" Idrius barked, as if he didn't hear.

"And I said no," Kel informed him patiently. "You may write to my lord Wyldon and send your complaint with the next courier. In the meantime, you are still dismissed."

The Tirrsmont people were trying to drag the purple-faced Idrius away. "You haven't heard the last of this!" he cried. "I won't be ordered about by some brass-faced wench!"

The soldiers stirred, their anger a rumble in their throats. Kel, chewing busily, shook her head. The soldiers quieted as the Tirrsmont refugees forced Idrius to sit at a table far from Kel's.

"Have you done the work schedules yet?" Kel asked Zamiel quietly after she'd swallowed her venison.

"I wanted to get the Tirrsmont people in before we did them," the clerk replied.

Kel spooned up a last mouthful of vegetables and gravy, then stood. "See that Master Idrius gets latrine detail for a week, if you please. Perhaps it will sweeten him."

"Not that one, milady," Zamiel replied. "Men like him eternally feel cheated of their due."

"Well, it will make *me* feel better," Kel said, gathering her dirty dishes. "I'll settle for that."

That afternoon she walked through the Tirrsmont barracks, greeting people, learning their names, making sure they settled in. She met the newborn Haven, a very small, very red scrap of humankind. She even held the girl briefly and competently, as she'd once held her nieces and nephews. After returning the infant to her mother, Kel finished greeting the newcomers, including the Valestones. Not once did she act as if she remembered her conversation with them in the mess hall.

Tobe and the rest of her spear class waited for her by the gate. None of the young people had quit. In fact, the group had increased by four; Tobe had recruited some Tirrsmont refugees already. One of them was a boy who looked to be only about five.

"Meech won't take part," his older sister, a moon-faced girl with frizzy black hair and pale eyes, assured Kel earnestly. "But Ma says watch 'im, an' I want to learn to fight. I don't want the enemy havin' 'is way with me."

Kel understood that. "As long as he behaves," she said, crouching so that her eyes were on the same level as the boy's. He clung to his sister's skirt, clutching a rag doll close to his side. It was grubby and battered, but obviously well made, right down to the shock of scarlet yarn hair that must have been salvaged from an expensive garment. "What of it, Meech? Will you stay out of our way?" The boy nodded soberly. "Very well." Kel straightened. "Let's go," she ordered the group.

On their way down the Haven road, she fell in step with Meech's sister. "What's your name?" she asked.

The girl smiled shyly. "Gydo—Gydane Elder, if it please my lady."

"Welcome to Haven, Gydo," Kel said. "Let me know if you'd like to try any other weapons besides spears."

Gydo's thin face lit. "Tobe says you teach 'im to shoot a bow, mornings."

Kel nodded. "You're welcome to join us."

When they reached the practice ground on the far side of the Greenwoods, Kel noticed that Tobe and his friend Loesia had found spears for the newcomers. Kel eyed the well-polished wood and razor-sharp points. She wouldn't ask where the weapons had come from. Few of the soldiers knew how to use a spear; fewer still wanted to learn. At least if the young folk used them, the weapons wouldn't go to waste.

8
FIRST DEFENSE

Kel rose at her usual time before dawn, heavy-eyed and achy. She had been up late the night before, working on the reports she would have to take to Lord Wyldon when she visited Fort Mastiff in a few days.

She cleaned up and got dressed, sniffling all the while. She was getting a cold; she needed to see Neal or his father sometime today. It vexed her to have to take the time for that when she had so much to do.

She watched Tobe as the lad pursued the morning cleanup she'd taught him, wondering if she ought to suggest once again that he at least remain in bed until sunrise. She decided it wasn't worth the effort. Tobe always refused.

This morning Jump and the sparrows settled onto Kel's still-warm bed after she made it. They had returned from their conference with Daine at some late hour.

Whatever they had been doing, it had exhausted the animals. Kel grimaced at them. "Some of us have the luxury of sleep," she complained, then coughed.

Outside, she walked into the open space between headquarters and the infirmary and began her practice dance with the heavy glaive. At her first spin she came to an abrupt halt. There was Tobe, as always. With him stood some of her other spear students, including Loesia, Gydo, and Meech. Meech yawned. Resettling his doll, he put his thumb in his mouth, almost asleep on his feet.

"You must be joking," Kel said, looking down into determined faces.

Loesia shook her head, curls bouncing. "We won't get good fast doin' this just once a day," she pointed out. "Barrabul, Keon, Dortie, and me practice extra when we've time—"

"'Cept lately, time's the last thing we got," the boy Keon interrupted.

Kel sneezed. If she weren't sniffly and achy, she would feel more pride that these youngsters understood the need for practice better than most adults. As it was, she smiled at them and croaked, "Very well. Form your lines."

Once their practice ended, all of them trooped to the mess hall for their morning meal. While the young people wolfed their food, Kel picked at hers. Neal, slow to wake though he was, saw she had a cold before he'd touched his breakfast. He required less time than it took to fry a slice of ham to work a healing spell on her. Once he had finished, he ordered Tobe to make sure that she drank the noxious tea he prescribed, three times a day for a week. As he did, Kel's appetite returned. She ate two bowls of porridge and two slices of ham, her sniffles only a memory.

Leaving the mess hall with Tobe and Jump, Kel asked, "I don't suppose you could be persuaded to forget the tea?"

Tobe looked at her with reproach.

"Yes, maybe it *was* a stupid question," Kel said in answer to his unspoken reply. "Just wait till *you* get sick."

Teaching the spear lessons meant that Kel hadn't gotten to do a complete pattern dance with her glaive. She collected it from her room and retreated to the corner of the fort where Daine had spent the previous day. She started slowly and speeded up through the dance until the staff was a brown blur and the blade a silver one as she spun, lunged, dodged, and pivoted.

"I'm always sorry I never get the chance to see you spar against someone who knows what they're doing," a familiar voice remarked as Kel finished her pattern dance with a stamp and a swirling flourish that brought the glaive to rest at her side. "Every time you practiced with the Yamani ladies on progress, I got called away."

Kel turned, panting, and smiled at Daine. The Wildmage sat with her back against the headquarters wall, a slender young woman in a pale green shirt, brown jerkin, and brown breeches tucked into black calf-high boots. Her masses of curling, smoky-brown hair were coiled and pinned at the back of her head, tilting it back slightly from the weight. She watched Kel through blue-gray eyes framed with long black lashes as she produced seed from her pocket for the sparrows who had come to see her.

"What were you doing with them yesterday?" Kel asked, leaning on her glaive. "I didn't want to interrupt." Now that she had stopped moving, her legs reminded her she'd just had a healing, albeit a small one. Telling herself that she was being polite, not lazy, she sat next to Daine.

"Oh, that." Daine looked at the ground, then shook her head. "I shouldn't have, but—Kel, the guard you've got is a fair disgrace. I know Lord Wyldon's stretched thin with troops in this district, but Vanget could spare more soldiers to ward these people. It's not right. And there's no talking to Vanget about things like that. He just tells me I don't see the larger tapestry, and sends me off to play with my animals."

Kel blinked. Vanget was known for being sensible. Now Kel had to wonder. She knew that no truly sensible man would make the Wildmage cross. "It's what we have," she said mildly.

Daine grimaced. "Oh, of course you'll agree. You're a warrior. You won't question orders."

I do, all the time, thought Kel. Then she remembered and told herself, I just don't do it out loud.

Daine went on. "But I'm no warrior. I can speak as I please. And I can help, which means a lot to me just now. I, well, there's a way of changing the People—animals—so their cleverness is more like two-legger—human—cleverness."

"That's happening at the palace," Kel reminded her. "Peachblossom, Jump, the sparrows, they're all wiser than other animals I've known. Hoshi, too."

"I can't help that," Daine said. "That's just . . . happening, and there's nothing I can do to change it, except stay away from the palace more. But what I did yesterday, that was stronger. Much stronger. I filled them with my magic."

"Filled?" Kel asked.

Daine smiled crookedly. "That's the best I can explain it. Your own sparrows already knew some hand signals. Now they'll learn them all; the dogs and cats, too. And they'll understand when you talk. I'd use simple words, though. Simple ideas. They'll patrol and fight for you on their own, and they'll report back to you. You'll have to work that out with them, animal signs you'll understand, besides the ones you already know."

Kel shook her head. It was wonderful and frightening and overwhelming. "Daine, I don't know what to say. I—"

The older woman held up a hand. "Say nothing," she said, her blue-gray eyes bleak. "I did them no favors, changing them, but they wanted it. I made sure of that. They want to help you, those animals who know you. They want to keep you and most of them that live here safe." The tiny lines around her mouth and nose deepened. "And the wild birds said it would be interesting, to see how two-leggers think. I wonder if they'll feel that way in a year. I hope they like it, because I can't undo what I've done. But you need the help so badly."

Kel laid a hand on Daine's arm. "I'll look out for them as best as I can," she said quietly.

"Oh, that I knew, or I'd never have agreed to it," replied Daine. "I don't know how you sleep, with so many to look after, and now I've added to your load."

"But I'm not the one galloping from fort to fort and sending animal spies to hunt for Blayce the Gallan," Kel pointed out. "You must be exhausted." She hesitated, then asked, "Any word of him?"

Daine shook her head, brown curls fighting their way out of her hairpins. "Word, oh, we've had that. None of it any good. None that tells us where to look for him. I'd settle for word of his man Stenmun, that captains his guard. You'd think even in Scanra it'd be fair hard to hide a man near seven feet tall, but all we ever get of Stenmun is a sniff here and there. He's bought supplies here, or he's carried killing devices there, but by the time I've word of it, he's gone." She pounded her knees with her fists. "It's so maddening, Kel! If I could lay my hand on that Stenmun, I'd have little birds follow him to doom and beyond, straight back to his master. It's like he knows to keep on the move, so we can't get word of his being somewhere." Her mouth tightened. "Well, sooner or later, I'll have him. I'd rather it be sooner, though."

Me too, thought Kel. She patted Daine's shoulder. "You'll feel better after you've eaten," she said. "Come to the mess hall. Our cooks have a nice way with porridge."

Daine rose, scattered more seed from her pocket for the flock of birds that had gathered around them, then offered Kel a hand up. "I like porridge," she admitted as she and Kel walked toward the mess hall. "And there you go, trying to take care of me, too." She laughed and reached up to give Kel's shoulders a quick hug.

Kel was keeping Daine company in the mess hall when Idrius Valestone stormed up to their table, crimson with fury. Gil and one of the other convict soldiers followed him. "These *criminals* tell me I'm to work!" Idrius snapped at Kel. "Clearing latrines! I'll have you know I'm a man of affairs and—" He threw up his hands as a small cloud of sparrows descended on him, their angry shrieks sounding like bird curses. "Call them off!"

"Nari," Kel said wearily.

As one, the sparrows turned and flew back to land on the table between Daine and Kel.

"Jump," Kel said in warning as the dog advanced on Idrius from behind. Jump raised his lone good ear and sat, panting, the image of canine innocence. Kel gave him a reproving glare, then regarded Idrius. "Everyone works here, Master Valestone. *Everyone.* The schedule changes every three days for all but the cooks, those who specialize in useful trades like carpentry and smithing, and the soldiers. That way no one gets stuck with one task for very long. I've done latrine duty. I've got it again next week. And if you don't quiet down and stop looking for special treatment, I'll make sure you are listed as having a talent for emptying waste tubs and getting rid of sewage."

The man had listened, clenching and unclenching his fists. "You hold a grudge because I named you for the trull that you are, is that it?"

Jump growled softly.

Kel sighed. "Go away, and take your bile as well," she recommended. "Otherwise I'll have to do something with you, and my schedule's busy enough as is."

Gil reached for Idrius's arm. The merchant yanked out of the convict's grip and stalked out of the mess hall.

"You'll have more trouble with that one," Daine remarked. "He's the kind that will complain if it's sunny or cool. And, don't bite me for saying it, calling you a loose woman is the easiest insult there is."

Kel smiled crookedly. "Why should I bite you for pointing out something I've known since I was a page?" she asked. "If talk were true, I'd be the easiest wench in Tortall. There's nothing I can do about that, so I may as well get on with my work." She sighed. "That's all this job is, Daine," she explained. "Trying to please everyone and pleasing no one. And it will only get worse, not better."

Outside they heard the shrieks of birds, not sparrows this time, but ravens and jays, dozens of them crying an alarm. Kel raced from the mess hall, Jump and the sparrows streaming behind her, headed for the gate. Merric, still half asleep, changed direction as he walked toward the cookhouse and ran with her, fumbling for the sword belt he didn't have.

Tobe poked his head out of Kel's window. "Tobe!" shouted Kel. "Sir Merric's sword!" Tobe vanished.

Merric let Kel precede him up the stairs to the ramparts. Someone thrust her spyglass into her hand.

"Thank you," Kel said, and put the glass to her eye. In the east, where the road from Fort Giantkiller emptied into the valley, she saw violent movement.

She turned to the gate trumpeter. "Sound call to arms," Kel ordered.

As the trumpet's blast carved the air, a raven soared overhead, coming out of Haven: Daine. She flew toward the distant struggle, calling to other ravens nearby. Stormwings also rose from the trees, shrieking with glee as they climbed into the air for a good view.

Kel passed the spyglass to Merric and turned to find Tobe and Loesia waiting by the stair. Panting, Tobe carried Merric's sword, helm, and cuirass. Loesia had Kel's helm and cuirass. Behind them, Keon, one of Kel's other spear trainees, held the glaive.

"Good choice," Merric informed Tobe, lifting the

cuirass over his head and shoulders. "If you've got to arm in a hurry, these are what you need first. Would you get those straps on each side?" he asked Tobe. "Yes, good, pull them snug."

Kel donned her own cuirass and helm. Loesia did up the straps without being asked.

"Kel, I'll need two squads, I think," Merric said as he buckled on his sword belt. "And we'd best have a third ready to go in reserve. You'll take that one?"

Kel nodded. "Sergeants Vidur and Connac?" she called, knowing they'd have come as soon as they heard the trumpet.

"Here, milady," they said in unison. All four sergeants had assembled on the walkway over the gate.

"You and your squads are with Sir Merric," Kel told them.

"Yes, milady," Connac replied. Boots pounded on the stairs as Merric and the sergeants ran for the horses. She hoped that by now their young stablehands would have at least a few ready to go.

It's too soon, all too soon, she thought, her mouth dry. *We aren't ready!*

There was no point in fussing now. She heard familiar trumpet calls in the distance: some of the embattled people on the east road were on their side.

"Sergeant Oluf?" she called.

"Milady?" Oluf, in charge of her second convict squad, and Sergeant Yngvar had remained on the walkway. If Kel's memory served her, Yngvar was that morning's watch commander.

"Have your squad arm up and hold themselves ready to ride," Kel ordered.

"Milady, we're better keeping them on the walls here," Oluf protested. "I wouldn't want them at my back—"

Kel faced him. She didn't like Oluf any more than his counterpart, Vidur. "Sergeant, I didn't ask you what you did or didn't want," she said quietly. *"Move."* She said it as she'd heard Raoul give such orders, as if there were no doubt she would be obeyed. Oluf wavered, then went to collect his men.

Neal and Duke Baird came running down the walkway from the stair near headquarters. Neal was buckling on his sword belt. "Tell me where you want me," he said, his voice crisp.

"Right here," Kel replied. "If Merric gets in trouble, I'll take Oluf's squad to back him up. You'll be in command."

"But surely you need me in the field," her friend protested.

"I need you *here.* People will obey you." Neal opened his mouth to argue further, but Kel cut him off. "We require a knight on these walls, and I'm not about to risk a healer out there. I'm afraid this time we'll have a lot more work for you and his grace." She nodded to Duke Baird.

"I'll ready the infirmary," the duke said immediately. "Don't waste the lady's time in debate, Neal. Let's go."

"Kel," Neal protested again, a hand on her arm.

"I'll send Tobe if I have to leave," she said firmly, with a little smile. "Don't damage the fort, all right?"

Whatever he saw in her eyes, it made him sigh in exasperation. He followed his father back to the infirmary.

"Tobe," Kel called, raising her voice, "I need Saefas and—"

Someone tugged her right sleeve. It was Tobe. Saefas and Fanche were right behind him, bows in hand. "Get every archer up and spaced evenly on the walls," Kel ordered them. "If they waste arrows shooting when the enemy's too far off, I'll flay them."

Fanche and Saefas went to rally the civilian archers. Kel chewed on her lower lip, reviewing the most recent dispatches. Under her feet the gate moaned as it opened. This commotion in the woods had to be the next lot of refugees from Giantkiller, those who'd come from Anak's Eyrie.

Merric and his two squads trotted through the gate and down the inclined road. As soon as they crossed the Greenwoods River, they spurred their mounts to a gallop. Kel looked around. Civilians from Goatstrack and Tirrsmont raced up the stairs to the ramparts, bows in hand. Kel heard raised voices. She saw Idrius arguing with Saefas, hanging on to the ex-trapper's arm though Saefas was plainly trying to get to his post.

"Sergeant Yngvar," she called to the watch commander, the only sergeant left to her, "have two of your men escort Master Valestone to the stocks and lock him in, immediately."

"Yes, milady!" the sergeant replied. He clattered down the steps with two of his soldiers.

Kel turned back to the distant conflict, bringing the glass to her eye again. It was hard to wait, seeing the fight, seeing wagons and riders flee across the valley floor, but she had no choice. Until Merric called for help, or until she saw something that meant he would need it, she had to keep Oluf's squad back to defend the walls. If another killing device attacked, they would be needed, even with the metal nets spaced at regular intervals on the wall against just that event.

The battle moved closer and closer to the Greenwoods River. Merric had rallied his soldiers and any civilians in the train who could fight into a circle around the refugees' wagons. The Scanrans were mounted and moving quickly, trying to take chunks out of that protective circle. Kel hoped her people got ahead of the enemy soon. She couldn't destroy the bridge to prevent a Scanran crossing unless Merric and the refugees crossed it first.

A raven perched atop the log palisade. Its beak changed shape until it could say clearly in Daine's voice, "There's Scanrans riding up from the south. They'll be clear of the trees in a moment."

Kel told Sergeant Yngvar, "Take your orders from Sir Nealan!" She raced down the stairs to find Oluf's squad, Tobe, and Peachblossom waiting. "Mount up," Kel ordered the soldiers. She passed her glaive to Tobe while she climbed into Peachblossom's saddle, then reclaimed it. "Tobe, get Neal. Tell him he's needed on the wall."

The boy raced off. Kel led the soldiers out through the half-open gate at a trot. Squinting at the southern woods, she could just see movement in the trees. There was no point in wondering how the enemy had crept behind the forts and patrols between Haven and the Vassa River. They were here, and she had to persuade them to leave.

Hooves thumped the ground, coming up beside her. Kel risked a glance to her left and saw Numair astride his spotted gelding. "They need you more over there," she told him, pointing to Merric's people.

"You need me in the middle," retorted the mage. He broke away and rode onto a rise in the ground squarely between Kel and Merric.

Screaming battle cries, the enemy in the southern woods charged. Only a third of them were mounted; the rest were foot soldiers. Kel noted the Scanran horseman who appeared to be the leader and gave her convict squad the signal for caution.

Shrieks sounded in her ears as her recently magicked and increased sparrow flock sped by, headed for the enemy. A flash of white on her left caught Kel's eye: Jump raced forward at the head of a pack of camp dogs.

Well, I said everybody at Haven works, she thought, grimly amused. I guess that means that everybody fights, too.

Fifty yards from the enemy, she signaled her men to form two lines at her back, leaving Kel at the point of their formation. Arrows from the enemy's archers zipped by them; Kel heard a man grunt. Then she was on the Scanran leader, chopping down with her glaive as she drew alongside him. The blond man raised his axe in time to block her. Peachblossom swung around, kicking a foot soldier with his hind hooves as he brought Kel into position to charge the Scanran leader again. Her gelding surged forward. Kel leveled her glaive and ran the Scanran through almost as neatly as she had once struck other knights' shields in tournament jousts. She jerked the blade free. Peachblossom reared and spun. Kel moved with him, her glaive sweeping edge first to cut down another mounted Scanran. Peachblossom dropped to all fours, landing squarely on a foot soldier's back.

"You have a mean streak," Kel murmured as she turned the gelding. She doubted that the man whose spine Peachblossom had just crushed would be getting up.

"Kel," a familiar voice said in her ear.

"Numair?" she asked, startled, looking around. The mage stood on his rise, well out of speaking distance. Hands tugged at her leg. Kel slashed the man trying to unseat her across the top of his head. Blinded with blood, he released her.

"Kel, get your people to retreat," Numair's soft voice urged in her ear.

And that griffin-feather band does a lot of good in my belt pouch. I can't tell if this is an illusion or really Numair, she thought bitterly as she looked for her men. Gil was unhorsed, his mount dead beside him. He was trying to hold off three Scanran foot soldiers with his longsword and shield. Riding down on Gil's attackers, Kel thought, I don't care how silly I look, I'm wearing griffin-feather ornaments in my hair from now on.

The sparrows swarmed one of Gil's foes, gouging his face with their tiny beaks and claws. They formed a cloud around his head, forcing the Scanran away from Gil. Jump leaped for a second attacker's sword arm and clung to it, powerful jaws locked around the man's wrist. Gil knocked the Scanran's other hand and the axe it held aside with his shield. He thrust in cleanly, his blade slipping between the bronze plaques sewn to a leather jerkin, all the armor his enemy had.

"Fall back!" Kel shouted, pitching her voice so her

men could hear her over the clamor of battle. She rode down the third Scanran foot soldier. "Fall back in order!" She killed the foot soldier, wrapped her reins around her saddle horn, and reached down to Gil with her free arm. "Behave, Peachblossom," she told the gelding. Peachblossom glanced back at her. Gil looked at the offered hand, then at Peachblossom, and gulped.

"Numair's up to something," Kel informed Gil. "Come or stay, but decide fast."

Gil seized Kel's hand and let her drag him up behind her. It was shamefully easy. That's it, thought Kel, I'm making sure these convicts are fed. Once Gil was settled, Kel shouted, "Fall back!" Hoisting her glaive, she waved it in a circle, the signal for a retreat. Her soldiers came, some without horses, to form a line on either side of Peachblossom. They moved away from the Scanrans. A pair of Tortallans were down, motionless on the churned and bloody grass.

The enemy stayed put for a moment, panting, gathering their strength to attack once more. Step by step, the Tortallan horses and the men on foot rode back toward Haven, weapons ready, putting ground between them and the foe. Kel glanced to her side. Sergeant Oluf swayed in his saddle, blood coursing down one arm.

The earth shook under Peachblossom, who pranced and whickered. "Stop it!" she ordered. "This is help—I think!"

Stone grated. The land moaned. Several of Kel's men dropped to their knees, making the sign against evil and muttering prayers. Kel urged Peachblossom over until she could poke the kneeling men with the butt of her glaive. "Up!" she snapped. They lurched to their feet. "When I say fall back, it's an order, lackwits!" She hoped they didn't hear the quiver in her voice. The hairs on the nape of her neck and her arms stood. The ground by Numair's rise sprouted a crack that raced across the land between him and the Scanrans Kel's men had just fought. The enemy huddled together in fear as the ground shook. When the earth opened in a massive yawn under their feet, they pitched into it. The ground snapped shut. Only a bare, narrow strip marked the ground where the crack had been.

"Why didn't I take up carpentry, like me ma wanted me to?" whispered one of Kel's convicts.

"And miss all this adventure?" someone else replied.

Kel turned Peachblossom so she could see them. "You act as if you never saw magic before," she said. "It's not like he doesn't do it all the time. Now fall back on the fort in proper order."

"You heard milady!" Sergeant Oluf forced himself to sit upright in the saddle. "Fall in! What of Laif and Adern?" He pointed at the Tortallans they'd left.

"Laif's throat's cut," one of the men replied.

"They got Adern clean through the belly," added someone else. They were all moving now, headed back to the road, the men on horses outside those on foot. Kel listened to them with one ear, trying to see how Merric fared. People approached them on the road, running, driving wagons, riding: civilians all. Merric and his two squads were protecting their rear, then.

A hand fumbled at one of her saddle fittings to unhook the water flask Kel always carried. Gil popped the cork out with a grimy thumb, letting it hang on its string as he offered the water to Kel from behind. Her mouth was dry as stone. She gulped at least half before she gave the flask back to him.

"Sergeant, we'll going to form line on either side of the road at the bridge," she said, trying to keep her voice level as the ground nearby began to shake again. "You take four men to the north side of the road. I'll take the south. Gil—"

"Gone," the convict said as he slid off Peachblossom. He'd kept his sword.

"But stay with me. You, you, you." She pointed to three other convict soldiers. "We'll hold the road on this side. Sergeant?"

He saluted and led his four men across the road, keeping out of the way of the civilians who fled for the safety of Haven. Their wagons were stubbled with arrows and marked by fire. One of them swayed and collapsed, its left rear wheel spinning free of its axle. The driver, a woman, got out. A teenaged girl, a baby in each arm, jumped out, followed by two boys. All of them raced across the bridge.

Light sparked where she'd first seen fighting on the Giantkiller road. Kel grimaced. Nearly twenty Stormwings mingled with the vultures to approach the dead now that the battle had passed that section of the valley. The noise of the earth creaking like an old ship brought her eyes back to the ground where Merric still fought. He and his men were now falling back. A tree near the Scanrans split in two. The ground under them opened and closed, swallowing them alive.

"He best leave us somethin' to farm," she heard a soldier remark.

"Don't worry. We'll farm, soon's he finishes wi' that new-style Scanran fertilizer," replied Gil. Some men actually laughed. Kel decided that life in the quarries and mines must create a morbid sense of humor.

She gnawed her lip, wondering if she ought to take her men forward to support Merric, but no. It was wiser to stay put. If the Scanrans she'd just fought had reinforcements in the southern woods, she dared not leave the road unguarded. And Merric was doing well enough. He was in view with his squads in good order. Beyond them the road was clear but for the bodies strewn along it. What looked like a wave of dark magic rose above Merric, about to break over him. Kel gasped, then realized the darkness was a cloud of ravens, lit by streams of bluejays like lightning. The crowd of birds grew wider and broader, then broke up to feed on the dead.

Haven was safe for the moment, provided no more Scanrans were in the woods. We need a burial detail, Kel thought, an eye on the Stormwings. And more weapons training. Four squads aren't enough to defend us, especially when we lose men. She squinted at Merric's approaching troops. He was short three soldiers. She had lost two. That was an eighth of their fighting force. She would have to ask Wyldon for replacements next week, when she was scheduled to report to him in person at Fort Mastiff. Even if he could replace those five, what of Haven's future losses? Forays into the valley to rescue people under attack could turn into a costly business.

One raven had not gone with the others. It swooped

around Numair and his spotted gelding, its movements frantic. Numair leaned against his mount, swaying.

"That must be Daine. And Numair's too exhausted to move," Kel whispered. She appraised Merric's troops and the refugees they ushered toward Haven, then her own men. "Sergeant Oluf," she called over the heads of a clump of refugees on foot, "stay here. You three." She pointed to three mounted soldiers. "Come along."

She turned Peachblossom toward the rise in the ground and urged him to a trot. "I know you're tired," she murmured to him. "I'll try not to ask too much more of you. We just need to get him off the field in case the enemy's still about."

Peachblossom shook his head with a snort as if to rid himself of unnecessary sentiment. "It's true. I mean every word," she assured him. She heard hoofbeats behind her: the men she'd chosen from what remained of Oluf's squad.

They reached Numair, who now sat on the ground, his head in his hands. The Daine-raven perched on his shoulder, preening him anxiously.

"Master Numair, come," Kel said as they halted beside him. The convicts' horses shied, nervous of the power that cloaked Numair.

The mage looked up, gray-faced, his eyes tormented. All my folk were so busy telling me how scared they were of him for making the ground rise for the camp, they didn't mention he must have been abed for days after, Kel thought. "Master Numair, come," she repeated. "Please, mount up—you're worrying Daine."

He put a hand up to the raven on his shoulder. "Yes—yes. Dearest, I'm fine."

Kel didn't think he meant her. "Do you need a hand?" she asked.

"No," said the mage, getting on all fours. The raven took flight, circling. Numair tried to stand and staggered. Kel dismounted and loaded him onto his gelding in sections, head and chest first, then the rest of him, using her cupped hands under one of his feet and all of her strength. Once he was settled, she gathered his reins and remounted Peachblossom.

"Let's go home," she told her men.

The raven settled onto Peachblossom's saddle horn. Its beak changed shape, enough that Kel understood when Daine said, "Kel, I mustn't stay. I think there's trouble over at Fort Giantkiller."

"Because Scanrans attacked on the Giantkiller road. I understand," Kel replied. She squinted at the road near the eastern hills. Ravens, buzzards, and Stormwings flocked to the dead Numair hadn't engulfed in the second crack he'd made in the ground. "Will you come back?"

"I don't know," the Daine-raven answered sadly. "If it's bad at Giantkiller, I'll have to get word to Mastiff and Northwatch. I hate to ask when you've so many to mind already, but will you keep an eye on Numair? He'll try to move about before he's rested, and he won't eat proper."

Kel smiled. "I'll take care of him."

The Daine-raven took flight and headed northeast.

The trot back to the bridge was uneventful, save for Kel's awareness that more and more Stormwings arrived every step of the way. At the gate she called for a fresh horse and dismounted from Peachblossom, taking her glaive with her.

"Find Tobe," she instructed her gelding. "He'll fix you up." Peachblossom shook his head, showering Kel with foam and sweat.

"Nonsense," Kel retorted as if he were a human. "You're all in. Do as I say."

He flattened his ears, then sighed, the fight going out of him. He trudged over to the waiting Tobe, weariness in every line of his body. Loesia brought Kel a fresh mount, a frisky mare, and held her as Kel swung into the saddle. Kel looked at Sergeant Yngvar, who stood by the gate. "May I borrow your crossbow?" she asked. "I'll bring it back." She opened her water flask and gulped the rest of its contents. Silently, Yngvar handed over his crossbow and quiver.

"Kel, where are you going?" demanded Neal. He'd been talking to the newly arrived refugees, soothing them as he looked for wounded among them and among the soldiers. "They're all dead, whoever's left."

"I know that," she replied. "Neal, we need burial details, just as soon as you can organize them." Someone prodded her arm. It was Gil, offering her a full, large, water skin. She murmured her thanks.

"But where are *you* going?" Merric wanted to know. He'd just handed his own mount over to one of the waiting stable hands.

Kel turned the mare and urged her through the gate. "To shoo off Stormwings," she called back over her shoulder.

April 30, 460
Fort Mastiff

9
MASTIFF

Kel's first emotion at the sight of Fort Mastiff was envy. Mastiff had a double set of log walls, the outer twenty feet high, the inner thirty feet high, with deep ditches before each. An abatis stood in the edge of the outer ditch, the sharpened logs offering an unfortunate end to anyone fool enough to try to jump them.

As Kel and her companions passed through the first gate, she heard a voice yell her name from twenty feet overhead. She looked up. Owen sat atop the inner wall, waving frantically. A hand grabbed Kel's impetuous friend by the sleeve and yanked him back onto the ramparts. Kel traded a head shake with Neal. Some people, like Owen, never changed.

The last set of guards waved them through the inner gate. Neal whistled, which made Kel feel better: she wasn't the only one who was awed. Mastiff housed three full companies of soldiers, plus an assortment of mages, clerks, healers, messengers, hedgewitches whose Gift could be turned to combat or medicine, and unimportant-looking persons in deep-woods clothing who looked like scouts, spies, or both. The barracks were military trim—no ropes of laundry flapping between buildings, no firepits and bubbling cauldrons at each barracks door, no debris or garbage on the ground. Chickens, ducks, and geese milled in pens instead of picking their way throughout the enclosure. There was no need to keep watch in case a toddler ran in front of the horses. The only raised voices she heard were those of sergeants shouting drill commands.

Owen came rattling down the stair from the ramparts. As Kel and her companions dismounted, Owen collected the reins of Numair's, Duke Baird's, and Neal's horses. He moved to take Hoshi's reins, but Tobe, who'd been in charge of the packhorses that carried Numair's and Duke Baird's things, was quick to add Hoshi to his charges. Owen nodded to him and told the others from Haven, "My lord says, you're all welcome to take your noon meal at the officers' mess, over there." He managed to point with a handful of reins. "Your men can eat at the common mess." He pointed it and the stables out to Sergeant Yngvar.

The squad dismounted and led their horses away, Tobe in the rear with Hoshi and the packhorses. Kel had brought the men as guards, but she had not been happy about removing over a quarter of Haven's trained fighters. She'd made Merric promise to stay in camp and conduct no patrols until her return.

"Hey, Rengar, c'mere," Owen called. A boy dressed in

civilian clothes trotted over to them. "Kel," Owen said, "would you give your reports to Rengar? My lord says that way you can eat while he reads them, and he'll talk to you about them when you're done. Master Numair, Daine said tell you she's up in the observation tower." Owen pointed out the tall wooden tower at the highest point of ground inside the walls. Numair immediately went to her.

"Daine's here?" asked Neal. "The last we knew, she was on her way to Giantkiller."

"She came to us from there," replied Owen, his face suddenly grim. Kel was about to ask him what was wrong when he trotted off in response to a call from the guard-post.

Still puzzled by Owen's change of mood, Kel passed her reports to Rengar and went to the officers' mess with Neal and his father. Harailt of Aili, a powerful mage and dean of the royal university, was there with his lunch. He greeted Duke Baird with pleasure and invited them to join him.

"I thought you were in Northwatch," Baird remarked as he set his tray beside his round-faced friend.

"I'm here for talks with Wyldon—the prince is, too," Harailt explained. "He's watch captain right now, but we'll see him at supper. Vanget decided some fresh air and a change of scene might do his highness good."

"Still missing Princess Shinkokami?" Duke Baird asked the question Kel was thinking.

"In part," replied Harailt. "Mostly he chafes at the bit Vanget's put on him. He has a full guard of knights when Vanget fights battles, and he's not allowed to patrol. After Roald snapped at a few people, Vanget saw he should do something for him, before his highness did something himself. It *does* run in the family."

Neal listened in silence as the older mages exchanged news. Kel was distracted by her own worries. She didn't want to give up Duke Baird or Numair, though she knew they had only been at Haven on loan and that they were needed elsewhere on the border. At least they had done all they could for her camp, Numair putting fire protections on the walls and roofs, Baird adding strength to the protections on their water and medicines. Kel would still miss the security two such powerful mages had given her. Neal would, too, though all he said within his father's hearing was that he would be happy when Baird was no longer underfoot. Kel might have scolded her friend, but she saw the look on Baird's face and realized he understood his son perfectly.

Owen joined them after grabbing his own meal: cold beef, cheese, hearty soup heaped with vegetables, and a tankard of milk. "Did you hear the news?" he asked, sitting next to Neal. "Giantkiller fell."

"What's this? When?" Duke Baird asked Harailt.

"Four days ago," the other man replied soberly. "The same day I hear you were attacked. The enemy there had killing devices and a battering ram. By the time Daine brought word of the attack to Lord Wyldon and my lord rode out to save the place, it was destroyed."

Kel shivered. In her mind's eye she saw the faces of those she remembered from her few days' stay at the fort. Dead, or taken?

"Did they catch the Scanrans?" Neal wanted to know.

"Our forces cleaned out the forest on both sides of the

ridge, but the enemy had gone. You can't leave soldiers in the wilderness forever, not in this war, anyway," Owen said with brutal practicality. "Everyone stays on the move."

Kel looked at her friend. Her throat went tight. So Owen, too, had learned about what the soldiers called seeing the kraken—being at war. "Owen," she began.

He shook his head. "General Vanget sent a company in to hold the area. He wants a new fort built in the same spot—we can't leave that gap unprotected—but my lord talked him out of it. He says the men will think it's a curse place and desert. They do things like that, never mind that they're supposed to defend their country." He scowled, vexed with anyone who gave way to fear.

"It's hard not to believe in curses when you've seen a killing device at work," Kel told him gently. "And it's hard to be brave when you feel the gods have turned from you."

"Is there any good news?" asked Neal. "King Maggur got lung rot, say?"

As the talk turned to the enemy king, Kel sent up a brief, silent prayer to the Black God for the dead of Giantkiller. Her post at Haven was rubbing her raw. Without Haven, without her duty to the refugees, she might have dared the Crown's wrath to cross into Scanra alone. She stood a far better chance of avoiding capture that way. She knew the language, and surely the Chamber would guide her to her long-overdue meeting with Blayce. The chance to wrap her hands around the Nothing Man's scrawny neck would be worth even disgrace and exile from Tortall.

But this is daydreaming, she thought bitterly as she finished her meal. Daydreaming. I *do* have Haven.

Owen raced off as soon as he finished eating. He returned with their supply lists just as Kel had begun to wonder what to do next. "Kel, my lord says he's ready to see you. Neal, he says, present your supply requests to the quartermaster. He approved just about everything." Owen gave Neal the lists that he, Kel, and Merric had labored on for the past three nights. "Rengar will show you where the quartermaster is." Kel smiled at the youth, who had followed Owen into the mess.

Neal got to his feet. "Time to earn my wage," he said. "Lead on, friend Rengar."

The tall youth bowed and blushed, then escorted Neal out of the officers' mess. Kel followed Owen to Wyldon's office. It looked much like the one Lord Wyldon had kept as training master, right down to the stone hawk figure at the corner of his desk.

"Take a seat, Mindelan," he said. "Jesslaw, post yourself outside in case I need you. And don't eavesdrop."

Owen bowed and left, closing the door behind him. Kel sat and remarked, "How can he avoid eavesdropping?"

"He can't," replied Wyldon. "But this way I will know how well he can hold his tongue. You requested more soldiers." Wyldon's lean, handsome face was expressionless as he looked at Kel.

"My lord, the request is reasonable," Kel pointed out. She refused to whine. "Merric takes a squad on patrol, leaving me with twenty-five trained soldiers to man the walls. The civilian fighters are coming along, but they're mostly fit for defense, not rescue work outside Haven. And—"

Wyldon raised a hand to silence her. "You'll have two

more squads and five replacements for the men you lost," he said evenly. "I know twenty-five isn't much, but it's what I can spare. Our patrols meet the enemy every day up here, and there's Giantkiller to rebuild."

"So I heard, my lord," Kel replied, bowing her head.

"We repaid the enemy for some of that," Wyldon told her. "Not enough, but some. Vanget beat roughly three thousand of the enemy two days ago, on the Vassa plain."

Kel knew the area he meant from the maps: between the border and the great bend of the Vassa River lay as broad a plain as could be found here in the north. "What were our losses, sir?"

"Fewer than we could have hoped," Wyldon said, pouring out two cups of amber liquid. Kel took one. It was cider. She drank gratefully. "Vanget lost ninety-eight men as the enemy attacked, so he started falling back," Wyldon explained after a swallow from his own cup.

Kel winced. That was nearly an entire company.

"The enemy gave chase," continued Wyldon, "and broke their formation. He turned and hacked them up."

Kel unconsciously clenched her hands. Why hadn't she been there, fighting the enemy, giving them a taste of all the ill they had doled out? She had become a knight to fight the realm's enemies, not to be a nanny for civilians!

"Maggur still hasn't made soldiers of his men," Wyldon remarked, not seeing Kel's frustration, or ignoring it if he did. "The moment they get excited, they break ranks and act each for himself, Mithros be thanked." The man shook his head, then looked at the papers before him. "You're up to four hundred and five refugees?"

Kel took a moment to register the change of topic. She

unclenched her fists. "The day after Giantkiller fell and the Anak's Eyrie folk arrived, we got a mixed group from Hanaford and Riversedge, and more from Fief Jonajin a day later." She recalled something Numair had told her. "My lord, I'm told there are plans to get the refugees out, with the danger from Blayce the Gallan?"

Wyldon sighed. "Even if the councils agree and vote funds for it, I doubt we'll get transport until summer's end."

Goose bumps rippled on Kel's arms. "Can't they move their behinds? Don't they see the danger? Blayce makes killing devices with captives!"

"They see danger everywhere, including at home," Wyldon told her. "We can't force action from them. The nobles fear the Crown will use the war to drain their purses, to make them dependent on the Crown should things go amiss on their estates. The commoners fear building the war up is an excuse to start pressing their sons into army or navy service. The king will wear the councils down, but not this week, or next."

Kel slumped in her chair. How would she last the summer penned up at Haven?

"Now, these letters of complaint from your civilians, particularly this Valestone fellow . . ." Wyldon began.

Kel sat up again. This was it. He would see she couldn't handle the refugees' constant squabbles and their demands on her time. This was the reason why she'd agreed to carry written complaints from Idrius and the other malcontents. It was silly to be pleased that Fanche hadn't written such a letter when it might have helped convince Wyldon to replace her, but Kel hoped that it meant Fanche had decided Kel was doing a good job. The respect of a woman like Fanche was surely worth one less complaint.

"Complaints go with command," Wyldon told her, not unkindly. "You'll never satisfy them all. You'd be foolish to try. Troublemakers come with every group, be they camp or company, village or palace. Valestone says you left him in the stocks for hours?"

So Wyldon would send her back after all. "I had other things to see to, including the dead," Kel replied steadily, trying not to show disappointment. "I couldn't approach without his starting to yell at me, so I left him until he shut up long enough to let me explain why I put him there."

"Very good," Wyldon said with approval. Kel blinked. "Sometimes you need to hit a man on the head to get his attention. He and his friends must learn to obey orders." Raising his voice he called, "Jesslaw!"

The door popped open and Owen stuck his head inside. "My lord?"

Wyldon offered him the sheaf of complaints. As Owen took them, Wyldon said, "Have one of the clerks write a single, general reply for my signature, saying that Lady Knight Keladry of Mindelan has my entire confidence and that all complaints in future will be addressed to her. She may rectify them or not, as dictated by the necessities of wartime. Have you got that?"

Owen recited the words perfectly. Kel raised her eyebrows, wondering how Wyldon had taught Owen that trick.

"Dismissed," Wyldon told Owen. The squire bowed and left the office. "Now," the man said, settling back in his chair, "you did not list their complaints in your reports. Why not?"

Kel was surprised he'd asked. "They weren't military problems, sir. Reports should include supply matters, the condition of the camp and its surrounding lands, military information and engagements with the enemy, and signs of possible mutiny. I did wonder about that last one, but"—Kel shrugged. She wasn't going to tell him about all the times she'd heard refugees say that no green eighteen-year-old could protect them and that nobles had no common sense. She certainly wouldn't mention the occasions her advice had been greeted with remarks like "What do *you* know, as young as you are?" or "The only reason you have this job is because they want you out of the way of the real fighting." Instead, Kel told Wyldon, "People dislike Idrius and his friends so much that the only mutiny we'll get is the others kicking them out. It may yet happen. I figure I have till the end of June before it gets that bad."

Wyldon smiled. He promptly covered the smile with his hand, trying to smooth it from his lips, but Kel saw crinkles at the corners of his eyes. She stared at her cup, her own eyes wide. *She* had made the Stump smile!

Wyldon cleared his throat and refilled their cider cups. "Now, let me fill you in on a few things."

Once they were done, Wyldon turned Kel over to Owen for a tour of Mastiff. Everywhere Kel saw Wyldon's firm hand on the rein. Of course it would be tidy and well organized, with him to run the place. She reminded herself that Wyldon dealt with soldiers, who were expected to obey when an order was given, but she also knew that civilians would not argue with Wyldon as they did with her.

There's no use pouting, she told herself as Owen showed her the mages' workshops. My lord wants me at Haven, so there I'll stay. I'll just have to make the best of it.

She tried not to drool over Mastiff's superior equipment, space, and well-trained men. That would make her too much like the many dogs who prowled the grounds or dozed in the sun. Owen told her most of the large, block-headed, brown and black war dogs and the scent-hounds with their drooping ears and wrinkled faces came from Wyldon's own kennels, trained by him and his wife. They were handsome creatures, but she preferred Jump and the dogs at Haven. Thanks to Daine, those dogs now earned their keep as sentinels and as hunters. They required no human archers to help them bring in small game like wild geese, grouse, or rabbit. If they killed a boar or deer, the dogs would summon humans to carry the heavier load. Kel nearly pitied the Mastiff dogs, even though she knew Daine felt that she'd done the animals of Haven a great disservice.

Supper was held in Lord Wyldon's dining room, with all the camp's senior officials present, as well as Prince Roald, Baird, Numair, Neal, Harailt, Daine, and Kel. Owen and his friend Rengar handled the service as officers and mages talked about the war, the killing devices, and the army's next assault on King Maggur's troops.

"The problem is that the chief damage is being done by these raiding parties," Wyldon remarked as the table was cleared. "Maggur sends his regular troops to nail down Northwatch, Steadfast, and Mastiff, then turns raiders loose in the country behind our lines to burn and loot. Some of those raiding parties fetch killing devices with them, and the humans kidnap more people than they kill. We're assuming the adults are made slaves, kept or sold to the markets in the south. The young ones all go to Blayce the Gallan."

"We need more troops," said one of the captains. "And soon. There's just too much border. We can't stop the enemy from crossing the Vassa. If we can get more men, we can turn the Scanrans away before they reach the back country."

"The killing devices worry me," Harailt said, his normally cheerful face troubled. "Until we learn precisely how Blayce makes them, we fumble for ways to stop the things. My biggest fear is that he'll get enough captives to create hundreds of them, or bigger ones, or a new kind even nastier. I'm not sure only children will serve as the power to make the devices work. In all my reading about this vile magic, I've found nothing that says the age of the spirit matters. I believe that Blayce uses children for his own putrid reasons. If some other mage learns how to do it, and starts using all the enemy's captives to make new ones, we could be overrun."

"You're certain it's just this one mage who builds the things?" inquired Neal.

"Definitely," replied Numair and Daine. They smiled quickly at one another before Numair continued, "Once you remove the iron, I find the same runes and commands, made by the same hand, cut into the bones that shape the limbs. And they're on the inside of the head-domes. Blayce had a reputation at the City of the Gods as one of those mages who feels that if others know his spells, he can be dispensed with. Unless he's changed completely, he'll keep the secrets of his devices to himself."

"So he tells King Maggur only he can do this," Baird said, his eyes bleak. "What a dreadful blessing for us."

"That's war," muttered one of the captains. "One dreadful blessing after another."

Kel fought to sit still, she was so upset. Blayce could do even worse harm if pressed to create more devices, and here she sat, useless.

"Do we know where this fellow is?" she heard herself ask. "This Blayce? Daine and Numair told me he's not in Hamrkeng. Has there been word?"

"None," said Harailt, his gray eyes sharp with anger and frustration. "Our spies—mostly Daine's spies—have searched the capital cellar to roof, with no success. And the place is so well protected from scry-searching in mirrors and crystals, magical searching in mirrors and crystals, we're lucky if we can as much as glimpse the laundry maids at work."

"I don't *understand* this!" cried Neal. "How can anyone give shelter to this creature? If we know how the devices are made, surely Maggur knows! How can he use such a monster as Blayce?"

Silence followed his outburst, until Wyldon sighed. "He wants to win," he said quietly. "Everyone with half an eye can see this war turns on the killing devices."

"If only it were a matter of armies and navies, we'd have sent Maggur into his mountains with his tail between his legs," added Harailt. "As it is, with more killing devices arriving each day, we can barely hold our own. It isn't just that they're fast and vicious—they're *terrifying.*"

"Troops who would face a giant without turning a hair are afraid of the devices," said one of the captains. "Two devices, they falter. Three, they break and run. Nobody wants to be cut up by a seven-foot iron insect with knives for fingers and toes."

"There are rulers and generals who would sacrifice anything for such a weapon." Numair looked grim. "Ozorne—the former emperor of Carthak—would have given his own children, and those of his nobles, for such a weapon."

"Maggur doesn't even have to risk his nobles turning on him," Prince Roald said, his eyes glittering like cold sapphires. "All he has to do is keep Blayce and his workshop hidden, and feed him a stream of *our* children. With no threat to their own children, and with slaves and loot to keep them happy, his nobles can pretend to know nothing about how the devices are made."

"Then why don't the gods put a stop to it?" demanded Neal. "All the legends say they loathe necromancy. It interferes with the balance between the mortal realm and that of the dead."

"Perhaps the gods *are* preparing to interfere," said Daine.

Kel flinched.

"But the gods have their own notion of time," continued the Wildmage. "It isn't ours, and sometimes they come at things in a way we see as, well, cockeyed. They may prefer to work through a human vessel."

Kel lowered her head, feeling more useless than ever. If she were such a human vessel, she'd have figured a way to get at Blayce by now. She bit the inside of her lip and pleated her napkin tightly as she made herself listen to the rest of the conversation.

The supper meeting continued past Kel's usual bedtime as information about the war was traded over the table. When Kel emerged from Wyldon's meeting room, she found Tobe waiting to guide her to the chambers they'd been given.

She was asleep and dreaming as soon as her head touched the pillow.

The big man, Stenmun, was putting tops on crates as Blayce watched, a finger digging in one ear. Kel walked over to the first crate. A killing device was inside, but this one didn't have that sharp, alien face with its visor-lips. It had a face, Loesia's face. Kel's body carried her unwilling spirit to the next box, which held a device with Meech's face, and the next, with Gydo's, and the next, with that of Tobe himself.

Your paths will cross, insisted the Chamber of the Ordeal. Its face was embedded in the stone wall of Blayce's workshop. Neither Stenmun nor Blayce seemed to hear it. *In time, your paths will cross. That is destiny.*

The door to the workroom opened. A line of children, all from Haven, straggled in.

"Lady!" A hand was on her shoulder, jostling her. "Lady, you're talking in your sleep again."

Kel sat up, bleary-eyed. "I'm sorry, Tobe. That's what, every night this week?"

"Good thing for you I'm a catnapper, myself," the boy informed her. He sat on the edge of her bed, eyeing her sternly. "You said them names again, Blayce, an' Stenmun. And the Chamber of the Ordeal. If I was you, I'd take a pickaxe to that Chamber, the way you're allus dreamin' about it."

"I'm sorry," Kel said apologetically, as she did every night she woke him up. "I keep telling you—"

"I'd be better off sleepin' someplace else," the boy recited, and rolled his eyes. "And how much rest would you get without me to wake you? Lucky you, dreamin' just once a night."

Kel got up. "Go back to sleep," she ordered, groping for her clothes. "I'll have a bit of a walk to clear my head."

Tobe shrugged. "As you will, lady." He wriggled under his bedclothes and was snoring by the time Kel left the room.

A walk on the ramparts would ease her mind. She climbed to the walkway around the inner wall as Fort Mastiff slept. Only the night watch was awake; they seemed used to visitors taking a late stroll. They kept their attention on the open ground around the fort and ignored Kel.

Owen leaned on the northern wall, staring gloomily at the moonlit ribbon of the Vassa River. She settled in beside him and admired the way silver moonlight turned the land into something magical, hiding the gouges and scrambled earth left from some recent attack.

"It's not what I expected, Kel," Owen told her suddenly. "Not at all. I mean, patrols, and fighting the enemy, that's just jolly. We gave them a pounding. They ran like rabbits. I would have followed, but my lord grabbed me and told me I could chase game another day." He was silent for a while.

Kel waited. It would be hard for the cheerful Owen to find words to describe bad feelings. When she saw a tear course down his cheek, she gently asked, "Giantkiller?"

He nodded and swiped angrily at the tear. "The dead were just strewn everywhere, like my sisters' dolls, all cut up. The ones in the sun were swelling. There were flies, and Stormwings and animals had been at them."

Kel nodded. At least she had gotten the Scanran dead burned and her own dead buried before the indignities of rot and scavengers settled on them.

"What chaps me is that by the time we got there, the trail was a day old," Owen said. "We'd no chance to avenge them. And so many were taken—civilians, mostly, waiting to move on to Haven. They killed the soldiers. Those refugees—some were children, Kel. I wish I could find that mage, that Blayce. I'd gut him and drag him around Scanra by his insides."

"Then you'd have another rotten body to deal with," Kel pointed out.

"No," Owen replied stubbornly, his chin thrust out. "I'd dump him on King Maggot's throne and let *him* clean up." He shook his head. "We fight and kill all these raiders, but we aren't getting anywhere. They just keep sliding by us, along with their thrice-cursed killing devices. This fortress is all very well, but if we stay in, the enemy goes around us. If we go out, we search miles of hills and canyons and forests, and *maybe* get something for our trouble. Mostly not."

"At least you're *allowed* to search, and fight," a new voice said on Kel's right. Prince Roald leaned against the wall, surveying the river below. "They have me so well wrapped in lamb's wool that I might as well be in Corus, for all the good I do. They only use me for magic, and that at a distance." He sighed. "People say they're grateful when I work a healing on them, but what if they hate me because I'm not allowed to take risks? Mithros knows *I* hate me."

Kel opened her mouth to say they'd get to do more sooner or later, but she didn't. She couldn't tell her friends something she didn't believe was so.

May 2–3, 460
Haven

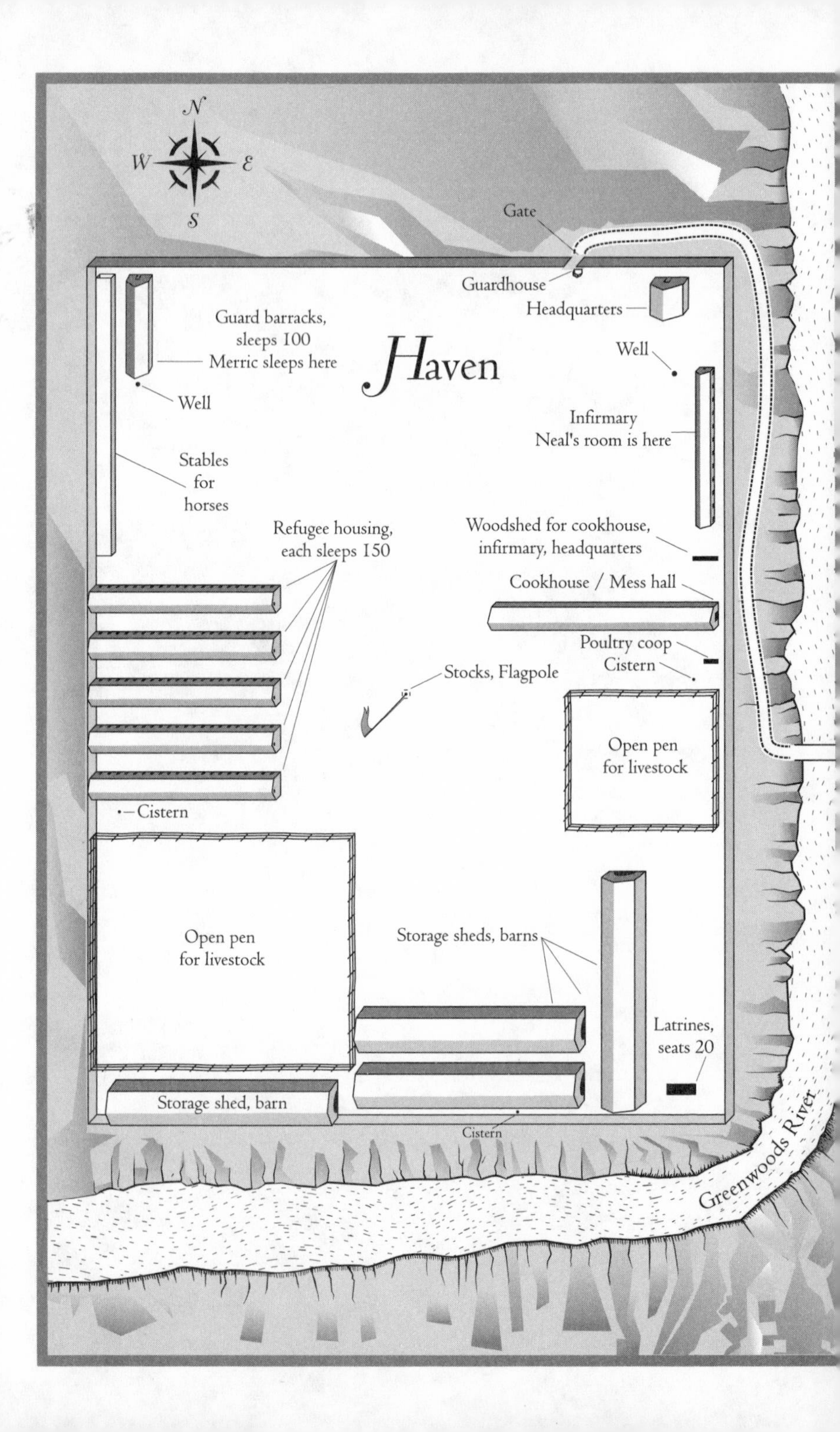
N
W
E
S
Haven
Gate
Guardhouse
Headquarters
Guard barracks,
sleeps 100
Merric sleeps here
Well
Well
Infirmary
Neal's room is here
Stables
for
horses
Refugee housing,
each sleeps 150
Woodshed for cookhouse,
infirmary, headquarters
Cookhouse / Mess hall
Poultry coop
Cistern
Stocks, Flagpole
Open pen
for livestock
Cistern
Open pen
for livestock
Storage sheds, barns
Latrines,
seats 20
Storage shed, barn
Cistern
Greenwoods River

10

THE REFUGEES FIGHT

Approaching Haven at the head of a train of soldiers and wagons, Kel fought the urge to turn Hoshi, cross the river to Scanra, and find Blayce on her own. So the realm's spies can't find the man, she thought as she guided Hoshi up the inclined road. *I've* been chosen by the Chamber of the Ordeal to settle Blayce's account. I might be drawn to him somehow.

"Lady?" asked Tobe, who had turned back to wait for her. "You've got your Blayce face on."

Kel tossed her mad daydreams aside. If she bolted now, who would guard Haven against the killing devices? Yes, her people trained with the nets and the pickaxes, getting faster at tossing the nets over those who played the role of the device, but Kel heard the refugees' whispers. They believed in their ability to best the devices because they knew she had helped to kill three of the things. Without Kel at Haven, its people wouldn't feel comfortable about their chances to fight off the devices.

Merric waited for them beside the gate, smiling as they rode in. Kel dismounted and passed her reins to Tobe. "Did you behave yourself while I was away?" she asked Merric.

"I was just as good as gold," replied Merric. To Neal he said, "A courier arrived from the south while you were gone. There was a letter for you. I left it on your desk in the infirmary. From the capital, and perfumed, no less," he teased.

Gydo took charge of Neal's mount. Meech followed her, clutching the scarlet-haired rag doll that was his eternal companion. Neal raced for the infirmary.

Kel looked around her as the refugees unhitched horses and oxen from the wagons and collected the supplies. She noticed unfamiliar faces among the population. "Merric, it looks like there are new people since I left," she remarked.

"That's because there are," he replied with a wry smile. "They came in late yesterday afternoon, both groups, from two little villages near Steadfast. Loggers and carpenters, mostly. And they don't complain as much as the Tirrsmont crowd."

"Could anyone complain as much?" Kel inquired absently. "Did the Tirrsmont folk behave?"

"Soon as you left, Valestone was all for having a meeting to choose him as headman, but no one was interested," Merric told her. "That was the only noise. The plowing crews did five acres yesterday, all on this side of the river.

The woodcutters brought more wood from where they're clearing trees to the south."

"Did you patrol?" asked Kel.

When Merric shook his head, his red forelock flopped against his forehead. "No, Mother," he said drily. "I knew you'd give me a spanking if I went out without doing my chores."

Kel looked at him and sighed. "I'm sorry, Merric. I wasn't thinking."

"You're in command here, Kel," he told her, his tone quieter. "You're doing a good job. I won't break orders to skylark."

"I'm not in command over you, precisely," Kel began.

Merric raised gingery brows. "Did you forget the day those bandits were set to cut us pages to dog meat? You saved all our lives because you think well in a fix. I know where *I'll* look for orders when the enemy comes."

Kel smiled crookedly. She just hoped he'd never be disappointed in her. "Very well. How many new people?"

"A hundred and twelve," he answered. "Gods be thanked that Numair made all this extra ground for the camp, or we'd be popping through cracks in the walls by now. What's the news from Mastiff?"

"Later," Kel said. "In private."

Merric winced. "That can't be good."

"Some is and some isn't," she replied. "Speaking of good news, I have some for you."

The sergeants of the two new squads of soldiers stood nearby, waiting. Loesia and other youngsters from Kel's spear class had taken the men and horses in charge and led them to the stables. Yngvar's men offered to show the fresh arrivals around. Kel beckoned the two new sergeants forward. "Sir Merric of Hollyrose, in charge of our outer defenses, may I present Sergeant Kortus and Sergeant Aufrec? The sergeants and their squads are permanently assigned to Haven, courtesy of my lord Wyldon. We've also brought five replacements for the men we lost."

Merric's face lit as the sergeants bowed. "Is that so?" he cried. "Welcome, both of you, welcome indeed! We need all the help we can get. Were you stationed at Fort Mastiff long?"

"Went in there with Lord Wyldon," said Kortus, who seemed to be the more talkative of the pair. "Stayed with him at Giantkiller last year. It's an honor to meet you, milord."

"Kel, do you mind if I introduce the sergeants to their counterparts?" Merric asked. "I'm sure they'll want to settle in."

Kel smiled, pleased that the new troops were so welcome to her year-mate. She knew he worried about guarding Haven with only forty men-at-arms, twenty of them convicts whose experience, until recently, was not gained on a battlefield. "Of course. Sergeants, we'll run into each other often," she assured them. "In the meantime, I leave you in Sir Merric's hands."

As the three men left, Kel heard Merric say, "Now, I handle the patrols outside the walls, but the lady knight governs all that's inside, and I take her orders in a fight. Don't look to this place as a restful one. You'll see combat here."

Kel turned to find Saefas and Fanche behind her. "I

heard Master Valestone tried to get elected headman," she remarked.

"He seems frustrated, poor fellow," Saefas replied with his easy smile. Kel had ordered the refugees to stop bowing when they talked to her or they would get worn out quickly. "He wants to be a leader even if he isn't one."

"We should set the young folk to making kites," added Fanche. "Someone ought to have fun, as much wind as he blows." She eyed Kel. "Good to see we've more warriors. I believe I'll keep practicing my weapons, though."

Kel grinned. "As will I."

Fanche nodded. "If you weren't a noble, I'd call you a sensible girl. You've commoner blood, that's the only answer."

She walked away, hands under her patched apron.

"Fanche missed you desperately, lady knight," Saefas assured Kel. "She just hasn't got the proper words."

"You are a flatterer, Master Saefas," Kel informed him.

"So she tells me, all the time," admitted Saefas, his eyes mischievous. "What do you think? Will I win her in the end?"

Kel looked at him. "She will make your life a misery," she told the man.

Saefas grinned. "That's what I hope for." He left to see if he could help with the wagons.

Kel looked around at the smoke, the dirty children underfoot, the ground churned by horses' hooves, the raw buildings, and the chickens that pecked everywhere. Home again, she thought, and walked to headquarters.

* * *

With Numair gone, Kel went back to eating in the camp's mess hall. That first night she sat among the newcomers, who had not yet worked out cooking arrangements in their new home. They watched Kel from the corners of their eyes as she worked her way through roast boar with mushroom gravy, noodles, and wild greens. From the other tables, Kel heard snatches of whispered talk.

"—have replaced her with a *real* knight . . ."

"Saefas says she's a good head on her."

"*Saefas?* You take his judgment? Mithros's beard, look at what he's courting!"

"—how many more are going to be sent here?"

"I'm off. Training first thing tomorrow. Sergeant Oluf says I've a knack for the spear."

Kel glanced at this speaker. It was a woman from Riversedge, so tiny she didn't look as if she could even hold a spear up. Just shows you can't judge us females by size, she thought with a smile.

Kel had planned to return to headquarters after supper. There was news to tell Merric and her sergeants, news she didn't want spread all over camp. Still, there were the newcomers who hadn't eaten in the mess hall to consider. They ought to see her so they'd know who to complain to. She trudged toward their barracks, listening to the sounds of a peaceful summer evening: someone playing a recorder, the clatter of pans, girls skipping rope. Jump and the pack of camp dogs trotted around her; the sparrows had gone to bed.

Shouts reached her ears. They came from the two barracks given to those from Hanaford and Jonajin. Kel picked up her pace. "Let me handle this," she ordered the dogs as they reached the edge of a noisy crowd.

There were times for polite entrances. This was not one of them. Kel shoved and elbowed her way through the crowd. She managed not to voice the famed provost officer's weary order: "Move on, nothing to see here, nothing to see."

At last Kel emerged onto the open ground around a barracks cookfire. Two young men, both larger than Kel, punched, kicked, and rolled on the ground, trying to rip one another apart.

Kel sized the matter up quickly. One of the brawlers she recognized as an Anak's Eyrie headache, a handsome fellow who doled out romance to as many women as possible, whether or not they already had a partner. The other brawler she didn't know. Neither did she recognize the young woman who stood closest to the fight, but she knew what this was just the same. Rather than choose one or the other man and put an end to the problem, this girl had let them go at it with their fists to prove she was desirable. It was in the way she stood hugging herself, her brown eyes eager as the men lurched to their feet.

Kel had seen enough. As the brawlers grabbed each other in bear hugs, she strode in. They were big, strong fellows, but she'd spent eight years strengthening her arms and learning the right time and place to attack. She grabbed both men by the hair and slammed their foreheads together. The watchers gasped in awe.

The men released each other. Kel hauled them apart without letting go of their hair. They were dazed, but that faded quickly. They tried to grab each other.

"Well, they say the front part of the head is the

hardest," Kel remarked. She smashed her captives' heads together a second time.

Now they staggered. Her grip was the only thing that kept them upright. One of them flailed at her arm. Kel shook him briskly, as a terrier might shake a rat.

"This saddens me," she informed them. "It does. Grown men brawling like apprentices. Now, here's what you may do for me. Promise to be good lads and go to your beds, and I won't remember your faces later." She turned their heads so they looked at her. Both sported black eyes and swollen mouths. The Anak's Eyrie man bled from a bite on his ear and the newcomer had a broken nose. "On second thought, if you promise to be good, I'll let you visit Sir Nealan. I won't even ask him to make sure the healing stings so you'll remember all this. Would you like that?"

Kel's voice was soft and reasonable. The look she gave them was anything but. She'd never beaten anyone and doubted that she ever would, but these two didn't know that. It was wicked of her to play on their fear of being flogged—it was a punishment favored by many nobles—but she would take what she could get in the way of good behavior, never mind why it was given.

The newcomer nodded agreement first. The Anak's Eyrie troublemaker required another shake before he, too, nodded.

"Clasp hands on it, like good lads," Kel told them.

Both men hesitated, then exchanged handshakes. Kel let go, and they stumbled off toward the infirmary.

The young woman who had set this in motion tried to melt back into the crowd. The row of women behind her refused to let her by. She glanced at Kel, who beckoned her with one finger.

"A word, if you please, Mistress . . . ?" Kel let the question hang in the air.

The young woman looked down at her patched skirt. "Peliwin Archer, if it please my lady."

Kel folded her arms. "Mistress Peliwin, on the coast, there is a way of doing things. If two men declare an interest in a woman, it's her duty to announce which she prefers, if she does prefer one. Then the second lover takes his leave. If he does not, the woman may bring him to the court of the Great Goddess for refusing to accept her right to choose. Does this custom not apply here?"

"It does." The speaker was a big, black-haired woman with sunken dark eyes and arms as muscled as a smith's. "It applies throughout the realm. It's how I got rid of my first husband and got another to suit me."

The other women nodded or murmured in agreement.

Kel looked at Peliwin. "Why did you not declare your choice, mistress?" she asked.

Peliwin twisted back and forth like a child who wished to go. "I couldn't decide, lady knight," she muttered.

"Then the custom is that you ask both to stand back until you do," Kel reminded her. "Instead, we now have two fellows who might be called to defend this place at the healer's. I think you need time to decide what is truly important here at Haven, and what only serves your vanity. I give you that time. Tomorrow morning you report for a week's latrine-cleaning duty."

Peliwin yelped, finally meeting Kel's eyes. "That's not fair! You can't expect—"

Kel interrupted, "I can and I do. At the end of that week, you will state your preference and that will be the last I hear of this, Mistress Peliwin. I'll have no trouble-makers here, understand?"

The young woman was still gasping in horror, hands over her mouth.

"Good evening to you, mistresses, masters," Kel said to the onlookers. They knew they were dismissed. The men bowed, the women curtsied, and the gathering broke up.

Kel wandered between the barracks, nodding to those whose faces she recognized. Two women approached her. Were they coming to praise her handling of the brawl or to welcome her back?

"Lady knight, you have got to tell this clay-brained besom that if she can't keep her bratlings from strewing my wash over half the camp—" one began.

"You've been nattering at my children since we moved in," the other woman interrupted. "Lady knight, it's enough to drive you mad, the way she goes on!"

Kel quieted them and sorted out the quarrel. She resumed her walk to headquarters, but it took longer than it should have. Other refugees asked her for news of the war, to settle a dispute over a litter of kittens, to learn the truth of a rumor that the crops sown in the newly plowed fields were to go entirely to the Goatstrack refugees. Someone else wanted to know why the newcomers had the barracks closest to the cookhouse. One of the cooks came to report that a keg of Haven's mead was missing. By the time Kel made it to the headquarters meeting room, she had a headache. She found Neal, Merric, and the chief clerk, Zamiel, already at work, mugs of tea at their elbows.

Kel dropped into a vacant chair and rested her head in her hands. Zamiel pushed a stack of reports toward her.

"Tonight I will name Lord Wyldon in my prayers," she muttered rebelliously. "Tonight and every night until I am freed of this gods-cursed, reeky-armpit ratsbane camp."

"You notice she didn't mention to whom those prayers might be addressed," Neal remarked. Zamiel sniffed and sipped his tea.

Merric nodded, checking duty rosters for the soldiers. "Given the rest of her statement, I believe they won't be addressed to any gods of happiness."

"What's the matter, love?" Neal asked, pouring a mug of tea for Kel. He watched her rub her temples for a moment, then added drops from a vial he carried in a pouch on his belt. "Did they wear you out with their exuberant welcome?"

"I broke up a brawl, sorted out a few quarrels—why in Mithros's name do they keep coming to *me*?" she demanded.

"Because they trust you," Neal told her. "They look up to you."

"They know you'll be fair," added Zamiel. All three nobles looked at him. While extremely competent, Zamiel seldom offered opinions.

"I hear them talk," the clerk explained. "I believe they think it's impossible for anyone to write and listen at the same time." To Kel he said, "They missed you."

"They surely did," Merric told her. "I'd ask if they wanted help with something, and they'd say they'd wait for you to come back." He grinned. "Frankly, I was glad of it."

"Oh," Kel replied, her cheeks warm. She wasn't sure

that she deserved such praise, not when she barely knew what she was doing. Changing the subject before she heard more unsettling remarks, she asked Neal, "What did you just put in my tea?"

"Something for your headache," Neal said.

"It's very good, and very fast," Zamiel added. "I recommend it."

Kel looked at Neal and sighed. "Thank you. I never had so many headaches before I came here." She picked up the mug and sipped. Almost instantly she felt her neck and shoulder muscles loosen. The throbbing in her skull eased.

"Kel, don't let these commoners impose on you so much, not if it makes you weary," Merric said, taking a drink of his own tea. "Tell them to clean up their own messes. You're too easygoing. You have to keep a proper distance, or they'll climb all over you."

Kel and Neal exchanged looks again. Zamiel's expression was carefully blank. Merric's views were common. Kel and Neal didn't share them.

"I have a suggestion," Neal offered. "It won't solve every problem, but fewer will get as far as you."

"Please, anything," Kel begged.

"Make each building elect two council members, a man and a woman. Have that council sit in judgment of quarrels," he suggested, leaning back in his chair. "Appoint one of the smarter soldiers—your ex-bandit friend Gil, say, or Sergeant Yngvar—as witness. If a vote is tied, his is the vote that decides the matter. Change the witness every two weeks. That keeps the soldier from getting tired or getting so friendly with individuals that it might affect his vote."

Kel sat up. She *loved* this plan! "Neal, you're brilliant!" she exclaimed.

Neal grinned. "I knew that."

"So what's the news from Steadfast?" Merric inquired. "I keep asking, but Sir Meathead says we should hear it from you."

Kel's good mood faded. "Tobe!" she cried.

The door opened. Tobe stuck his head in. "Lady?"

"I need all of the sergeants who aren't on duty," Kel said. "Get them, please?"

"It's that important?" asked Merric. "You know how hot it gets in here when there's a crowd."

"It's that important," Kel replied grimly. "Giantkiller has fallen. I'll tell the rest when the others are here. It's not a report I want to give more than once."

Merric and Zamiel, their faces ashen with shock, sketched the sign against evil on their chests.

The next morning Kel returned to her routine: glaive practice, with Tobe and his friends doing spear exercises beside her; breakfast; then archery practice on the riverbank. She was about to return to Haven with her archers when a plowman on his way out of the fort approached her.

"They've got you listed for kitchen cleanup. A big lass like you's wasted on scrubbing pots," he informed her. "D'ye know how to plow?" Kel shook her head. "Then it's past time you learned," the man informed her. "That idyit Edort went and sprained his ankle. Whilst he's getting coddled by Grandma Nealan, we could have more acres done."

Kel met the plowman's eyes. He was a stocky older

man, black-eyed, his hair silvery, his mustache salt-and-pepper. Like the other refugees, he looked as if he'd seen better days, but there was an imp of spirit in his eyes. "You do understand I've never plowed in my life, Master—"

"Just Adner, no 'master' in me," he retorted. "And if you keep that attitude, you'll never learn. Carry on, y'ens," he ordered Kel's archers, using northern slang for "you people." "I'll give 'er back to yez unbroke." He took Kel by the arm and steered her toward the fields being readied for planting.

"But that's the lady knight!" cried one of Kel's archers, shocked. "You can't just carry her off!"

"I can unless one of y'ens will plow in her stead," he called over his shoulder. Kel waved the archers on. They were bakers, laundresses, and carpenters, all with their own work to do. It was vital to get as many acres plowed and seeded as they could, as soon as they could. They needed all the food they could produce.

Trudging along with the men and women who managed plows and animals with easy familiarity, Kel was glad to see something familiar to *her:* bows, quivers of arrows, and staves. Adner bore a crossbow that must have been his. Longbows were easier and cheaper to make in the north, so few people outside the army used crossbows. She wondered what kind of shot Adner was. Maybe he would shoot against her some evening when they had time.

At last they reached the ground beside the acres that had been plowed while she was away. Adner chose an ox for her and showed her how to hitch him to a plow. "You'll pick it up," he assured Kel, indicating the strip of ground that was hers. "There's some good dirt here. Toss what rocks y'hit over aside the river, not onto ground we've yet to plow." He looked Kel over as she gathered the reins in her hands. "I'm workin' that strip there. I'll keep an eye on yez."

Kel faced the ox's rump. I ride Peachblossom, she thought. An ox will be no trouble at all.

The plowing should be easy enough. She'd watched plowmen and -women all her life. All she had to do was flap the reins now and then, keep the plow moving in a straight line, and turn the thing at the end of the strip.

"Easy as pie," she said, and flapped the reins gently against the ox's back. "Come on, big fellow," she called softly, so the others couldn't hear. "Let's bustle a bit."

The ox didn't wish to bustle. He was more interested in the grass. Kel flapped the reins harder, then harder still. She thought she heard snickers from the others, but when she looked at them, they were in motion, calling encouragement to their own horses or oxen. It took Jump and five sparrows to get Kel's beast going. When he did plod forward, it was not in a straight line. He veered as Kel fought both reins and plow to straighten the ox's course. She stepped three times in lumps of fresh dung she was sure the ox had left for her on purpose. At the end of the furrow she wrestled the plow and ox around to prepare for her second furrow. The evidence of her long, sweaty labor was a meandering furrow that stretched the width of the field.

She looked at the others' results. Their furrows were straight. They'd plowed more of them, too.

"If they can do it, we can," she said grimly. This time she set the ox forward by thrusting the plow through the ground toward his rump. The ox looked around, startled by the sudden slackness in his reins. He saw the approaching threat to his tail and ambled ahead, away from both plow and Kel. Finally, Kel's animals, who seemed to have learned a great deal from their time with Daine, made their own choice to help. Each time the ox tried to swerve left, Jump leaped up beside his left eye, startling him back to a straighter course. If he tried to swerve right, the sparrows fluttered around his right eye until the ox straightened his path again.

By the time Kel reached the end of her second meandering furrow, she had begun to think longingly of latrine duty. She stopped for a ladleful of water, envying the way Adner and the others moved steadily across the ground, making rows as neat as razor cuts, turning up rich black earth.

Her fingers twinged as she took up the reins again. Kel looked for the source and found, to her horror, that she was developing a blister.

A blister! she thought, cross. These reins were nothing like those she used in riding. As if I were some lily-handed noble, good only for poems and dancing! She smacked the ox with the reins more firmly than she had before. The ox looked back at her, startled. Something in the way Kel scowled at him seemed to convince him that she would accept nothing but motion.

Kel was turning him a third time when sparrows darted out of the woods thirty yards ahead, cheeping the alarm. Seconds later came horn calls. Merric had sighted the enemy in the woods. The sparrows flew straight at Kel. All but one dropped to the ground and nibbled grass seed.

The one was a bird Kel recognized, the male she called Duck because his lack of a tail gave him a duck-shaped behind. He hovered before her.

"How many?" Kel asked, and stretched her hand out, palm-down. Duck stooped to tap her hand three times before he lit on the plow. "Fifteen, is it?" Kel murmured. She listened to horn calls as she trotted back to the spot where her glaive leaned against the water cart. Merric had the Scanrans on the run. He wanted soldiers from Haven to strike the enemy as he drove them toward the river. Unless he'd lost men, his strength was at eleven, counting his own sword, against fifteen Scanrans. Haven's soldiers might not reach the field before the enemy came into sight. She had an opportunity here, if she cared to take the risk.

Kel looked at her companions: they were trying to unhitch their plows. She held up a hand palm-out, the "wait" signal, and walked over to them.

"Get your bows; prepare to shoot," she called, her voice no louder than necessary. In the distance she heard the sounds of battle approaching. "They'll come out of the north woods. Turn side-on to them so they won't see your bows. As soon as you have a clean shot at one, *in your range,* take it. Try not to shoot our soldiers. Lord Wyldon won't give me any more."

Adner grinned wolfishly as he stood clear of his plow. His stance was easy, his crossbow held down against his side. It was already cocked with a bolt in the notch. Unlike longbows, whose strings went loose if the bow was kept strung for too long, crossbows could be readied to shoot and set aside until needed.

The other workers, women and men, didn't share Adner's comfortable readiness. Some fumbled as they strung their bows. One dropped an arrow. Kel didn't even try to reach her bow nearby. If these people could help Merric's soldiers without her assistance, it would be a victory everyone in Haven would celebrate.

She saw movement among the trees. The sound of men's shouts and the crash of running horses announced the arrival of the fight. Out of the woods burst eight or nine men in Scanran dress: rough reddish tunics and strapped-on leggings. One of them went down, an arrow in his back. Then came Merric and his squad, ducking to avoid the last branches of the trees, swords unsheathed.

Once the Scanrans reached the open field, they ran for all they were worth. They raced straight toward a handful of civilians who were too terrified to run for the shelter of the fort.

Wait for it, Kel thought. Her farmers had to decide the timing for themselves. To her left she heard Haven's gate open and the thud of racing horses. Rescue would arrive in a moment if her people froze.

Adner's muscled arm swung up. He braced his crossbow against his shoulder. He shot almost as soon as he leveled the weapon, hardly stopping to aim. A Scanran went down with a bolt in his throat. Adner bent to cock and load the crossbow again.

Two farmers' arrows struck a Scanran; another arrow from Merric's soldiers brought down a second man. A Scanran stumbled and dropped, a civilian arrow above his knee. A slight, weathered older woman shot the enemy's biggest man in the chest. He spun with a cry and was shot in the back by Adner.

Merric's archers killed two more Scanrans; a farmer shot the last. Merric rode up to Kel, sweeping his helmet from his sweat-soaked, flame-red hair. "Sorry to interrupt the plowing," he said, ablaze with combat fever. "If I'd known your lot would do the heavy work, I'd have continued on patrol." He looked at the farmers and grinned. "Nice to know you can do it without us, eh?" he asked them.

"Next time leave us a few more," the older woman informed him, coiling her bowstring. "We need the practice."

From the walls of Haven they heard the sound of cheers.

May 6–June 3, 460
Haven and Fort Mastiff

II

SHATTERED SANCTUARY

About fifty of the enemy attacked from the east three days later. Sparrows got word to Kel, who had taken her young spear trainees to the riverbank. They raced back into Haven. Sergeant Yngvar took out two squads to support Merric's patrol. While those squads fought the enemy—a mixed force with more foot soldiers than horsemen—on open ground, civilian archers held off twenty more Scanrans who tried to clamber over the boulders and up Haven's west wall. Idrius Valestone was a cool head in that fight, calming the civilians around him as they steadily aimed, shot, and put fresh arrows to the string.

When she guessed the enemy would break with a little extra push, Kel led a fourth mounted squad to the battle. What was left of the main body of attackers fled. There was no one alive to flee among those who had tried Idrius and the archers on the western wall.

As the refugees piled and burned the Scanran dead, Stormwings circled above, jeering at them. More than one archer tried to shoot them down without success. The creatures were nimble on the wing, easily dodging all the arrows that came their way.

Two days later couriers rode in from Northwatch to deliver reports to Kel before they pressed on to Fort Mastiff. Vanget's words, set on paper in a clerk's polished writing, were as blunt as ever. Giantkiller was being rebuilt. Until it was finished, the workers and soldiers lived in mines in the hills between the old Giantkiller and Haven. Vanget also wrote that King Maggur's army had lost two pitched battles, one to Vanget, one to Lord Raoul and the King's Own. It was good to read about victories, particularly after Vanget also wrote that the sieges of Frasrlund and the City of the Gods remained firmly in place.

"Write a notice for our people about the battles won," Kel told the clerks. "If folk ask for word on the sieges, just say that there's no change."

Five days after the couriers' visit, eighty-five more refugees came in from the south in time to join in the elections for the civilian council. Kel, who had looked forward to a decrease in civilian complaints, discovered instead that she now had a clump of angry, quarrelsome people in the shape of the elected council to seek her out day after day. Sorting their arguments out led to such long, late discussions that Kel had to wonder if it had taken as long to arrange Prince Roald's betrothal to Princess Shinkokami.

"This was *your* idea," she accused Neal as the council

left headquarters one night.

"It seemed like a good one at the time," he replied, yawning.

"For two copper bits I'd toss the whole mess into your lap," she threatened.

Merric, reviewing supply sheets, commented in unison with Neal, "And let you miss such fun?"

Kel scowled at them and went to bed.

With the arrival of still more working hands, Kel found herself eased off the work rosters. Tobe, Loesia, and Gydo explained that Haven's residents thought it was beneath their commander's dignity to scrub pots and cut up wood, especially now that there were so many who were used to the work. "I was getting better at sowing," Kel protested, wondering what she had done to make them think she had dignity. The youngsters only grinned and shook their heads.

With fewer chores, Kel worked more as a weapons trainer. There she was welcome. The more trainers they had, the more civilians received individual attention and the better they got. Kel took pride in the improvement of Haven's students, young and old. They were eager to learn self- defense. As their training progressed, they walked less like victims and more like people proud of their skills with staff, bow, spear, and sling.

Kel also worked with the animals and humans together, settling on signals everyone could use. The humans had to learn what a dog's circling, a bird's string of peeps, and a cat's sharpening her claws in the dirt meant. The animals had to learn what humans meant even when they spoke with various accents. The animals learned so quickly that some people would have spent all day talking to them if they could. Other men and women were nervous, though they insisted on staying to learn all the signals. "The starving can't choose what tools to harvest with," Sergeant Vidur commented. "Even when it seems plain unnatural."

Four days before Kel and Neal were due for their next visit to Mastiff, a raiding party of sixteen mounted Scanrans tried their luck on Haven. They were dead before any soldiers reached them. Civilian workers placing stones on the height above the boulders shot the enemy off their mounts with arrows, then finished them with axes, staves, and even the rocks they carried.

That night the refugees celebrated loud and long. They had fought for themselves and won! Kel didn't mind if they made noise about it, but she did wonder if, with the enemy close enough for one attack, she ought to put off her trip.

"Don't do that, lady," Tobe protested when she mentioned it to him. "Maybe himself will give you more soldiers. We'll be fine."

"*We?*" Kel asked. "Weren't you planning to go with me?"

Tobe grinned. "I guess if you go away, you're prolly comin' back."

This was the nicest thing she'd heard in days. Kel couldn't help it: she leaned down and kissed her young henchman on the forehead. "Thank you," she whispered.

He looked up at her with suspicion. "Are you goin' t'act like a girl now?" he demanded.

"No," Kel said, stifling a giggle—something that really

would have frightened him. "It won't happen again."

When she broached the subject of a delay to the headquarters meeting room, Neal frowned. "I do need fresh supplies of the herbs that don't grow locally," he reminded her.

"Don't be ridiculous," Merric said, covering a yawn. "You trained them to fight. How will it look if you won't leave them for two days? Even with you taking a squad, I'm not staying inside the walls this time. We've got four squads, *and* your fighting farmers. Cut them off your apron strings, Mother."

"He's right," Neal said. "They'll think you don't have faith in them. We need supplies, and you know the Stump wants our personal reports."

Zamiel looked up from his work. "They take confidence in what they can do from the confidence you show in them, milady," the clerk informed her. He smiled crookedly. "So do I. Give us a bit more confidence, and keep to your schedule. We can hold our own, should the enemy visit."

Kel knew they were right. She did no one any favors by acting as if they couldn't manage without her. At dawn four days later she, Neal, Jump, a fistful of sparrows, and Sergeant Connac's squad prepared to ride to Fort Mastiff. Peachblossom would come this time, as would Neal's and Merric's warhorses. Haven's smiths could shoe all kinds of mounts for commoners, but they feared the warhorses. Mastiff's smiths could handle them, and Peachblossom had thrown a shoe. The knights decided it would be good to have all three warhorses checked.

"Don't skip practice," Kel warned Tobe, Gydo, and

Loesia. "Loey, mind your footing on the long side cut. Tobe, practice that middle hold—a straight line—"

Tobe rolled his eyes. "Aye, milady Mother," he said, every inch an exasperated male. Then he colored. "Meanin' no dis—"

"And eat your vegetables," Kel told him with a grin. She was flattered that Tobe might call her Mother, even in jest.

"Me'n Gydo, we'll watch 'im, milady," promised Loesia. "Safe journey."

Kel nodded to them and clucked to Hoshi, leading their small group out of Haven's gate.

Owen was as delighted as ever to see them. He and his civilian friend Rengar made them comfortable as Wyldon read Kel's reports. Afterward the two boys waited on them at table as they took their evening meal with Lord Wyldon and his officers. Most of the talk was about the war, news from the City of the Gods and Frasrlund. The City of the Gods, with its concentration of mages, was proving costly to King Maggur, and the Tortallan navy had gone to attack the Scanran ships that blocked Frasrlund's harbor. If Blayce had been found, word had not yet reached Mastiff.

So the war progresses without me, Kel told herself grumpily as she got ready for bed. And I'm no closer to Blayce than ever.

Horses raced up the road to Haven. Kel, frightened, looked for her weapons, but she was naked. She opened her eyes inside Mastiff's guest quarters. She'd been dreaming.

If it was only a dream, why did the horses' hooves continue to thunder?

She jumped for the door and yanked it open. A soldier lurched in, hand still raised to pound again. "Lady knight, see my lord at headquarters."

Kel stuffed her nightshirt into her breeches and pulled on her boots, leaving her stockings aside for the moment. She didn't bother to comb her hair or clean her teeth; she just rattled down the stairs of the guest barracks. Jump was at her heels as she dashed to headquarters. Neal, Sergeant Connac, and seven other men, all dressed much as she was, ran with her. They raced into Wyldon's office and halted, trying to catch their breath.

Wyldon, also in nightshirt and breeches, sat before the hearth, helping a boy to grasp a heavy mug as the lad drank from it. The boy looked up, searching the eyes of the new arrivals. His face was dirty and scratched, his clothes muddy and tattered.

It was fortunate Wyldon gripped the mug. Tobe let go of it and scrambled across the room with a cry of "Lady!" He wrapped his arms around her waist and buried his face in her nightshirt.

Kel hugged her boy. Sobs shook his frame, though he refused to make any noise. Soothing him, she looked at Wyldon. That Tobe was here, at night, in such condition, told her what had happened.

Wyldon stood. To the men of his command who'd come with Kel, Neal, and Connac, he said, "I'll take

Company Eight and Company Six. Battle mages, twenty scouts. Jesslaw?"

"Sir!" Owen said behind Kel. He wore only boots and nightshirt.

"Get me a clerk, and messengers for Northwatch, the garrison near Giantkiller, and Steadfast."

"Tobe, how long have you been on the road?" Kel asked the muddy head buried in her nightshirt.

"Not th' road, th' woods. Since noon," he said, his voice muffled. "They hit mid-mornin'. The iron mantises, with the knife fingers an' toes, they climbed over the walls on three sides. Master Zamiel sent me out the hidden tunnel. I left Loey an' Gydo an' Meech an' Saefas—"

"Stop," Kel ordered softly, her pulse beating in her throat and wrists. She was enraged, but it was a distant feeling, one that made her cold. "You did right, Tobe. You've been on the move ever since?"

He nodded against her shirtfront, trembling from head to toe. As the boy continued, Neal came over to place a green-glowing hand on Tobe's back. "I had t'go the long way 'round, t'keep 'em from catchin' me," explained the boy. Though he'd spent weeks trying to speak properly, fright and exhaustion reduced him to talking as he had when Kel first met him. "The sparrows led the way. I heard Sir Merric's horn calls—they was fightin', in the east woods. I kep' low and kep' movin'. I daren't try the road, but the sparrows couldn't go after dark, so they fetched me an owl. Th' owl brung me here."

"Aren't you glad Daine has friends everywhere?" Kel asked gently. Tobe nodded. She looked at Neal. "What's the matter?" she asked her friend. "He's cold and clammy."

"He's chilled," replied Neal. "His body's in shock. He hasn't drunk enough water, and he hasn't eaten since breakfast, I'd guess. He needs rest."

Disentangling herself from Tobe, Kel knelt so she could look him in the eye. "I must go to Haven. *You* stay here," she told him firmly. "Do as you're bid." His chin jutted out mulishly. Kel went on, "You're no good to me if you're sick. Obey the healers. Eat, drink, sleep. Understand me, Tobe? You did a man's work today. Now you must still act the man and rest."

Grudgingly, he nodded. Kel guessed that he knew he couldn't do anything else right now. His eyelids slid down and jerked up: he was literally falling asleep on his feet. Kel nodded to Neal, whose hand was still on Tobe's back. A moment later the boy sagged, truly asleep. Kel caught him and passed him to a healer who'd just arrived.

"Change and arm up, Mindelan, Queenscove," Wyldon ordered tersely. "Your riding mounts are being saddled."

Wyldon led their force, leaving Mastiff in the hands of one company while two went with him. One company spread through the woods on either side of the road, beating the brush for the enemy, but the Scanrans were long gone. The forest was eerily silent, even after the sun rose. Wild creatures did not like the killing devices and fled when they were near, taking days to return to their homes.

The scent of smoke and Stormwing reached them as they emerged from the trees onto the flatlands where Haven's fields lay. Kel's instinct was to kick Hoshi into a gallop, to leave Wyldon and the others behind in her frantic need to see what had become of her people. She bit her lip until it bled and made herself keep Hoshi at a steady trot in the vanguard of Wyldon's troops. She knew that what had taken place at Haven was over.

When they reached the crossing with the road to Fort Giantkiller, they halted. The Giantkiller road was a mess of churned and rutted earth bearing the marks of hooves and wagon wheels. The enemy had gone that way.

"Company Eight," Wyldon called. The captain rode forward as Wyldon added, "Couriers—Northwatch, Mastiff, new Giantkiller, and Steadfast." Once the men surrounded him, Wyldon handed out orders. "Company Eight, follow the Giantkiller road. These tracks are nearly a day old. I see a lot of riders, but the wagons will slow them down. Maybe you'll catch up. Pursue as far as you can, but be sensible. Return here to report. Couriers, take word to the district forts and Northwatch. Make sure right now you have your protective charms with you." Each courier reached into his belt purse. Only when they all showed him their charms dangling from loops of cord did Wyldon nod. "Dismissed."

The captain waved his flag-bearer up. They turned onto the Giantkiller road, mages, couriers, and a hundred mounted troopers in their wake.

Wyldon beckoned to Kel. "It's your command," he said. "Lead us in."

Kel set Hoshi forward, bound for the walled heights. Stormwings circled among the ropes of smoke that rose from inside Haven. Wyldon and his troops followed Kel as she rode to the rough bridge the enemy had thrown across the Greenwoods River. It seemed that the watch commander had used the mage blasts to blow up the original bridge, for all the good it had done. She saw bodies around the bridge's ruins, Scanran by their clothes. The sour breath of smoke and the red stink of blood drifted down the high ground from the walls.

Kel guided Hoshi up the inclined road, around the bodies of the dead, Scanrans and defenders alike. The mare snorted at the stench and rolled her eyes at the corpses but pressed on. "Good girl," whispered Kel, patting her neck. "Good girl."

Looking at the walls, she saw pale chips in the dark wood, the marks of killing devices. From the look of things, three had climbed the east wall. One hung partway over the top, snared in one of the nets Kel had ordered made for the purpose. Someone must have cracked the thing's head-dome while it was entangled, letting out the spirit that made it work.

Kel paused at the ruins of the gate. Here the Scanrans had used a battering ram. One side of the gate tilted half off its hinges, logs dangling from its crosspieces. Two logs had been knocked from the other half of the gate. Around the gaping entry lay the dead.

Haven was in ruins. Every building showed signs of attack. Doors were gone or hung crazily from their hinges. Shutters had been chopped off windows. Smoke streaked every opening. The enemy had tried to burn the place, but Numair's fire protections had saved the walls, if not the contents of the buildings. The only place he had not protected, because the traces of his spells would interfere with the healers' magics, was the infirmary. It was a burned-out ruin, a mass of charred, smoky wood. If she had felt anything at the sight, Kel would have prayed for anyone trapped there, but all her emotions were bound into a small, tight knot in her heart. If she prayed, the knot, and her heart, would go to pieces.

On the ground lay a few dead sword- or axe-cut animals. Most of them were dogs; some were cats. All had bloody muzzles and, in the case of the cats, bloody claws. Changed by Daine to help the refugees, they'd fought alongside their humans, and they'd paid for it. Some of the other animals lay in heaps: chickens, geese, and ducks, animals that hated to be cooped up. They'd been trampled.

Kel dismounted. She fumbled the reins as she looped them around Hoshi's saddle horn. With Jump at her heels, she climbed one of the stairs to the ramparts.

"Dismount and fan out," she heard Wyldon order. "Let's have the wounded and the dead laid out here by the gate. Search every building."

Kel stopped halfway up the stair. On one side of the hole where the gate had stood was a maroon-and-brown pile. There Oluf's cold, dead face, his eyes wide, seemed to stare right at her. He lay on a stack of dead men, all in army maroon. A massive sword cut opened his chest, telling Kel how he'd died.

I never liked him, she thought distantly. He beat the convicts until I stopped him. But he fought for us. He fought for us, and they threw him on a pile like trash.

She finished the climb to the ramparts. The sparrows met her there, perching on the sharpened logs. Dead soldiers and civilians littered the walkway. Many sprouted arrows as porcupines sprouted quills. She and Jump walked the entire circuit of the camp on the walkway they'd fixed after Numair had dropped logs on it. She recognized everyone she saw. This fellow mashed all of the food on his plate into a single mound, then ate it as if it might be snatched away. His throat had been slashed. This woman often sang counterpoint with Tobe, her mellow alto voice intertwined with his pure soprano. She had been cut in two at the waist, probably by the killing device ensnared beside her. It had gotten one hand free of the net that trapped it, enough to kill the singer before someone opened its head with a pickaxe. This man had been handsome before summer's heat bloated his dead face. He'd been much sought by the girls, but Kel had seen him with a lover, a man, hiding in the shadows one night as she walked the camp. He at least had been shot, not cut up by killing devices. Others on the walkway had lost their heads or an arm or both legs. Blood had dried everywhere on the wall and on the planks under Kel's feet. Stormwings had left their unmistakable mark on all of the dead, here and on the ground. The stench coated her tongue, throat, and nostrils.

She finished her circuit of the camp and descended the stairs near headquarters and the ruin of the infirmary. She had counted more than fifty dead on the walkway, soldiers and civilians shot or cut apart by killing devices. The pile on which Oluf lay looked to hold about ten bodies. Sixty or so dead, most of them soldiers, out of nearly five hundred people, Kel figured. Where were the rest?

Sunlight on steel lanced her eyes. A Stormwing glided down until she landed in front of Kel.

Kel locked her hands behind her back. The last thing she wanted right now was a chat with a Stormwing. This one had bronze skin a little darker than that of the Yamanis, with similar wide, almond-shaped brown eyes. Had she been human, she might have been attractive in a cold way, Kel thought, noting the creature's cap of glossy black hair roughly cropped around a small, well-shaped head. Her mouth was plush, her face marked by high cheekbones and a small, rounded chin. It was the rest of her that Kel loathed, the steel and human flesh streaked with reeking fluids.

"We are sorry about this, a little," she said, spreading her metal wings to indicate the ruin around them. "We were not certain if the rules applied, this being a refugee camp, not exactly a fort." The creature frowned. "But then the enemy came with their weapons, and their giant metal insects, and their shamans. Your people included soldiers, they carried weapons . . ." The Stormwing shrugged. "We did what we live to do. It is the first proper feast that we've had in this place, without you to run us off."

A dagger of something white-hot pierced the ice that had encased Kel since she had woken that morning. She took a step toward the creature. "And it meant nothing to you, that my people took up weapons, and fought for their lives, and their families, and their home, when otherwise they'd never fight at all."

The Stormwing shrugged again, light rippling over her feathers. "I said we were sorry. If only you were not stingy, perhaps we might have held off. Practically everyone else lets us have the enemy dead, at least."

"The enemy dead," Kel repeated with numb lips. "They *let* you have the enemy dead."

"Who cares about the enemy?" the Stormwing wanted to know. "Probably just you." She smiled cruelly. "We are done now. You may bury what is left." She took off, half blinding onlookers with the sunlight reflected by her wings.

While Kel had been circling Haven on the walls, Lord Wyldon's men had searched the buildings for survivors. No one had entered headquarters yet. Jump whined as he and Kel approached the building.

"I must," she told him gently. The sparrows fluttered down, some landing on the headquarters hitching posts, some on Kel. "Where are the others?" she asked the birds. "Merric and his soldiers? Find them. They would have been on patrol."

Nari, clinging to Kel's tunic, peeped. The birds took to the air.

Kel walked into headquarters. She found Zamiel fallen on top of his desk in the clerks' office, a pile of reports under him, a sword in one hand. He was the worst swordsman I've ever seen, Kel thought, her heart locked in ice. He made sure Tobe got out, but he didn't run himself.

She went into her bedroom and dragged her blanket from her cot. With it she covered Zamiel, tucking it gently around his body. At least the Stormwings hadn't found him.

Except for Zamiel, the clerks' office was empty. The room where the command staff held their nightly meetings was deserted. She climbed the stairs to see the guest quarters and the storeroom. They were empty, the storeroom cleared of supplies. She found no bodies. Where were Gragur, Hildurra, and the other clerks? Where were the children who carried their messages through the camp?

She went out the back to be confronted by the smoking heap of the infirmary. One of the Goatstrack midwives Neal had once called a "crabby old besom" lay across what had been the door. Three dead Scanrans were sprawled in front of her with no wounds but those inflicted by Stormwings after their hearts had ceased to beat. Kel had known the woman had a magical Gift for healing but not that she could wield death as well. She was cut nearly in two from behind. Apparently a killing device had ended her life, not another human.

Neal leaned against headquarters, weeping silently. Kel gave him a handkerchief. Shock still gripped her.

From the infirmary she walked the camp building by building, her eyes and nose burning from smoke. Inside, the barracks floors and walls were only scorched, tribute to the power in Numair's spells against fire, but the refugees' belongings lay in black and ashy heaps.

She found one more lifeless killing device behind the latrine. It lay half free of the metal-and-hemp net the defenders had tossed over it. Its arms were free. Kel wondered how anyone had gotten close enough to crack the dome. She crouched to inspect it and found that a sparrow had wedged himself into one of the device's eyepits. On that side the thing's dome had been smashed in to free the captive spirit. Kel guessed the weapon had been an axe. The impact had crushed the bird. He'd given his life so a human could attack the device on its blind side and kill it.

Kel gently extracted the sparrow from its metal tomb.

"Daine was right," she whispered softly. "We do you no favors, teaching you to think like us." She wrapped the bird in one of her spare handkerchiefs and used her dagger to dig a grave for him.

Wyldon, his men, Sergeant Connac and his squad, and Owen found the dead. They placed them in double lines on one side of the ruined gate. Kel tried not to watch. Some of the dead were in pieces when the grim-faced soldiers laid them out. She would have to look at them soon, but not now, surely, when some had to be reassembled like puzzle toys. Despite the men's care, a head or foot sometimes thumped the ground as those lowering a corpse slipped. Coming out from behind the looted storage sheds, Kel noticed that someone had found the head of the carpenter Snalren and was placing it in its proper position atop his neck. Snalren had once told Kel that Dom had informed him she was a disaster as a carpenter, so she must not work those chores. Kel shuddered. Was this how she would always remember him, as a corpse in pieces?

Wyldon came up beside Kel and laid a hand on her shoulder. "You couldn't have known that this was coming, Mindelan. It's not your fault."

"Yes, sir," Kel replied softly. She wasn't going to point out that in her shoes, he would feel it was his fault. He'd know that already.

Sparrows darted over the wall, cheeping urgently. They swirled around Kel. Wyldon frowned. "Mindelan, what is the problem with those birds?" he demanded.

Kel looked at the sparrows. Since Daine's work with them, her original flock had doubled. The new additions were far more upset over their news than the veterans,

Nari, Arrow, Quicksilver, and the rest. The newer birds swooped and fluttered, chattering in panic.

"Nari, calm them down," Kel ordered. "I can't think with all this noise."

The queen of the sparrow flock peeped once loudly. The frightened birds landed on the backs and heads of the camp dogs who had returned to Haven or on the shoulders of the nearest men. Wyldon's captain jumped as five selected him as a perch, two on each shoulder, one clinging to his beard.

"Nari, Arrow, report," Kel told the sparrows who had settled on Wyldon. The two immediately took to the air and flew in a small, tight circle, the sign for "friend." Then both dropped to the ground and hopped around, one wing dragging. "Hurt friend," Kel interpreted. Nari and Arrow rose in the air and came together in mock battle, tiny claws extended. Arrow fled while Nari fluttered, dipped, and swerved around Kel. "Some of our people are alive, but hurt," Kel told Wyldon. "They're due south of us. The birds will lead."

"Captain Tollet, take five squads," ordered Wyldon. "Proceed with caution. I believe whatever took place here, we missed it, but there's no point in carelessness."

"Very good, milord," the captain replied. He glanced at his shoulders. "Uh . . ."

Kel raised her hands. The birds who had chosen the captain for a perch took off. Tollet saluted Wyldon properly, then turned and bellowed five sergeants' names.

Kel walked down the rows of the dead. Here was Uttana, she who had spun the finest thread in camp. If Kel kept her eyes on Corporal Grembalt's face rather than the ruined flesh below his belt, he appeared to be sleeping. A redheaded toddler had been struck by a crossbow bolt. Ilbart, he won all the horse races against his fellow soldiers. Oswel, he brewed illegal mead and started fights when drunk. Waehild, a hedgewitch who told off-color jokes to see if Kel would blush. Sergeant Kortus, slashed crosswise from collarbone to hip. Aufrec, another sergeant. Neum, he won any wrestling match, whether against fellow soldiers or against civilians who fancied that all that marching meant soldiers had weak arms.

Uniforms. Most of the dead wore uniforms. Kel frowned and went back along the lines. Sixty-three dead, over thirty-five of them in army maroon. Sergeants, corporals, privates. Soldiers. Some part of her mind stirred under the weight of her shock. Here was Oluf, who had commanded a squad of eight convicts and two corporals. She looked and spotted his corporals: one had been shot; one was missing his right arm and leg. Here was Vidur, whose men were also convicts.

Where was Sergeant Yngvar? His corporals were here, but not Yngvar.

Kel walked the lines of the dead again. Only sixty-three, sixty-four including Zamiel. No one had found more bodies in the wreckage for some time. She stopped and rubbed her temples, calling the duty roster up before her mind's eye. Merric had meant to patrol with a convict squad today, Vidur's squad. Yet Vidur was here—not his corporals, nor his convicts. Yngvar was not here, but his corporals were.

She looked around and found Connac at her elbow. The man was a twenty-year veteran in the royal army. She knew he'd seen all kinds of dreadful things, but this had left him gray-faced, a white line around his tightly shut lips.

"Where are the wounded?" she asked, gripping his arm. "Were they in the infirmary when it burned?"

The man shook his head. "No wounded, Lady Kel," Connac replied numbly. "Not a one. We looked. Under the barracks, in the cisterns, the garrets. No one at all, and the infirmary was empty."

No wounded in a camp of nearly five hundred people? Only sixty-four dead, most of them soldiers?

"Have you seen our convicts?" she asked, her dazed mind struggling to think clearly.

The sergeant shook his head.

Kel looked around, seeing the camp afresh. Her thinking was sluggish. Clearing her mind was like fighting her way to air from underwater. Doors and shutters were ripped from buildings, as if the enemy had been hungry children scrambling to crack a nut for the treasure inside. Animals . . .

"Horses?" she demanded.

Again Connac shook his head.

Where were the survivors? Where were the dead? They hadn't located even a fifth of Haven's population. More people had to be alive somewhere. Perhaps the men hadn't looked hard enough. There would be survivors hidden away.

Kel went to the back wall of the camp and began another search. This time she went through every nook, cranny, and cubbyhole. She knew them all. She even checked the secret exit, emerging between the boulders below Haven's western wall. From a nearby stand of trees some cows gazed at her.

They took the horses and left the cows, she told herself. Hearing a squeal from near the river, she added, And the pigs. Meat animals. They left good meat animals behind but not a single living human.

She cut a willow switch with her belt knife and drove the cows toward the gate. Standing below it, she yelled up for men to take charge of them and to round up the pigs.

As five men raced down the slope over the boulders, Wyldon came to the gate. "We've got Merric!"

June 4–7, 460
Haven and Fort Mastiff

12
RENEGADE

Kel abandoned the cows and ran up the slope, clambering over boulders. At the top she paused to catch her breath. There had been new arrivals while she had searched for one more survivor. Their horses were troopers' horses with military saddles and sweat-dark coats, some with long, blood-caked scratches on their hides. Inside the chipped walls she found convicts at last, six of them, the silvery mark blazing through blood and grime on their foreheads. All showed signs of a hard fight. Some wore crude bandages; one corporal sat on the gatehouse bench, his left leg straight out in front of him in a crude tree-limb splint.

Kel ran for headquarters. In the clerks' office Sergeant Yngvar lay on a long worktable. One of Vidur's corporals, a sallow, black-whiskered man who had a nasty way with a riding crop, occupied a cot someone had found. Yngvar sported a large black knot on his forehead. He grinned at Kel, revealing broken-off teeth between swollen lips. He pointed to the lump on his skull and said with pride, "Ma always said I had the hardest head south o' the Vassa."

Kel rested a hand on Yngvar's shoulder. "Your mother was wise, and you are fortunate," she informed him. "And so are we, to get you back only a little dented."

Yngvar nodded, grim. "Thanks to Sir Merric, milady."

"Where?" Kel asked.

"Your room," said Wyldon.

Kel found Neal beside her cot. He occupied a stool and was holding Merric's hand as the emerald fire of his magic rolled over his friend. Merric was ghost-white with blood loss. Kel watched, hands clenched, as Neal's green fire pooled in an ugly stab wound on Merric's right side and on a long slash down his left thigh.

Merric saw Kel and smiled thinly. "Thirty of them. They caught us at the southern part of the sweep. Not that we *chased* thirty, mind. The sparrows fetched us. I should have waited for their count, they've gotten so good at counting, but we saw only seven, so we followed. I swear the sparrows called us ten kinds of idiot when we did it. Stupid thing . . ."

"How were you to know more would be waiting?" Kel demanded softly, crouching on Merric's free side.

"*You* would have been suspicious," Merric said. "You'd've waited for the sparrows."

"Neither of us can know that," Kel told her friend. "I might have done the same thing. So stop torturing yourself. What next?"

Merric grimaced. "We heard the horn calls from the

fort just when they ambushed us. We tried to get past, go back to Haven, but there were too many. They drove us south, but then they broke off. I think they heard one of their own horn calls. They weren't really *interested* in a fight, Kel. Just in getting us away from Haven. As it was, we lost two men—Leithan and, and Qafi, that Bazhir convict. Fought like a wolf, he did. Kept me from being cut in two." He was sweating. "Kel, I'm sorry. We should have been more careful. How many dead?" His hands clenched the sheets. "How many?"

"We don't know," Kel replied honestly. Leithan had been a street robber, Qafi a horse thief, both hard fighters. They had done good work for Haven in other attacks. "We're still looking."

Neal raised his head. "Look, if you can't hush—"

"Save your strength, Queenscove," Wyldon ordered from the door. "Get him so he can be moved without hurt, but we've other wounded. Mastiff's healers can finish up once we get there."

Neal looked up, green eyes blazing, and opened his mouth to argue. Kel scowled at him. Neal closed his lips without a sound.

"My lord, I'd like to search the area for survivors," Kel said. "I'm hoping they used the tunnel to get out."

Wyldon looked at her. She saw he thought it was unlikely, but he kept that to himself. "Take three squads. Be wary, Mindelan."

"Merric's fine for now," Neal said, the green fire of his Gift fading. "He can be moved safely."

"Too contrary to get yourself properly killed," said Kel to her redheaded friend.

Merric smiled. His eyelids drooped; he'd be asleep in a moment. "Sorry I let you down," he whispered. His eyes closed.

"You didn't—" Neal and Wyldon said at the same time. Both looked horrified at having the same thought as the other.

"I know," Kel said. She went to gather the squads she would need, Connac's and two of Captain Tollet's.

"Mindelan," Wyldon called.

Kel turned to see what further orders he had.

"Round up any animals—cows, sheep, pigs, and so on," he told her. "We're not so oversupplied we can leave them for anyone to take."

Kel had been thinking the same thing. "Yes, my lord," she said.

She was positive they would find people in the woods around Haven. The refugees knew the area as well as she did. Given warning, they could have fled. She led the troopers on a search, using the spiral pattern they followed on Haven's patrols. They were a mile out, having found signs of people only where the enemy had lured Merric away from Haven, when they heard horn calls demanding their immediate return.

Wyldon, Captain Tollet, and five mounted squads were riding down the road from the gate as Kel and her soldiers arrived with the livestock they had found in their search. Tollet and his men crossed the bridge as Wyldon stopped to talk with Kel. "Courier rode in from Company Eight," he said tersely. "Scanrans left a trap on the Giantkiller road—four killing devices. Our mages are holding them, but they need help. Get those animals inside your walls and put men to grave-digging, but close by, understand?" Kel nodded. Wyldon ordered, "Wait here until I send word, Mindelan." He galloped on to catch up with Tollet's force.

"Get them in," Kel ordered her sergeants. "Try to pen them somehow. I'll be along in a moment."

The soldiers obeyed, urging the cows, pigs, sheep, and goats they'd found up the road, helped by the camp dogs. Kel stared at the troops headed to the rescue of Company Eight, her thoughts bitter. The army had mages who could actually *hold* the killing devices—not kill them, perhaps, but hold them. Stop them from advancing. Company Eight had mages to hold *four* killing devices at once. Haven was forced to rely on metal-and-hemp nets, pickaxes, and local hedgewitches who struggled with unfamiliar spells. Haven's mages struggled and their efforts left only blackened outlines of killing devices next to their own mangled bodies, while one company *held* four of the things.

Kel's hands shook, her rage was so intense. Companies. That was another thing. Wyldon had companies at his disposal. So did Raoul and General Vanget. Haven had been granted six squads, four if she was at Mastiff to report to Wyldon and Merric was on patrol. Six squads and over five hundred civilians with scant combat training . . . They had been left out here in harm's way, and harm had come calling.

In quiet moments Kel knew the shape of the war, the way Tortallans were forced to protect a lengthy border through forests and on mountains. When they met the enemy in force, they beat him resoundingly, but such battles were few. As head of their defenses, Vanget did his best. The whole realm was in danger, not just a camp of homeless people. Vanget's first priority was the use of his armies to defend strategic sites. Those armies could only be so many places at once.

But this was not a quiet moment. Kel didn't care about the large tapestry, about thousands of miles of border to protect, two cities under siege, the movement of armies, raiding parties, and ships at sea. She hadn't even been here to defend Haven with her own body. She had been at Mastiff, reporting like a good little clerk and gathering what supplies could be spared by those who did *serious* fighting.

Jaws clenched, she rode back to what was left of her command. There she chose ground for the graves, then helped the men find any shovels that had not burned and make new ones. The graves would have to be common. She doubted that Lord Wyldon would stay here long enough for her to dig individual ones. The ground she picked belonged to Haven itself. She marked off four large pits around the flagpole. It stood untouched, its banners flapping. Their sound was a slap to Kel, another reminder that she had failed her people.

During breaks in digging, she continued to search. Surely someone had escaped and was hidden somewhere, in the heaps of burned furnishings, in a hidey-hole under or behind the buildings. She couldn't believe all they had was sixty-four dead.

At mid-afternoon Wyldon sent a messenger to summon Kel and Neal to meet him at the intersection with the Giantkiller road, with instructions to bring Merric and the other wounded. He also wanted four of the squads he'd left with Kel. Neal growled curses at people who thought to ride with half-healed men and showed the soldiers how to rig stretchers that could be hung between two mounts. Merric, Sergeant Yngvar, and two corporals were loaded onto the stretchers and carried down the Haven road. The procession crossed the river and rode to join Wyldon, Tollet, half of Company Six, and what remained of Company Eight.

"It was a trap," Wyldon confirmed. "Four of the monsters, no humans. The mages had to melt them completely to stop them. Company Eight got badly chewed up before the spells took hold. Queenscove . . ." His voice trailed off as he stared into the distance.

Neal waited silently until he realized that Wyldon was thinking of something else. "Excuse me, Lord Wyldon—you had orders for me?"

Wyldon looked at him with a frown. "I did? Yes, of course. You're the strongest healer in the district. You must check each man as we ride."

He stared at the Giantkiller road to the east, his eyes bleak. Stormwings followed it already, knowing they would find Company Eight's dead in the hills. "The refugees are gone, long gone," Wyldon said crisply. "The devices slowed us down long enough for the trail to go cold. I can't waste more time searching when they're across the Vassa by now."

"But sir," Kel began, her mouth dry, "we haven't found but a tenth—"

"We have other problems, Mindelan," snapped

Wyldon. "Maggur's got that cursed pattern, remember? Two or three attacks at once. I want us in Mastiff before he strikes, if he hasn't already. And there are other factors. I can't explain them right now. Here are your orders: I leave you Sergeants Connac and Hevlor. Bury your dead. Ride to Mastiff at first light. You'll be reassigned. Bring those farm animals and *keep your eyes and ears open.* If Mastiff is besieged, report to Lord Raoul at Steadfast. Do *not* engage the enemy at Mastiff. Understood?"

"But my lord, if the refugees are still alive—" Kel pleaded.

Wyldon cut her off, his dark eyes hard. "We have bigger problems to concern us, Mindelan. You have your orders. Bury the dead and get your troops to Mastiff." He signaled the captains at the head of the column of soldiers. They set out. The squads from Company Six who had followed Kel until now fell in with their comrades.

She'd thought Neal would protest, given his inability to keep his mouth shut, but one of the wounded from Company Eight started to bleed through his bandages. Neal went to look at him. Merric passed her on his stretcher, hung between two troopers. "Take care. I'll see you at Mastiff!" he called to Kel.

Kel and Hoshi stayed at the side of the road. Jump and the camp dogs sat at their feet; the sparrows hopped on the ground, eating grass seed. They've given up, her mind whispered over and over. *Wyldon* has given up.

You know he's right, a second part of her insisted. Maggur does like to hit more than one target at a time. You saw that last summer. It's a good strategy for him. It forces us to split our armies, and it frightens us, not knowing what else he's up to. And now he's got armies of his own to do it with, so he can cause greater harm.

Kel turned Hoshi and rode back along the Giantkiller road. She wanted to see if the raiding party had left any trailsign that had not been destroyed by Company Eight's passage.

The sparrow Duck peeped and bounced into the grass. He returned to her with a twist of bright red yarn. Kel's heart thumped in her chest. It looked like it came from Meech's rag doll.

Kel stared at the yarn, bright against her dirty palm, then tied it around her right ring finger. That done, she turned Hoshi and rode back to Haven, with Jump, his crew of dogs, and the sparrows swirling around her.

The graves were finished by dark. While the convicts made supper outside Haven's ruined gate, cooking flatbread and some ducks and chickens, Kel and the other soldiers buried their dead, murmuring prayers as they filled the graves first with the bodies, then with dirt. The Scanran corpses they laid on a pyre on the far side of the river and burned. Kel was the only one to pray for these men, sent by their king to die so far from home.

Back at Haven, they washed their hands in a cistern, now that there was no need for an emergency supply of water, then went to eat. After supper everyone sat around the fire and told stories of the fallen. Their best whittlers cut names into the planks that would serve as headstones.

Kel prowled, unable to sit. She walked through Haven, in and out of buildings. She half expected the missing to crawl out from under the floors and shout "Surprise!" when they saw her. She climbed to the upper walkway, where she listened to the woods peepers and considered plans. Was this the moment the Chamber had spoken of, when her path to Blayce the Gallan became clear? She hoped it was, because she was about to destroy all she had worked for to recapture her people. If she could. She was only one person. She wasn't god-touched, as Alanna the Lioness was. But she had to try, because she couldn't live with an obedient return to Mastiff, leaving her people to the Scanrans. She had promised to keep them safe. She had failed at that, but she must not fail to bring them home.

It was fairly simple, put in those terms. There were a few complications. Connac and Hevlor, their men, and the convicts who had ridden with Merric that day: they had to reach Mastiff and safety, or at least as much safety as any part of the north offered this summer. Jump and his friends would follow her, but she must talk to the sparrows and see if some of them would act as lookouts for Connac and Hevlor to make sure they weren't ambushed. And she would have to time her departure very carefully. She couldn't leave tonight. Hoshi wouldn't fit in the hidden tunnel, and Kel needed a horse. More than anything she wished she had Peachblossom, but she would have to manage without him. She also didn't want to keep these soldiers here, searching for her, when they should be safe at Mastiff. She would have to give them the slip on the road. That meant she would lose more precious time riding back to pick up the trail on the Giantkiller road.

You're going to take them all by yourself, are you? jeered part of herself. *Just you, your glaive, and some ragtag dogs and birds.*

I'll think of something when I see what I'm up against, she told that part firmly. I can't plan with no information. Once I know more about their numbers and how far we must go to reach safety, then I'll worry about how to do it.

And Tobe. She would break her promise to him. She would disappear.

All she could do was pray he would understand. Surely he'd know that she had to try to recapture his friends, to keep them from Blayce.

So many things could go wrong. If she were caught by Tortallan patrols, she'd be sent to Corus in chains and put on trial for treason. If she were caught by Scanran patrols or war parties, she'd be cut to pieces. She would have to go quickly and silently. She had to pray that her reckoning with Blayce wouldn't be scuttled by an overeager trooper or a killing device.

At Fort Mastiff the next afternoon, Sergeant Connac finished his report and waited. Sweat rolled down his face. Sergeant Hevlor, at his side, was sweating, too. Both men, hardened veterans who feared very little, dared not move.

"Surely I misheard," Wyldon said quietly, his voice as crisp as a late frost. "I could have sworn you just informed me that Lady Keladry of Mindelan is not with you."

"She said she heard sommat in th' woods, milord," Connac replied, staring over Wyldon's head. "She told us she'd check it out and catch up down the road. On'y down the road never came, no more than she did."

Wyldon rested his head in his hands and called himself seven kinds of idiot. He knew her better than anyone but Raoul of Goldenlake. If he hadn't been pre-occupied . . . Mithros curse him, it had been right under his nose. He *knew* the chit, knew that once she'd taken up those refugees, she'd guard them with her last breath.

The office door slammed open, admitting the guest who had come while he had been at Haven. "Please say what the Haven convicts just told me isn't true." Lord Raoul's voice was a rumble in his chest. "Please tell me Kel did not go haring off on her own."

"I can't tell you that, Goldenlake, because she cursed well did," snapped Wyldon, upset enough to break the leash on his own contained temper. "Eighteen combat veterans can't keep their eye on one green knight—"

"She *ordered* us on, milord," protested Hevlor. "We can't disobey an order from a noble, and she didn't look at all odd. . . ."

Wyldon's cold stare silenced him.

Raoul crossed his arms over his chest. "Would you men excuse us." Despite the phrasing, it was not a request. The sergeants fled, pulling the door shut after them. Once they were gone, Raoul spoke again, his voice ominously soft. "I thought you knew her. Did you believe she would let them take her people? And yet you left her, just told her to bury the dead and report here. . . . I'd've wrapped her in chains and brought her back over her horse. This is the girl who risked having to repeat all four years as a page to find her *maid*."

"Gods all bless, Goldenlake, you think I don't know I made a mistake?" Wyldon asked. He sat back with a sigh. "I wasn't thinking. I had a dozen things on my mind. You would have, too, in that spot. Mithros! All those killing devices just thrown away for a refugee camp? I was sure it had to be a diversion."

"If it was, then our information about next week's attack here is wrong," Raoul informed Wyldon. "No, Haven was another matter entirely. Five hundred–odd slaves will fuel a lot of iron monsters, don't you think?"

"I know I erred," Wyldon said through numb lips. "You're not saying anything I don't know."

Raoul shook his head. "If she dies, Mithros forgive you. I never will," he informed the other man. He walked out of Wyldon's office.

Instead of returning to his room, Raoul wandered the grounds of Fort Mastiff. He was looking for the two squads who had come with him as guards. They were sparring in the practice grounds between Mastiff's first and second walls.

Subtly Raoul hand-signaled Dom to gather his squad and meet him at the stable where their mounts were kept. As Raoul trudged uphill through the gate in Mastiff's inner wall, he saw Dom stop by each of his men briefly. Raoul took a moment to talk to Mastiff's watch commander. Afterward he returned briefly to his quarters, then ambled down to the stables, pausing now and then to chat. Dom and a few of his men casually drifted to the same destination.

By the time Raoul reached the stable where the Own's mounts were housed, all of Dom's squad was there. The men climbed to the loft, where they could talk in privacy. The stable was deserted, but Raoul took no chances.

"I have a mission for you lot, if you'll take it, but it's risky. Volunteers only. If anyone wants out when I'm done talking, I'll understand," he told them softly.

The men exchanged puzzled looks. Since when did the Knight Commander of the King's Own give anyone a *choice* in duties?

"This isn't a fight or a patrol," Raoul continued. "It's behind the enemy's lines, I've no doubt—way behind."

"We're following Kel?" asked Dom eagerly.

The men looked from him to Raoul. "What's this about milady?" asked Fulcher, one of the corporals. "We've heard nothing."

Raoul looked at Dom, who shrugged. "I had to use the latrine," he explained. "I overheard Connac and Hevlor in there."

"As long as I've been soldiering, you'd think I'd know how fast word gets around," Raoul commented ruefully. "Tell them."

"The rest of the Haven burial detail got here safe," Dom told the men. "They managed to lose Kel, though." He looked at Raoul. "She went after her refugees, didn't she?"

Raoul nodded. "Alone. I need volunteers—" Every man's hand went up. Raoul smiled grimly. "Very well. Quartermaster's people will leave packs with supplies here shortly. The story is, I'm sending you to Northwatch with urgent messages for Vanget. Here's a purse for bribes and road expenses." He plunked a leather pouch of coins on the floor between him and the men. "Saddle up, get your gear, prepare for hard riding and combat. I doubt she's reached the border yet if she's following the refugees' trail. I just spoke to a couple of the men who rode with her till she went off on her own. The refugees were taken along the Giantkiller road. She'll follow that." Raoul reached into his tunic and pulled out the maps he'd retrieved from his quarters. Placing them on the loft's floor, he traced Kel's probable route with a broad finger, showing the men where they might intercept her. "Or, if she's moving faster than I think she can, just follow the refugees," he said at last, passing the maps to Dom. "From what I heard, the Scanrans aren't trying to hide—speed's what they want."

"The wagons'll slow them down some," remarked Corporal Wolset. "And I doubt those civilians will go quietly. They're tough, and she's been teaching them to fight. We'll catch them."

"But probably not this side of the border," Raoul pointed out. "You'll be in enemy country. Once you find her, take your orders from Kel and stay with her. Questions?" Dom's men, combat and tracking veterans, shook their heads. Raoul nodded. "Then don't waste daylight. Try to come back with her, and yourselves, in one piece. You know I hate training new men." He stood with a grimace as his knees protested. "Mithros bless you all. Go."

"But that's *treason,*" Merric protested, sitting up in his bed. Neal, Owen, and two of Kel's other year-mates, Seaver of Tasride and Esmond of Nicoline, had come to his room in Mastiff's infirmary to relay the news about Kel. "Deserting in the face of the enemy, that's what they'll call it. She'll have destroyed her life, just for commoners."

Neal frowned, but it was Owen, standing beside Neal, who said, "She cares about commoners."

"And these were her people. She promised she'd protect them," Neal added. "You know how she is. She's been jumpy all summer, worried something like this would happen."

"She was afeared," a small voice remarked from the corner. The young knights and the squire turned. Tobe stood there, unnoticed until this moment. "She was dreaming all the time, talking in her sleep about slaves, an' Blayce, an' death magic."

Neal's jaw dropped. "The killing devices. She thinks the Scanrans took her people for Blayce to use."

"You can make a lot of killing devices with five hundred people," Owen said quietly. "Or even just two hundred children."

"She thinks she can retake them *alone*?" demanded Merric, his voice rising.

"She'll try," Neal said. "Even if she loses her shield."

"Or her life," murmured Owen.

"We can't let her." Seaver kept his voice low so no one passing outside might hear. "She's saved all our lives at one time or another. At the very least we can bash her on the head and bring her back. We'll tell people the men got it wrong, she was ambushed by the enemy. I bet my lord won't ask questions, if we move fast."

"Are you *mad*?" whispered Merric. "Break your vows to the Crown? If you stay out too long, you'll be guilty of treason, too."

Seaver looked at him scornfully. "Nobody asked you to

go," he snapped. "And I *know* we're talking treason here. That's why we need to move fast."

"I'm going," Owen said.

The four knights stared at him and said, "*No!*"

A healer came to the door, her eyes flashing. "If you can't be quiet, get out," she told them. "I have people who need rest, including *you,* Sir Merric."

"We'll be quiet," Neal promised her. "We're sorry. It won't happen again."

"I'll kick you out if it does," she threatened. After a moment she left.

"You'll be twice foresworn if you try it," Esmond told Owen. "Not only would you be a traitor to the Crown, you'll break faith with my lord Wyldon."

"I know," Owen whispered, staring at the floor.

"Well, you see? It's quite impossible." Esmond looked at Neal. "I'm in."

Neal smiled. "Thought so."

Seaver nodded.

Smashing his fist into his blankets, Merric growled, "I'm still weak as a newborn lamb. If only we could wait a day or so—"

"We can't," Seaver pointed out. "Not if we're to get her back soon enough that my lord will accept our story."

Merric looked up at Neal, his blue eyes ablaze. "Tie me to my horse," he said. "If you go without me, I'll tell Lord Wyldon. Somebody ought to be there to chance bashing her on the head and fetching her home before it's too late."

Neal looked at his year-mates and Faleron. "You do realize we should all be put in a nice, cozy room somewhere with muscular people to keep us from harming ourselves?" When no one replied, he shook his head. "I'll pack your gear," he told Merric. "I think I can get us out the gate at dawn, just before the watch changes."

None of them noticed that Owen and Tobe had left.

It was late. The watch had called the hour not so long ago—"Midnight, and all's well."

Except all was *not* well, not by Tobeis Boon. The lady had broken her promise and vanished on him, but he couldn't fault her for that. He could and did fault her for going alone, without him to look after her. That was plain not right. Dogs and birds could only do so much for her. She would need him, particularly if she had to take enemy horses when Hoshi got tired. The lady was good with horses, for a noble, but she couldn't talk to them as Tobe could. And if her helm-headed friends caught up with her, they might try to stop her unless she was warned. He supposed they meant well, but they were dead wrong. Bringing the lady back would save *her,* maybe, but what of Loey, Gydo, Meech, and Saefas? What of Einur the cook, and Mistress Valestone, who was as kind as her husband was mean, or Gil and the other convicts? Neither the lady nor Tobe would let them be killed or enslaved, not if they could reach them in time.

And it wasn't like he would be missed.

While everyone was at supper, he collected food, rope, a couple of daggers, tree-climber's spikes, a spear he'd cut down to fit his size, and a compass. He'd watched the guards, and he thought he could get over the first wall and up the second if he moved fast once they passed him. Now, his supplies in a rough pack, he stood at the foot of a stair to the walkway around the inner wall. His sole regret was that he couldn't fetch Peachblossom along. Peachblossom would be as good as a squad of soldiers. Moreover, he'd have made it possible for Tobe to reach Kel quickly.

He'd just set his foot on the stair when someone tapped his shoulder. "Not that way," Owen of Jesslaw told him softly. "Come on."

Wyldon was right. Owen eavesdropped diligently and kept his mouth shut about what he knew. One of the first things he'd overheard was the location of the secret exit required by Daine and approved by Lord Wyldon. The entrance was set in the floor of the warhorses' stable.

Around suppertime Owen had found a chunk of lard and used it to grease the hinges on the escape hatch. Bit by bit he'd assembled all he would need and hidden it in an empty stall. Now he led Tobe to the stable, keeping to the shadows so the watch wouldn't see them. No doubt he was being overcautious, since the watch's attention would be on the land outside the fort, but Lord Wyldon had taught him to be thorough.

As Owen readied his own warhorse, Tobe saddled Peachblossom. Owen was glad to be spared that chore, though he was fairly sure the gelding would have let him do it if he had explained matters carefully. Once the horses were ready, Owen slowly raised the large section of stable floor that was actually a gate. Unlike the escape tunnel at Haven, this one was large enough for horses to use, so that Lord Wyldon could send couriers out while Mastiff was under attack.

Lantern in hand, Tobe led Peachblossom down first,

then asked the gelding to keep going. He returned for Owen's warhorse, a deceptively mild-looking liver chestnut stallion named Windtreader by Wyldon, who had given his squire a mount from his own stables. Owen called the big animal Happy. With Tobe's soothing hand on the reins, Happy allowed himself to be led through the tunnel. Owen gathered the last of the packs and his own lantern, then lowered the heavy piece of stable floor into place, letting it close without a sound. No one would know where they had gone, though Wyldon might guess.

The thought of his knight-master's wrath didn't upset Owen, although he knew he'd destroyed his own name and his chance to become a knight. Wyldon's disappointment in him would cut far deeper, but there was no choice. Kel needed an army to get her people back. If Neal and the others caught up, that would be good, but at least Owen and Tobe could fetch Peachblossom and Happy to what promised to be an interesting fight.

The gray light of pre-dawn was gilding the eastern hills when four young knights assembled with their mounts in the shadows near the inner gate. Esmond led Neal's mount. Neal himself crept up behind the sergeant in charge of the watch, emerald fire quivering inside his closed fist. A touch of it would send the man into a half hour's sleep, enough for Neal and his friends to make it out of Mastiff once he had done the same to the guards at the outer gate.

Neal stretched out his arm to shift sleep from his fingers to his victim. The guard turned to him and grinned. "Now, Sir Nealan, is that any way to treat a friend?" Sergeant Connac asked. "I thought you got training in manners bashed into you before they'd give you a shield."

Once matters were sorted out, they left the fort with no trouble whatsoever. Connac had told Mastiff's guards that all they had to say to Lord Wyldon was that Sir Nealan had ordered them to open up. Who were they to question a group of nobles? All their group's plans for secrecy now looked silly, but Neal didn't mind. This way there was no risk that someone would note their odd behavior and sound the alarm. When they rode through the outer gate with Connac, they found his squad and the six convict soldiers left from Haven's fall ready to go with them.

"Don't worry about it, milord," Connac assured Neal, seeing chagrin on his face. "Us soldiers just see things simpler than you noble folk. We don't let our plans get too complicated." Neal was grateful then for the faint light; it hid his blush. It was a lesson he'd remember all of his life, or at least he would remember it if he survived this particular venture.

As they rode out, no one noticed as three Stormwings perched in trees close to Mastiff took to the air. They soared high overhead, following the men up the Vassa road.

13
FRIENDS

Not until she reached four puddles of molten iron surrounded by Stormwing-ravaged bodies did Kel wake up to the fact that what she was doing was insane.

Her lips quivered as she dismounted to inspect the scene, her eyes stinging. Twice, she thought as she crouched beside the dead. She had failed her people twice: once by being away when the enemy had come for them, and once by riding off to their rescue alone.

She looked up, blinking away tears, and surprised herself with a strange giggle. She clapped her hand over her mouth, but the giggles bubbled insistently in her throat. How could she think she was alone? After all, she had a horse, a flock of small birds, Jump and twelve motley dogs, and ten cats.

"This isn't a rescue," Kel whispered. "It's a joke."

She could still turn back and tell Lord Wyldon she'd come to her senses. He might let her off easy if she returned soon. He was a commander; he knew that losing so many people could make anyone run mad.

She straightened. About to take the reins and mount Hoshi again, she glimpsed something that was not a shredded soldier's corpse at the far side of the road. She lifted her glaive from its rest and went to investigate. It was a heap of clothing. From the feel as she prodded it with the butt of her glaive, it covered a civilian's body. She approached, holding the glaive point down in case this was someone pretending to be dead. Kel reached out with her free hand and tugged on the clothes. The body rolled over.

Though animals had fed on the dead woman, the Stormwings hadn't touched her. The earth had protected her face. Gently Kel brushed the mud away. Through the dirt, bloat, and darkening of dead flesh, Kel recognized Hildurra, Zamiel's assistant clerk and one of Fanche's best friends. From the caked places on the dead woman's clothes, Kel guessed that she had taken a number of wounds during the attack and had bled dry as the raiders fled. There were healers among the refugees, but Kel guessed the enemy hadn't allowed them to care for the wounded. So Hildurra had died. The Scanrans had thrown her aside like so much rubbish and ridden on.

Kel sat back on her heels. The icy grip of rage settled around her heart once more. I can't even bury her, she thought. I can't slow down at all if I'm to catch them before they kill any more of my people. Before they give the children to Blayce the Gallan. I'll free them, somehow.

Knowledge struck her like a sudden ray of sunlight. What am I thinking? she asked. My people are trained with weapons. They'll fight if they think they have a chance. And I didn't see any of Gil's squad among the dead, which means they have a squad of convict soldiers among them. Mithros, even the children can fight. All I need to worry about is finding them and getting weapons into their hands. We'll manage just fine. Once they're on their way home, I'll find Blayce and finish him.

Kel stood and found one of the many handkerchiefs tucked in her armor. She laid it over Hildurra's face. "May the Goddess bless you, and the Black God grant you a place of peace in the summer sun," she whispered. "Mithros grant you justice."

She swung onto Hoshi's back and rode on through the warm afternoon, following the broad, churned-up path left by the raiders and their captives. The sparrows flew in a broad circle, watching for enemies in the brush.

With Hoshi as her only mount and no replacements available, Kel took extra care of her. She watered the mare often, dismounted and walked her to relieve her of Kel's weight, and rested her from time to time. The slow pace chafed Kel, but it was better to move slowly than to kill her only mount.

The Scanrans would be slow, too. While they seemed to have put many captives in wagons, those who rode were not bred to it. They would fall, they would run into each other, they wouldn't care for the horses as an experienced rider might. Some might even do those things on purpose.

Kel knew her people. They would make the enemy's retreat a misery. Kel smiled at the thought. Wagons would develop lost wheels and tangled reins. Things would fall off the horses' tack. Cooking food would burn. Unpleasant herbs picked when no guards saw would find their way into the Scanrans' tea. She might not reach her captives before they crossed the Vassa, but she would find them eventually.

Kel had been able to get few supplies in the way of food, but when night came, she didn't go hungry. One of Jump's friends, a big, wire-haired, boar-hound herd dog mix named Shepherd, dragged a freshly killed small boar to Kel's fire as she made camp. Kel accepted the gift with thanks, skinning and gutting the catch before she cut it up. She kept a chunk to cook for herself, then shared the rest out with the dogs and cats. The sparrows, able to eat grass seed all day, slept.

There wasn't enough boar to fill twenty-three meat eaters, but four dogs found squirrels and rabbits. Kel soon understood that the animals saw her as a convenient way to get at supper without dealing with the nuisance of fur. She did her part of the task, skinning and gutting; her companions did the rest. She left entrails and furs in a heap, murmuring a Yamani prayer to the local forest god to accept the offering from her and her companions, then finished cooking what would be her supper and two of the next day's meals.

Once that was done, she doused the fire. Her eyes had adjusted to the dark by moonrise. She could take up the trail again. The sparrows dozed on Hoshi as Kel led the mare through the balmy summer night. The dogs and cats spread out into the brush once more. They would alert Kel if they found any humans.

Down the kidnappers' trail she walked, Hoshi's reins light in her hand, the three-quarter moon silvering the shadowed woods. In the distance she heard a wolf pack sound the first note of their evening howl. She listened as voice after voice rose, each pack member joining the song. Her dogs kept silent. None of them wanted to cross a wolf's path.

When the pack's song ended, Kel listened to the sigh of the cool wind in stands of pines and the rattle and rustle of the undergrowth as her companions startled nearby wildlife. Once, she rounded a pile of rocks to find a doe and two fawns in an open stretch of meadow. They darted into the trees as Kel whispered, "Shepherd, leave 'em be!"

Whether the biggest dog actually obeyed or refrained because he was well fed, he didn't give chase. Neither did the other dogs. Jump, beside Kel, snorted. Kel wasn't sure if he was pleased with his friends or vexed with her for being silly enough to think they would neglect guard duty to chase deer.

The brief summer night was half over when Kel saw the remains of Giantkiller's walls. The Scanrans' trail continued past the fort, but Kel had to sleep and Hoshi needed a proper rest. Giantkiller would give them shelter. Few Scanrans would face any ghosts that remained there to enter it.

Stopping at the open, wrecked gate, Kel spat on the ground, an offering of herself to the restless dead. She added a soft Yamani prayer in praise of the nobility and strength the ghosts showed in allowing her onto their ground without harm. It seemed to work with most ghosts. She'd never seen any in the Yamani Islands. While the Tortallan dead may have only spoken Common and Scanran when alive, priests said that after death souls understood everything. Kel was fairly certain this included Yamani prayers.

Dogs and cats streamed around her and her mare as they walked into what had been one of the barracks. Its walls and floor appeared to be solid. Kel unsaddled Hoshi and rubbed her down. She tied the mare to an empty bunk and set down her packs, then removed the plate armor she wore over her chain mail. She placed her glaive and axe beside the area where she would sleep, then lay down with the saddle blanket for cover and the saddle itself for her pillow. She did not remember closing her eyes.

The smell of cooking meat reached Kel's nostrils, bringing her to instant, tense, complete wakefulness. Making as little noise as possible, she picked up her weapons. The light coming through the shutterless windows and gaping door was that of barest dawn. Outside her sanctuary she heard men's quiet voices and the chatter of sparrows. There wasn't a dog, cat, or horse in the barracks with her. Had some mage killed them all, or lured them away? Frowning, Kel got to her feet, thrust her axe into her belt, and held her glaive in both hands.

She eased across the floor into the shadows by one of the whole walls. She thought she'd made no noise, but a handful of sparrows darted through a window. They flew in small, tight circles, the signal for "friends."

Kel looked out the window and scowled. She knew those horses picketed outside: geldings and mares, their markings and colors as familiar as Peachblossom's or Hoshi's. Hoshi stood with them, feeding from a bag marked with the blade-and-crown insignia of the King's Own.

Irate, Kel left the barracks and located the fort's well. She used the charmed cork on her bottle to ensure that the well's water was still good. She drew some to wash the sleep from her face and rinse her mouth, then slicked back her hair.

Dripping, she marched over to the campfire, where ten men lounged, grins on their faces. They wore chain mail, but their tunics and breeches were light brown with green trim, not the bright blue that was their normal uniform. Their mail wasn't parade gear, polished to silver, but plain dull steel. These men weren't on a pleasure jaunt; they had come for deep-woods work. Despite their casual postures, she noticed that their weapons lay within reach. They also had companions: the Haven dogs and cats.

Kel knew them all, including the corporals Wolset and Fulcher. If they were here, then the man who sat with his back to her, cooking strips of bacon threaded onto sticks, was Sergeant Domitan of Masbolle. Jump sat next to him, intent on the meat. On Dom's other side, oatcakes cooked on a flat rock.

"What is going on here?" demanded Kel, her voice harsh. "Are you out of your minds?"

"We wondered if we should wake you, but your breakfast isn't done yet." Dom handed the sticks of bacon to Wolset and turned to look up at her. "We figured you could use as much sleep as you could get."

"We haven't run mad, Lady Kel," said Fulcher. "We're under orders. My lord sent us to do whatever you say needs doing." He was broader and taller than Wolset, with brown hair and a trimmed, full beard. He balanced the other corporal, who, in addition to being only five feet seven inches tall and hostile about it, was a quick, dark worrier. Fulcher provided ballast, Wolset brains.

Kel refused to admit, even to herself, that she was glad to see the squad. "My lord sent you," she said, leaning on her glaive as she scowled at each man impartially. They were feeding their breakfast odds and ends to the dogs and cats. "And you got here all the way from Steadfast in, what, a day?"

"No, milady Kel," said Wolset. "Us and Aiden's squad rode to Mastiff with my lord—some parley with my lord Wyldon. We were there when Connac and Hevlor got in. My lord told us you'd likely be about here by now."

"You can't do this," Kel argued. She began to feel silly, looming over them. "You don't know what I'm doing, the laws I'm breaking—"

"Well, actually, we have a good idea," Dom remarked. "Here, eat this before it gets cold. Which of you hedge pigs has the honey pot?"

Someone took charge of her glaive. The others made room for her. She began to sit, then had to straighten to pull the axe from her belt. The honey was produced. At last she was able to devour hot bacon and oatcakes with honey, a feast after last night's unadorned boar meat.

Dom waited until her mouth was full before he produced his final bribe. He held up the roll of maps. "You don't get these unless we come too," he teased.

"Don't forget the purse my lord gave us for bribes," Wolset pointed out.

"That's blackmail," Kel said through a thick piece of bacon.

"Actually, it's extortion." That was Lofren, whose father was a magistrate. "Blackmail implies—"

His squad-mates dragged him to his feet and took him to saddle their mounts. Kel was grateful. Lofren was happy to talk about matters of law at length, in detail, to anyone who would listen.

In the confusion of cleanup and preparation to ride out, Kel lost the chance to argue further about their involvement in her rescue attempt. If Raoul had ordered them to come, they at least wouldn't have to pay the price she did for disobeying Wyldon, she thought. Besides, they had maps. Resigned, Kel took out her griffin-feather band and tied it over her forehead and ears. As always, she felt ridiculous, but it was better to feel like a fool than to be caught napping by a Scanran mage.

She was saddling Hoshi, the sky overhead going from pink-tinted gray to hazy blue, when her placid animal reared and whinnied loudly. Swearing, Kel dragged her down by the reins. "What's the matter with you?" she whispered. "Anyone could be outside!"

Two distant horses answered with loud neighs. The men, who had been joking as they prepared to go, jumped into the saddle, swords or bows out, their faces grim behind the nose pieces of their helms. The dogs and cats raced toward the sound, Jump and Shepherd in the lead. Sparrows darted inside Giantkiller's damaged walls, again flying tight circles before Kel.

"*More* friends?" she asked, leading Hoshi to the gate. "What is this, a cavalcade?" She pulled her spyglass from a saddlebag and focused it on the shadows under the northwestern trees. The dogs had formed a running pool of fur around two riders. She recognized one horse, and his tiny rider, immediately. "I'll kill him," she announced. "I'll kill him very dead and leave him for the border ghosts. . . ."

"Can we do it later?" asked Dom. "We lose daylight if you kill him now. Besides, Peachblossom is as good as a squad in himself." He collapsed his own spyglass.

Kel could not deny that. What she wanted to deny was the identity of Tobe's companion.

They left—they couldn't afford to lose precious daylight—but they argued with Owen on the way. Nothing they said had an effect. Owen refused to return to Lord Wyldon. Kel gave up at last. She knew Owen as well as she knew Tobe. Neither would back down. And she had no time to deliver them to any authorities, not if she wanted to catch the refugees before they vanished into the heart of Scanra.

Tobe's determination to come was understandable. He had friends among the kidnapped refugees, and Kel must not be permitted to vanish from his life. She could hardly deny him. But Owen's presence broke her heart.

"Don't be upset," he said, drawing level with her on the broad trail left by the fleeing raiders. "I had to come. We owe these people our protection. My lord was just stuck. General Vanget sent word that the enemy will cross the

Vassa into our district in five nights, when the moon's full—"

"Owen, you shouldn't tell me this!" Kel whispered, keeping her voice as low as Owen had kept his. "I doubt Vanget wants others to know!"

"But you *have* to," replied her friend, his voice and eyes intent. "I know you didn't understand why my lord turned his back on all those civilians. Well, that's why. King Maggot wants to cross with a thousand men two miles downriver from Mastiff. My lord and Lord Raoul and General Vanget are smuggling companies and mages into Mastiff before the enemy comes. Kel, it must've *killed* him to refuse to save your people. That's why I had to tell you." Owen settled back in the saddle. "I think he knew I was going. He didn't say anything, but . . ."

Kel shook her head. Let Owen believe Wyldon had guessed what he planned if it made him feel better. At least she knew why Wyldon had apparently turned his back on her civilians. He had a much bigger headache to deal with.

The sun had just cleared the eastern mountains when the sparrows came zipping back to them, peeping the alert. When Kel stretched out her open hand, Quicksilver bounced down to tap her twice, then lit on her forefinger. Three other birds flew in the figure-eight pattern signaling they were unsure if the eleven who approached were friend or foe.

"Maybe a patrol from the new fort," she whispered to Dom, who had ridden up beside her. "What do you want to do?"

He raised his eyebrows, looking so like Neal that Kel didn't know whether to laugh or groan. "Your party, Kel," he murmured. "Your orders."

Oh, we'll have to talk about this later, Kel thought as she hand-signaled everyone to hide off the road. I'm not about to command a squad of men older and more experienced than I am.

She wouldn't have thought her friends could hide so completely, but they did. The men's tunics and breeches helped them blend with the background, and their horses were all in colors that mixed with brush and trees. They'd even used dark saddle blankets and plain tack, another sign that they'd come prepared. The cats and dogs vanished easily; the sparrows fanned out once more to act as sentries.

Kel and Hoshi chose the shelter of a cluster of rocks hemmed by mountain laurel bushes. Soon they heard the approach of horses. Here came the patrol, as Kel had guessed, a squad of soldiers and a knight—Quinden of Marti's Hill, one of her year-mates. They should have scouts in the woods, Kel thought. If we were Scanrans, they'd be dead in moments. She stifled the urge to grab Quinden and tell him so. He would have to arrest her, and she had no time to deal with that.

Once the patrol was out of hearing, she signaled her men to move out. As they mounted and headed back to the refugees' trail, riding in the direction opposite the patrol's route, Kel noticed that Tobe shook his head. She nudged Hoshi closer to Peachblossom—she still rode the mare, who was fresh from her night's rest, leaving Tobe on

Peachblossom, who'd been going all night. "What is it?" she asked the boy softly.

"They shoulda had scouts, lady," he replied, just as quiet. "If we'da been the enemy, they'd be dead now."

Kel smiled ruefully, thinking, What a grand world, when boys understand the tactics of war. "When we come back, we'll tell their commander," she assured him.

The sun was halfway up the morning sky when sparrows came in, signaling the arrival of even more friends. "Go back," Kel snapped when Neal, Merric, Seaver, Esmond, Connac, his squad, and her six remaining convict soldiers were within earshot. "Have you lost your minds completely? You're needed at Mastiff!"

"We're needed more here," retorted Seaver, his dark eyes level. "You'll have a fight on your hands when you reach your people."

"I have warriors, and my people can defend themselves, given weapons. *You* have an oath to the Crown!" Kel shouted, tested at last beyond the limits of her patience. "This is treason, you sapskulls! You can't just decide when you're in service to the realm and when you're not!"

"Like you have?" Neal asked sweetly. The young knights halted in front of Kel.

"This is different," Kel snapped.

"Of course it is," Faleron said, leaning on his saddle horn. "That's why we're here."

Kel scrambled for another argument, any argument she could use. She looked at the white-faced, swaying Merric. "*He* should still be in bed!" she cried. "You had to tie him to his horse to get him this far!"

Merric smiled. "But I'm really *well* tied," he explained

in a tone of utmost reason. "I slept most of the way here."

"Why are you upset?" Owen came up beside the mounted soldiers. "It's going to be a jolly scramble now."

Kel gathered her breath and wits to argue, then surrendered without a word. There was no point to it. They had made their choice, as she had. She would just have to do her best to make sure they came home alive, if they had a home to return to.

"Hey, Sir Meathead," Dom called, riding up to them. "You took long enough to get here. Sergeant Connac, good to see you."

"Sergeant Domitan," replied Connac with a grin and a bow. "Good to see you again, sir."

Kel fumed silently. I never asked for help, never wanted to ruin anyone's life but my own, she thought wrathfully. What is the matter with them? Can't they see we'll die if this goes wrong? Don't they *care* that we've earned a warm and lasting reception on Traitor's Hill if we choose to return? Why do men always have to *complicate* things?

"She'll be all right," she heard Owen say confidently. "She just needs to get used to things."

What I need is a barrel full of dreamrose to dose your supper with, she replied silently. Then, while you slept and maybe came to your senses, I'd get so far ahead of you that you'd never catch me. You'd give up and go home, if you're all as sensible as I used to think you were!

They set out again on the trail of the refugees. A mile down the road Kel spotted a bit of gaudy red on a bush. She reached down and picked it up: red yarn. Someone was taking Meech's doll apart to leave a sign for pursuers. Kel tucked the yarn into her belt pouch.

Maybe having company isn't so bad, she thought, more relaxed now. After all, if the Haven folk are making it easy for us to follow, then they deserve a proper rescue. She glanced back at the two columns that rode behind her and Neal. And at least I have a better chance to save them than I did all by myself.

14
VASSA CROSSING

Five miles down the road they found other, less heartening signs that the refugees had passed that way. A woman lay crumpled at the roadside. Kel thought her skirts were dull maroon until she saw that they were stained with blood. She knew the woman, the young, pregnant wife of one of the Hanaford loggers.

Neal dismounted to examine her. "Dead over a day," he said, his green eyes dull as he looked up at Kel. "She lost the baby. I'd say she hemorrhaged—bled out. It happens, sometimes, if there's no healer."

A hundred yards down the road they found the woman's husband hanging from a tree. His hands were marked with bruises and cuts. Kel guessed that he'd fought the disposal of his wife and the Scanrans had hanged him for it.

Biting the inside of her lower lip to stop herself from crying, Kel rode over and stood in her stirrups, wrapping her arm around the dead man's legs. Flies, disturbed at their business, buzzed around them. With her right hand she took her glaive from its saddle holster and cut the rope. As the man's weight fell onto her shoulders, hands reached to take him from her. She glanced down. It was two of the convict soldiers, Jacut and Uinse.

"Give 'im to us, lady," Uinse told her gently. "What was you wishful of doing?"

Kel fumbled her glaive back into its socket. The buzzing of the flies gave her the shudders. "Place him with her, please," she replied. "We—we haven't time to bury them, but at least they can be together."

"Aye, lady knight," replied Jacut. He and Uinse took the dead man back and laid him gently beside his wife, then bowed their heads. Kel bowed hers, too, saying a prayer. She'd known them both, their names, their families, their hopes for the future. Now their future lay in some other realm than the mortal one. All she could give them was her word that she would try to send those who had killed them to the Black God's domain, where his judges would punish them for their crimes.

Sunlight glinted on steel. She looked up and saw a female Stormwing, freshly streaked with blood and flesh. It was the same female who had talked to Kel back at Haven.

"Rot your eyes, they didn't die in battle!" Kel shouted. "Leave them be!"

The Stormwing licked a wing feather. Her metal parts seemed as flexible as her human ones. "Mortals," she remarked. "Always jumping to conclusions." She took wing and flew in circles over Kel's head. "I'm just hoping you'll provide us with a meal soon. With Scanrans all over this border country, the least you could do is give us a snack."

Kel took up her longbow, braced it against her stirrup to string it, then grabbed one of her griffin-fletched arrows. "Why don't I turn *you* into someone's snack?" She put the arrow to the string and raised the bow. The Stormwing was nowhere to be seen.

"Don't take them so personally," Neal advised. "They are what they were made to be." When Kel glared at him in reply, Neal smiled crookedly. "I'm sorry—I forgot," he admitted. *"You are what you were made to be, too."*

They rode steadily through the morning, taking their noon meal in the saddle, stopping only to water and rest the horses. As the animals relaxed, the men and knights would pair off to spar with weapons or fight hand to hand, keeping their bodies ready.

As scouts, the dogs, cats, and sparrows were priceless. They gave Kel's people a degree of safety they couldn't expect with two-legged scouts. Humans missed things. Daine's wild magic had transformed Kel's animals so that they cared about the same things she did. They missed nothing, and they could pass unnoticed through the forests between the old Fort Giantkiller and the Vassa River. They warned their humans of a column of Tortallan soldiers headed west and steered Kel's people around them. Kel silently promised the sparrows that if she lived through this, they would have dried cherries every day, and the dogs and cats fresh meat.

Five miles from the river, the refugees' trail turned due north. Their tracks went down gently sloping ground to the shores of the Vassa, where flat-bottomed boats left distinctive marks in the stone-and-mud shore. The boats were gone. Kel used her spyglass to look across the river. They were beached on the far side. Beyond them the captives' trail began again.

Dom reined in beside her. "Rafts, do you think?" he asked, blue eyes measuring the far shore. "Or Fulcher and I can swim across, and start bringing those boats here."

Kel grimaced. The Vassa was no Olorun, flowing calmly to the sea. It tumbled and roared in spots, rushing along its bed. The waters were icy, even this late in the year.

"Swimming that is just mad, Dom," she replied.

He dismounted and stuck his hand in the water. Pulling it out, he winced. "I'd cramp up ten yards out. Doesn't this river know it's *summer*?"

"Even if it could be swum, does anyone know *how* to use one of them boats?" asked Connac, scratching his head. "They got to be poled across, fighting the current all the way."

"It's that or build rafts," Esmond pointed out wearily. "I doubt we'll be any better with rafts."

"More like have 'em bust up mid-river," grumbled one of Connac's men.

"If we string ropes across, we could pull the boats over. The horses might swim it," offered Jacut. "Maybe it takes us all night to get there. We sure don't want to do this in the daylight."

"Military folk," Neal said with comic patience, shaking

his head. "The only way you know to solve problems is by beating them with a stick."

"And you're not military folk?" asked Seaver. "Oh, I forgot—you're a mage. Mages think, if you can't twiddle your fingers at it, what's the point?"

"Lads," Kel began, "this isn't valuable in the least."

"I wasn't referring to magic," Neal said loftily. "I was referring to a scholar's way to solve problems. When a situation arises, rather than bungle it yourselves, call in an expert. Follow me."

He said it, but he and everyone else waited for Kel to speak. She shifted in her saddle, not sure that she liked the way they looked at her, as if she knew things they did not. "Will your solution get us across sometime before next week?" she asked Neal.

"Considerably," Neal assured her, his tone serious, not mocking. "It's not entirely legal, but I won't tell anyone if you won't."

Kel bit her lip, but her need to reclaim her people was stronger than her need to find out which legality Neal meant. "Let's go, then."

Neal rode down a track that followed the high ground as it rose above the Vassa, until they rode single file along the edge of a forested bluff. Kel was fascinated. The path looked like a game trail until she noticed the hoofprints on the edges. The path was also beaten down at the center, as if it were used regularly by heavier animals than deer. By the time they had ridden three miles, fording the Brown River in the process, she knew they had technically crossed the border into Scanra. Fortunately, no one lived in these surroundings to tattle. Every farmhouse and woodsman's shack was either smashed and empty or burned and empty. No one stayed to see if they could survive in border country when two lands were at war.

The trail rose, taking them in sight of the river, until it descended into a broad clearing. At the far edge stood a cluster of Scanran-style longhouses inside a log palisade. Chimney smoke rose inside the palisade, a hint that this place, unlike others, was still occupied. The noises of goats, chickens, and geese added to the impression that peaceful life continued behind the log wall. Kel would bet that the residents were either Scanran allies or smugglers.

"Wait," Neal told their companions. "String out along the trees so they can see how many we are. Kel, you're with me."

"How did you know this was here?" demanded Seaver, his dark eyes suspicious.

Neal smiled crookedly. "You meet the most interesting people, riding with the Lioness," he replied. "They're usually friends with her husband. Kel?" He urged his mount down the track.

Kel told Seaver, "Relax. He'd never risk his own skin, let alone ours." She rode after Neal. Double fistfuls of sparrows, as well as Jump, five dogs, and three cats, came with her.

"No!" someone protested. She turned. Tobe and Peachblossom broke away from Dom's restraining hand and followed her.

"Tobe, Neal said just me," Kel told her young henchman.

"He can come, just be quiet," Neal called over his shoulder. "Look like we know what we're doing." The palisade gates swung open. Four men and three women, all Scanran, walked out, armed with crossbows.

Air rippled behind them. Kel drew the griffin-feather band down closer to her eyes and saw a tiny old woman doddering in their wake, using a cane to make her way. She was a mage, concealed by spells that made her look like her surroundings. "Neal!" Kel whispered. When he looked at her, she hand-signaled a warning about the mage.

"Fine," he whispered. "Now, you and Tobe stay here, and look serious." He rode up to the local people. Kel, ten yards back, couldn't hear what he said, but she saw its effect. The man who led the group stepped back as if startled, then grinned and walked forward to slap Neal familiarly on the leg. His companions lowered their crossbows.

Neal twisted in his saddle and waved Kel and Tobe closer. As they advanced, Kel heard him remark in Scanran, "—brisk of late."

The man shrugged as he surveyed Tobe, then Kel, with the hardest blue eyes Kel had ever seen. "Business is always brisk, one way or another," he replied, also in Scanran. "We survive."

Kel propped herself on her saddle horn. "Were you part of that interesting business two or three miles downriver?" she asked in Scanran, her voice as cool as she could make it despite the furious pulse beating in her throat. "The very noisy and complicated business, with nearly five hundred captives?"

"Strangers. Pah!" said a short woman, and spat on the ground. "They had naught to do with us, nor we with them."

"Not their slaves, not their vile metal beasts," added another man. He, too, spat, the spittle landing an inch from Peachblossom's right front hoof. The gelding regarded the man with one large, brown eye.

"And you didn't think to warn anyone?" Kel asked, struggling to breathe normally.

"Not our lookout," replied the man who seemed to be in charge. "We do business with all up here, whoever they be. It's the only way to live, on the border." He looked at Neal. "Not one of the Whisper Man's, is she?"

Kel raised her eyebrows. What was a Whisper Man? Despite her curiosity, she remained silent. When negotiating with possible enemies, her people had to show they were united and sure of their loyalties. She would ask Neal about the Whisper Man later.

"No," replied Neal to the stranger's question, "but she's all right. You don't want to get on her bad side."

Kel wanted to roll her eyes at his extravagant claim but didn't. Neal was in charge here. Instead, she tried to appear imposing, and hoped she looked like something other than a complete stick. Out of the corner of her eye she glimpsed the man who had spat near Peachblossom. He sidled closer to the big gelding and Tobe, his eyes on the reins.

"I wouldn't do that," Tobe remarked to him in Common. "He's smarter than he looks."

The man reached anyway. Peachblossom whipped his head around and grabbed the man's outstretched forearm, big teeth closing on cloth and flesh.

"Peachblossom, let go," Kel ordered in Common. In Scanran she told the man, "He's not for sale or for stealing.

He'll kill you. He's killed men before, he doesn't seem to find it difficult."

Peachblossom released the man after a wait to show Kel he didn't take orders. He then spat foam onto the man's shirtfront. The man backed away, grimacing as he tried to wipe gooey green saliva from his clothes.

Kel looked at Neal. "We're wasting time," she told him.

"We're here to do business, coming and going," Neal said to the smugglers' leader. "Us and our friends back there."

A loose feather in Kel's band tickled her nose. In a moment she would sneeze. "Grandmother, come out from behind your veils," she suggested, looking straight at the old woman. "It's uncomfortable, pretending you aren't there."

Cackling amusement, the old lady shed her magical concealments with slow flicks of knobby fingers. Neal and Tobe started when she seemed to appear from the wood of the palisade. "Now *there's* a toy I wouldn't mind having," she said, pointing to Kel's griffin-feather band.

"It has its uses," Kel replied. She pushed the band higher, where it was less likely to drop over her eyes. The errant feather she pulled free and offered to the old woman. "A good-faith gift, Grandmother," she said.

The mage lurched forward and accepted the feather. "A useful thing," she remarked, turning it over. "Amazing how many folk try to lie to those who are just trying to survive in a cruel land."

Neal and the leader had embarked on a harsh, whispered argument. Kel and the old woman looked at them as the leader said, "—out of my mind! I don't care if you *are* from the Whisper Man, I know trouble when it rides up on warhorses!"

Neal reached into his belt purse and drew coins from it. He held up three gold nobles.

"Not if it was a thousand gold!" snapped the leader. "You think I'm blind? Your lot is plain dangerous, and I won't risk my people!"

Neal produced two more gold nobles. Kel resolved to pay him back somehow. Perhaps it was time to sell some griffin feathers.

"I'm not trying to drive up the price," the man growled.

"Do it," said the old mage abruptly. The leader—there was enough resemblance that Kel thought they might be mother and son—glared down into the old woman's faded blue eyes. "The hand of fate is on them. On *her.*" She pointed to Kel and ordered, "Bring your people inside the walls till moonrise."

"Mother," protested the leader, "just *look* at them!"

"I did," retorted the old woman. "Maybe you should look harder." She turned and hobbled back through the gates.

The leader sighed and looked at his companions. They shrugged as one.

"Call your people in," he told Neal, exasperated. "The Whisper Man owes us large for this."

Neal turned and waved the others forward, down off the ridge. Kel and Tobe followed the smugglers inside.

It was the slowest evening of Kel's life. From the signs left by the river, their quarry was only half a day ahead, but here was another delay. She understood the smugglers' need for caution, but her heart shrieked that every moment the enemy stayed ahead of her was a moment when someone else might die. She paced until she realized all of the smugglers watched her nervously, hands on weapons. Then she went outside into the soft night air.

The old mage stood at the half-open gate, staring blindly at the clearing before her. Kel hesitated, not sure if she ought to distract the woman.

"You're better mannered than most nobles," the old woman remarked without turning her head. "Not that we're experts, but we see more than we ever wanted to. That moon won't rise any faster however much you fidget."

She was right. Kel took a deep breath and thought of a broad, calm lake, its surface glassy and serene. Slowly she drew breath in and released it, until she felt more like that lake. Once she had recovered some of her calm, she looked at the mage again. "I thought smugglers worked in the dark of the moon."

The old woman grinned at her. "Not on the Vassa, girl. You need all the help with the Vassa you can get. We have our little arrangement, both sides. They're well paid to overlook us on the far bank, and we've a friend who explained to Vanget we do more good than harm."

"You mean the Whisper Man," Kel guessed. "Who is he?"

"He buys and sells information. More than that, I can't tell you," the woman said. "Mayhap your friend will say, or not. Look. There's a fox, with her cubs."

Kel looked over the woman's shoulder to see a vixen

and two cubs. They trotted across the clearing, the mother alert for enemies, then vanished into the trees near the wider path from the woods.

As the mage turned back toward the longhouses, Kel remembered something she had wanted to ask. "You said I had the hand of fate on me," she reminded the woman as she thrust the gate closed and barred it. "How could you tell? Do you have the Sight as well as the Gift?"

The old woman cackled. "Who needs Sight to tell that much?" she asked. When Kel offered her an arm, she latched onto it with her free hand, her grip like an eagle's claws. Together they walked slowly toward the woman's home. "A wench in armor, wearing a griffin-feather band. You've got a clever set of animals about you, and you're leading four knights and a bunch of men who don't look sentimental. Oh, yes! And you're chasing after two hundred warriors and nearly five hundred prisoners, led by Stenmun Kinslayer." They entered the longhouse as the old woman continued, "You don't need magic to see the fate in that, any more than you need a healer to know you and your folk are deranged."

Kel hung her head. "I tried to stop them," she muttered.

"That's your fate, too," the mage said, releasing her arm. "Be happy they respect you so much they didn't listen. It's not like you're off to a May fair, not with Stenmun against you." She tottered off to a seat by the fire.

Kel sighed. She *was* grateful. She just wished she didn't know how little chance they all had to return alive.

The smugglers served a very well made dish of murrey. Having seen no cows anywhere, Kel was wondering how their hosts got the veal that set the pork off so well when Merric sat across from her. Kel eyed him as she briskly wiped the inside of her bowl with a piece of bread. She was fairly certain why he'd come and would have avoided this argument, but she knew him. Nothing would stop him from saying his piece. He'd been asleep since the smugglers had taken them in. If he were to speak freely, it had to be now, before they crossed the river or not at all.

When he opened his mouth, she quickly asked, "Feeling better? That's the trouble with healings, you could sleep for a week. You shouldn't be here." She grimaced. In her eagerness to distract him, she'd given him the perfect opening.

He took it. "Kel, *we* shouldn't be here, none of us. It's not too late. My lord's practical, he'll overlook—"

Kel met her friend's eyes squarely. "It doesn't matter. I can't leave my people to the enemy. To Blayce. I can't. Even without what I know—" She stopped herself, grinding her teeth in frustration. She must be tired. Either that or the smugglers had put something in the food to make their guests talkative. She wouldn't put it past them.

Merric pounced on the hint. "What do you know? Kel, if there's something you're not telling us, you owe it to us to spit it out."

She was shaking her head. "You won't believe me."

Merric sat back with a frown, puzzled. "Come on, Kel. Give me the benefit of the doubt. I'm a gullible lad. I believe all sorts of things."

"If it's knowledge you're after, try Neal," suggested Dom. He straddled the bench Kel sat on. "It looks to me like he's gleaning from the crop of spy fields."

They looked across the hall. Neal sat in deep conversation with a knot of smugglers, unaware that his friends looked his way.

"What does Lady Alanna know of spies?" demanded Kel. "That's how he said he knew of them, from riding with her."

"He also mentioned her husband," Dom reminded Kel. "I think that's more to the point."

"Enough!" snapped Merric. "Kel, just say it, all right?"

"It's sommat to do with Blayce, an' Stenmun, an' that Ordeal room," Tobe said. He'd come up behind Kel. "She dreams about 'em all the time. How can anybody talk to a room?"

"*Tobe,*" Kel began, and sighed. "It's not just a room. Or there's a thing in it, a god or something." She looked at Merric, Dom, and Esmond, who'd come to listen. "I—I had reason to talk to it, before we left Corus."

Merric blinked. "*You* talked. To the Chamber."

"I said you wouldn't believe me," Kel reminded him. "It told me that my path and Blayce's would cross." The words were as bitter as gall when she said, "It just wouldn't—couldn't—tell me when, or where, or how many would die beforehand."

"Well, that answers that. I'm so glad I was a younger son and never wanted a knighthood," remarked Dom, getting to his feet. "I wouldn't go in the Chamber once, let alone twice. Not to be abrupt, but it looks like we're getting ready to move."

He was right. Everyone was standing. As Kel and her people walked to the door, the old woman met them, holding a large, open cup of the sort known in Scanra as a krater. "Some protection for poor folk ground between two countries," she said, meeting Kel's eyes.

Kel sniffed the steam rising from the krater. "Neal," she called.

He took the cup from its bearer. Emerald fire rose from his hands to drift over the liquid inside. He raised his eyebrows, impressed. "Very nice," he said with considerable approval. "I don't suppose you have the recipe?"

"I'll give it to you when you return," the old woman said. "Now reassure the lady, here, before she sets her birdies on me."

Neal grinned and took a swallow from the krater before offering it to Kel. "It's a very neatly specialized bit of magic," he explained. "If anyone tries to learn how we crossed the river, or who helped us, we'll forget. It's keyed to the spot where you drink the potion, you see. Harmless, except if we're questioned by mages or torturers, we won't give this place or these people away."

"You're *sure*?" demanded Esmond.

Both Kel and Neal looked at him, Neal with more wrath than Kel. "Do you think he'd have taken the first drink himself if he weren't?" Kel asked Esmond.

"Not our Sir Meathead," Dom commented behind Kel.

"You're like a dog with a bone about that name," growled Neal as Kel slid the krater from his hands.

She ignored Dom's reply as she sipped. Her tongue found hints of lavender, rosemary, and peppermint mixed in with other strong herbs. She grimaced—maybe healers like Neal lost their sense of taste after drinking their own nasty teas—and passed the krater to Dom.

When it reached Merric, he looked at it and sighed. "Why didn't I start my page training with year-mates who were sane?" he asked sadly, then drank.

"You're not looking at this the right way," Owen told him sternly as he accepted the cup. "Here we are on an adventure. It's glory, and fame, and all those people the Scanrans took. It's *not* counting troops or finding ways to bury the dead so they won't rot into the drinking water. And if we die in battle, Mithros will speak for us in the Black God's court. You ought to be more grateful." He took a gulp from the krater, nearly spat the mouthful out, and forced himself to swallow it instead.

Once all of them had drunk, the smugglers led the way down the moonlit trail to the river. The sparrows rode, fast asleep for the night; many of the dogs and cats were tucked into saddlebags. They could rest their paws for a while, at least, after their long day's run. Everyone in armor and mail wrapped themselves in blankets so no glint of polished metal gave them away. Even the horses' armor was wrapped in large canvas sacks and carried.

The smugglers' boats were well hidden, covered in nets through which leafy branches were laced. From the water they must look like greenery, Kel guessed as she led Peachblossom onto a flat-bottomed boat. She hadn't realized how nervous she was about the crossing until the smugglers cast off and poled the boats into the current. Then she made the sign against evil on her chest, closed her eyes, and prayed. It could be worse, she told herself as the boat wobbled, rocked, and bounced under her feet. You could be falling off a cliff, or climbing one.

A warm, solid weight leaned against her left calf. A bigger, more solid weight pressed against her right side. Kel peeked. Jump had come to steady her on the left as Peachblossom braced her on the right. "It's as easy as pie," she told them. "A really *bouncy* pie."

Once the boat slid to a stop on the far shore, Kel disembarked. It took three trips for the smugglers to land them all in Scanra, necessary with the large, skittish warhorses. Owen's Happy did not live up to his name. He balked at the sight of the boat, fidgeted all the way across, and leaped off the boat as soon as he could, nearly yanking his master into the Vassa.

"I'm with you," Neal told the stallion as Owen led him to stand beside Kel. "I felt safer on ocean ships in the middle of a storm."

"The Vassa keeps what it takes," Sergeant Connac murmured, repeating an old northern proverb.

Once they were across, the smugglers left them without prolonged farewells. If their Scanran kin were anywhere near, they refused to show themselves. Kel looked around, wondering if she would need the maps, but there was a good-sized trail along the river's margin. They could follow it to the spot where the raiders had landed with their refugees.

"Let's get ready," she ordered her friends softly. Those closest to her passed the order down the line. "Tobe, I'd better take Peachblossom now. You ride Hoshi."

Tobe nodded and got to work saddling the mare. Kel put saddle and armor on Peachblossom, then mounted up. The dogs and cats had already spread out to cover the ground between the river's edge and the bluffs that rose a hundred yards away. They scouted for lurkers or enemy soldiers, sniffing the evening's mild breeze.

As soon as everyone was ready, Kel signaled them to move out along the riverside trail. Merric rode beside her. For a mile or so he was quiet. Suddenly he asked, "The Chamber of the Ordeal?"

Kel nodded.

"You said you talked to it before we left Corus. You—you went *inside*?"

Kel nodded a second time.

"You went *into the Chamber* a second time."

Looking at her friend, Kel sighed. "I had to."

"And you're allowed to talk about it? Your Ordeal?"

"Not the *Ordeal,*" Kel said patiently. "It said I could talk about the second time, the task it set me, if I could find anyone who would believe me. Do *you* believe me?"

"I have no idea," replied Merric, his face troubled.

"Then we don't need to keep talking now," Kel pointed out. "That would be a good thing, seeing's how we're in enemy territory. Don't you think so?"

Merric took the hint and returned to his place in the column.

Two miles of brisk riding brought them to the wide, mangled grassy verge where six large flat-bottomed boats had been pulled onto the land and covered over with branches. Kel's instinct was to put holes in them in case the enemy meant to use them for the assault on Mastiff. At the same time, she knew they could be used to take the refugees home.

The three-quarter moon settled her mind: it was edging toward the treetops. They had to ride now. They were in the open and needed to find cover before moonset.

Raising her hand, she signaled her people to follow and turned Peachblossom. They rode down the broad, messy path left by raiders, wagons, and horses. It led northeast, toward the rise of the bluffs, deeper into Scanra. High overhead, moonlight glittered on Stormwing feathers and claws as a lone scout flew overhead.

June 8, 460
Scanra,
between the Vassa
and Smiskir Rivers

15
ENEMY TERRITORY

They followed the refugees' trail across the Vassa road to the foot of the bluffs, where an unpleasant surprise awaited them. Beside the trail the raiders' mounts had left, five dead people hung from trees. Into the ground before them someone had thrust a plank of oak with a sign cut into it: "Rebellious Slaves."

Kel knew them, of course, even with their faces swollen and dark from being hanged. Two were a husband and wife from Riversedge, both smiths. One was a convict soldier from Gil's squad, one a Tirrsmont man who was forever losing his temper. The fifth was Einur, the cook.

They cut the bodies down and covered them with leafy branches. There was no time to dig graves. Kel tried to speak the prayers for them and failed. She had *liked* Einur. He'd been one of her first supporters at Haven, someone she knew would always be honest with her. It was Neal who finally prayed.

They rode on along the foot of the bluffs until Kel called a halt at a place where the trees at the base of the rising stone offered plenty of cover for them and the horses. Once the animals were tended, they worked out guard watches and settled for what remained of the night. Kel thought that she wouldn't be able to sleep. Heartsick over the dead and worried about the time and distance they had lost, she hadn't known how exhausted she was. The moment she pulled her blanket over herself, she was asleep.

Tobe woke her around dawn. Kel blinked at him and thought of a new concern. "Did I talk in my sleep?"

"No, lady," he assured her.

"It could be that now you're on your way, you'll stop dreaming about it," Dom pointed out from nearby. He was cutting slices of cheese and cold sausage: no one wanted to risk a fire in enemy territory. The rest of the men were up and about, eating their cold breakfast as they fed and saddled the horses. One of the convict soldiers skinned rabbits as the dogs and cats waited patiently so they could eat, too.

They're getting spoiled, Kel thought as she cleaned her teeth as best she could. Next thing you know, they'll start thinking we're *their* pets. She combed her hair, then got out the maps. If she had judged their crossing and the direction of the refugees' trail properly, she and her friends were tucked into a broad angle formed by the Vassa road and the Smiskir road, which followed the river of the same name, a tributary of the Vassa. Now that

Stenmun was in home territory, he would be relieved of the need to move secretly and quietly. Judging by what she saw of his trail from her camp, he was headed straight for the Smiskir road. She folded her maps, accepted cold sausage and cheese from one of the men, and mounted the already-saddled Hoshi. Tobe immediately hauled himself into Peachblossom's saddle.

"Doesn't it hurt you to ride him for so long?" Kel asked, seeing the boy's feet didn't come near the stirrups.

"He don't mind if I fidget, long as I don't fall off," said Tobe, patting the gelding's neck. "If it gets too bad, I ride sidesaddle."

"You could ride a packhorse," Esmond pointed out. "They're smaller."

Tobe shook his head. "Thank you, sir, but me'n' Peachblossom do fine."

"Suit yourself," Esmond replied with a shrug, then mounted his own horse.

Kel sent animal scouts out in a wide circle around her group and placed humans on either side to look for things the animals might deem unimportant. She then led her column of men single file over the ground already covered by the refugees to ensure that enemy patrols would confuse their tracks for those of the refugees. On they rode through forests that looked the same as those they had ridden through the day before, hearing the same kinds of birds, seeing the same kinds of trees. Kel realized that she'd expected things to look different once they were in another country. She shook her head. The land didn't change because humans divided it with an invisible line. Birds weren't stopped from going where they must for food, and the Scanran side of the Vassa ran as hard, fast, and cold as the Tortallan side.

She also knew she should not let the similarities in countryside soothe her. The rocks and trees might look the same, but she and her men were in enemy territory, far more so than when they'd been on the smugglers' land. She was especially wary, as if the trees might have eyes. Every twig snap, every rustle in the bushes, was a hunter in search of supper, a farmer's child looking for mushrooms, or an enemy scout.

A glimpse of bright color grabbed her attention. With a thin smile, Kel leaned down from the saddle and plucked a bit of red yarn from the end of a twig. "That doll will be as bald as an egg by the time we find Meech," she murmured to Neal.

He grinned. "They're tough, those young ones," he remarked, his voice also quiet. "It amazes me, how tough they are."

Kel sobered immediately, remembering Blayce's workroom and a white shape that called "Mama?" Their young people would have to be tough, to get away from the mage and his dog, Stenmun.

They reached the Smiskir road by the time the sun was clear of the eastern mountains. Kel had worried that her quarry's tracks might be lost among others on the road, but it seemed five hundred people and their guards were enough to make an impression even on a major highway. Jacut, the human scout on their group's left flank, found a game trail that paralleled the road: they could ride there with trees and brush to hide them from passersby.

The sun was halfway up the sky when sparrows came back to warn them of the approach of twenty-five enemy soldiers. Owen, the scout on Kel's right, on the far side of the road and well ahead, came right behind the birds. He risked a dash across the open road to reach Kel.

"We've got company," he said, eyes blazing with excitement as he reined in beside her. "They're hard men, fighters. Five carry shields. Weapons are longaxes, spears, and swords. I think they're bound for Mastiff, right, Happy?" The stallion, scenting battle, snorted and pawed at the earth.

"Don't let him do that. Brush it away. People will be able to tell we were here," Kel said absently. Owen tugged Happy away from the spot and dismounted to sweep the mark away with a branch.

Kel looked at her men. All together, they outnumbered the enemy, barely. A fight seemed unwise; she might lose some of her people. They could hide from the oncoming scouts—there had been another road a hundred yards back that would keep them away from the warriors.

If they avoided the enemy, where did that leave them? This war party and their supplies might turn the course of battle in the attack on Mastiff. She'd bet her shield the Scanrans were headed there. She owed it to Wyldon to reduce the Scanran numbers if she could. Moreover, if she and her men found her refugees and freed them, they would have to ride back this way, with this Scanran war party between them and the Vassa.

If they fought the Scanrans, they'd have to kill all of them. They couldn't risk one man getting away to cry the alarm. They dared not take prisoners who might escape. But surely it would be murder, if a man lay on the ground and begged for his life.

Her lips trembled. She had not set out to kill every man in a group simply because they were in her way. What did that make her?

She realized she was rolling something between her fingers: the red yarn she'd taken from the bush not so long ago. That settled her mind, though what she was about to do would haunt her all her life. So much thinking and feeling in so few breaths of time, she thought, knowing that it had only been that long since Owen had brought his news.

She hand-signed the men to prepare to fight. "Jump," she whispered. The dog trotted over to Hoshi. Kel dismounted, beckoning for Tobe to take the mare. She knelt and looked into Jump's tiny, triangular eyes. "I hope you really do understand what you're told," she remarked. "There are enemy scouts riding in the woods on either side of the road. You and the others must take them. Hamstring the horses if you must, but don't let them escape. Get their riders on the ground. Kill them if you can, or fetch one of us. Understand?"

Jump whuffed quietly, his agreement noise. He turned and trotted into the brush, a cluster of dogs and cats at his back. Kel straightened. The men had gathered around her. She checked the fit of her armor as Tobe waited, holding her glaive and helm. "The animals will tend to the scouts, I hope," she said, keeping her voice low as she tested each strap and buckle. The other knights did the same. "Dom, you and your boys get behind the men on the road, like yesterday. Esmond, go with them to hold the enemy at the rear. If you don't mind, let Dom give the orders—he's been fighting longer than either of us." Esmond and Dom nodded. Kel went on, "Wait till you hear noise from the front before you start shooting. Don't let the horses get away"—she gulped, then continued—"and don't let a man get away. Not one, do you understand? Get the dead off the road as soon as you can. Nari, Quicksilver?"

The sparrows fluttered over to Kel. "Take some of the flock. Get in front of Dom, further down the road. Warn him if anyone else comes." The sparrows darted away. Dom and his men mounted and rode off after the birds. "Uinse, take your lads to the far side of the road, get into the trees with your bows. Seaver, you're with them." The six men didn't wait; they hurried to cross the road before the enemy came in view. "Owen, Neal, Merric," said Kel, "you've got this side of the road. Neal, do not heal anyone. Do you understand me?" She held his gaze until he lowered his eyes.

"I understand," he replied huskily.

"I'm sorry," Kel whispered, resting a hand on his arm. The two knights and the squire mounted up. "Tobe, stay with Neal, do as he tells you," ordered Kel. "I don't know if you can call the enemy's horses to you once their riders are off them, but now would be a good time to see if you can." Kel looked at Connac. "Your boys and I will hit them from the front. Duck, Arrow?" The two male sparrows sat on Peachblossom's mane. Both regarded Kel with black button eyes. "Let us know when the enemy's three horse lengths back from that rock." She pointed out a rock at the bend in the road: it was just visible through the trees. The birds left. Connac's men already rode toward the rock as quietly as they could. Kel mounted Peachblossom. Tobe passed her helm up. She settled it on her head, then flipped up the visor to keep the stench of oily iron and sweat-soaked padding from overwhelming her. She accepted her glaive from Tobe, then set out after Connac.

It seemed like forever before Duck and Arrow came shrieking around the curve in the road, but the sun had barely moved. "Charge!" Kel shouted to Peachblossom and to the men with her. Peachblossom leaped forward, hooves digging into the packed dirt of the road. The big gelding hurtled into the mass of men just around the bend.

Chaos erupted as arrows flew from the woods behind and on either side of the Scanrans. Horses reared, throwing off their riders, then trotting into the woods. Kel barely noted their departure. She was too busy fighting. She clung to Peachblossom's back as the gelding wheeled, striking out with his front hooves. Down he went onto all fours. Kel wrenched her glaive free of a Scanran and grabbed the saddle horn one-handed as Peachblossom kicked out to smash whoever had come up behind him.

It was a short fight. The Scanrans, relaxed and comfortable behind their own border, were not prepared for an attack. Those who cleared their weapons to deal with Kel's small group in front of them barely lived long enough to realize that more enemies harried them: archers and knights boxed them in while sparrows darted at their faces, pecking and scratching, distracting them enough for a fatal blow or shot.

Stormwings circled overhead as Tobe returned to the

road with packhorses and mounts, the Scanrans' as well as their own.

Kel wiped sweat from her eyes and looked at the boy. "Would they stay here if you asked them?" she inquired, curious. "In case we need them on the way home?"

"It's better over by the river," replied Tobe. "There's grazing and water."

"Do that, will you, please?" Kel asked. As he led the horses away, she called for the sparrows, twisting the stopper from her water flask. Two birds she didn't recognize immediately came to her. "See if the road is clear ahead." Off they went.

Kel drank almost all of her water, her mouth and throat caked with road dust. Someone took her flask from her to refill it. She looked around. Neal was fixing a shallow gash on a convict's forearm as the man gulped the contents of his water flask. Here came Dom, Esmond, and the men of Dom's squad, some with cuts or scratches, all on their horses. She counted her knights. All were present.

Owen had a long cut across one cheekbone. He demurred when Neal reached for him with a green-glowing hand. "I want a scar to impress the girls," he informed Neal. "They like a man who looks dangerous, and my face needs all the help it can get."

"At least let me clean it," Neal growled. "Unless you think you'll look *really* dangerous with your face rotting off."

Owen submitted. Kel looked around. "I want their weapons, all of them," she croaked. Someone shoved a full water flask into her hand: Jacut. She thanked him, then gulped another bellyful. I'll need to stop behind a bush before we ride on, she thought ruefully, but at the moment she didn't care. She was alive, and so were her people. "Strip them of their weapons and supplies. Put it all under canvas, hide the whole mess behind that rock," she ordered. "You never know when a cache of supplies will come in handy. Let's drag the bodies into the woods, so it'll be a few days before they can be smelled."

"Spoilsport!" jeered a Stormwing from above as the men got to work to hide the dead.

Kel, who had joined the effort to get the Scanrans out of sight, dropped the legs of the body she was hauling. "Tobe, my bow and arrows," she called. By the time he reached her with the weapons, the Stormwings had fled.

After she'd helped to strip the dead of their weapons and hide the bodies, she washed her hands. Silently she apologized to the men they had left in a graceless heap. I am sorry to leave you without proper burial rites, she told them. Maybe you leave enemy dead like this, but I hate doing it.

Kel squared her shoulders and walked over to Peachblossom. "We'd best mount up," she said. Tobe came to her with her helm and glaive. Kel donned the helm—she would feel very foolish if she were shot in enemy country because she had left it off—and accepted the glaive. Tobe jumped into Hoshi's saddle. Kel sent her human scouts out, two forward, two to her rear, and led the way once she could no longer see them in the trees.

They met a second party of ten warriors around noon and dealt with them just as they had the earlier enemy party. When the first Stormwing appeared, Kel shot at it, not particularly trying to hit it. She missed. At the same time, she'd come near enough that the creature swore at her and fled. She didn't want the presence of Stormwings to alert Scanrans that battle had come to their side of the Vassa.

As they rode on, Kel thanked Mithros and the Goddess for her animals and for Tobe. Without them, she and her men might well have been caught; with them, no enemy soldier or horse got away to warn the local people. She also thanked all the gods for the two farmsteads they found later, both abandoned weeks ago.

"Well, of course," Dom remarked when the scouts reported that the second cluster of buildings was empty. "Smart people. They decided maybe they could live with Grandmother's belches and Brother's sharp tongue if it meant getting clear of the war."

"Smarter than Maggur," Owen muttered as they rode on.

"You think he's stupid?" Neal demanded. "He's just united a country of men who live to take chunks out of one another. What better way to keep them from rebelling against him than by starting a war with us?"

"And they're hungry," the convict Uinse added. "Their lords tell them how rich we are, and they want to be rich, too." He smiled thinly. "I can understand that."

"Understanding that is what got you hard labor to start with," Jacut pointed out.

"Hush," Kel told them softly. A scout was coming in, one of Connac's men.

"Lady, have a look," he said, offering her a blob of horse dung in a gloved hand.

Kel poked it and discovered it was soft yet, only dry on

the outside. "We're close," she whispered. She glanced at the sky, judging the angle of light coming through the trees. "Where are we?" she muttered, opening a map.

"I'd guess about here." Dom leaned across to tap a spot on the map below the joining of two rivers. From that point the Smiskir flowed northwest; the second river was the Pakkai, flowing down to the Smiskir from the northeast. "It's almost dark. They'll pitch camp."

"Where the rivers meet?" suggested Owen.

Connac shook his head. "Too damp. But close, for the water."

"I want three scouts, on foot," Kel said. "Dom, Connac, Jacut"—she had noticed that the other convict soldiers followed Jacut's lead—"your quietest people, right now. Send them forward along the road, *with care,* mind. I need to know where the refugees' camp is and where the guards are positioned. We'll be there." She pointed to the woods to her left, where a few fallen trees gave them something to duck behind.

The foot scouts were chosen. Kel sent Jump, his dogs, and his cats to call the mounted scouts in. They returned to eat cold sausage, bread, and cheese with the rest while the horses were fed. The sparrows came in for the night, settling drowsily on packs, saddles, and manes. Kel envied them the ability to stop for the day and leave the work to others. She wished she could do as much. Instead, she tended her weapons, cleaning her glaive thoroughly, then sharpening the edge on it, her sword, and her dagger. She was checking the straps on Peachblossom's armor when the foot scouts returned. The sun gilded only the tops of the trees when they arrived, shadows thick in the low ground between the foothills and mountains.

Everyone but the four men on watch gathered around the scouts. The men scraped a square of ground clear of grass so the scouts could draw a map for them. Tobe produced a lantern and lit it so everyone could see as the scouts drew the enemy camp with sticks.

"Here's the ford," said Dom's chief scout. "The two rivers, and this level patch. Then there's a rise on the far side of the road, our side. That's their camp."

"There's about two hundred fighters. Only a hundred are soldiers, and sloppy ones at that." Uinse had scouted for the convicts. The silver mark on his forehead shimmered in the dark like a pale moon. "I got close enough to hear their talk. They had two hundred more soldiers, but they rode west on the Vassa road after they crossed back to Scanra. These civilian slavetakers was waiting here. They took charge of our people. It don't look like they expect trouble. I saw one guard nodding off, and it not even dark."

"They've set the wagons in a circle on the west side o' camp." That was Connac's scout, Weylin. He drew lines to indicate the wall of wagons. "Horses are picketed here. Our folk is chained inside the wall. I heard a couple of the slavetakers say they're never takin' unbroke slaves again, however cheap. Seems they've lost wagon wheels, their horses keep goin' lame, an' even using the whip it takes forever to move out or make camp."

"They whipped our people?" cried Tobe, furious.

Dom clasped the boy's thin shoulder with one big

hand. "That's what slavers do. Like some whip a horse to break him to bridle."

Tobe's hands clenched.

Kel grinned for the first time in what felt like years. She had known her people would not go tamely or quickly. They could fight even without weapons. She looked forward to putting real weapons into their hands once more. "Uinse, did you see the other squad of convicts? Gil's squad?"

Uinse nodded.

"Can anyone on that squad pick locks?" she asked.

It was fully dark when the dog trotted into the slave camp. "As bold as brass," said one of the guards. They decided the scarred, ugly animal might have belonged to one of the families that had fled the border country. It had certainly seen hard times, as shown by his missing ear and broken tail.

The only further notice the guards took of him was to warn the slaves that if they fed the animal, it would come out of their rations. The guards were angry and irritable after a day when a single vexation had spawned twelve more. All they wanted was their supper and bed after their watch.

They didn't notice the slaves had gone quiet at the dog's appearance. They also didn't see the dog leave several thin pieces of iron next to the convict Morun, whose criminal life was laid on a foundation of locks.

As the night passed, the guards didn't see the trickle of dogs and cats that entered the camp while the slaves pretended to sleep. Each animal carried something. Dogs quietly set belt and boot knives next to selected people. The last two to visit, both rangy cats, left packets for the women who'd been forced to cook for the guards. Each packet was filled with herbs and marked with a dot of emerald fire that vanished as the women took them. The herbs went into the guards' pots.

The civilian slave-merchant guards who stood the night watches were not the most attentive. Fighting drowsiness, not as wary as the soldiers this close to the border, they failed to notice when their fellows on watch began to disappear. They also didn't see the ugly dog pull up the stakes that picketed the horses.

For every three civilian guards there was a soldier, bored, angry, and tired. One of them ordered a slave woman to bring him a cup of tea as the sky began to lighten in the east. She brought it with a wink and a sidelong glance that told the man he might have company in his bed that night, if he wanted it. He gulped his tea, thinking it was time these women realized how to make their lives easier. He nodded approval as the woman carried tea to the other guards, but he also watched to make sure that she gave none of them the same flirtatious glance.

The tea, hot and strong as it was, didn't make the guard feel wakeful. If anything, it made him sleepier. He was about to call for another mug when the arrows flew out of the dark, hitting the soldier guards first. Most went down immediately and did not rise again.

The refugees who had received knives during the long

night slipped out of unlocked manacles. They came up behind their captors, killing them as quietly as they knew how.

Warriors attacked the slave camp on foot. They wielded swords, axes, and in one case a heavy Yamani glaive with deadly force.

It was soon over. Afterward Kel found that every slave guard and soldier lay dead. She wasn't sure if she was relieved or not. Had any survived, she would have ordered their deaths to keep word of the Tortallans' presence from getting out, but the refugees had taken revenge on each of their captors. Kel wasn't sure if she ought to thank Mithros for sparing her the need to give the order, but she thanked him all the same.

Checking the dead, she saw a flurry of movement in the road. Peliwin Archer hacked at a dead guard, chopping his body repeatedly with a longsword she could barely swing.

Kel stopped her. "Peliwin, he's dead. Enough." Gently she unwrapped the older girl's fingers from the hilt of the sword.

Peliwin looked at Kel, despair in her eyes. There was a long, purpling bruise on the side of her lovely face and bruises around her neck as well. "He hurt me," she replied, her voice a croak.

Kel wrapped an arm around her shoulders and led Peliwin away from the dead man. "You've fixed it so he'll never hurt anyone else. You can forget about him." She winced, knowing she'd just said a very foolish thing. "I mean, you can live your life. I guess you won't be able to forget him." She took her arm away.

"No," Peliwin admitted, tears streaming down her cheeks. "No, I don't think I will." She took a deep breath and squared her shoulders. "I'm going to the river, to wash."

"Stay in view of our people," Kel told her. As Peliwin made her way down to the water's edge, Kel saw Olka Valestone, Idrius's soft-spoken wife, join her. The quiet woman had a way of soothing people. Kel hoped Olka would be more comfort for Peliwin than Kel herself.

All of the refugees showed the effects of their time with their captors. Fanche's back was bloody from shoulders to waist. She had particularly annoyed her guards. Saefas had a whip weal across his face and more on his back. Idrius Valestone, unusually quiet now, had been punched until he was barely recognizable.

Kel was refilling her water flask when Tobe raced up to her. "Lady! Lady Kel, they ain't here! Loey and Meech and Gydo and them, they ain't here!"

Kel nodded. "I know." During the fight she had noticed there were no children in sight. She had expected it, in a way. "They were taken?" she asked Fanche.

"Sunset last night," Idrius said through puffy lips and broken teeth. "Across the ford. They're with a hundred and fifty soldiers and that animal Stenmun, riding."

"You'd've been proud," Fanche said wearily. "They fought like wildcats, all of them. We were terrified they'd be killed, but Stenmun wouldn't let them be hurt. Now he has them. Gods know where they're going."

"Across the ford *where*?" demanded Owen.

"Upriver," said Adner the ploughman. "Up the Pakkai."

Kel nodded. They were on their way to Blayce. She summoned her soldiers. "Drag the bodies and the wagons into the woods," she ordered them. "Get them out of sight. I don't want anyone who rides this road to know a fight took place here. Merric, post watchers on the road here and to the ford. We don't want surprises. Tobe, round up the horses, get them ready to go. Everyone, collect weapons and food. You'll need them on your way back."

Even those who had started off to do as she ordered turned back.

"What do you mean, '*you'll* need them'?" demanded Esmond suspiciously.

"Exactly what she says," Neal replied wearily. "She's going after the little ones, and Stenmun, and Blayce." He spoke as he worked, one hand on Fanche's shoulder, one on Idrius's chin, green fire streaming through his fingers to heal them. "You'd better tie me to my horse after I get this lot fit to ride," he told Kel.

She propped her fists on her hips. "I want you to return with them."

"Not a chance," Neal said crisply, looking into her face.

Kel wanted to argue, but his eyes were as hard as emeralds, daring her to try it. She knew him. There would be no talking Neal out of riding on with her.

"They go without me and my boys, too," said Dom as he handed a sword to Gil. "My orders were to stay with you."

"We're stayin', too, me an' my squad," Gil announced.

Kel looked at Owen and Tobe. Their eyes were as steady as Neal's, Dom's, and Gil's. She didn't feel like arguing. "The rest of you," she began.

"You're not going without me," announced Fanche.

"Or me," Saefas instantly added.

Kel rubbed her temples. She felt a headache coming on. "Merric, you're in charge," she ordered. "Get them back across the Vassa and safe home, to Mastiff if you can. Neal, tell him how to contact the smugglers."

"But *Kel,*" Merric protested.

"It's our *duty,*" she replied, stubborn. "These people are under our protection. I *can't* go back, do you understand? I *have* to get the little ones, and I *have* to settle with Blayce and Stenmun Kinslayer. Otherwise they'll be making almost two hundred new killing devices for us to fight."

"Oh," Merric said quietly, understanding at last. "What the Chamber wanted you to do, right?"

Kel nodded.

"But our children," a refugee protested. "Oughtn't we go after them?"

"I have a reasonable certainty we'll meet killing devices," Kel replied. The refugees paled. "In any event, I need to move fast, and I need to know you're safe. That means you go home. Esmond and Seaver, Connac, you're all with Sir Merric, understand?" She looked at the refugees again. "We know the rest of you can fight at need. Take your orders from Sir Merric. If I live I swear I'll bring your little ones back. But I can't be worried about protecting you as well."

"You could die out there," whispered Olka Valestone.

"I hope not," Kel replied, trying to sound casual. "I put eight long, hard years into this. I'll feel very foolish if I'm killed with the paint still wet on my shield. Now let's get moving."

June 9–10, 460
the Pakkai road

16

OPPORTUNITIES

Now Kel was free. She was surprised that she didn't float despite her mail and armor. The confusion, frustration, and uncertainty of the last few months were over. Her path was clear. Stenmun was in her way, as were the soldiers he commanded, but Kel had an idea or two about how to deal with the odds against her and her people.

Most of the cats and dogs had gone back to Tortall with the refugees, but Jump and ten camp dogs were part of her group, as was a cat who had tucked herself into one of Dom's saddlebags. She'd hissed and clawed when he tried to give her to Merric's group. Dom informed Kel he made it a rule never to argue with a lady, and the gray-and-orange-marbled female rode like a queen before him, viewing the landscape with pale green eyes. Kel had negotiated with the sparrows until the flock split. Part went with Merric; part stayed with Kel. Nari, Arrow, Quicksilver, and Duck were the four Kel knew were with her, but there were eight more, all eagerly scouting the trees.

They couldn't range far on either side of the Pakkai. Between the river and the mountains that bordered it lay just a mile of ground, thick with trees and brush. It was forsaken country, given over to deer, elk, boar, wildcats, and the occasional bear. On the far side of the river was a scant border of trees at the edge of steep, hard cliffs. The Pakkai itself ran fast and cold, as cold as the Vassa. All Kel needed in such restricted country was a handful of human and animal scouts.

The road showed signs of recent horse traffic. She hoped that was Stenmun and his men, not a sign that the road was much used by anyone else. When they stopped to rest and water the horses, Kel beckoned to Fanche, Saefas, and the convicts who had been taken by the raiders. "Tell me about Stenmun and his command," she ordered.

It was Fanche who spoke, her eyes as hard as jet. "He's a big one," she said, arms wrapped around her knees, skirts neatly drawn over her legs. "Six foot five?"

"Six foot seven," amended Saefas. "A broadsword of a man."

"Handsome enough in a Scanran way," Fanche continued. "Long blond hair, beard. Graying at the sides and in the beard, but he's fit."

"More than fit," grumbled Morun. "Backhanded a man at Haven in the throat and crushed his windpipe."

"He favors a double-headed axe," continued Fanche.

"He's as fast with it as you are with your glaive, Lady Kel. Brown eyes, thin nose, hard mouth."

"He wouldn't let 'em hurt the little ones, for all their mischief undoing laces and saddle girths," Gil pointed out.

"He said his master, Blayce, wants them unmarked," Saefas replied. "He didn't so much as look at the grown folk, 'less we crossed him." He frowned at Fanche. "You kept needling him."

The woman shrugged, stiff despite Neal's healing. "I wanted to see if I could make him slip. Lots of control, that one. The men were afraid of him, you could tell."

"One of his soldiers said he'd a man skinned alive for liftin' supplies," one of the convicts volunteered. "I believed 'im. He'd the look of a man that's seen a skinnin'."

"I don't mean to let him skin any of us," Kel said.

"But what can we do?" Owen asked. "There's five of them to one of us, just about."

Kel smiled at him. She had wondered when they'd remember that. "I learned something from Lord Raoul," she said, looking at Dom, who stood nearby listening as he watched Neal eat. His cousin leaned against a tree, exhausted by the healing he'd done just so the refugees could make it back to Fort Mastiff.

"Which lesson would that be?" Dom asked. "He teaches so many useful things."

"When the odds are against you, change the odds," she explained. "We don't throw a log down and try to light that for a fire. We whittle it to kindling. That's how we'll treat this Stenmun and his folk. We'll whittle them down. First, though, we narrow the distance between us and them." She stood and twisted her shoulders back and forth to loosen her spine. "Mount up."

On they rode, as silent as mounted warriors could be, straining eyes and ears for signs of the enemy. They set as fast a pace as the warhorses could manage. It wasn't as quick as they could have traveled with lighter animals, but it had to do. They needed all the fighters they had, and that included the warhorses. When Tobe said they had to rest, the company halted. Kel would take no chances with the health of Peachblossom, Neal's Magewhisper, or Happy.

All along the way they found signs of Stenmun and his captives. There was no need for Meech to strip his doll of hair when buttons, buckles, food, coins, and scraps of leather and cloth littered the road. Haven's children were not cowed by Stenmun's soldiers. Their courage gave Kel hope.

She was thinking that it was almost time to stop for the night when sparrows and the forward scout, Owen, rode in. "They're camped three miles up," he told Kel. "They're well settled and have sentries posted."

"Good enough." Kel looked around. There was a clearing inside the trees that bordered the road. "We'll stop here for now."

"Fires?" asked Uinse.

Kel shook her head. "Take care of the horses, eat something, but we're just resting till moonrise."

Owen grinned, his eyes shining. "Time to start whittling?" he asked.

Kel nodded. "Care for your horse," she told him. Turning to the big dog, Shepherd, she said, "Bring Jacut in." The dog galloped off to collect their rear scout.

Kel worked on Peachblossom and Hoshi, thinking. They would have to get as many of Stenmun's command as they could at dawn. If they picked off too many sentries in the early watches, Stenmun would know there was an enemy on his tail. He'd take precautions, perhaps even attack. Kel wasn't about to risk her tiny company in a battle with over a hundred soldiers. The best time to strike was at dawn, when the Scanrans would be sleepy, cross, and bored. She wished she could send dogs with weapons to the children, but she didn't have the courage. Saving them from Blayce meant nothing if she got them killed by Stenmun.

Besides, the big man had to keep some captives. He was going to lead Kel to Blayce the Gallan.

After dawn, the game would be up. Stenmun would know he'd been followed: he'd be watchful. Kel and her people would be reduced to picking off his scouts, the tail-end riders in his column, and the men he sent for water—at least until he realized their weakness and started to send children for it. Sooner or later he would think to protect his men by allowing them to ride with children on their saddles.

How to get rid of the soldiers without endangering the children? she wondered as she watered her horses. Tobe. Tobe could call the horses to him. Her people could then drag the riders down, sparing the children. Mithros, god of warriors, must have sent Tobe to Kel. The boy was worth his weight in gold.

She gnawed a cold sausage, got down some mouthfuls of cheese, and made herself eat a wedge of bread. She wasn't hungry, but fainting later because she hadn't eaten would be foolish. More than at any time in her life, she could afford no mistakes.

Once the moon was high enough to see by, they resaddled their mounts and put the spare horses on lead reins. Kel and Dom checked each mount for the slightest jingle in its tack and muffled each piece with cloth. Only when they could move quietly did they head toward the enemy camp.

The moon was overhead when they took places in the woods around Stenmun's camp. The man had chosen carelessly, halting in a pocket formed by the land at the foot of a set of bluffs. From those bluffs Kel and her people could look down into his camp. The children slept, some restlessly. Those who tossed soon woke up. It was a little while before Kel saw why. Each of them was picketed next to a soldier by a stake and a chain. If they moved too hard, the soldier instantly awoke. He would give a yank on the chain until the child tethered there huddled unmoving once more.

It was time. Kel snapped a branch. Humans might think an animal made the sound, but Jump would know his signal.

Furious yowling split the air, the sound of a cat in combat with a hated enemy. The cat's yowls and the crash of battle in the underbrush were loud even on the bluff. Dom turned to Kel and grinned. All over Stenmun's camp everyone woke, the men flailing for their weapons. The gray-and-orange cat, all fur and claws, raced through the camp and back, screaming her rage. Jump and another dog, a brown, black, and white fellow, with lungs of leather, charged here and there among men and children, baying as they "chased" the angry cat.

One of the soldiers got to his feet, a big, double-headed axe in hand. He swung and just missed hacking the cat in two. She raced up his legs and chest before he knew what she was doing, gouging his flesh. She sank all four sets of claws into his scalp before she launched herself from his head into the dark. The dogs had vanished the moment that axe came down.

Kel surveyed Stenmun in the scant moonlight: here at last was one of the enemy. Not only was he big, he handled that axe as if it were made of straw. She would have her work cut out for her if she fought him.

"Animals!" she heard him roar. "It's just animals—all of you shut up and go back to sleep!" His was a battlefield voice that could be heard over the clash of weapons and men's yells. Kel admired the order, though she thought Stenmun didn't know babies. His roar on top of the dog and cat fight just made the five infants in the camp shriek all the louder. The men who cared for them had a dreadful time calming them until they could sleep. Some of Kel's men stuffed their forearms into their mouths to stifle laughter.

Kel watched the camp, marking who had the babies, where the horses were picketed, and where the sentries were posted. Obviously Stenmun felt safe here. He took no care to conceal his people. One of her human scouts reported the two men now detailed to watch the road and the river had sat down to drink and dice against one another. A woods sentry between the road and the bluffs sat on a stretch of rock lit by moonlight, biting his nails and scratching his scalp. He'd taken his helmet off, something his relief scolded him for. At the far end of the bluffs, the silhouette of the man on watch there was clear against the sky. His relief was no smarter, because he took the same place out in the open.

Kel poked Dom after the new watch was posted and the old had gone to bed. Dom poked the man next to him, and so on down the line to Neal, who tossed a pebble down below. Shepherd, hidden in the brush, began to howl. The dogs of Kel's command lifted their heads and joined him. In the distance wolves heard and began their own song. The babies came to immediate, shrieking wakefulness; the soldiers scrambled to their feet.

They had barely settled down to sleep again when Kel signaled Tobe. She couldn't see or hear what he did, but suddenly the picketed horses went mad, neighing and trying to free themselves. They yanked and plunged, forcing the men to rise once more to calm them and make sure their tethers were secure. Some men couldn't lie back down. They had the next watch.

Everything was going as planned. Kel rolled onto her back and took a nap.

A hand nudged her. She sat up, blinking sleep from her eyes as she reached for her bow. From the sounds of the birds and the ghostly light that filled the air, it was almost dawn.

The others had fanned out to assigned positions. Kel rose to her knees, squinting in the iffy light, set an arrow to her bow, and sighted on her target, a man in the woods. He crouched by a stream that fed the river, splashing water on his face. Kel loosed. Her first arrow skimmed over his head. He scrambled to his feet, looking around in panic. Her second arrow killed him.

Around her rose the soft twang of bows. Saefas and Fanche shot, as did Gil, Dom, Uinse, and Fulcher, the best of Kel's archers. Six more sentries died as quietly as Kel's had. A signal came up the chain of watchers: Owen had killed the road sentry. Lofren of Dom's squad had killed the man on the riverbank.

Once the easy shots were over, everyone but Kel retreated to the spot two hundred yards back where Tobe and the dogs waited with the horses. Kel found a hiding place in a massive tree, one that still gave her a good view of the camp. She'd had to argue with Neal and Dom, but at last they'd seen that she had a point. She could weigh their future tactics by observing how Stenmun reacted when he found all of his sentries for the pre-dawn watch dead. They had killed nine, almost a tenth of Stenmun's force. Not bad for a night's work, Kel thought grimly as she shifted so a knot in the tree wouldn't dig through her mail into her kidneys.

The raiders' camp slept through dawn. The sentries were to rouse the camp as they came off duty, except that none lived to do so. Predictably, it was the babies who woke first. They began to cry from hunger or wet diapers. The toddlers and slightly older children woke to strange, uncomfortable settings and the faces of strangers and joined in the infants' wails.

Stenmun lunged to his feet with a roar of fury: "Can't a man *sleep*—"

Kel, watching through her spyglass, saw the big man

notice that the sun was well over the horizon. He scowled and barked orders. A handful of men scurried out to check their sentries.

They returned at a run to tell Stenmun that the last guard shift of the night was dead. This was the moment Kel had waited for. In Stenmun's place she would have searched the woods, taking hours if necessary to track down who had killed her men and ensure the safety of those left. If her notions about Stenmun were right, though, Blayce and the killing devices would be of greater concern than his soldiers. If that was the case, Stenmun would rush on to his master with his prizes. She hoped that wouldn't sit well with his men: angry men were slipshod. It would mean she could pick off more soldiers as the Scanrans fled.

After the last searchers returned to tell the big man what they had found, Kel watched as Stenmun thought. He pulled on his lower lip and scowled, then glared at the men who'd brought the news and gave them an order.

The men argued fiercely. By their gestures and their expressions, Kel guessed that they wanted to properly bury the dead and say prayers. Stenmun cut them off. The argument got worse; one man slapped his chest as if asking, "Will you do this if *I* am killed?"

Stenmun's answer was a snarl and a blow that knocked the man back six feet. The men got to work. Once the horses were ready, they untethered the children, tied their hands together, and helped them onto horses. Some children rode with a soldier; others paired up on a horse that was led by one.

Her lads had to be careful, thought Kel as she waited

for the Scanrans to ride out. Those children were the soldiers' best protection. Stenmun would know that as soon as he found time to wonder why only his sentries had been killed. She'd be reluctant to tamper with any man who rode with a child, and she couldn't let Tobe call a horse that might throw a child and kill him or her by accident.

Once the Scanrans were gone, Kel climbed down the tree and ran back to her men to describe what she'd seen. As they mounted up, Neal handed Kel a slice of bread covered with melted cheese, followed by another. Kel wolfed the food. She looked at him reproachfully as she ate.

"We used dry wood," he said. He knew she was thinking that a fire was risky. "No smoke at all."

"Smell," she mumbled around a mouthful.

"The enemy was upwind," Saefas replied. "They'd have to be gods to smell it."

"Mother gets so upset when she thinks we lads have been careless," Dom teased Kel as she gulped some water.

"If I'd been your mother, I'd've beaten you," she informed him, swinging onto Hoshi's back. "Bows, everyone. We'll use the road till our forward scout spots the enemy. After that, we take to the woods. It's risky, but we have to chance it. They've got little ones with all the men. No shooting unless a man dismounts and leaves the children on the horse. Remember the plans we made last night. We can do this if we go at it *carefully.*" She'd had to work to persuade her companions not to kill Stenmun or all his men. Stenmun had to lead them to Blayce.

They rode at a trot, doing their best to go easy on the warhorses, gaining on Stenmun. They had not gone far when Dom tapped Kel's shoulder and pointed up through a gap in the trees. Kel looked and growled under her breath. Four Stormwings flew lazily along the road, closer to Stenmun than they were to Kel and her fighters. If Stenmun didn't know that someone followed him, he does now, she thought grimly. Within moments the trees closed in again, which stopped her from having to choose between pursuit and a brief halt to shoot Stormwings.

At last the convict soldier who rode as forward scout returned with the sparrows to say the enemy was in sight. Kel and her people fanned out in the northern woods. That slowed them, forcing them to watch the ground for rabbit holes and other hazards that might cause a mount to break a leg or a rider to bang his head. They'd been in the woods long enough for Kel to realize she needed to find a bush where she could relieve herself in private when the forward scout returned a second time. Their quarry had stopped to water their horses.

Kel hand-signaled for Gil, Fanche, and Owen to dismount, go forward, and pick off any soldiers they could. When they were gone from view, Kel signaled four more of her people to go forward with their bows. She and the others drew back to a stream they'd just crossed.

There they waited. Kel relieved herself, then returned to gnaw a handful of the dried dates favored by the Bazhir among her companions. She made a face as she nibbled. They were sticky sweet. To the man who'd given them to her she whispered, "Your people *like* these things?"

"If you don't want them," he began, reaching for the handful.

Kel yanked them back. "I need the food," she confessed, trying not to yawn. She was tired despite two naps the night before. Catnapping in hostile country was not restful.

They heard crashing in the woods. The sparrows came winging back to signal the approach of friends. It was Fanche, Gil, and Owen, sweating and bright-eyed with success. Gil raised a bony fist, extended his thumb, and dipped it four times. They had shot four men.

They heard more crashes and battle sounds. Kel and the others grabbed their weapons and waited. Five horses, riderless and wild-eyed with terror, galloped through the trees to halt beside Tobe. The four archers who had gone to cover Gil, Fanche, and Owen returned, wiping sweaty faces on their sleeves. One of them, Lofren, grinned as he raised his hand, made a fist, extended a thumb, and dipped it five times.

"Old Stenmun must be wetting his breeches," Dom murmured to Kel. "He's down eighteen men."

When a scout reported that Stenmun was on the move again, Kel and her people returned to the road. They could speed up now, Kel decided. Stenmun knew the enemy was still with him. If he wasn't going to send anyone after them—and his departure after they'd killed nine of his men told her that he wouldn't—he'd ride for Blayce as fast as he could. His captives would slow him down even more as they now outnumbered his warriors. It was time to see if they could recover some of the children.

The problem with catching up to Stenmun was that with fewer men to burden the horses, his train could ride faster. Wolset, Kel's latest forward scout, sent word back that horses without soldiers to ride them had been put on lead reins, children tied to their saddles. Kel ordered him to keep Stenmun always within sight. She thought as she rode. There had to be a way to separate some of those horses from their lead reins.

"What about the sparrows?" Neal asked softly as he drew even with Kel. "If they came at the faces of the men holding those lead reins, the men might drop them. Tobe could summon the horses back to us."

Kel smiled at her friend. "I always knew you were the clever one," she said. To Nari on her shoulder Kel explained what she wanted. Nari listened, then rounded up those of her flock not on scout duty. Tobe, Gil, and Saefas followed the birds down the road.

"You know, when I was growing up, talking to animals was considered more than a bit cracked," Kel remarked to Fanche, who had come to ride on her other side. "But the more I do it, the more reasonable it seems."

"It helps that you know they understand," replied the woman. "I wouldn't want to visit that palace of yours."

"Why not?" chorused Neal and Kel, startled. In their travels they were always asked to describe the palace and the people who lived there. When they did so, the usual responses from their audience were sighs and the wish to actually *see* it, just once.

"Just your animals *here* are unnatural. What if you return to find the horses have decided not to work for men and the dogs are running the courts of law?" Fanche asked.

Kel grimaced. Sometimes she wondered the same thing.

When she heard Stenmun's roar of frustration, she knew he must be in an area hemmed in by rock, which bounced the noise back along the river. I hope you told Blayce how many children you would bring, she thought with grim satisfaction. I hope he holds you to account for the missing ones.

Tobe came back on Peachblossom, three horses trailing him. They trotted along the road neatly, taking care not to spill their precious burdens, two girls in their early teens, three boys of seven to nine years, a toddler, and one infant. Kel welcomed each with a smile, a clasp of the hand, or a ruffle of the hair, but her insides twisted. Stenmun still had more children, including Loesia, Gydo, and Meech.

She sent a convict soldier up to take over as scout. Wolset, when he returned, was sweating hard. Kel gave him her second-to-last handkerchief.

"Thanks, milady," he said gratefully, wiping his face. "They won't make that mistake a second time, I fear. Stenmun ordered them that's leading horses to wrap the lead reins around their waists or their saddle horns. Where we are now? In about five hundred yards the land starts rising. It looks like there's a castle on a mountainside ahead, with the river in front. Ten miles, perhaps? I think they're riding for the castle."

Kel gnawed on her lip. She couldn't push the horses any harder, not the warhorses, anyway. "Gil?" she asked, waving the grizzled convict soldier to her. "Take your lads and Saefas. Try to get into the road in front of them. Start shooting, but don't hit anyone. I want them stopped or slowed down, not killed. Tobe, take Hoshi." She dismounted and collected her weapons as Tobe climbed from Peachblossom's back to Hoshi's. Kel took Peachblossom's reins. "Ask Stenmun's horses to slow down if you can."

Tobe rubbed his forehead. "If I can. It's easier with just two or three."

Within moments the convicts, Gil, Saefas, and Tobe were gone, dust rising from the road in their wake. Kel swung herself into Peachblossom's saddle with a grateful sigh. She didn't want to exhaust the gelding by riding him too long and too fast with the burden of her weight, armor, and weapons, but it was *very* comforting to be on him again. She looked at Neal. "Shall we?" she asked.

They had not gone far when her advance party returned at the gallop. Kel drew up. They wouldn't have returned unless something was direly wrong.

"There's an army ahead, beyond a rise in the ground," Gil reported, his weathered face ashen. "Or at least a company, ready to do battle. If their scouts find us, we're dead."

Kel frowned. Surely the sparrows would have reported an army. She and her people spread out in the woods and rode up the hill ahead, ears straining for the faintest sound. A hundred feet from the crest, Kel and the others dismounted, leaving Tobe with the horses. As they crept through the undergrowth toward the peak in the land, the road barely visible on their right, she realized that the dogs were also relaxed and comfortable. They trotted gleefully through the brush, pouncing on hidden mice, acting not at all like her fierce scouts and defenders.

Slowly and carefully the humans crawled the last yards to the break in the ground and peered over. Neal and Owen went pale and made the sign against evil on their chests. Dom made the sign as they did, but his frown indicated puzzlement, not fear. Kel was the last to find a spot from which she could see into the small valley below. When she did, she noted forest, open fields, a small, ill-kept village on a creek, and the road. At the far end of the valley she saw Stenmun's group, riding on for all they were worth.

"Where's this army?" she whispered to Gil on her right.

"Milady—are you well? It's there, across the road," he said, pointing with a bony finger. "They're at least two hundred strong, maybe more."

Kel wondered if her bandit had cracked under the strain of fumbling through enemy territory. It startled her to see him giving her a similar look.

"Two hundred without the mages," Neal added in a husky whisper. "Five mages, and they look like real trouble."

Owen frowned. "Why are they here?" he wanted to know. "Are they on their way south? You'd think they'd be on the road if they are, not camped."

"Their banners don't flap," said Dom, his brows knit. "We've a good wind, but their banners hang limp."

Kel took her griffin-feather headband off. Suddenly she could see the army, sprawled and waiting on the road. Dom was right. Their banners didn't fly on the wind.

She put the griffin band on. The army vanished. "It's an illusion, lads," she told them. "Just a village down there."

"I *hear* them," Saefas insisted. "I can smell their horses."

"It's a very *good* illusion," Kel admitted, though it seemed the griffin feathers protected her from the part of the illusion that smelled, too. "But it's an illusion. And Stenmun's getting away."

She got halfway to her feet. Neal yanked her flat. "Are you mad?" he demanded hoarsely. *"I see their mages!"*

Kel lifted her face out of dry leaves and dirt, blowing them out of her mouth and nose. If he wasn't my friend, I'd hit him, she thought, wiping her hand over her nose. She yanked the feather band from her head and thrust it onto Neal's.

He looked at the valley and turned beet red. "Oh," he said, and slipped off the band. "Very well, then, it's the best illusion *I've* ever seen."

Dom surveyed the griffin feathers with thoughtful eyes. "Almost makes it worthwhile to raid a nest," he murmured.

"I wouldn't, if I were you," replied Kel. "They're nasty beasts."

"Are you *sure* it's an illusion?" asked Owen. "What if it's an illusion that we're hearing you and Neal say it's an illusion? It could all be a fakement. We wouldn't know until it was too late. If we're smelling illusions, maybe we're hearing them, too, and we'll be chopped up before you can say 'King Maggot.'"

Kel got to her knees. A headache brewed behind her eyes, and Stenmun was gone from view. "Since I don't feel like going to every one of you and jamming this curst itchy thing onto your faces, you'll have to take my word for it," she growled. "While we pick our noses the quarry's getting away, and there's still a village to worry about!"

This time Fanche, who had remained mercifully quiet until now, spoke. "There's a village?"

Kel thumped her forehead with her fist. Dom gently pulled her arm down, then borrowed the griffin-feather band. He didn't put it on, only laid it on his forehead. "Looks pretty dead. I don't see movement, but there's smoke coming from the bakehouse. There's tools just lying about."

"Jump, Nari," Kel said wearily, sitting back. "Take some friends. See if anyone's down there." As they obeyed, Kel looked at her companions. "The sparrows and the dogs didn't see it. That's why they didn't warn us," she explained. "It's a very good illusion—"

"Layered," Neal remarked with a sigh of envy. He took the griffin-feather band from Dom and laid it above his own brows. "Beautifully detailed. Almost perfect. Putting enough power into the mages so another mage would believe they were real, now *that's* brilliant."

"If it was truly brilliant, the banners would flap in the existing wind," retorted Dom.

"Probably figured we'd just see the army and run," commented Fanche.

"An illusion." Tobe shook his head. "No accounting for these mages, what they'll come up with, eh, lady?"

Kel rubbed the back of her neck. "No accounting at all," she replied.

Soon the dogs and birds returned. "Anyone?" Kel asked Jump. The dog shook his head. "But there *are* people living there." He nodded.

"Cleared out," said Gil. "And not for us. For Stenmun. They don't even know we're here."

"They're afraid of their own people?" Owen asked. "That's sad."

"I wonder how many children they have," murmured Fanche.

Kel chewed her lower lip, thinking. "Let's risk the village and the road," she decided. "We need to catch up to Stenmun. Gil, those of you with the last forward party, ride. Try to reach them before they get to the castle. There aren't enough of us for a siege. You have to slow them down before they reach Blayce. Sparrows, some of you fly ahead. Try to get Stenmun's horses to slow down without scaring them. Tobe will help once he's close. Go, go, go!"

Saefas, Tobe, Gil, and the remaining convict soldiers rushed back to their horses. Kel looked at the others. "We'll have to push the warhorses, I'm afraid," she said regretfully. "If we catch the enemy soon, we should be all right. Please, Goddess," she added. Horses were dedicated to the Great Mother.

They mounted and rode, the dogs and birds spreading into the woods to scout. As they passed through the village, Kel noticed a dropped broom, a tipped-over bucket, a lone chicken pecking at the dust. The people had left in a hurry. She had to pray that her animal scouts would find them if they waited somewhere nearby with bows, ready to shoot her and her companions in the back.

The road followed the rise out of the small valley that cupped the village. When it leveled, Kel found that her advance party had come to a halt. Their horses reared and danced in the road, their eyes panic-white all the way around the irises. They were terrified despite Tobe's reassurances.

Sparrows flew shrieking around a bend in the road ahead, crying their most serious alarm. Kel's scalp prickled. She put two fingers to her mouth and whistled. Saefas turned to look, and she waved him and the others back to her. Though the advance group's smaller, lighter horses were terrified to advance, they weren't too scared to return to Kel and the others. They came at the gallop.

The only bird sounds Kel heard were made by a few sparrows. The dogs and cat burst from the woods ahead, racing until they could stand in the road with their people. Jump and Shepherd came last, hackles raised, lips peeled away from their teeth as they voiced low, shuddering growls. They backed down the road to Kel, eyes fixed ahead. Beyond the sounds they made, and those of riders trying to soothe nervous mounts, Kel heard none of the noise of normal forest life. She got her bow and strung it, bracing its lower end against her boot in the stirrup. "Ropes," she called. She had the feeling that just now readiness was more important than secrecy. "Dom, you remember the last time the birds got this upset?" she asked, making sure she could reach her quiver easily.

"I do," he said grimly. "Boys, let's have the special ropes out." The men of his squad turned pale and moved the coils of rope they carried from the back of their saddles to the front. "We borrowed a page from your book. Ropes with a chain core," Dom explained. "Oh, look, Mother. We have company for supper."

Three black metal killing devices walked around the bend in the road. The hammered-iron domes that were their heads swiveled to and fro on the neck grooves, questing for their quarry.

The things stopped and fanned out. The sparrows attacked two, swooping and dodging, circling the devices' heads like a swarm of flies. Both halted, confused. Helm-heads swiveled as they tried to follow the birds. Kel hoped none of the birds would try to climb into the things' eye-pits, as the bird that died at Haven had done.

The third device strode toward them on the grassy border to Kel's left. Its steps were uncertain, its movements slow and uncoordinated. New? she wondered. Or was something not right with the child whose spirit gave the thing its unnatural life?

She selected an arrow and put it to the string. She rose in her stirrups, aiming at the slow one's helm as two of Dom's men galloped toward the closest device, a rope stretched between them. They spread apart to avoid the thing's knife-clawed hands.

Kel loosed her arrow. It sped across the distance between her and the slowest device and punched into its iron dome. Shepherd raced over to the thing and leaped, twisting to avoid its wildly flailing knife-fingers and gripping the arrow's shaft in his jaws. His weight snapped the arrow, allowing its head to fall into the dome, opening a gap for the child-spirit to escape. The dog's momentum carried him free as the device collapsed in a heap.

"Can I have one of those arrows?" asked Fanche. Kel handed one over and selected a third for herself.

Dom's first two riders galloped past the device in the center of the road. Their rope snagged neatly under the thing's chin, in its neck groove. The riders then galloped at each other, crossing the rope so it encircled the device's neck. It snapped off its feet, crashing onto its back. Two more of Dom's men rode forward, twirling rope lassos. The nooses settled over the device's arms and pulled tight. Behind them came more of Dom's men to lasso the thing's feet.

Kel and Fanche shot the third device in the dome, nicking a feather on a sparrow who didn't move quickly enough. Both arrows struck the device and punched through. It began to spin, clawing at the arrows. Its knives sheared through the shafts, allowing the arrowheads to drop inside the dome. A small cloud issued from one of the holes, wailing like an infant. Its iron prison collapsed as the wind blew the infant's ghost away.

The third device hung in the air between five horsemen, spread-eagled by tightly drawn ropes. It fought to get free as the men wrapped the ropes around their saddle horns and backed the horses until the thing's limbs were stretched to their limits. Dom got down from his horse, choosing an axe from his weapons. It was like Kel's own war axe, with a blade on one side and a sharp spike on the other. Dom smashed the spike into the device's helm. When he yanked it free, the white ghost-cloud flowed out and broke up. The device went dead, and his men recovered their ropes.

"Lady," Tobe called, "we got visitors." Kel looked back.

From the trees on either side of the road came the missing villagers, men and women, armed with scythes, axes, flails, crude spears with knives strapped to them for blades, whips, and a few clumsily made bows. They spread out across the road.

Kel looked at Gil. "Take a scout and go ahead, in the woods," she ordered. "I need to know what that Stenmun is doing."

"This day just gets better and better," groused Owen as they turned their horses. "Why can't we fight real warriors, who know what they're doing?"

Kel and Peachblossom advanced as her people moved aside. Neal and Owen followed on either side of her; Tobe rode beside Owen. The animals came with them, but for the sparrows who left with Gil or went to search the woods. Kel held up a hand; she and her immediate companions halted out of the range of the villagers' weak bows.

"We don't want trouble," she called in Scanran. "Our business is with those who just rode through your village. We mean no harm to you if you mean none to us."

A girl of no more than six or seven years trotted out of a clump of bushes to stand at the center of the road. She clutched a floppy rag doll to her chest. Kel thought of Meech and twisted her ring of bright red yarn, wanting to scream with impatience. Her problems were *ahead,* not behind. If she'd been alone, she might have run, but she didn't want farmers who knew this area to be after her people.

The child stared up at her and smiled. She had vivid dark green eyes rimmed with long lashes as brown as her waving mass of hair. Her smile was full of innocent goodwill. When she grinned, she revealed a missing front tooth. After looking at Kel for a moment, she faced the villagers. "That's the one, all right," the girl announced. "I told you she would come, the Protector of the Small. And she's got her knowing animals, the healer, and the horse boy, the armed men and the marked men, the trapper and the bitter mother. They're all here. Blayce will fall."

A man, sharp-featured and lank-haired, came up to stand beside the child. "She is a seer," he explained, his dark eyes hard as he looked Kel over. "She prophesied that you would come and save us from the Gallan. You had better be worth the wait."

"I'm not interested in waiting," Kel replied, happy that her mail hid the goose bumps that rippled over her skin when the little girl spoke. "Every moment I sit here puts Stenmun closer to the castle and its walls. If you don't mind, go home and let me do what I came to do."

"You must come with us," the little girl said matter-of-factly. "They're closing the castle gates now. Blayce has your children."

Kel's heart froze. She turned Peachblossom and set him racing down the road toward the castle. She had not gone a mile when she met Gil, his companion, Morun, and the sparrows. The bleak look in the men's eyes told Kel the young seer was right. Stenmun, and Kel's charges, were in Blayce's hands.

How could she get in? They couldn't lay a siege here, not twenty-odd fighters without supplies or catapults. Were they completely helpless?

She rode on past her scouts. The castle. It wasn't as far off as it had looked from the ridge above the village. The trees ended where the castle's owners had cleared the land to leave half a mile around its walls with no cover for attackers. Armed men trotted to positions on the walls: Kel's people were expected. She saw no moat or abatis. Her men might try to scale the walls that night. Dom and Connac had brought grapples.

The castle itself was not particularly big. The river flowed along its east side, a brisk, deep obstacle. On the north side a sheer stone cliff soared hundreds of yards into the air. The north and east walls, then, were well defended. The west and south walls might be climbed in the dark, if the guards were distracted, and if the mage had set no further illusions or killing devices to protect the place. Kel didn't like to calculate with so many ifs to consider.

The wind stirred. It bore a stench and a clacking sound. Gripping her spyglass with hands that trembled with frustration, Kel opened it. She found the source immediately. Corpses hung from the walls in iron cages. Some of the bodies were beginning to fall apart. At least two looked fairly recent. Some cages hung empty. The dead looked to be adults, not children. Kel wondered who had been so unfortunate as to suffer Blayce's wrath.

Slowly she rode back, considering. They needed a distraction, a good one. An assault had a better chance of success after dark, but she feared to wait that long. How many children would be dead by the time she got her plans in order?

When she rejoined her force, the villagers were still there. "Come with us," the little girl said. "We'll help you."

Kel looked bleakly down at her. "How?" she demanded. "And when?"

"Tonight," said the man who had spoken before. "We know a way inside."

It took a moment for his words to penetrate Kel's gloom. When they did, her nerves came to fiery life. "A way in? Then we can't wait. We'll distract them, draw them off."

"We wait," the man replied stubbornly. "There's no cover, and the way lies right under their walls. Unless you've a mage who can hide everyone, we're not killing our own so you can bravely charge in."

Kel leaned forward, clutching her saddle horn tightly in her effort to be patient. "You don't understand," she told them fiercely. "They have nearly two hundred of our children. I want them back—*all* of them. How many will he slaughter between now and dark?"

"None," said a hollow-eyed woman. She wiped her mouth on a grimy sleeve. "Right now he's arranging for them to have baths, and have their hair combed and curled. He's showing them rooms of toys and beds with clean sheets and silken comforters. Later they'll eat food the likes of which they've only dreamed."

"He'll talk to them, and tell them they're safe," added the lank-haired man. "He'll make Stenmun apologize on bended knee for scaring them. They'll play games tonight and tomorrow. They'll have kittens and puppies and more baths. They get balm put on their chapped little hands to make them as smooth as a lady's. He won't pick his first one for a couple of days, and that only if he's in a hurry."

"How do you know all this?" asked Neal. "How can you be sure?"

"My daughter worked there, till he found she was smuggling poppy to the ones he'd chosen," said the hollow-eyed woman. "She's hanging on the walls right now."

"And my daughter's there, and my son," the lank-haired man told them. "My grandchildren went in there and never came out."

"Your children *work* for him?" demanded Owen. "They lend themselves to that?"

"He says if they don't, he'll kill us," retorted another woman. "He tells us that if we refuse to till his fields, he will kill them."

Kel sat for a moment, looking at these people. They were ragged, thin, and dirty. She remembered the homes in the village, the bad thatching, the windows with shutters made of trash wood, the crudely made pens and coops. These people got no profit from the creation of killing devices. They looked as if they were near starvation.

"I don't understand," Neal said abruptly. "He doesn't need that for death magic. Clothes, or food, or toys. Bathing, maybe, for purification, but the rest makes no sense."

"He doesn't do it because it's *needed,*" said the hollow-eyed woman, her voice thick with scorn. "He does it because he likes it."

"He could use any ghosts for his magic," the girl seer added, rocking her doll in her arms. "As long as the king in Hamrkeng gets his evil metal creatures, he doesn't care who Blayce uses or how he uses them."

"At least, he doesn't care if our children are used, or yours across the border," said the lank-haired man, his voice cracking. "It would be different if Blayce wanted nobles' children." He shook his head as if to clear it. "Well?" he demanded, brown eyes fierce as he glared at Kel. "Do you want in, or don't you? Will you rid us of him, or will you stay here like a herd of cows?"

Everyone looked at Kel. She wished they wouldn't.

"You're sure he isn't killing them right now?" she asked the child seer.

She closed her eyes. When she spoke, it was in a thin, whispering voice that Kel knew. *He welcomes them as his own,* the Chamber of the Ordeal said. Everyone around her made the sign against evil on his or her chest. *He says they are safe now. They are to have sweets, hot baths, a feast, easy dreams. He makes his dog, Stenmun, grovel for them. It is your time, Keladry of Mindelan, Protector of the Small.*

The child staggered as the Chamber released her. The lank-haired man swept her up in his arms and walked down the road, bound for the village. Kel followed, weary.

Neal stopped her with a hand on her arm. "Kel, who *was* that?" he wanted to know. Kel turned. All of her people stared at her.

She sighed. "It was the Chamber of the Ordeal," she told them. "It sent me here. Sort of."

A convict brightened. "Then we're to succeed? If it's been foretold?"

The hollow-eyed woman had stayed within earshot. She faced them with a crooked smile. "Irnai—the seer child—she says your chances are one in two. Since that's better than ours, we'll pray for you."

June 10–11, 460
Blayce's Castle

17
THE GALLAN'S LAIR

After a look at the villagers' meager rations, the Tortallans added their own supplies: sausages, stale bread, hunks of cheese. The men of the Own produced noodle balls, dried noodles and herbs that made a decent soup when dumped into boiling water. Kel, restless, walked around the village. The farm animals had returned. The villagers had concealed them from Stenmun. At least the fowl, goats, and cows looked decently fed. The dogs and cats were as rail-thin as the villagers. The grain and vegetable fields were rich and green, the orchards flourishing. Why did these people go hungry?

The lank-haired man—he'd introduced himself as Zerhalm—laughed bitterly when Kel asked. "We've a mage in the castle, in case you'd forgotten," he informed her. "Most of it goes to him, and he knows what's due. If we hold anything back, like our children, Blayce has Stenmun grab one of us, skin him, and hang him from the castle walls to wait for death. Or her, in my wife's case."

"Why don't you go to his overlord?" demanded Owen. "Or even to the king in Hamrkeng, and ask for justice?"

"We did," Zerhalm retorted. "King Maggur has made a pet of this mage from Galla. Couriers say we'll eat like kings when we've land in the south, but we don't hear of any great victories."

The phrase "like our children" had sent a shock wave rolling through Kel. She'd thought—hoped—that their young people were hiding. "Have you no children left?" she asked. "He took them *all*?"

"First it was just the prettiest girls and boys, around ten years old," Zerhalm replied, his eyes seeing a horror invisible to Kel. "Those days, we didn't know it was him. We'd go to bed and wake in the morning to find them gone. Next went the pretty ones who were nine, eleven, twelve. Around then we found our weapons had gone missing; our bows, our spears, all we used to defend ourselves from raiders. We went to him for help against the thieves and for weapons to fight them with. Stenmun had his men beat us, demanded our older boys and girls as servants, and kicked us back home. We were told to feed the castle and not ask questions. Then the young children went. The warlord Rathhausak, King Maggur now, he came to the castle. We begged *him* for help. He had ten of us killed and hung on the walls."

"Your children?" repeated Kel softly. *"All?"*

"Even the ugly ones, the crippled ones, the slow ones,

the babes in their cribs, over winter this year," Zerhalm whispered. He trembled from head to toe. "All. And in every village hereabouts."

Kel remembered the three devices she and her people had just killed. One had seemed slow.

"They brought more children in by cartloads, under Maggur's banner, so no one would try to save them," Zerhalm went on. "Our neighbors, folk beyond—the lords of Scanra were afraid to protest. By then Rathhausak had *their* wives and children."

"What about the seer?" Owen asked. "The little girl, um—" He looked at Kel.

"Irnai," Kel said.

"Why doesn't Blayce have her?" demanded Owen.

"I don't believe he knows she exists," replied Zerhalm. "She walked in here a month gone. Never said where she lived, who her people are. Told us the Protector of the Small was coming. Told us it was our best chance." He looked around at the soldiers, the young knights, Tobe, and Fanche, all sharpening their weapons. The dogs and the lone cat sprawled in the sun, asleep. The horses grazed in a nearby field. "Forgive my saying, but you don't look like much of a chance to me, not against Blayce and Stenmun and a hundred fifty men-at-arms in the castle."

"He had a hundred seventy at midnight last night," Gil pointed out.

Zerhalm grunted.

"Pessimist," Neal remarked as he healed an ulcer on an old man's leg.

"Four years of Blayce the Gallan does that to a man," retorted Zerhalm.

"Then he wasn't always here," commented Fanche, looking up from the arrow she was checking.

"Not if we call him 'the Gallan,' mistress," Zerhalm told her. "That's where he said he was from."

Fanche and Saefas glared at him.

The Scanran sighed. "This was Fief Rathhausak, once," he explained more patiently. "The line dwindled. Young Maggur went off to foreign lands to be paid for fighting. He came home but once, took his family with him, just his mother and an old aunt. We were happy with no lordling over us, till Maggur gave the castle and lands to the Gallan."

Kel's gut twisted. Instead of caring for his people, Rathhausak had given them to a monster who murdered their future. Did it bother him that those who should be his first concern were now preyed upon by his successor? Or were the killing devices so important that he didn't care?

She crouched by a patch of dusty ground and, using a stick, began to draw a rough map of the castle wall and the surrounding lands in the dirt. Someone knelt beside her. It was the hollow-eyed woman, Agrane. She picked up her own stick and added to the map. "I was cook," she explained as she worked, "until the Gallan decided I was too old and too ugly to keep. Would I had put metal shavings in his food before that. It wasn't until after that we learned he was taking our little ones. We'll bring you up through the cellars, past the dungeons. Now, here's the underground level. Here"—she began a second sketch next to the first—"is the ground floor and the castle grounds inside the wall."

Kel watched the lines form in the dust. Other villagers added what they knew to the maps and made suggestions for the assault. Kel went over the maps again and again, making sure the distances were as accurate as the villagers could make them. Once she had the layout fixed in her mind, she worked out her plan of attack and presented it. Some villagers, Agrane and Zerhalm included, would go with them. Kel refused to let Irnai the seer child or any of the children she had recovered accompany them. They were to stay hidden in the village. Only Tobe would go, for the warhorses. Kel, Neal, and Owen would fight afoot, but the horses would be as good as four men in a battle with the castle's soldiers.

By the villagers' count, there were a hundred and forty-six armed men inside the walls, not counting those Kel and her people had killed on the road. "The main thing is to hit fast and hard," Kel told them over supper in the village alehouse. Outside, the shadows grew long as the sun dropped toward the horizon. "We take them by surprise, before many can so much as grab a weapon. If you don't like hitting them when they're defenseless, remember that they help Blayce. Now rest, all of you. We leave at moonrise."

She walked outside to enjoy the cool air and clear her head. She paused under the tree where her sparrows had settled for the night to thank them for their help that day. Footsteps made her turn. Neal and Dom approached.

"I wish you'd let one of us go in with you," Neal began.

Kel shook her head. "Connac's squad and Gil's convicts will do very well inside. Dom and his lads on horseback will create more confusion when they get in. You're best placed with Dom—your group will be in more danger from archers than mine. You must also take command if I don't make it," she added quietly but firmly. "If I die in there, you have to get our people home. Listen to Dom—he's more used to commanding groups. But your duty is to take our folk back to Tortall."

"We'd best take these people, if they'll go," Dom pointed out. He lounged against the tree trunk, hands in breeches pockets. "Leaving them here for King Maggot seems like a bad idea."

Kel scowled. He was right. "Will you talk to them?" she asked. "After, I suppose, if we *get* an after."

"We'll get it, Kel," Dom replied, his eyes serious. "I have faith in you."

"So do I," said Neal, though he still looked troubled by her orders.

"Me too," said Owen. None of them had heard him come up. "It'll be jolly, Kel. An evil mage destroyed, a chance to take a bite out of Stenmun and his men—isn't this why you became a knight?" He looked from Neal to Kel, who both watched him, speechless. "It's why *I* want to be a knight," Owen insisted. "I may not get to be one now, but it'll be almost worth it, to rob Maggur of the killing devices. And I thought we were supposed to rest, and here you three aren't doing it."

"We're coming, Mother," Kel told Owen with a crooked smile. "Or did you learn that from Wyldon?"

Owen beamed at her, gray eyes bright with mischief. "Nope. I learned it from *you,* Mother," he teased. He ducked Kel's swipe at him and ran back to the house where they were to rest, a bounce in his step.

"That boy makes me feel old," grumbled Neal.

The path they followed under the castle walls along the Pakkai River was little more than a goat track. The ground dropped sharply into the icy river not a foot from the trail. The moonlight shimmered on the briskly moving water but granted only a little light for their feet.

Kel stepped on some fallen rock and slipped. Zerhalm, ahead of her, and Gil, at her back, grabbed her before she fell. Afterward Kel was grateful for the dark that hid her shakes. She had largely conquered her fear of heights, but she doubted any knight didn't fear the result of falling into deep water in full armor.

Agrane led, in front of Zerhalm. She guided them to a runoff tunnel from the castle's depths. Kel did not look forward to entering it—human waste was dropped into runoff tunnels—but once inside they would be out of the open, safe if the guards chose to send out a patrol.

Zerhalm came to a stop. Kel sent the signal back to her troops through Gil: wait. Kel peered around the villager's broad shoulder to see what caused the halt. Agrane stood a few yards up, running her hands over a large, grate-covered opening as if they touched a solid wall. "I don't understand!" the former cook hissed. "It was right here. I *always* counted the steps in and out!"

"They bricked it up?" asked Zerhalm. He, too, ran a hand over the opening as if it weren't there.

"Can I get by?" Kel whispered.

Zerhalm backed into a niche in the rock. Kel slid by, though a touch of her foot made the edge of the path crumble slightly. I will be *so* happy to leave through the gate, she thought as she reached Agrane. If I live to do it.

As always now, she wore her griffin-feather band. "It's an illusion," she told Agrane. "An illusion that they filled it with rock." She tested a bar of the grate. Ancient with rust, it broke in her hand, fragments dropping around her feet and rolling into the river. "That's so shoddy," Kel whispered in disgust. "He expends magic to hide the thing, but then he doesn't replace the grate. Mages—so many are lazy." She broke away more bars until she could walk into the tunnel. There was a faint clank: her helmet. She wouldn't be able to wear it in this cramped space. With a sigh Kel removed it and laid it inside the grate, out of people's way. When she re-entered the tunnel, she stooped to fit. Her glaive and longbow, strapped on her back, scraped the ceiling. Rolling her eyes, she took them off and leaned both against the wall. "Agrane, Zerhalm, come on," she whispered. "The rock's an illusion. Grab my tunic."

Agrane gripped Kel's tunic, closed her eyes, and let Kel draw her into the tunnel. Once inside, the woman looked around. "Mithros's mercy!" she exclaimed softly. "But I *felt* rock."

"Lantern," Kel urged her, helping Zerhalm to enter. While Agrane fumbled to light their lantern, Kel helped the others past the illusion. Once the humans were safely inside, the dogs and the cat trotted through.

The other lantern holders lit their wicks from Agrane's, then spread out to light the way. The dogs and the cat went ahead, scouts once more. Kel gathered her weapons and followed Agrane, her neck and shoulders aching as she tried to keep from knocking the ceiling with her head. Her glaive and bow were encumbrances that she worked around. She was certain that she would have to go through Stenmun to get to Blayce, which meant she needed both weapons.

Soon the reek in the stone passage made her eyes water and her nose itch. She breathed through her open mouth to avoid the worst of the stink, fought the urge to sneeze, and smacked her head on moldy stone. Biting her lip to stop curses from escaping her, she trudged on, catching up to Agrane.

They walked for some time. Finally Agrane halted and raised her lantern. Overhead, Kel saw a grate. This one had solid bars, but it was not anchored and a little pressure raised it. Kel handed her weapons to Agrane and carefully pushed the grate up. Once it was clear of its stone rim, she eased it to one side. Gently she lowered it to the floor overhead. With it out of the way, Kel placed her hands on either side of the opening, jumped, and levered herself out of the tunnel. Agrane passed up her glaive, bow, and a lantern: Kel took them and set them aside before she reached down to grip the woman's arms. Lifting Agrane and then Zerhalm was too easy. These people needed a proper meal.

With them to help the rest, Kel held the lantern up to view their surroundings. They were in a clearly long-forgotten storeroom. Everything was shrouded in burlap and covered with an inch of dust. Mouse droppings lay everywhere; an assortment of rustles and squeaks came from the shadows.

Kel burrowed in Agrane's pack until she found a

rugged sack attached to a coil of rope. She passed it to Agrane. As Zerhalm helped Connac, his squad, the convict soldiers, Fanche, and Saefas up, Agrane lifted out bagful after bagful of dogs, and one cat.

At last they were all in. They wiped themselves clean of tunnel muck using the burlap in the room. Kel pinched her nose against sneezes as dust rose everywhere and mice scattered in panic. The cat spotted a mouse by the door. Her forelegs went down, her bottom wriggling as she prepared to attack. Kel nudged her with a booted toe. "Don't," she whispered. "We have work ahead."

The cat gave her a glare that would peel paint. She then sat and began to wash a paw, as if washing had been her intention all along.

Once everyone was ready, Kel tried the door. It was unlocked. She slid through the narrow opening, glaive at the ready, Agrane at her back. They were in a shadowy corridor. At one end light flickered and bounced: torches in the next hall. Kel snapped her fingers softly, a signal to Jump. He trotted forward to the junction of their corridor with the one that was lit. He looked at Kel and shook his head. No one was there.

They moved quickly and silently, trying not to scrape the wall as they oozed into the next corridor. The light came from a pair of torches at an intersection ahead. Once more Jump scouted and signaled that the hall was empty. The third corridor was better lit and punctuated with closed, locked metal doors. Kel waved up the picklock, Morun, then indicated each door. He nodded his understanding and got out his picks. As Kel and Zerhalm watched the stairs to the castle's upper levels, Morun opened lock after lock. Out came the castle servants, imprisoned after supper was served because Blayce feared they might use the nights to escape. The servants looked haunted. Kel tried to send them out through the tunnel and back to their village, but most refused. Instead, they showed her to the guardroom, where they helped themselves to axes, maces, and swords.

The dogs and cat trotted upstairs to scout as Kel listened for humans. She didn't think the animals would draw attention: people rarely noticed a castle's rat catchers or hunting dogs. Agrane had said, and the present servants confirmed, that once they were locked up for the night, Blayce retreated to the upper floors to toy with the children and to conjure in his workroom. The soldiers went to their barracks, where they could ignore what went on in the keep. Kel hoped that was true, but she had to ensure that Blayce had not changed his routine tonight. Lord Raoul had drummed it into her that more expeditions went awry from bad scouting than from bad planning.

One after another the dogs returned to report. The ground level was empty. The children were in rooms on the second floor, and a lone adult male was on the third floor in a room with a closed door. The villagers and servants watched with quiet astonishment as Kel and Jump quizzed the other dogs, who conveyed answers by tapping their paws, standing on their hind legs, shaking or nodding their heads, or giving very quiet yips.

The humans climbed to the ground level and the main hall. It was a gloomy area, lit just enough to keep them from stumbling. Kel glimpsed tapestries and the usual lord's trove of weapons on the shadowed walls: spears, swords, axes, bows. The hearth fire was banked for the night, the tables and benches cleared for morning use. Here the men ate and toasted their master while Blayce fed his children dainty bits and planned their murders.

More than anything, Kel wanted to charge up to his workroom and finish him off. Somehow she kept herself in hand. Ignoring her carefully laid plans would get her and those who depended on her killed. Instead, she resettled her armor and waited. Jump, Shepherd, and two other dogs led Agrane, Gil, and Gil's five convict soldiers, all armed, upstairs. They wore soft cloth wrappings over their boots or shoes to muffle their steps.

Kel went to the foot of the stair to listen, straining to hear anything that did not sound right. Time slowed. A few of the servants, Connac, Zerhalm, Fanche, Saefas, and Connac's squad went to the kitchen, where a side door led outside. It made a better exit for their purposes than the front door, which was framed with torches that burned throughout the night. If they went out that way, in all likelihood the guards on the castle walls would see them and alert comrades in the barracks.

Sweat trickled down Kel's temples. So much could go wrong here. . . . Blayce might want a late-night snack; a messenger from King Maggur might arrive. A restless soldier might wander and glimpse her people. The children might make noise.

Stop it, Kel! she ordered herself. *Neal's the one with the imagination, not you.*

At last a child appeared at the top of the stair. He was dressed in a white velvet tunic, hose, lacy-collared shirt, gold chain belt. If it hadn't been for the half-bald doll clutched in his arms, Kel would never have recognized Meech in this pretty lordling. He saw her and raced down the steps to hug her fiercely around her armored waist. Behind him came a flood of children, all barefooted, all clean, dressed in silks, velvets, lace, and brocade, their hair brushed and ordered. They trotted down as quickly and quietly as Meech had, though a few wept silently: Kel saw the glitter of tears in the faint torchlight. Meech wasn't the only one to seize her in a frantic hug. Kel kissed the heads of any she could reach and traded handclasps with the rest.

Here came Agrane and the convict soldiers with the infants. The youngest children made no sound, either. Neal had given Agrane drops to make them sleep until dawn. The dogs swarmed around them as they descended the stair.

Kel waved the remaining servants in and hand-signed slowly, making sure they understood her. They were to help Agrane take the children to safety through the tunnel, *now.* Each time a servant opened his or her mouth to argue, Kel put a finger to her lips. When it was clear that she wouldn't take no for an answer, they gathered the children and led them downstairs. If this attack goes wrong, at least the children will escape, Kel thought.

As the last of them vanished on the stair to the dungeon, Kel turned to discover that not all of the children had left. Gydo and Loesia stood there, armed with spears they had taken from brackets on the wall.

Kel draped an arm around each girl's thin shoulders and murmured, "You could get killed."

"We'll fight till then," Loesia replied, her voice barely

a whisper. Gydo nodded. Kel looked from one girl to the other. At twelve she had battled bandits and spidrens. She doubted that commoner girls had any less courage than noble ones did. She motioned toward the kitchen hall.

The people who had gone ahead waited there. Some of the men carried three long kitchen tables. Kel nodded when she saw them. They could block some barracks exits with these. Handing her glaive to Gil, she strung her bow and checked her quiver of griffin-fletched arrows. She chose several and handed them to her best archers: Fanche, Saefas, Gil, and one of Connac's men. This was the trickiest part, dividing Blayce's soldiers into bite-sized groups and opening the gate to Dom's squad, Neal, Owen, and the warhorses.

Once the arrows were distributed, Kel went for a look outside. The inner courtyard was just as Agrane had described it, torchlit all the way around on the lower part of the wall. The barracks stood at a right angle to the kitchens, with the privy a separate building behind them. The stables stood on the opposite side of the courtyard; the main gate was directly across from the keep. As a castle it was just enough to hold off bandits and neighbors. It was also a perfect isolated location for a mage who worked death magic.

Hidden from the sentries by a low woodshed, Kel scanned the wall. A couple of wagons stood against the wall between kitchen and barracks. She pointed them out to Connac, who hand-signaled his men. Four of them followed him through the shadows to the wagons. They, like the kitchen tables, could barricade the rear and side exits of the barracks once things got moving.

First they had to deal with the sentries who paced the walls. The portcullis was down, the gate up. With no soldiers on the ground, Kel guessed that Stenmun didn't think she could attack the castle in any strength.

And maybe if he'd treated the locals better, he wouldn't have to worry, she thought, counting the sentries. There were five, all in view. With the castle's curtain wall built snug against the cliff, Stenmun couldn't post guards there, out of Kel's sight, even if he'd wanted to. Kel shook her head at this further sloppiness and signaled her archers one by one, indicating which sentry to bring down. Carefully she fitted a griffin-fletched arrow to her bow.

Her people were as ready as they could get. Kel stepped into the open, sighting on the guard she had chosen. All wore leather jerkins with iron plaques sewn to them, scant protection against big longbows, which could punch an arrow through plate armor. Kel loosed; five more bowstrings snapped around her. Her sentry went to his knees as her arrow struck him in the back. Gil's arrow hit his man on the helm and glanced off. He instantly put another arrow into the air before the man could shout the alarm. The sentry went down with an arrow in his eye. Kel made sure of her guard with a second arrow, conscious of the thuds of falling bodies and the creak of wooden wheels as her men pushed wagons toward the barracks.

The men carrying tables quietly braced them against three sets of shutters. Kel saw no light through the shutters or under the barracks doors, but she still approved of her people's stealth. The more exits they could block before the soldiers woke, the better their chances for survival.

Uinse appeared around the far side of the barracks and waved. Kel motioned to those whose chore it was to open the gate, then pointed her archers to their positions on the keep steps and the far side of the barracks, where they could shoot anyone who escaped. She and Connac stood on either side of the only barracks door that was not blocked, the front one. Other men took places on either side of the shutters that opened onto the courtyard, their own weapons ready.

Kel looked at the men at the gate. They had their hands on the winches that would raise the portcullis. Once it was up, they could admit the rest of their friends. Kel raised her arm and let it drop. The men put their backs into the winches, straining to raise the heavy portcullis. The thing made a crunching noise that Kel would have sworn was audible in Corus, but long moments passed in silence before she heard the pounding of feet inside the barracks.

The door opened and a man stuck his head out. Kel cut him down. Another man stumbled across his body to die at Connac's hand. Inside, Kel heard men hammering at the blocked doors and shutters. Here came another soldier, half armed over a nightshirt. Kel rammed her glaive into his unprotected side while Connac chopped at the next man's neck.

Yells and the crash of wood told Kel the unblocked shutters near her were open. The men positioned there did their best to kill anyone who came out. A second crash: the other shutters didn't fly open as much as they shot off their hinges. Three men tumbled out of the barracks into the courtyard dirt. Her fighters were on them.

A Scanran in chain mail swung at Connac with a big hand-and-a-half sword, forcing the soldier back. Kel darted in and blocked his stroke with her glaive. Sparks flew as glaive met sword: the Scanran's weapon was made of good steel. Now Kel had a fight on her hands. She parried the man's next swing and jabbed at his middle. He lunged back, then leaped forward again, chopping. She parried as she backed up a step to give herself room. He chopped down a third time. Kel came up inside his weapon's reach, driving her blade up into her foe's armpit. The glaive parted his mail like a hot knife passed through butter, biting into the big veins in the armpit. Kel freed her glaive and thrust at a new attacker, a blond man who advanced on her, howling, axes in both hands.

"Idiot," Kel muttered. She swung her glaive up between his legs, slashing his thigh muscle. The man went down. She killed him.

She glanced at the gate. The portcullis was up; her men fought to lift the heavy bar on the wooden gate. One last shove and it was off. Eagerly they thrust the halves apart to admit Dom's squad, Neal, Owen, and the warhorses.

It was a mess after that, one Kel was hard put to follow. Two of the tables failed, giving the men in the barracks less hazardous ways to leave the building. Peachblossom saw three of them race around the corner of the barracks and plunged into their midst, spinning as he lashed them with his forelegs, then dropping to kick out with his hind legs. The men flew into the air. When they landed, Peachblossom was waiting for them.

Kel was holding off two men with swords, both veterans who respected the reach of her glaive, when Owen rode up behind them, cutting one man down from behind as Happy butted the other with his armored head. The second man fell and Kel finished him off. She hated to kill men on the ground, but it had to be done. She couldn't let word of their presence get out. She did it, but she knew she would feel the glaive cutting flesh and bone for a very long time.

There was Dom, calling out orders to his squad, blade flashing as he rode down two men who ran out of the barracks. There was Neal, crouched beside Gil as one of Blayce's soldiers ran at him, sword raised high. Kel was about to scream a warning when Neal turned on his knees, the sword in his hand biting deep into his attacker's side. It seemed he had learned more than just healing from Alanna the Lioness.

Morun, her picklock, was dead on the keep steps. Loesia, Gydo, and Tobe circled a soldier, their spears leveled at him. Shepherd hung from a man's throat despite his prey's frantic hammering on his ribs. Jump seized the wrist of a man who was about to stab Fanche as she knelt over Saefas. As Jump swung from the man's sword arm, Fanche gutted the attacker, hate in her eyes.

Throughout the entire mess Kel was aware of a tall man, his long, gray-blond hair loose, bellowing orders as he cleared the ground around him with a big double-bladed axe. He briefly managed to get a few soldiers into a position they could defend, their backs to the keep wall, but Peachblossom, Owen, and Happy rode at them, the horses as bent on victory as Owen. The men scattered.

Loesia screamed. Tobe was shot, an arrow in his side. Kel leaped to fend off the men who converged on the girls and Tobe. Jump, the gray-and-orange cat, Dom, and Neal's horse, Magewhisper, all followed her. Within moments the younger fighters' attackers were dead. Kel brought Tobe to Neal herself.

It was nearly over. A few soldiers fought to reach the gate, but they wouldn't make it: Kel could see that. What she couldn't see was Stenmun, but she knew where to find him.

"Neal," she said. He looked up as he held a green-glowing hand over a deep gash in Gil's chest. "I'm going after Blayce. If I'm not out when you've secured this place, take our people home."

He nodded, half of his concentration on Gil. "I'll remind 'im, lady," croaked Tobe. Loesia wept as she knelt with her friend.

"Good," Kel said, trying not to show her fear for her boy. Later she could give way to emotion. Right now, if Blayce and Stenmun escaped, all this would mean nothing. "Try to stay alive, will you?" She turned for a last survey of the battle scene. Her people had won. That was as plain as the glaive in her hand. They could finish up. She wiped her forehead on her sleeve before remembering her sleeve was mail, grimaced, and headed into the keep.

"Gods all guard you, lady," she heard Tobe call.

The main hall was empty. Kel climbed to the second floor as Jump, the cat, and several other dogs spread out around her. She listened for any sound of an ambush. The second floor, where the children had been kept, was also empty. She hadn't expected anything else, but she waited until the dogs returned to let her know they had found no one. Just because she didn't expect to find Stenmun or

Blayce here didn't mean she could go on as if they weren't. Mistakes like that got people killed.

Again the dogs and cat preceded her up the stair. She *did* expect to find Stenmun here, guarding his master's workroom. Stenmun was Blayce's dog: he would guard the mage and leave the men who looked to him for leadership to die.

Jump yelped and leaped to the side as an axe blade cut the air where he had been. Sparks flew when the blade hit the stone steps. Kel instantly lunged up the stair as Stenmun recovered. She kept low, her glaive held over her head as a shield. When the axe came down again, she parried it with the teak staff of her weapon, wincing as the axe cut chips from the wood. She parried a second lunge and made it to level flooring. Stenmun swung his axe sidelong, chopping at her armored waist. Kel knocked the heavy blade aside and slammed the iron-shod foot of the staff into the big man's ribs. They circled, eyes intent on one another.

It wasn't often that Kel had to look up to a man, but Stenmun was a head taller than she, a big, hard-muscled warrior with the merciless stare of a water snake. Though she was armored and he wore only a shirt and breeches, she knew he was going to make her work for victory.

The muscles in Stenmun's arms flexed, making Kel think he would try a big chop. Instead, he jabbed with the pointed, spearlike tip between the twin crescents of the axe blades. Kel knocked the axe aside just enough that the point punched through her mail into her left shoulder instead of into her throat. A blaze of fire leaped in her left side. She stepped back to get her bearings.

"I just want to know," she said as they circled each other once more, "why do you do this? You bring the children, you know what he does—why?"

Stenmun raised his eyebrows as if he were shocked by the question. "He pays me well," he informed Kel.

"That's *it*?" Kel demanded, shocked. "Just *money*? Are you mad?"

"Isn't that just like a noble?" asked the Scanran. "Only you rich folk think money doesn't mean anything. Listen, these commoners' brats die all the time. Famine, disease, war—something gets them." He feinted at Kel, who dodged and feinted back. He blocked, still talking. "At least Blayce's way they have a bit of fun and a decent meal before they go, and *we* have King Maggur's gratitude."

He closed in, his eyes alight, thinking he had her. With a yowl that made the hair stand on Kel's neck, the cat who had made him bleed on the road once more launched herself onto Stenmun's head. She clung to his scalp with three sets of claws and swiped at his eyes with the fourth. Stenmun yowled and flailed at the cat one-handed, using his other hand to try to keep his axe between him and Kel. Jump leaped and grabbed the big man in a place no human male should be grabbed. Stenmun roared. He tried to smack Jump away while throwing himself backward at the wall in an attempt to jar the cat from his scalp.

Kel lunged, bracing her glaive with her right wrist and elbow so she could wield it one-handed. She thrust at Stenmun's belly. He kicked her weapon aside and struck Jump with the butt of his axe. The dog let go. Stenmun hit the cat against a stone arch. She tumbled from his head, leaving ribbons of blood to flow from the wounds she'd inflicted.

Now Stenmun charged Kel, bringing his weapon up in a two-handed chop. She swung her glaive up to block the axe and twisted the teak staff, locking it and the axe haft together. Stenmun leaned into the jammed weapons, forcing them back on Kel. They strained. Kel's arm trembled with the force he put on it.

Stenmun smiled. "Too bad for you, little girl," he said, his voice tight with triumph.

Kel gave him her politest Yamani smile, hooked her leg around one of his, and jerked, a leg sweep from her studies in hand-to-hand combat. Her legs were powerful and he wasn't braced. He went down on his back, hitting so hard the breath was knocked from his lungs. His fall jerked his axe clear of her glaive. Kel didn't wait for an invitation. She brought the iron-shod butt of the glaive down with all her strength, striking him right between the eyes, breaking through his skull. That probably finished him, but to be sure, she cut his throat.

For a moment she stood over him, leaning on her glaive, gasping for breath. Then she looked for her friends. The other dogs stood in front of a closed door. Jump limped toward them, a long scrape on his left shoulder bleeding sluggishly. Kel couldn't even remember when he'd been hurt. She looked for the cat. The animal lay against the wall, unmoving.

"I hope the Black God has something tasty for you," she whispered to Stenmun, and spat on him. Then she cut strips from his shirt to bandage the hole he'd put in her, so that she wouldn't bleed to death. The wound hurt sharply as she pressed a wad of strips against it and bound them tightly around her shoulder and under her arm. Only when she finished did the pain settle into a dull, steady pounding. The cut didn't seem to be too deep, though it was cursed inconveniently placed.

She looked at the door where her dogs stood and stepped toward it. The door moved away. Kel stepped again to close the distance. Now it seemed a hundred yards away, which was much too far for the size of the keep. A third step took the door two hundred yards back. She could barely see the dogs.

Kel put her good hand to her head and ground her teeth. At some point, a missed blow had cut the griffin headband from her forehead. She looked until she found it hanging over the top step of the stair. Kel lurched over to the band and picked it up, balancing her glaive against her shoulder. When she straightened, the room spun.

"Blood loss," she said aloud. "Never mind." She turned and laid the band over her eyebrows. The dogs and the closed door were just ten feet away. *Is it locked?* she wondered. It might be. She made herself go to Stenmun's body and grope in his belt pouch. Here was the key.

It took her a moment to get the key in the lock. Her hand shook as badly as the rest of her. Finally the stiff mechanism opened. "I hope the Chamber was right and he's out of killing devices," she muttered. "Else I'm dead and am just about to find it out." She thrust the door wide. The dogs streamed in ahead of her as Kel walked straight into her nightmare.

18
BLAYCE

Here was the smithy, and the shelves, and the table. Here were the barrels of iron-covered giants' bones and the guttered table. The reek of old blood was even stronger than it had been when the Chamber had shown her this place the second time.

The Nothing Man paced back and forth before the ordinary hearth, not looking at Kel as he gnawed a thumbnail. "Stenmun, tell me how you let them get in," he whined in Scanran.

"I'm not Stenmun," Kel replied steadily in Common.

The mage turned to stare at her, his brown eyes wide with shock. The hand he'd been gnawing on went to his chest. He held the other up to her, palm-out, as she advanced on him. He was as pasty-skinned as she had dreamed, small, and unhealthy-looking, with nails bitten down to the quick of his fingers and strips of angry red flesh around them where he'd picked away bits of skin. His robes were ratty and stained, his brown hair short and uncombed. "I don't know who you are or what you are doing here, but King Maggur will be most displeased when he finds you've interrupted me at my work. It's vital to the war. You've broken my concentration. You'll pay, my overeager friend. If you want to keep even a shred of life, you'll get out and fetch Stenmun to me."

"I don't answer to Maggur, Stenmun, or you," Kel retorted. "I just came to see what a monster looks like."

Blayce opened his mouth, then closed it. He peered at her for a moment, obviously confused. At last he said, "You're not Scanran."

"They said you were clever," Kel told him bitterly. He was the worst letdown of her life. She had expected someone with Numair's or Daine's air of hidden power, or Baird's suggestion of iron strength, not this ratlike creature. He truly was a Nothing Man. How could the gods have let such a creature wreak so much havoc?

"You're Tortallan," Blayce said, now speaking in Common. "You—you've . . ." His eyes darted around the room, as if he were looking for an escape hatch. "Gods be praised, you've saved me!"

He lurched toward Kel with open arms. She brought up her glaive, its point aimed at his throat. "Not another step," she warned.

"I don't know what your masters told you, but it was lies. Stenmun forced me to do it, for King Maggur. I had no choice. They said they'd kill me. You've saved my life." He fiddled nervously with a jeweled pendant around his neck. "Gods, I thought I'd never be free."

"Liar," Kel told him softly. "The lives I'm saving are those of the children you had fetched to you. I thought Stormwings were monsters, but they aren't. They're what they were made to be. You chose your path." She made her voice hard, but her soul was in an uproar. How could she do this? Was she going to cut him down in cold blood? He was no more able to physically defend himself than Meech. "*You're* the monster, Blayce the Gallan."

"*Chose?*" he whined. "I didn't choose where my greatness lay. Don't you think I'd rather make a place in the world by healing, or bringing rain to places stricken by drought? Necromancy is where my talents are. I must work with what I have."

"Liar," retorted Kel. "You *like* what you do."

He drew himself up. "I'm a great mage, whoever you are, and you'll treat me with respect." He attempted to sound haughty but only sounded anxious as he fiddled with his pendant. "Don't think yourself fit to judge magics you can't comprehend, or great mages. A sword thug like you couldn't hope to understand the subtleties of my mind."

"You torture and murder children, then enslave their spirits for conquest and more murder," Kel told him, leaning on her glaive for support. It was hard to remember if she had ever been so tired. "That's all I *need* to understand." She wished he would leave the pendant alone. The light that glanced from it felt like needles in her eyes.

"You don't want to be rash," Blayce said. The pendant he fiddled with so nervously held a jewel of some kind. "Think. Your king could win this war if I helped him. Not only do I have the secrets of these devices, but I know King

Maggur. I know his plans. That could be worth a great deal to you. Honor from the Crown, perhaps more land, more gold, more respect at court."

Kel swayed and dimly realized what he was doing. He was using the pendant to try to catch her mind, just as Numair had warned some mages could do, back when he'd visited Haven.

With a growled curse she swung the glaive at Blayce as she might swing a club, with no thought but to break his hold on her. He was an illusion: the glaive passed through him. Kel turned around, searching for the real Blayce, sweeping her glaive in front of her.

"You really ought to listen to me, sir knight." His whine came from every direction. Kel advanced, hoping to hit him if somehow he'd made himself invisible, swinging her glaive left and right. "Trust me when I tell you I know kings. They use every tool they can find. Your monarchs will welcome any chance to defeat King Maggur and save themselves a long war. My devices will give them that power. You don't want to throw away the most powerful weapon that your king can put his hand on."

"He would never take help from the likes of you," Kel said, trying to pinpoint the location of his voice. "Never." She advanced, thrusting her glaive into the room's nooks and crannies.

"For all you know, I'm not even in this room," Blayce taunted.

Kel halted. This was foolishness. If she weren't dizzy from blood loss, she would have known better than to hunt a mage unaided. She groped in her belt for the pieces of the griffin-feather band, then held them over her eyes.

"What are those?" Blayce demanded sharply. "There is power in them, but not the Gift. What hedgewitch made that?"

Kel turned. His voice still came from all around. But now she saw him, standing on top of his worktable.

She thrust the pieces of the band into her breastplate. She knew she had to kill him quickly, before he caught her in the mind-gripping spell of his pendant, or with any other magics.

She brought up her glaive in a controlled slash, one-handed, part of the staff lined up against her arm to steady it. She caught Blayce at the knees, cutting the muscles behind them. He dropped, turning visible to her unaided eyes, his control over his invisibility spell gone. Kel seized her glaive two-handed and yanked the blade toward her, neatly beheading the Gallan.

She swayed, exhausted. That was it. The man who had haunted her for nearly six long months was dead at last.

"You're wrong about my king, I think," she told the body. "But better that he not have the chance to be tempted by the likes of you. And frankly? What you just got was far more merciful than you deserve."

She stopped, thinking about what she'd just said, and smiled briefly. He *had* deserved worse, yet she had not given it to him. That was something to be proud of, and it made up for her carelessness in almost getting trapped by the pendant spell. With a sigh of relief, she leaned on her glaive, trembling with exhaustion. What next?

Jump pawed her leg and whined. When Kel looked at him, he took a dog's pointing stance, his twice-broken tail quivering as he stared at the door.

Using the glaive as a crutch, Kel turned. What she saw was not the door she had come through, but another, familiar entryway lined in bright blue light. She now looked at the door to the Chamber of the Ordeal from the inside. The face sculpted in its keystone looked at her. It eyes shone yellow, as they had during Kel's previous experiences with the thing.

Very tidy, its voice announced in her mind. *I said you would do it, and you have.*

Kel gripped her glaive until her fingers creaked inside her gloves. "Yes, it's done," she replied. "I 'fixed' it. I killed a swordless man and saw a lot of good people murdered. Now you have your balance, I have the little ones, and you and I are quits, understand? Find someone else to do what you can't."

Yes, we are finished. Do you think this makes you free of your fate? asked the Chamber. *You are the Protector of the Small. You see real people in the humans and animals overlooked by your peers. There will always be work for you.*

Kel scowled. "I don't mind that," she retorted. "It's what I mean to do, though I'd never call it by as silly a name as Protector of the Small. At least now I know where I'm going and what I'm doing, which I never did with you. I can find my own road from here." She strode toward the door, praying it would open in Scanra. Jump and the dogs followed her.

As she put her hand on the latch, she heard the voice say, *Gods all bless, Keladry of Mindelan.* She stepped outside. She was still in Blayce's keep. Before she could shut the door, the Chamber added, with something that sounded like wicked humor, *Protector of the Small.*

Grumbling about Chambers that thought too highly of themselves, Kel stumbled down the hall. She blinked at Stenmun's corpse: her fight with him felt like something that had taken place years before. Looking past him, she saw the gray-and-orange cat against the wall.

It was a foolish thing to do. She knew that as she did it. Somehow she got down to one knee, hanging on to the glaive as if her life depended on it. Carefully she leaned it against the wall until she could gather up the cat's body and drape it over her good shoulder. She didn't want to leave so brave a fighter in the same building as Stenmun and Blayce.

Dizziness flooded her as she fought her way to her feet. The floor seemed to roll and lurch. Wetness on her left side told her she had bled through the makeshift bandage on her shoulder. She had forgotten all about her wound during her fight with Blayce.

"Sometimes battle fever is a good thing," she mumbled to the anxious dogs. For a moment she rested against the wall. Then, with a grunt of effort, she took up her glaive and hobbled slowly across the yawing floor, bound for the staircase. Her head swam as she took first one step, then another. The stair rail she clung to began to sway along with her body.

Once she reached the ground floor, she stopped. Just for a moment or two, she told herself. Somehow she propped herself against the wall. Gently she placed the cat's body on the floor beside her. Then Kel closed her eyes.

* * *

When she woke, it was past sunrise. She lay on a pallet in the courtyard of the castle. Her first sight was of Stormwings lined up on the outer wall, watching greedily as the Tortallans built a funeral pyre for their dead. The Scanran dead had been left where they fell, except for two. Stenmun and Blayce—his head and body—lay in an open part of the courtyard, their faces bluish white.

Kel struggled to sit up. Her blankets felt like sheets of lead. Dogs who sat in a ring around her moved up and dragged the covers away. Putting a hand down, Kel found a small, warm body at her side. She looked down into the emerald eyes of the gray-and-orange cat. The cat blinked, and began to purr.

"She was only stunned." Tobe knelt beside her. He sported a set of bandages. "Bad stunned, but Zerhalm has the Gift with healing animals. She's near as good as new."

"That's good indeed, then. Saefas?" asked Kel.

Tobe pointed. Dom was helping the trapper mount a horse. Kel was glad to see that there were plenty of castle horses in addition to their own. Escape from Scanra would be much easier if everyone, adult and child, was mounted.

Hands—Fanche's and Gydo's—helped Kel sit up. Woman and girl both looked the worse for wear, but Kel saw a new, fierce gleam in their eyes. "They call what happened to you seeing the kraken," she told them, her voice a croak. "It means you've survived the ordeal of war."

"An honor I'd as soon have done without," retorted Fanche. "You look like the kraken found you too tough to chew and spat you out."

Kel looked at her left shoulder. The bandage was fairly clean and unstained by blood. She felt pounding there that would probably get worse, but at least she was no longer bleeding.

Kel looked for Neal. Dom's remaining corporal, Wolset, was helping him lurch over to Kel. Like most of Kel's people, Wolset wore bandages, his on his arm. The bandages meant that while Neal had done his best, he had been forced to spread his Gift thin to keep as many people alive as he could. Only the gravest wounds had been tended. The rest would have to wait.

She inspected Neal as Wolset brought him over. Her friend had seen better days. His skin was pale and sweaty, his eyes feverish. When he saw her, Neal glared. "You call that mess you had on a bandage?" he demanded sharply. "I was picking threads out of your wound. I stopped the bleeding, at least, and cleaned it. What business did you have getting wounded in the first place?"

"You, you should—" croaked Kel. Her parched throat refused to emit another sound.

"She's bone dry," snapped Neal. "Any of you battle baits have a water flask?"

Someone offered her a full water skin. Kel drank, and drank, and drank. When she felt halfway human again, she told Neal, "You should see the other fellow." She looked over at the bodies of the mage and his protector. "What are Blayce and Stenmun doing out here?"

"The local folk wouldn't believe they were dead till they saw the bodies," Fanche explained. "Can't exactly blame them for that."

"No, I suppose not," Kel whispered. She drank some

more water, then struggled to her feet. "Let me think a moment."

Someone put her glaive into her right hand. Kel used it like a staff as she looked around the courtyard, trying to decide what to do next. The Tortallan pyre was nearly ready, which was good. She hobbled over to measure their losses. They were harsh. Gil lay there; Neal hadn't been able to save the former hill bandit. So too did Sergeant Connac, Morun the picklock, Lofren and Corporal Fulcher of Dom's squad, and three of Connac's men. The pyre also included animals: Owen's Happy, the dog Shepherd, the hound Owen had wanted to take back to Wyldon, and two more dogs. Kel would cry for them later, in private. She had other problems now.

In a corner by the gate Kel saw Tobe's friend Loesia, hidden in the shadows. She walked over, her legs stiff, to find the girl kneeling beside one of the Scanran dead, her face in her hands. A spear was buried in the man's body.

"Loey, what's the matter?" she asked, using Tobe's nickname for her.

"Him," said the girl, showing Kel a tearstained face. "He was—he was good to me. He took care of me all the way here, he was nice, and I killed him."

Kel shook her head. "He couldn't have been that nice," she reminded the girl. "He was bringing you here to die."

Loey wiped her eyes, leaving streaks of dirt on her face. "I know I ought to think of that, Lady Kel," she whispered. "But he was nice when I was scared. How can I feel good about killing him?"

Kel sank to one knee, still hanging on to her glaive. Awkwardly she put her wounded arm around the girl's velvet-clad shoulders. "There would be something wrong with you if you did," she said quietly, thinking of the men she had killed. "Try to think of the young folk who will live because he and his master are dead. And come on. It's time to go home."

It took Loesia and Dom to get Kel on her feet again. Her people gathered around her with that look on their faces, the one that said they trusted her to see them through the next bit of madness. Kel took a deep breath and plunged in. "We need to get out of here sooner rather than later," she told them. "I want the torch put to the keep—make sure the level where Blayce kept his workroom burns in particular. Take nothing out of there. I mean *nothing*." Her worst nightmare was that someone might find Blayce's workbooks and commit his crimes all over again. She watched as a handful of men and women ran to take care of the keep, then continued, "The keep burning will be a torch for the countryside. The quicker we go, the safer we'll be."

Tobe brought Peachblossom to her. Dom and Zerhalm helped her mount up. She was steadier in the saddle, more clearheaded. She took part in the prayers for the Tortallan dead from Peachblossom's back and watched as Owen lit their funeral pyre. The young squire's chubby face was set, his mouth a grim line.

Slowly, one by one, her people mounted up. Some formed strings of free horses and placed them on a lead rein. They would carry the rest of their company, the children, back to Tortall.

By now the upper floors of the keep were burning well. Smoke poured from every window. The heat of the keep and the funeral pyre slowly drove Kel and her people back toward the gate.

"Lady Kel?" asked Saefas. He was still on foot. "The Scanrans? Douse 'em with oil and light 'em up?"

Kel looked at the bodies of the soldiers who had carried children into Blayce's grasp, at Stenmun, who had commanded them and who had killed so well and efficiently for pay, and at Blayce, the most commonplace monster she might ever meet. Was it a curse on the world, Kel wondered, that Blayce managed to find empty men like Stenmun to carry out his wishes? But if that were so, what manner of curse harmed so many unrelated people, Scanran and Tortallan?

No, she decided, the gods always had good, clear, plain reasons for curses and blessings alike. The bloody triangle made by Blayce, Stenmun, and Maggur was sheer, clumsy, human bad luck.

She lifted her eyes to the walls. The Stormwings were restless, watching the fire consume the Tortallan dead. They sidled to and fro, one eye on Kel's people and their bows. Only the female who had insisted on talking to Kel all along remained still, her dark eyes fixed on Kel's face.

"Someone ought to get some good for this. Leave them for the Stormwings," Kel told Saefas, and rode out of the gate.

It took them five days to return to the Vassa River. The children, those villagers who refused to stay in a place that had so many painful memories of their dead, the freed castle servants, and the seer child, Irnai, couldn't ride for as long a time as warriors. Kel's band took as much care to hide their presence leaving as they had on their way north, the sparrows and the dogs alerting them to any human presence. They lit no fires as they worked their way down the Pakkai and along the Smiskir road. When they set watches, the servants and villagers from Blayce's domain stood guard alongside the soldiers.

At last they reached the Vassa. Neal disappeared briefly with Dom and Owen to find the Scanran relatives of their smugglers. These men and women looked every bit as hard and wary as their Tortallan counterparts. Kel would have grinned at the obvious shock on their faces when they saw how many children were in their company, but her sore shoulder left her with almost no sense of humor. She knew she would be better once a healer was able to finish the healing Neal had started, though she didn't look forward to being made healthy only to face execution.

Once they were in sight of Tortall, she considered deserting her people but knew that she couldn't. She owed it to the children to get them to a place of safety, for one. For another, flight would mean that she took no responsibility for what she had done. That was unacceptable. She had done what was necessary. She would take the consequences.

Owen and Neal, who had as much to lose as she did, made no mention of flight. Kel thought that was simply the result of what they had gone through: Owen was still too grief-stricken over the loss of Happy, Neal too exhausted from keeping a number of wounded people alive to reach Tortall. Kel wondered if she should ask them if they meant to run but decided not to. They were grown men; they knew the risks as well as she did.

The smugglers took forever to get them across: they had not anticipated being used as ferrymen for crowds of escapees and their escorts for free, they told Kel. She realized they did not just mean her and her group. When she asked, they told her that Merric and his people had crossed three days before. They were quarreling with each other nonstop, according to the smugglers, but all were alive and well. Kel was freed of that worry, at least.

She, Jump, and Peachblossom were on the last boat with Neal, Dom, Owen, Tobe, and their mounts. If the crossing was as bumpy as it had been on her way north, Kel didn't notice. She was asleep by the rail before they cast off.

As the boat ground against the river's Tortallan shore, Neal shook her awake. Kel groaned, stood, and led Peachblossom onto solid ground. Only then did she see that a welcoming committee awaited them: Lord Wyldon, Lord Raoul, and Duke Baird. Behind them stood Merric, Seaver, and Esmond.

Kel knelt and bowed her head in submission to Lord Wyldon, awaiting his judgment. Neal and Owen knelt on either side of her. Jump and the sparrows put themselves in front of Kel. She felt Peachblossom's warm breath on the back of her neck.

"Sergeant Domitan, tell me these children aren't the result of your squad's Scanran frolics," Kel heard Raoul say cheerfully. "Though I do admit, some of them look a little old to be yours."

"Well, sir, my men helped," Dom said, the picture of boyish mischief.

Kel almost smiled. At least Dom would get away from this with a whole skin, it seemed. She'd wondered if his tale of Lord Raoul's sending his squad to help had been just that, a tale. It was a relief to know it was the truth and Dom had been acting under proper orders.

"You missed a tidy fight," Raoul said. "Smashed one of King Maggot's little armies all to bits. Come along and I'll tell you about it." Dom and his remaining men followed him up the path.

Kel looked sideways when she picked up movement on the edges of her vision. Duke Baird was gathering up the children who had already landed. He was telling them, "We'll just have a look, to see how well you are. I know some mothers and fathers who are eager to see you all." To the civilian adults, Scanran and Tortallan, he said, "And you look as if you could use proper meals and beds. Come along."

Kel lowered her head once more. Only she, Neal, and Owen remained with Lord Wyldon and the friends who had brought the adult refugees home.

Owen was the first to break the silence. He looked up at Lord Wyldon, tears running down his face. "My lord, I'm sorry, but I got Happy killed. I didn't mean to—he fought as hard as any knight—but he got killed anyway, and I never wanted that."

"Is that all you have to say to me, that your horse is dead?" Kel heard that familiar cool, measured voice say over her head.

"No, my lord." Owen bowed his head. "I disobeyed you. I betrayed you. And I'd do it again, under the circumstances, not meaning any disrespect, sir. But I miss Happy."

"And you, Sir Nealan, have you any comments?" Lord Wyldon inquired, his voice quite mild.

"No, my lord," Neal replied.

"I believe, Owen, that you are familiar with my dislike of needless dramatics," Lord Wyldon said. "I am not about to declare you a traitor because the mount I gave you was killed in battle. He did what he was trained to do. I am sad for the loss of the horse—he was one of the best I've raised—but I would be sorrier still for the loss of a squire in whom I can take pride."

"Sir?" chorused Neal, Owen, and Kel, all staring at their former training master.

Wyldon stood iron straight, arms crossed over his chest, his dark eyes observant as he looked at them. "One of the hardest lessons for any commander is this: it is a very bad idea to issue an order one knows will not be obeyed. Lady knight, had my mind not been on other things, I would have known better than to forbid you to rescue your people. I had placed them under your care, knowing you would protect them with every skill at your disposal. I cannot now say I didn't want you to take your responsibility too seriously. The same applies to Sir Nealan and to Sir Merric, who were also charged with their well-being. If I do not punish you, then I cannot in fairness punish those who aided you."

Kel glanced past Lord Wyldon to Merric, Seaver, and Esmond. All three looked sheepish.

"But my lord," she began to protest.

A hard arm wrapped around her head; a callused palm sealed her mouth. *"Not a word,"* Neal whispered in her ear.

"For once in your life, will you take a gift without arguing that you aren't worthy of it?" He looked up at Wyldon. "She took a blow to the head, I think," he said, falsely earnest. "It leads her to say odd things. She needs a stay in the infirmary, just until she comes to her senses."

Wyldon sighed and resettled his sword belt. "It appalls me to say this, but for the first time I find myself in agreement with Sir Nealan." He warned Neal, "Do not let it go to your head."

Kel, Neal's hand still firmly over her mouth, blinked up at Wyldon. She was free? She wasn't to die a traitor, or be forced to leave Tortall?

Wyldon looked at Owen, then at Neal. "I would like a moment alone with the lady knight," he said more formally. "Go with your friends."

Slowly Neal withdrew his hand as Owen looked suspiciously at his knight-master. "You're not going to yell at her, are you, sir?" he asked. "Because you can't."

Wyldon looked at the younger man, brows raised. "I beg your pardon?" he inquired. Kel expected frost to issue from his mouth with the words.

The Owen of a month ago might have ducked his head and fled. This Owen remained where he was, meeting Wyldon's stare with resolve. "She doesn't deserve to be yelled at, not after losing so many people and killing Blayce and being wounded and keeping us alive."

Wyldon sighed and fingered the raised scar on his temple. "I do not intend to yell at her. *Now* will you go away?"

Before they went, Neal and Owen dragged Kel to her feet. As they trudged off, Kel tried to knock away the pieces of grass and damp earth on her knees. Once she knew her friends were out of earshot, she straightened and met Lord Wyldon's eyes. "You have every right to yell at me, my lord," she said. "Go ahead. I deserve worse."

Wyldon took a step closer to her, cupped her head in both hands, and kissed her gently on the forehead. "You are a true knight, Keladry of Mindelan," he told her. "I am honored to know you." He steered her down the path her friends had taken. "Interesting news came from the battle-fronts this morning," he said. "Apparently the killing devices at Frasrlund and the City of the Gods collapsed in the field and move no longer. King Maggur's troops are plainly frightened, though he is still in control. The spy-masters plan to set it about that a powerful new mage has entered the war on our side, one who did away with the devices."

Kel smiled crookedly.

"Not that we're done fighting," Wyldon continued. "Frightened Scanrans are dangerous, and Maggur is still king. Have you thought about your duties now, where you will be assigned?"

His question took Kel by surprise. She searched for a coherent answer until at last she said, "My lord, up until we landed I assumed my next assignment would be on Traitor's Hill, and not as a guard."

Wyldon nodded. "Very proper. As your punishment, then, I assign you to find ground for a new refugee camp, build it, and run it. Continue to instruct the people in how to defend it. I give you the entire valley of the Greenwoods River as your subdistrict of my command. You will hold it and make it safe against Scanrans and anyone else who thinks those people will be easy pickings."

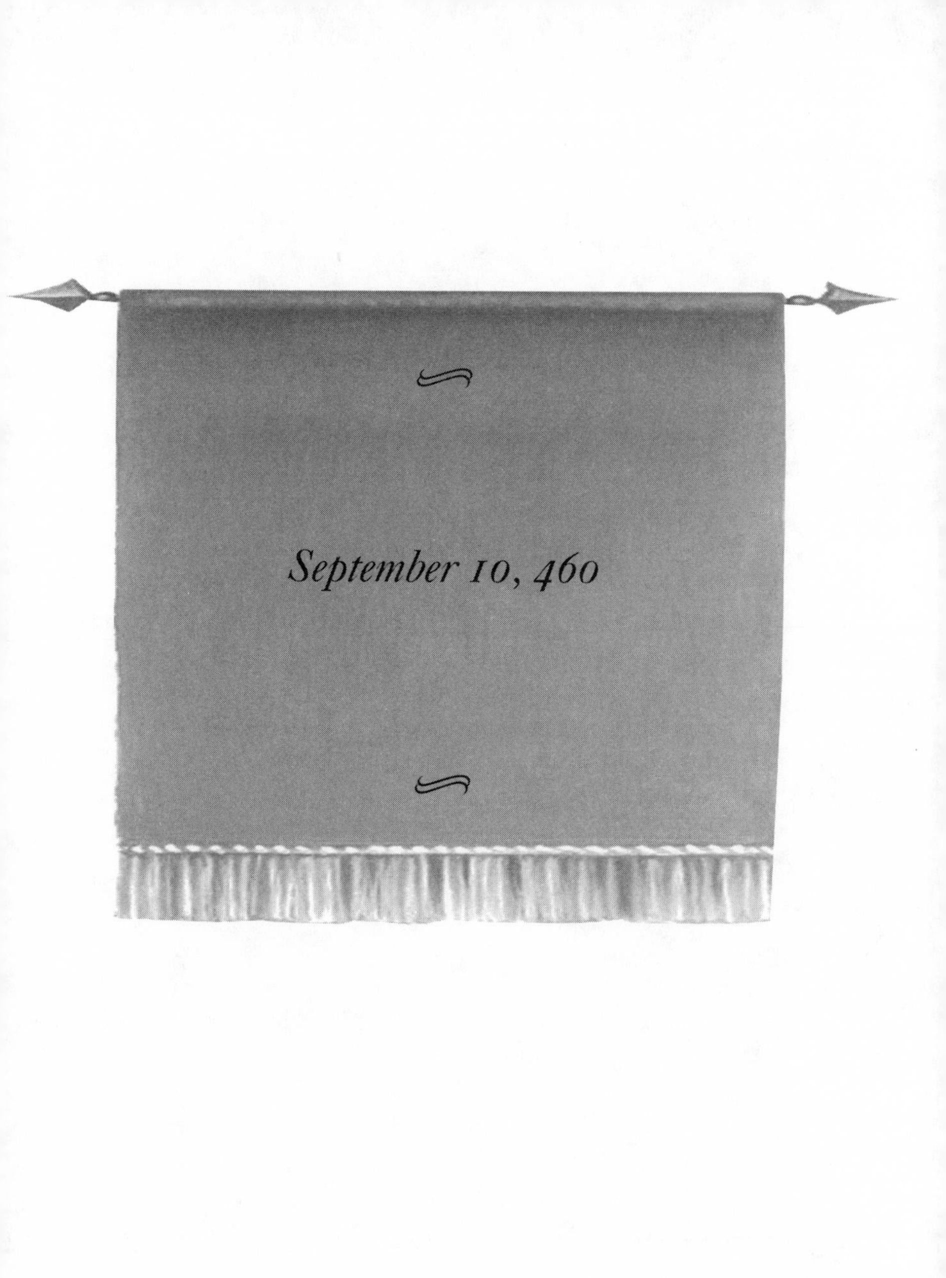
September 10, 460

EPILOGUE

Kel swung herself into Hoshi's saddle, taking one last look around her. After two months or so the fortified town of New Hope still looked raw, but it was starting to resemble an actual town rather than a logging camp thrown together in a week. The sight of cart after cart bringing their hard-earned harvest to the storage barns filled her with profound satisfaction. Not for the first time, she blessed Lord Raoul for waiting until the crops were in before he set his wedding date. She wouldn't have been able to enjoy herself at Steadfast if her people had still been in the fields. With the crops taken care of, she could feast with a carefree heart.

"Stop fussing," Fanche commented. She stood near Kel, hands on hips, her dark eyes amused as she looked up at the younger woman. "You'll be away for a week—if we can't manage for that long, what good are we?"

Kel grinned at New Hope's headwoman. "Actually, I was trying to remember if there was anything I hadn't done. Shutters left open—"

"Shutters closed," said Tobe, mounting a small, spritely, piebald mare who had taken a liking to him in Scanra. The greatest change the events of June had made in him was that he no longer trusted Kel out of his sight unless they were inside New Hope's walls. Kel understood and hoped he would relax as the winter's snows made it impossible for either of them to go very far. "Shutters closed, bed made up, leave-behind weapons and armor cleaned," Tobe continued to rattle off, "don't have to worry about feedin' your animals because they're comin' along with us. Duty rosters for the week in Master Terrec's hands." Terrec was the clerk who had taken Zamiel's position.

"She's fussing, isn't she?" Merric strolled out of headquarters, his hands tucked comfortably in his breeches pockets. "You women are forever fussing." Things with their fighters had reached the point where occasionally Merric would let a sergeant command a patrol rather than do so himself. Today was Sergeant Jacut's day to patrol with his squad of former convicts and men of the town intermingled. While there had been no official attention paid to Kel's Scanran journey, a week after her return the silver marks on the convicts' foreheads had faded, a sign that someone somewhere had decided they were pardoned. As mistrustful as Tobe in their own way, they had elected to remain with the army, in the north, with Kel. Merric's staying in town while a convict squad patrolled showed all of New Hope that he trusted them not to return to their criminal habits.

"I'm not fussing," Kel retorted. "And where's Neal?"

Neal came racing up to them, windblown and hands only partially cleaned of blood. "I'm sorry! I don't tell babies when they're allowed to get born."

"Neal," Kel said as he reached for the horse Loesia held for him.

Neal looked at her, his green eyes feverish. He was in a hurry to get to Steadfast. His betrothed, Lady Yukimi, was there. Like Raoul's betrothed, Buriram, Commander of the Queen's Riders, Yuki had tired of waiting for her man to return south. As soon as the celebrations for Prince Roald's wedding to Princess Shinkokami had ended, Buri had resigned her post as commander, to be replaced by her assistant commander, Evin Larse. Together she and Yuki had bought passage on the first ship north, then traveled overland to Steadfast.

"Your hands," Kel pointed out as Neal simply blinked at her. He looked, saw they were not entirely clean, and released a sound that was a cross between an anguished cry and a wail. Back into the infirmary he went.

"If he's like this now, how will he stay calm when his daughter tries for her knighthood?" a youthful voice asked.

Kel looked down at Irnai. The girl was one of several homeless children who had come to live in headquarters with Kel, Neal, Merric, and Tobe. She did her best to act like a normal child of her age, but when she foresaw things, she sounded as world-weary as Neal at his most sophisticated.

"Perhaps we won't share that knowledge with him just yet?" suggested Kel. "Let it be a surprise for him."

Irnai grinned up at her. "He doesn't like surprises, and the road of his life is littered with them. I like that."

Kel couldn't help it; she grinned at the child. "I do, too," she admitted. "It will be good for him."

Neal came back, hands dripping wet and clean. He flung himself into the saddle and raked his hair back from his eyes. "I'm ready," he declared. "Let's go."

Kel led the way, Neal on one side, Jump trotting on the other. People waved as Kel and Neal rode by but immediately returned to their work, putting on roofs and shutters, making the nails, preserves, and kindling New Hope would need to see them through the winter.

Passing through the gate, Kel waved at Sergeant Adner, who now commanded the village guard. He waved in reply. "Bring back some pretty, meek girls," he called. "Ours is too quarrelsome." Agrane, whom he was courting when he was off duty, elbowed him.

"Enjoy your holiday, Lady Kel," Irnai called as they rode down the inclined road that served the village. "There will be work for the Protector of the Small soon enough."

Kel shook her head. No matter what she did, she couldn't stop people from calling her that.

She let her guard escort, Neal, and Jump ride ahead as they crossed the Greenwoods Bridge. She looked north. The dark high ground of Haven, now their burial ground, lay two miles upriver, too far from New Hope for an enemy to use it as an attack base. She had also asked Numair if he could raise the ground they would need forty feet rather than twenty, to put off all but the most determined attackers. This time Numair had kept his health and shared the work with Harailt of Aili and a few other mages who had responded to his call for assistance. Lord Raoul had confided that Kel should ask for all the extra help she needed. Giving her all she asked, within reason, was a kind of silent apology from the Crown for putting her people in harm's way.

Kel turned Hoshi to look up at New Hope's walls. She thought the battle flags and shields taken from those Scanrans who had attacked her people that summer gave the walls a nice, homey touch. They also served as a warning to any raiding parties that New Hope had teeth.

"*Kel!*" shouted Neal. "Are you going to dream all day? She's waiting for me!"

Lovers, Kel thought, rolling her eyes. At least there was one headache she *didn't* have. She was about to tell her friend he could wait when she remembered that she'd get to see Dom while at Steadfast. It would be nice to be able to sit and chat for a while without kidnapping, flight, and war to distract them.

She nudged Hoshi to a trot.

CAST OF CHARACTERS

Adner	ploughman and archer, refugee
Agrane	female villager
Alanna of Pirate's Swoop and Alau	the King's Champion, lady knight
Alvik	abusive innkeeper in Queensgrace
Arrow	sparrow
Aufrec	regular army sergeant at Haven
Baird of Queenscove	duke, chief palace healer
Blayce the Gallan	mage, works for Scanrans
Breakbone Dell	deceased outlaw
Cleon of Kennan	knight, Kel's friend
Connac	regular army sergeant at Haven
Domitan of Masbolle	called Dom, squad leader in the King's Own, Kel's friend
Dortie	female child refugee
Duck	sparrow
Edort	clumsy ploughman at Haven
Einur	cook at Haven
Esmond of Nicoline	knight, Kel's year-mate and friend
Eulama	Tobe's deceased foster mother

Faleron of King's Reach	knight, assigned to coastal conflict
Fanche Weir	miller's widow, tough villager
Fulcher	corporal in Dom's squad of the King's Own
Gilab Lofts	former hill bandit, now convict soldier
Gothar Weir	Fanche's deceased husband
Gragur Marten	apprentice clerk at Haven
Grembalt	regular army corporal
Gydane Elder	called Gydo, girl refugee, Meech's sister, Tobe's friend
Harailt of Aili	mage, head of the royal university, serving in the North
Hevloc	regular army sergeant at Fort Mastiff
Hildurra Ward	female clerk at Haven
Hobard Elbridge	regular army captain, sets up Haven
Idrius Valestone	self-important Tirrsmont refugee
Ilane of Mindelan	baroness, Kel's mother
Ilbart	regular army soldier at Haven
Irnai	female child seer
Jonathan of Conté	king of Tortall
Jump	Kel's very intelligent dog

Keladry of Mindelan	called Kel, lady knight, in command at Haven
Keon	boy refugee
Kortus	regular army sergeant at Haven
Leithan	convict soldier at Haven
Loesia	called Loey, girl refugee, Tobe's friend
Lofren	private in Dom's squad of the King's Own
Lukin	soldier at Fort Mastiff
Maggur Rathhausak	warlord and now king of Scanra
Meechiyel Elder	called Meech, Gydo's five-year-old brother, refugee at Haven
Merric of Hollyrose	knight, Kel's year-mate and friend
Morun	convict soldier at Haven, pickpocket and lockpick
Nari	chief sparrow
Nealan of Queenscove	called Neal, knight, healer, Kel's friend, Baird's son
Neum	regular army soldier at Haven
Numair Salmalín	powerful mage, Daine's lover
Olka Valestone	Idrius's wife, Tirrsmont refugee
Oluf	regular army sergeant in command of convict squad at Haven

Oswel	refugee
Owen of Jesslaw	squire to Lord Wyldon, Kel's friend
Peachblossom	Kel's strawberry-roan gelding destrier, temperamental
Piers of Mindelan	baron, Kel's father
Peliwin Archer	female refugee
Qafi	Bazhir convict soldier
Quicksilver	female sparrow
Quinden of Marti's Hill	knight, Kel's year-mate, not of her circle
Raoul of Goldenlake and Malorie's Peak	Knight Commander of the King's Own, Kel's former knight-master
Rengar	boy at Fort Mastiff
Roald of Conté	prince, knight, heir to the throne
Saefas Ploughman	refugee trapper
Seaver of Tasride	knight, Kel's year-mate and friend
Shepherd	Haven camp dog
Snalwin	refugee carpenter
Stenmun Fodeben	chief guard to Blayce the Gallan
Terrec	clerk at New Hope
Thayet of Conté	queen of Tortall

Thurdie	female refugee
Tobeis Boon	called Tobe, boy/horse mage Kel hires
Tollet	regular army captain under Lord Wyldon's command
Travr	male refugee
Uinse	convict soldier
Uttana	female refugee
Vanget haMinch	supreme commander of Tortall's northern armies
Veralidaine Sarrasri	called Daine, also known as the Wildmage
Vidur	regular army sergeant in command of convict squad at Haven
Waehild	female refugee and hedgewitch
Weylin	regular army private in Connac's squad
Wolset	corporal in Dom's squad of the King's Own
Wyldon of Cavall	in command of northern border district to which Kel is assigned, her former training master
Yanmari	stingy female refugee
Yngvar	regular army sergeant at Haven

Yukimi noh Daiomoru	called Yuki, Neal's betrothed, a Yamani
Zamiel Fairview	senior clerk at Haven
Zerhalm	headman of Blayce's village

GLOSSARY

abatis: a wall-like defense of logs sharpened on one end and set in the earth with the points facing outward against attackers.

Anak's Eyrie: a fiefdom in northernmost Tortall.

basilisk: an immortal that resembles a seven-to-eight-foot-tall lizard, with slit-pupiled eyes that face forward and silver talons. It walks upright on its hind feet. Its hobby is travel; it loves gossip and learns languages easily. It possesses some magical skills, including a kind of screech that turns people to stone. Its colors are various shades of gray and white.

Bazhir: the collective name for the nomadic tribes of Tortall's Great Southern Desert.

Bearsford: a town on the Great Road North.

Carthak: the slaveholding empire that includes all of the Southern Lands, ancient and powerful, a storehouse of learning, sophistication, and culture. Its university was at one time without a rival for teaching. Its people reflect the many lands that have been consumed by the empire, their colors ranging from white to brown to black. Its former emperor Ozorne Tasikhe, was forced to abdicate when he was turned into a Stormwing. (He was later killed.) He was succeeded by his nephew Kaddar Iliniat, who is still getting his farflung lands under control.

City of the Gods: the religious, magical, and educational center in northeast Tortall.

Code of Ten: the set of laws that form the basis of government for most of the Eastern Lands.

convict soldiers: convicted criminals who are given the choice to fight in the army if there is a war on rather than go to prison. There may be a pardon at the end of their service if they survive; since they are poorly trained, and feared by normal citizens, they rarely survive. In the Eastern Lands, convict soldiers carry a silver mark on their forehead that cannot be removed or covered, to identify them as convicts.

Copper Isles: a slaveholding island nation to the south and west of Tortall. The Isles' lowlands are hot, wet jungles, their highlands cold and rocky. Traditionally their ties are to Carthak rather than Tortall, and their pirates often raid along the Tortallan coast. There is a strain of insanity in their ruling line. The Isles hold an old grudge against Tortall, since one of their princesses was killed there the day that Jonathan was crowned.

Corus: the capital city of Tortall, located on the northern and southern banks of the River Olorun. Corus is the home of the new royal university as well as the royal palace.

dragon: a large, winged, lizard-like immortal capable of crossing from the Divine Realms to the mortal ones and back. Dragons are intelligent, possess their own magic, and are rarely seen by humans. The infant dragon Skysong, known as Kitten, lives in the mortal world with her foster mother, Daine Sarrasri.

Eastern Lands: the name used to refer to those lands north of the Inland Sea and east of the Emerald Ocean: Scanra, Tortall, Tyra, Tusaine, Galla, Maren, Sarain.

Frasrlund: the Tortallan port city at the mouth of the Vassa, on the other side of the border with Scanra.

Galla: the country to the north and east of Tortall, famous for its mountains and forests, with an ancient royal line. Daine was born there.

Giantkiller: a fort built by Third Company of the King's Own in *Squire,* given its name in honor of Lord Raoul after Raoul killed two giants there in a Scanran raid; Lord Wyldon's temporary command post.

Gift, the: human, academic magic, the use of which must be taught.

glaive: a pole arm, including a four- or five-foot staff capped with a long metal blade.

Goatstrack: a destroyed village near Fort Giantkiller.

grapples: large, three-pronged iron hooks that can be attached to a rope and tossed over a wall or cliff to be used as an anchor for a climber.

Great Mother Goddess: the chief goddess in the Tortallan pantheon, protector of women; her symbol is the moon.

Greenwoods River: the river that flows past Haven.

griffin: a feathered immortal with a catlike body, wings, and a beak. The males grow to a height of six and a half to seven feet at the shoulder; females are slightly bigger. No one can tell lies in a griffin's vicinity (a range of about a hundred feet). Their young have bright orange feathers to make them more visible. If adult griffin parents sense that a human has handled their infant griffin, they will try to kill that human.

Hamrkeng: the capital of Scanra.

hand-and-a-half sword: a longsword with a longer-than-usual hilt, which may be wielded single-handed or with two hands.

Haven: refugee camp.

headman: the leader of a tribe, or the mayor of a small town.

Human Era (H.E.): the calendar in use in the Eastern and

Southern Lands and in the Copper Isles is dated the Human Era to commemorate the years since the one in which the immortals were originally sealed into the Divine Realms, over four hundred and fifty years prior to the time covered by *Protector of the Small.*

hurrok: an immortal shaped like a horse with leathery bat wings, claws, and fangs.

Immortals War: a short, vicious war fought in 452 H.E., the thirteenth year of Jonathan and Thayet's reign, named for the number of immortal creatures that fought, but also waged by Carthakis (rebels against the new emperor Kaddar), Copper Islanders, and Scanran raiders. These forces were defeated by the residents of the Eastern Lands, particularly Tortall, but recovery is slow.

indenture: contract of service under which a buyer pays a certain amount and in return is granted a person's service for a set length of time, usually seven years. During that time the buyer must provide basics—food, clothing, shelter, education (in Tortall)—in return for the servant's work.

King's Council: the monarch's private council, made up of those advisers he trusts the most.

King's Own: a cavalry/police group answering to the king, whose members serve as royal bodyguards and as protective troops throughout the realm. Their Knight

Commander is Lord Sir Raoul of Goldenlake and Malorie's Peak. The ranks are filled by younger sons of noble houses, Bazhir, and the sons of wealthy merchants. The Own is made of three companies of one hundred fighters each, in addition to the servingmen, who care for supplies and remounts. First Company, a show company, traditionally provides palace bodyguards and security for the monarchs. Under Lord Raoul, Second and Third Company were added and dedicated to active service away from the palace, helping to guard the realm.

logistics: the military study that involves the purchase, maintenance, and transport of supplies, equipment, and people.

longhouse: a long, barnlike structure that provides housing for several families or for an extended family and their animals (in winter). A typical Scanran home, it can also be found in both northern Tortall and Galla.

mage: wizard.

mage mark: a silvery circle on the forehead, used to identify a convict soldier.

Maren: a large, powerful country east of Tusaine and Tyra, the grain basket of the Eastern Lands, with plenty of farms and trade.

Mastiff: the new fort that serves Lord Wyldon as command post during events in *Lady Knight.*

mess (hall): the building in which military meals are eaten; sometimes cooks work in the same building.

Midwinter Festival: a seven-day holiday centering around the longest night of the year and the sun's rebirth afterward. It is the beginning of the new year. Gifts are exchanged and feasts held.

Mithros: the chief god of the Tortallan pantheon, god of war and the law; his symbol is the sun.

naginata: the Yamani term for the glaive used by Kel.

Northwatch: the command base for Tortall's northern defensive, currently the headquarters for General Vanget haMinch, commander of the northern armies.

ogre: an immortal with aqua-colored skin, shaped like a human, from ten to twelve feet in height.

Pakkai River: a small river in Scanra.

pole arm: any weapon consisting of a long wooden staff or pole capped by a sharp blade of some kind, including spears, glaives, and pikes.

Queensgrace: a town on the Great Road North.

Queen's Riders: a cavalry/police group charged with protecting Tortallans who live in hard-to-reach parts of the country. They enforce the law and teach local residents to defend themselves. The basic unit is a Rider Group, with eight to nine members. Rank in a Group is simply that of commander and second-in-command; the head of the Riders is the Commander. They accept both women and men in their ranks, unlike the army, the navy, and the King's Own. Their headquarters lies between the palace and the Royal Forest. Buriram Tourakom is now the Commander; Queen Thayet was the Commander but has since passed the title to Buri.

regular army: foot soldiers, cavalrymen, catapult operators, quartermasters, scouts, and their officers; uniformed troops.

remount: a rider's second horse, to ride when the primary horse gets tired. In the case of knights and the King's Own, remounts are often warhorses, heavier mounts trained to fight.

River Olorun: its main sources are Lake Naxen and Lake Tirragen in the eastern part of Tortall; it flows through the capital, Corus, and into the Emerald Ocean at Port Caynn.

Riversedge: a town near Fort Giantkiller.

Scanra: the country to the north of Tortall, wild, rocky, and cold, with very little land that can be farmed. Scanrans are masters of the sea and are feared anywhere there is a coastline. They also frequently raid over land. Their government is a loose one, consisting of a figurehead king and a Great Council (formerly the Council of Ten, expanded in the disruptions following the Immortals War) made up of the heads of the clans. Maggur Rathhausak, a warlord stirring up trouble for Scanra's southern neighbors, has taken the crown at the start of *Lady Knight.*

scry: to look into the present, future, or past using magic and, sometimes, a bowl of water, a mirror, fire, or some other device to look through.

Smiskir River: the Scanran tributary to the Vassa River.

Southern Lands: another name for the Carthaki Empire, which has conquered all of the independent nations that once were part of the continent south of the Inland Sea.

spidren: an immortal whose body is that of a furred spider four to five feet in height; its head is that of a human with sharp, silvery teeth. Spidrens can use weapons. They also use their webs as weapons and ropes. Spidren web is gray-green in color and it glows after dark. Their blood is black and burns like acid. Their favorite food is human blood.

squad: ten soldiers commanded by a sergeant and two corporals.

standard-bearer: the young man or boy who carries the company flag.

Steadfast: the fort built to serve as headquarters for Third Company of the King's Own and Lord Raoul.

stockade: a wall made of whole logs, their upper ends cut into rough points.

Stormwing: an immortal with a human head and chest and bird legs and wings, with steel feathers and claws. Stormwings have very sharp teeth, but use them only to add to the terror of their presence by tearing apart bodies. They live on human fear and have their own magic; their special province is the desecration of battlefield dead.

strategy: the plans for a battle or war from a distance, working out the movements of armies and setting goals for them.

tactics: the plans for a battle at short range, as it happens.

Tirrsmont: a fiefdom in northernmost Tortall.

Tortall: the chief kingdom in which the Alanna, Daine, and Keladry books take place, between the Inland Sea and Scanra.

Tusaine: a small country tucked between Tortall and Maren. Tortall went to war with Tusaine in the years

Alanna the Lioness was a squire and Jonathan was crown prince; Tusaine lost.

Tyra: a merchant republic on the Inland Sea between Tortall and Maren. Tyra is mostly swamp, and its people rely on trade and banking for income. Numair Salmalín was born there.

Vassa River: the river that forms a large part of the northeastern border between Scanra and Tortall.

warhorse: a larger horse or greathorse, trained for combat—the mount of an armored knight.

wildmage: a mage who deals in wild magic, the kind of magic that is part of nature. Daine Sarrasri is often called the Wildmage for her ability to communicate with animals, heal them, and shapeshift.

wild magic: the magic that is part of the natural world. Unlike the human Gift, it cannot be drained or done away with; it is always present.

Yamani Islands: the island nation to the north and west of Tortall and the west of Scanra, ruled by an ancient line of emperors, whose claim to the throne comes from the goddess Yama. The country is beautiful and mountainous. Its vulnerability to pirate raids means that most Yamanis, including the women, get some training in combat arts. Keladry of Mindelan lived there for six years while her father was the Tortallan ambassador.

NOTES AND ACKNOWLEDGMENTS

Anyone who reads this and knows where I live will see clear parallels to the events of September 11, 2001. This is and is not a coincidence. I had planned the fate of Haven and its inhabitants since the mid-1990s, when Mallory said she would love to see a new series about a new girl knight, and I began to work out the course of Kel's adulthood. I forgot where in *Lady Knight* I had stopped writing when September 11 swept us all into the real world. Afterward, all I knew was that I needed to get back to Tortall. I *had* to get back to Tortall. I wanted to immerse myself in fantasy because reality was "way too much." I wasn't able to sit down at my computer for five days, and when I saw where I had stopped—on Kel's second return to Haven—my hands began to shake. It took me two weeks to write the next twenty pages, the hardest twenty of my life. I did it because it had to be done; I had to write the book, awaited by so many faithful readers. And then, I confess, when I did the rewrites, I expressed my feelings about war, refugees, and disaster a bit more forcefully than I had in the first draft. So September 11 did and did not shape this book; maybe the right way to put it is that it added muscle and my own personal trauma to what would have been a strong story in any case. Make of it what you like. Think about what's here and come to your own decisions, that's all I ask.

As ever, my heartfelt thanks goes to my wonderful

editrix, Mallory Loehr, whose idea it was to make Kel a commander (I wasn't sure I could write anyone who works and plays well with others), and whose enthusiasm for Kel's story from the very beginning has kept me moving forward. Books are very much co-productions, and without input from Mallory, my agent Craig Tenney, my beloved Spouse-Creature Tim, and my English editrixes Holly Skeet and Kirsty Skidmore, the Kel you read about now would be very different and not as solid. These people help me to tell my story in a straightforward way, make sure I explain things that are confusing, notify me when something is unneeded, and give me the ideas that get me unstuck and writing again.

My thanks also to Rick Robinson, geometer (map-maker and -reader) extraordinaire, and Raquel Starace and Tracy Schlabach, whose continued horse input gave birth to Peachblossom.

To my mother, my stepbrothers, my sister, my husband, and all the family clustered around us, well, the old eagle flies free at last. I just hope he flies slow enough that we can catch up to him when it's our turn to fly.

TAMORA PIERCE captured the imagination of readers everywhere with *Alanna: The First Adventure.* As of August 2002, she has written nineteen books, including two quartets set in the fantasy realm of Tortall, The Song of the Lioness and The Immortals, as well as the now complete Protector of the Small quartet. She has also written four Circle of Magic books and the first three books in The Circle Opens series. Her books have been translated into many different languages, and some are available on audio. Tamora Pierce's fast-paced, suspenseful writing and strong, believable heroines have won her many fans and much praise; *Emperor Mage* was a 1996 ALA Best Book for Young Adults, *The Realms of the Gods* was listed an "outstanding fantasy novel" by VOYA in 1996, and *Squire* (Protector of the Small #3) was a 2002 ALA Best Book for Young Adults.

An avid reader herself, Tamora Pierce graduated from the University of Pennsylvania. She has worked at a variety of jobs and has written everything from novels to radio plays. She has also teamed up with writer Meggin Cabot (*The Princess Diaries*) to create Sheroes Central, a discussion board about female heroes and remarkable women in fact, fiction, and history.

Tamora Pierce lives in New York City with her Spouse-Creature, Tim, and their four cats, two birds, and various rescued wild animals.

Visit Tamora Pierce's Web site for more information at:
www.sff.net/people/tamora.pierce

Sheroes Central at:
www.sheroescentral.com